The Twelfth Physician

The Twelfth Physician

by Willa Gibbs

FARRAR, STRAUS AND YOUNG
New York

for

FLOYD C. MILLSAP

Acknowledgment

To John Homer Woolsey, M.D., much gratitude is owing for his adroit use of the scalpel as well as for invaluable aid in preparing this manuscript. Don King, M.D., and O. C. Railsback, M.D., are other names that occur among many, as the author acknowledges here a debt to the men and women of the medical profession for their kindness and skill.

ONE

The Street Singer

1

TWO

The Medical Students

36

THREE

The Bonnet Rouge

90

FOUR

Sinnamarie

122

FIVE

Miasma

140

SIX

Bonaparte Again

178

SEVEN

The Oath Broken

211

EIGHT

The Oath Fulfilled

261

"And that physician who makes only small mistakes would win my hearty praise."

—Hippocrates, *On Ancient Medicine*

ONE

The Street Singer

THE SKELETON was old, and held together with silver wires. When first her husband had brought it, Diane Florian used to speculate about it. How had he met his death, how old had he been, what nationality? Farmer? Priest? Merchant? Soldier?—anonymous bones, polished by time. Tonight she could not seem to keep her eyes away from it. Charlot was nearly an hour late. Every day innocent persons disappeared off the streets, and never were heard of again.

The five young men had little to say, and they avoided her eyes. They too waited, listening for him, hearing only the storm sounds. Poor young things, they are as frightened as I am, she thought. She had stopped resenting them. Charlot had so many duties and responsibilities—consultant physician at the Hôtel Dieu, consultant at the Bicêrte, his private patients—Diane had felt she would be robbed of what little time she had with him. Instead, husband and wife had drawn even closer in a shared effort to help the young men. They are like grown sons of ours, Diane thought, and this seemed true, although the oldest, Oliver Gris, was nearly her own age.

Her eyes were drawn back to the skeleton. Its enigmatic grin mocked her. Charlot was never late to the meetings. What had happened? Why did human beings consent to live as they lived? It was as though the French people had been condemned to death en masse, and it was only a matter of time before the individual was summoned to his fate. Everyone had hoped for so much from the Revolution. Charlot, for instance, had hoped for a new renaissance in medicine, a golden age, with France the threshold over which the rest of the world would pass into the dawn of scientific enlightenment. Instead had come the brutal and foolish laws that closed all schools, including medical schools, and that permitted unlicensed, untaught men to practice. The other professions, the Army excepted, had been as badly hurt. Then unorganized chaos gave place to organized Terror as Robespierre, the blood drinker, seized power. The French people were like a band of chickens who are

1

commanded by a hawk. In time he noticed you . . . swooped.
. . . Charlot's tardiness tonight could mean that he had been noticed
at last. It was against the law to teach medicine; had he been found
out about that? He, Diane too, were well-born. Had the ever-active
agents penetrated the simplicity of "Citizen-Doctor Florian" and
found whose son he was? Under the Law of the Hostages, both had
committed a capital offense in belonging to noble families who had
emigrated. If Charlot has been arrested I'll denounce myself, Diane
decided. I won't live without him. She was frightened at her own
boldness, yet the decision brought a measure of peace. The leering
skeleton held her gaze in its bony stare.

Deliberately she forced her eyes away. She studied the tense faces
of the young men. Their nervous gestures betrayed fear as sharp
as her own. She noticed Robert Lasné glance at the skeleton, and
away again, so he felt it too, the symbol. I could tell them to put it
away, she thought, but then they would know how deeply afraid I
am. We must not admit it, the waiting will be unbearable if we do.
She tried to think of something to say that would reassure them,
but nothing occurred.

I'm glad they are here with me, she thought. They love him too.
Their stake in his safety is nearly as great as my own, and gives me
something to worry about besides myself, and him. She noticed
Legouvé looking sternly in her direction. She realized he was worrying about her. She smiled weakly; he smiled back before their
eyes parted. His tenderness toward her remained like a benediction
on her troubled heart. This is what Robespierre can't kill in us, she
thought with a flash of angry courage. He can't drive us to the final
depths of animal terror because he can't stop us from caring about
others. He would if he could, but he can't do it. Every day, every
death, he is defeated by persons whose last thoughts were of someone
else, in love and pity.

"The storm has made the doctor late," Diane said, in a voice con-
vincingly light. The tension in the room relaxed slightly.

Robert Lasné said with eagerness, "He'll be walking against the
wind. It's so strong." Immediately Diane could see him walking
against the wind, in their direction, free. Her smile to Lasné was a
finished one. But then the awful silence came back, and their
strained faces were pale in the firelight while all senses were subordinate to that of hearing as they listened for the sound of the
door opening and closing downstairs.

What would happen to the young men if Charlot had been taken?

They would have to surrender their dreams. What they wanted so much, what they had battled so valiantly to have, would become impossible. No one else in France would break the law to teach them. There was no way out of France except through her Armies, where France held you as tightly as she did here. No one could replace Charlot because no one was willing to take the risks he took. It is a terrible thing to break the dreams of young men, she thought.

Only two of them had so much as seen the inside of a medical school. Monteil and Legouvé were in their first year when the schools were closed. They had struck a pact to go on by themselves, each helping the other to learn. But they did not know enough to do this successfully; anyway, the right books and equipment were not available. Robert Lasné first, then Oliver Gris, and finally Jouvancy, had joined them. Each new, stray fact or theory that fell their way became the subject of passionate conjecture until, worn threadbare, it ceased to make sense. This was torment, yet they could not stop; unless they could become doctors their lives were without direction or purpose, it seemed. Charlot had made Diane understand that. "Their feeling for medicine is the same as my own. Don't you see how that makes me responsible for them?" It had taken time for her to see, but she understood now. After all, nothing prevented them from starting their practice at once, as others no better fitted had done. One of the Rights of Man conferred by the Revolution was the right to practice medicine without knowing anything about it. All over France, hordes of wandering, unlicensed doctors were second only to Robespierre himself in the number of Frenchmen they had killed. But these five know-nothings had the hearts and souls of real doctors. They wanted to learn.

Again and again they had been rebuffed. The few trained physicians who remained in Paris, in public posts usually, were overworked; the young men had no funds to pay for instruction. But the real reason for curt refusal was that a meeting of more than three persons could be termed seditious assembly. It was dangerous to consent. Dr. Florian had been the twelfth physician to be approached by them. They had asked without hope, knowing in advance what the answer would be. Instead he had quoted the high brave words: "I will teach the healing art to any who may ask me, and without recompense to myself," then he had told them how those words had been set down centuries earlier by Hippocrates of Cos, the first doctor. Although that injunction had become meaningless with the establishment of the great schools, Salerno, Padua and Pavia, Mont-

3

pellier, Paris, Leyden, yet that part of the Oath had never been stricken out. Perhaps it had been kept in wise foreknowledge that times would come again when individual doctors must be responsible for keeping medical knowledge alive through private instruction. In words as courteous and graceful as he himself was, Charlot had given them more than mere assent, he had given them stature as well. "It is your right to demand this of me. Of course the answer is yes." My heart hurts from loving him, Diane thought.

He had been teaching them for six months now. They met three evenings a week, in the apartment. Diane attended the teaching closely. She had always liked learning things, but no other chance had come her way once embroidery and music, dancing and languages, had been mastered. Charlot liked having her follow the lessons, he did not share the opinion that knowledge in a woman is ungraceful. The apartment was shabby actually, but it must seem exotic to the young men. Charlot had told her how they lived in order to learn from him. They slept under roofs that did not keep out rainwater, on pallets thrown down on a floor. They subsisted on sourbread and herb soup on the good days and roots, leaves, sawdust, blubber oil, frogs and snails on the bad ones. They wore rags, they lived under debt, they broke the law daily to become doctors. They were, he believed, the only medical students in France. A feeling of being part of something valiant and fateful had been with her since.

Her eyes moved to the table, where their poor gifts of food were waiting. Salt herring was Lasné's contribution, the loaf of black bread was Legouvé's, and a small cheese nearly devoured by mold, Monteil's. Jouvancy, the most prosperous of the five, had brought a bottle of red wine, and Gris had supplied coal for the fire. Diane had wanted to stop them from bringing things. "It's silly. Our sacrifice in eating what they bring is as great as theirs. We like good food, and we can afford it." But Charlot had made her see that the twice-monthly custom was important to them. They saved mightily to acquire these tidbits in order to share them with the Florians. From doing it, they gained a feeling of manliness, of returning favors handsomely. Once it was explained to her, she did not err again in lacking appetite for black bread and smelly dried fish.

Jouvancy spoke, startling her. "Perhaps the Citizeness would prefer that we wait in the foyer. If he's under suspicion and they come here, it won't help her case to have us hanging around like conspirators."

4

It was a reasonable suggestion, but Diane did not want to be left alone. She made a soft negative sound. The other young men looked at Jouvancy coldly as though suspecting the concern he was feeling might be for himself. For some reason, his words started a flurry of small activities. Oliver Gris counted out three small pieces of coal which he added to the fire to keep it going. Legouvé and Monteil began rearranging the few things on the supper table, in a finicking effort to improve its appearance. Robert Lasné picked up his threadbare jacket from the fender where it was drying. "I'm going to look for him." He went out.

Diane, watching after Lasné, felt she was being watched and turned quickly. But it was only the skeleton's bony glare that had drawn her to look around. Silently, she began to cry.

❖   ❖   ❖

Lasné picked his way down the dark, steep board staircase, into the street. He started in the direction of the hospital, the Hôtel Dieu. His clothes had not dried out from the soaking he had gotten coming here, and were wet through again as soon as he left the protecting portico. He had no real hope of finding Dr. Florian. In his mind, he was saying goodbye to the only good thing he had ever known. He was not sure if the irritating trickle into the hollows of his nose was rain, or tears, or a mixture of both.

He was a stumpy, short-sighted youth, slow to learn, overanxious about everything. Unlike most shy people, he possessed deep feelings. The pulse of Diane Florian's suffering had reached across the room to him, and was partially responsible for his being out in the storm again. She had looked beautiful and sad in the low firelight, and he had almost forgotten what Florian's death would mean to himself and the others in realizing the grief that would be hers. No one who knew them could mistake the closeness that existed between them. It was Robert Lasné's first experience in observing married love. If he married someday he would want to love and be loved in the same way, though no woman as beautiful as Diane Florian would ever feel interest in him. But it's the loving that counts, he decided, hurrying along, his wet clothes slapping him dismally.

In his sympathy for Diane, he tried to go on thinking about her, as if his concern would defend her in some obscure way. But he could not; after all, she was only an adjunct to Florian. If Florian had disappeared into one of the terrible prisons from which death was the only escape, Diane meant nothing any more, nor did anyone else. The absence of that one man emptied all of Paris as far as Lasné and the others were concerned. He looked down the dark, rain-glossy street, seeing Dr. Florian clearly in thought. He was slender, but wiry and strong, and his movements were easy and correct. His young face was thin, its pallor emphasized by straight black hair he wore neatly clubbed and his black level brows. He was kind, yet he demanded so much, and when you were with him you felt yourself trying to transcend yourself. It was an exhilarating feeling. Afterwards, you tried to copy his mannerisms, his turns of phrase, feeling that you captured something of his uniqueness. Yet the guillotine could cut him out of life completely and quickly; a doorway slammed shut, a world aspired to, irrevocably lost. How many like him, beloved and necessary, were dying every day in the anonymous batches Robespierre's penstroke sent to death? Hatred of the dictator rose sourly. Then he began imagining himself in Robespierre's presence, and explaining why Dr. Florian must be saved. A shadowy figure was behind a big desk, listening. He could not see Robespierre in his mind because he had no idea what the dictator looked like, but he could see himself, admirably self-contained, with his hands jammed in his pockets the way Florian did when he wanted to hammer something home to them. He told Robespierre how Florian had studied at Pavia under the great Scarpa, had stood at Scarpa's right hand during dissections that proved Galen's sacrosanct teachings were mistakes or lies. And then for Florian, Leyden, the only school in Europe where bedside medicine was taught. Leyden had a twelve-bed hospital, he told Robespierre; six beds for women and six for men, and the doctor-teachers took to these bedsides students as slow to understand as Lasné himself, and *showed* them the typical signs of disease at onslaught, in progress, and at termination in death or restored health. Robespierre was fascinated of course, and readily saw how important it was . . .

I've never seen a real dissection, even, Lasné thought.

He began telling about the time he himself had boldly brought the body of a three-year-old girl to the apartment. She was small, easily carried, easily concealed, and she had died of being hung from a lamppost. When he had produced her little body, Diane Florian had cried out softly and looked at him from horror-stricken eyes. Oliver Gris had said something harsh about ghouls being worse even than murderers. Ashamed and frightened, Lasné had shrunk back, seeing himself ugly and unnatural, but then Florian's hand

6

rested on his shoulder lightly and Florian said, "Robert didn't kill her, Oliver. He brought her here so she might have a kind of life after all. None of us can give back what was taken from her, but we can remember with amazement and devotion what she taught us. Isn't that better than the Republic's lime pits?" Don't you see, Lasné said earnestly to the listening shadow behind the big square desk with corners jutting sharply, don't you see this man must not die? And the shadow nodding, echoing . . . must not die. But no one was allowed to see Robespierre, and he never had spared anyone, never.

      *   *   *

"Thank you, Doctor," she whispered.

"You're a brave girl," he said.

"It didn't hurt much."

"I know better. It hurt dreadfully."

Her bitten lips tried to form a smile for him. Her eyes were full of trust. Where had she come by her quite incredible courage? He brushed lank, sweat-damp hair away from her forehead, feeling a sorrow that was violent and despairing. Strong men had to be held down forcibly by the orderlies but this girl of the streets, untaught, valueless to society, had accepted the bone-saw without flinching, her eyes full of trust. "Damn him, whoever he was," Dr. Florian said softly. She rested, watching him. Soon the full force of pain would strike again. "Will you promise me never again to let a doctor touch you who can't first show proof that he was properly licensed at one time?"

"I'll never go to anyone but you." Her voice was soft and exhausted.

He was very late now. Diane would be worried about him, and the five young men who were waiting were to him the most important persons in France. Yet it was hard to leave her in the dark airless old hospital, to face alone the horror of what he had been compelled to do. He could not help her further. She would have to figure out for herself how to go on living with the handicap of an arm missing at the shoulder. At one time he would have accepted full responsibility; he would not have let her go out of his life until he had found a place of some kind for her. But the sad cases multiplied themselves too fast. More than a year ago, he had laid down an ironclad rule for himself: do your part to help them, then forget them. It was hard and his innermost nature still rebelled at it, but he

7

had to save himself for his real work. He sat crosslegged by her pallet and watched the orderly wash up. That much he could and would do for her—stay until the brute finished. He knew what treatment the patients received when the doctors left too quickly.

She asked him, "Why does the government let them pretend they are doctors when they're not?"

"I don't know, my dear. It's a terrible mistake, and they will see that themselves someday, but meanwhile, hundreds of other people will be mutilated and killed. I'm doing what I can to get things changed back but there is so little I can do."

He talked to her a while longer, then, promising to see her the first thing in the morning, he left her. He was surprised at how hard it was storming outside. A strong wind whipped the rainfall into driving lances. He would have to walk; the Hôtel Dieu district was too poor to support hacks. He started out, her plaintive question ringing in his ears.

Three-fourths of his work nowadays was correcting blunders made by the charlatans. A populace scourged by poverty and fear of the guillotine on the one hand, was preyed on by a horde of wandering illiterates on the other. Curiosity may have led some of these into dissecting a pig or a chicken; on that they based what knowledge they might have of anatomy, yet they boldly attempted the most delicate surgical operations. In internal medicine, they prescribed phlebotomy as a cure for anemia, or treated fatal diseases by the laying-on of hands; they dosed all who were ailing with antimony, a poison. In obstetrics, they understood less than the midwives, who at least knew simple version: the new "doctors" performed embryotomy in every case of birth complication. Yet, before the Revolution, there was Senac on the heart, Puzos and Baudelocque in obstetrics —where were those men now? The colleges in Paris and Montpellier had been schools of immense reputation. They were abandoned piles of stone. It had taken centuries to build all that; in these few years, where had it gone?—vanished as completely as if it had never been. The laws that proclaimed liberty and equality only made it unsafe to speak your mind. The laws were intended to benefit everyone, yet somehow resulted in imprisonment and the guillotine for men and women of all classes. And the laws hung the long robes of physicians and the short robes of surgeons on the shoulders of imbeciles and assassins. A sore spot on a young girl's hand . . . an ignorant fool with a knife fit only for cutting bread. . . . Amputation at the shoulder that he, Florian, had to do to save her life.

8

The Paré technique he had used had been developed on the battlefield, where amputations were necessary after swordstroke sheared through bone, or cannonballs shattered limbs to splintery pulp. But until the charlatan with his bread-knife had come into her life, nothing was wrong but a sore spot on her hand. Wicked and criminal folly! In his anger, he paid no attention to where he was stepping. He nearly fell over the body before he noticed it.

Like a child asleep, a young man lay on the cobblestones, one arm outflung. His shoulders and head were in a pool of muddy water. The rain beat down, but he did not stir.

Dr. Florian assumed that he was dead simply because the dead were a common sight on Paris streets; sleeping persons less so. But he bent down to make sure and smelled brandy. There were no street lights. A dim glow came from behind the dirty windows of a café. Florian found a wound over the man's temple that could have been caused by a blow or a fall. Rain had washed the blood away. The sleeper's heartbeat was strong.

It seemed to the doctor that he might have seen that face before. It was almost a famous face, yet he could not place it. The man was young, in his mid-twenties probably, reckless and swarthy. An impression of animal vitality came from him even as he slept. Florian did not fail to notice the heavy development of the chest, the resiliency and firmness of his flesh. It seemed a pity for a person in such magnificent health to die of foolish exposure. Florian shook him and slapped his cheeks. Not so much as a mutter rewarded him.

He swore gently. Even granting he could manage it, he could hardly afford to take the fellow along with him. That face was certainly familiar. If he were a Deputy, say, or a member of Public Safety, and he wakened in the middle of their illegal proceedings, there might be trouble that would involve Diane. Perhaps someone in the café would have a taste for Samaritanism.

He entered it. But the place was one that springs up wherever poverty has been so long and hopelessly sustained as to change the people who have endured it, wearing away their humanness, reducing them to a kind of soulless ferocity. Behind their vicious masks, he knew, were frightened helpless human beings, warped by constant pressures toward which they had no understanding. But to hand the man outside into such care as they would give would be worse than leaving him where he was. Florian backed out of the place without speaking to anyone.

Again he stood by the fallen man. There was no real reason for him to feel responsibility; the fool had drunk himself into this plight. Worthier persons in need were to be found everywhere; that girl he had left in the hospital, for example. And yet Florian's years of training simply did not permit him to walk away from a fellow human who might require medical assistance.

He tried to lift the sodden human bundle. Florian was the taller man but was slender, and this one was stocky and strong. He floundered along a few steps. It was impossible, the man was dead weight. He let him down gently. He heard someone trudging toward them and muttering. It sounded like a debate of some kind, yet there was only one voice and one set of footfalls. A moment later he recognized Robert Lasné's querulous tones, and spoke to him.

"Is that you, Doctor?"

"Bless you, Robert, were you looking for me? I don't think I could have managed without you. Come and help me."

"We thought you had been arrested!" Lasné said, hurrying up.

"I know I'm late. I couldn't help it. Take the other side, that's right. Now, up with him. Good. Can you manage?" Together they wrestled the sleeper's heavy body through curtains of rainfall. "Did you recognize him, Robert? He seems familiar to me."

"I didn't particularly look at him, Doctor, but I don't think so. We've been so frightened!" Lasné said. "I wondered if we'd ever see you again."

"Something came up at the hospital, another mutilation case. I'll tell you about it tonight. Is Diane worried?"

"She was crying when I left."

Florian did not say anything. What was there to say? This sort of thing was one of the conditions under which the French people lived. While he lingered by the girl's pallet, he had known what torments of anxiety his tardiness would impose on his wife. But if he should begin neglecting his patients to spare her, some fundamental virtue would go out of him. He loved Diane more than life, and medicine more than either. This is a splendid era for the haters, he thought, but it's doubly hard on those of us who love. The haters can get quick and easy revenge through denouncing those whom they hate. But there is nothing we who love can do to protect whom we love.

❖   ❖   ❖

The sound they waited for so tensely, the opening and closing of the downstairs door, was followed at once by awkward noises on the staircase. Diane blanched and the young men traded nervous glances. Florian's step should be light and quick. This sounded like one of the arresting patrols. It was now too late to act on Jouvancy's sensible suggestion that they not be found up here.

Oliver Gris, the boldest, opened the door a crack and looked down. Then he threw back the door and ran downstairs two steps at a time. "I'll take him, sir," Gris said.

"You're more than welcome to him," Dr. Florian said. "I've kept you waiting. I'm sorry."

Diane recognized his voice. She sank back in her chair, rubbing her cheeks briskly to remove the marks of her tears. In such small ways as this, they tried to spare each other.

"Let go of him, Lasné. I can manage better alone," Gris said.

Jouvancy began calling to the others in the room, "He's brought us a real corpse. An adult male! We can dissect in the bathroom. Get things ready."

Florian said drily, "For God's sake, Jouvancy. Examine your man before you dissect him. This one's alive." He came in, and went to Diane. He took her warm hands in his that were clammy and shaking with cold. "I'm sorry, my darling. I couldn't help it."

"I know. It's all right." Her lips felt stiff, but she formed a smile of sorts for him. "I'll get dry things for you."

"Get something of mine for Robert too, he's wetter than I am, if that's possible." He spoke to Oliver Gris. "Put him down on the floor there, he won't know the difference and there's no point in ruining Diane's couch. What, Monteil? What did you say?"

"It's Ange Pitou!" Monteil repeated.

Florian said in deep alarm, "I thought I had seen him before! Maybe you shouldn't stay. He might overlook it that one man tried to help him, but six of us would certainly look like sedition or conspiracy. Which one is Ange Pitou? I know I've heard the name. Is he likely to denounce me for that blow to his head? Go on, Monteil, tell me."

"He's the street singer, sir."

"What?"

"He's Ange Pitou. The street singer. You must have seen him. He walks around singing and talking, and crowds follow him. He's the most seditious man in France, sir."

Legouvé took it up. "He calls himself the truthteller. I don't know how many times he's been arrested. Somehow he always gets out."

Dr. Florian made a little puff of relief. "No wonder I thought I

11

knew him. So my fright was for nothing, eh? It's easy to see witches and Deputies on every streetcorner when it's storming like this. Let's put him to bed. The cut on his temple doesn't amount to anything, I see now, but I don't know how long he was lying out there before I found him."

Jouvancy said, "Ange Pitou won't denounce you, sir. But some one else might, if it became known that you ever had him in your house."

"Oh." Florian looked thoughtful.

"It might be a good idea to put this fish back in the water where you found him."

"I hate to put an unconscious man out on a night like this. What do you think, Diane?"

Mere existence was risky enough. She did not want Charlot to take extra chances. But she tried to answer as he would wish. "If they took him that seriously, I would think they'd have guillotined him before this."

"Yes," he decided, proud of her logic. "There can't be too much danger. Take him to the other bedroom, then let's get on with our meeting. I brought you a pair of lungs, they're in my pocket. But first, a change of clothes for Robert and me, and some supper." He noticed the table, their gifts of food laid out. "Ah, good. Salt herring again. I'm very fond of it," he said heroically.

The sudden end to long tension had given Diane a feeling of headiness. She could not stop a spontaneous giggle, he was so dear and funny, the rain running off him, and gallantly claiming a fondness for salt herring which he loathed. And human lungs in his pocket! Was there ever another like him? He looked at her sharply, increasing her amusement. Then he smiled. His thin, hard-planed face came alive when he smiled like that. Suddenly they were laughing together, enjoying the ridiculous, while the sober-sided young men watched them from puzzled eyes.

II

DIANE FLORIAN was mistaken in thinking that the street singer's freedom indicated that he was not taken seriously. Ange Pitou's movements were under surveillance most of the time, and it was dangerous to know him. Fear of him, and not indifference, had so far prevented his own death, but at least a dozen others had died because they knew him. If he had been drinking the night before,

Ange sometimes wakened in terror, feeling there were dead men around his bed who were angry because he went on living.

The loyalty of the Paris crowds protected Ange. Each day he was expected at ten o'clock exactly at the west door of the church of Saint-Germain l'Auxerrois, from where he proceeded to the Rue de Coq and the Rue de L'Arbre-Sec, gathering new followers all the way. If he failed to appear, the crowds knew that he had been arrested again. This had happened fourteen times. Fourteen times they had gone to the prisons in turn, demanding Ange back, and had made furious demonstrations at the police bureau and before the Convention itself. Their numbers provided anonymity and saved them from retaliation, and fourteen times Ange had been restored to them. He was one man the all-powerful dictator dared not kill. But this immunity of his did not protect others.

Ange's singular career had been launched during the early days of the Revolution, before Robespierre's bloody-minded Deputies of the Mountain had wrested control of affairs from the moderate party of the Plain. In those days, the accused were still being given trials, which was how Ange came to survive his first escapade, before he became famous. One day, while he was hungrily tramping the streets of Paris, he met a classmate at the divinity school in Normandy where he had studied for Orders before the schools were closed by the Revolution. This classmate, Pascal, had been luckier than Ange; he had made friends and connections in the capital. Ange confessed his difficulties to Pascal. What little he got from begging and stealing was hardly enough to satisfy his own roaring appetite, and he was responsible for his twin sister Angélique since her husband's conscription into the Army of the Rhine. Angélique was pregnant, the time for her accouchement was drawing near, Ange told Pascal. Could Pascal help him? Pascal could. A certain Citizeness Morlay, once of Lyons, a fairly well-known hostess, was giving a dinner party that same night. Important people would be there. Perhaps something would fall Ange's way; anyway he could be sure of a good dinner. Ange borrowed a coat from Pascal and went to his destiny.

As good as his word, Pascal introduced him to everyone. Over and over he told how clever Ange was, what an amusing gift Ange owned for mimicry and rhyme. Meanwhile, lean with hunger and ragingly athirst, Ange ate and drank everything that was offered. By the time the company called on him for song, he was drunk. When he attacked them and their Revolution with effective savagery, Pascal, appalled, tried to stop him, but Ange shook his friend off and roared out verse after verse of mocking insult. Next morning his hostess and a guest named Hyssmann denounced Ange as a traitor to the Republic, and denounced Pascal as well for being his friend.

Ange saved himself with song. He stood in the box with the blood-hunger ravening around him, and sang fiercely patriotic words to a military tune that he composed on the spot. The delighted jury-men carried him out on their shoulders. His song was published as the *Réveil d'Epiménide* and was still being sung, though its author had repudiated it as soon as he was free. But meanwhile, the charge against Pascal had been allowed to stand. Pascal was guillotined on a charge of consorting with a traitor (Ange) and Hyssmann, who had denounced them both, was guillotined on a charge of falsely accusing a patriot (also Ange), and no doubt the Morlay woman would have been guillotined too except for an accident of the court summoning before it another Citizeness Morlay, who could testify to nothing. . . . The confused affair presaged the future as Ange, the storm center, continued to live, while the bolts of lightning he attracted to himself fell instead on his hapless friends. This was the man Dr. Florian had brought into his house; the man of whom Diane had said, "If they took him that seriously, they'd have guillotined him."

*   *   *

Ange Pitou wakened in the dark, in a strange place. While it was not uncommon for him to do this, it was always startling. He felt around with his hands, trying to identify his surroundings. He was not in jail again, because the bed was a good one, and freshly made up with fine old linen sheets. His head hurt him. When he put his hand there, he discovered a neat bandage on the left side of his face. From this it did not seem that he had fallen into the hands of enemies. He moved around in the bed tentatively. All of his limbs were in good working order.

"I guess I got drunk again," Ange said softly.

It was not very wise for him to go roaring about Paris and drink-ing himself into insensibility. He kept promising himself not to do that another time, but it kept happening that he did. Already, at twenty-three, Ange had lived too long. He had had his bellyful of horrible sights. He had lost the power to weep for his fellowman or hope for him either. The dead nudged him, whispering of their innocence, of his part in their deaths. His restlessness increased to such a pitch that he jerked in the bed. Then a familiar phenomenon started up, a stinging and crawling sensation across his back. Long ago, he had decided this meant they were beating Angélique again. It seemed unlikely that anyone would trouble himself to whip her in the middle of the night but they were conscientious about their "treatments," he knew, and Ange had faith in his symptom. The sensation increased. Unquestionably they were beating Angélique again. If only he had not been sent to the Bicêrte that time—then he would not have known what she endured! Doctors, he thought. My God, how I hate doctors! They are the real murderers. They murder slowly, with enjoyment, their little sharp eyes taking note of everything we feel. The guillotine is swift, but doctors torment you out of your senses, then try to torment you back into them again. He pushed the clinging dead away from him angrily. Their sufferings were over. I've got to have a drink, Ange thought, or talk to someone. In the dark like this, I see things that are terrible.

He felt around for a tinderbox. There was none that he could find, but a dim line of light showed him there was a doorway across the room. A doorway, and the light, meant people, and he needed people badly; anyone, anything but this loneliness in the dark with his knowledge of his sister's sufferings, in the company of his dead friends. He eased out of the bed, holding his throbbing head with both hands. He was wearing a long nightgown of some soft stuff, very warm and nice. He had no idea where his clothes might be, so he was going to have to present himself as he was.

He crossed the room quietly and found the latch on the door without any trouble. He moved it open, careful to make no sound, because he wanted to reconnoiter before he was discovered himself. He looked out.

What he saw was as bad as anything he had seen in the Bicêrte itself, with the added horror of being absolutely strange. From the trained lungs of Ange Pitou, a scream was a blast of marvelous sound, rounded and whole, dramatically conveying the limit of his ability to react. Then the sight vanished as he pitched forward into the unfamiliar room that contained the new and ultimate in horror.

❖   ❖   ❖

The scream, and the body falling forward as though dead, struck

15

them all with the same terror. Diane started out of her chair with a soft cry. Her husband, who was standing, merely stiffened and whitened; he made no gesture of self-defense. Robert Lasné moved abruptly nearer to Florian, as though he would use his own body to shield the doctor. Jouvancy bolted toward the stairway, and Oliver Gris faced the danger, whatever it was, with a poker held up threateningly. Monteil and Legouvé flattened themselves against the wall.

Florian was first to recover his composure. "It seems we are mutually frightening to each other. He's fainted already, Oliver, there's no point hitting him with that. Will you help me get him back into the bed?"

Jouvancy, shamefaced, closed the door he already had opened to escape through, and Gris replaced the poker. Silently, four of the five young men lifted the street singer, Florian going ahead with the light, and Lasné and Diane trailing the others. They stood around the bed looking down on the unconscious man, their faces curious. Florian was feeling a sort of generalized indignation, a sharp clean disgust at the state of mind that could produce such ludicrous results from an encounter however unexpected. How could anything worthwhile root and flower in this chilly climate of fear? Compassion for his wife claimed him next. Her head with its gift of shining hair drooped wearily. He dismissed the young men. It was nearly midnight; anyway they could not be expected to concentrate after such a fright. When they were gone, he helped Diane to the other bedroom and put her to bed gently. She was as relaxed as a child. Her eyelids were still trembling. Fierce protectiveness rose in him.

"Aren't you coming to bed, Charlot?"

"I'll sit with him until he becomes conscious. He had a bad fright of some kind."

"But hold me—just for a minute—"

He lay down, gathering her against him, smelling the gentle fragrance of her hair and skin. She sighed, nestling. "You're tired too," she said.

"Yes. I can't remember being so tired."

"It's been a horrible day."

"Yes."

"But this is nice."

"I wish there was some way of getting you out of France."

"I wouldn't go without you," Diane said.

His arms tightened. He did not argue the point because there was no way he knew of; the borders were closed tightly. He kissed her. Her lips were warm and soft and answering. "Do you have to go back there?" she whispered.

"I should. I can't imagine what frightened him, but something certainly did. He's among strangers and he's been hurt—are you laughing?"

"Don't you really know why he was frightened? I do."

"No. Why?"

"Don't you recall what you were doing when he screamed?" He drew away to look at her. The familiar glint of mischief in her eyes warned him that she found him droll. Being laughed at was a condition of loving Diane. "Midnight," she said. "A hard storm. Demoniac rites." She chuckled, delighting in his puzzlement. "Oh, Charlot, he's not a doctor or a medical student! He saw you fitting a pair of human lungs into a human skeleton. Why wouldn't he scream and faint?"

"Of course. How stupid of me. If you weren't around to point out the obvious, I'd never understand anything, would I? I suppose we did make a weird impression." He shook her gently, lovingly. "That's enough! Stop laughing at me." Though he half meant it, one of his gravest fears was that her ebullience and sense of fun would be destroyed by the rigors under which they lived. She was made for gaiety and light. Robespierre's austere and blood-drenched State must weigh on her as heavily as fetters. He had been wrong not to take her away while emigration was still possible. Now it was too late. "Don't change," he whispered, rocking her gently. "Don't you change. I love it when you laugh at me."

"I thought you told me to stop."

"I did, but I didn't mean it."

He made himself leave her. He went into the next room. The street singer was still unconscious, though a hard frown furrowed his low, swarthy forehead. Florian mixed a stomachic for him, then sat down by the bed and waited for the shock of what Pitou had seen to release its hold. The candles burned dully, with a flickering, unsteady light. They were poor candles, but all that could be had these days. The storm lashed Paris as his thoughts lashed his tired mind.

In spite of his own alarm Florian had not missed any detail of their several reactions, and Jouvancy's panicky flight disturbed him. Jouvancy was quicker of mind than any of the others, the best of the students, but tonight had shown that he was a frail, flawed vessel for the storing of treasures. No, Florian decided, it is not my place

17

to criticize them. I never was called on for so much patience and faith when I was that age. Certainly the incredible hardships of their studentship were in sharp contrast to golden days he remembered poignantly. I wish I could take Diane to Italy, he thought. She could be truly happy there, and I could. The gracious, unhurried land . . . he could not remember anything cruelly sudden ever happening there. His whole being yearned back.

The man on the bed stirred and groaned. "You're all right," Dr. Florian said, his voice quiet and kind. "You fainted. You're all right now, you're warm and safe, in bed." The singer's hand crept toward the bandage on the left side of his face. "Does that hurt?" Florian asked him. "It's nothing really, a little cut not more than an inch long."

"I saw something," Pitou said. He moaned again, and turned his head away from the light.

"I know. It was a shame to frighten you like that. My name is Florian, I'm a physician. The young men you saw are medical students, so you see there is a reasonable explanation. Come now, look at me, you're all right."

Pitou opened his eyes long enough to give Florian a glance of hard suspicion, then he closed them again. "Here. Drink this," the doctor said, touching his shoulder.

"What is it?"

"It will make you feel better. You had too much brandy, you know."

"I'm not drinking anything any doctor gives me," Ange Pitou said angrily. "Where are my clothes? I want to get out of here."

"It's storming hard. It would be better to stay."

"I'm not staying in any doctor's house. I know what doctors are like."

"Do you? What are we like, then?"

"Where are my clothes?"

"They're drying in another room."

"Where that skeleton is?"

"It's been put away. The lungs have been burned. There's nothing there now to frighten you. As I said, I was using them for purposes of instruction. We meet secretly because it's against the law. That's all there is to it."

"You trust me a lot." His voice was sullen and ugly.

"I'm not alarmed that Ange Pitou will denounce me."

"How do you know who I am?"

18

"I've followed you a time or two, and listened to your songs. You're very clever. And very brave."

Mollified, Ange looked at Florian. He had to admit that he liked what he saw. The face was strong and kind, handsome, indefinably aristocratic. It was not at all like the butcher face of the surgeon who had hurt Angélique. But her name crossing his mind brought back all his distrust and hatred. "Do you know what an embryotomy is, Dr. Florian?" he said in his bitter voice.

"Why do you ask?"

"That's what the doctor did to my sister."

"Why did she permit it?"

"He didn't tell her anything until it was over. She's in a madhouse because of that doctor."

Florian said, "That's a cruel and horrible practice. It was repudiated as far back as Soranus of Ephesus. No doctor would do such a thing except under a set of circumstances so extreme and peculiar that I cannot even imagine what they might be. Did he say why he did it?"

"I hate doctors. They are butchers."

A weary bitterness rose in Florian. Only too well, he understood the uselessness of arguing. This young man's sister was one of the legion of the maimed, and of course he blamed the medical profession for it. He was silent, the bitter weariness clamping his heart.

"Angélique would be better dead than where she is," Ange Pitou added sullenly. "I was in the Bicêrte myself."

"Were you?" Florian said. "Why?"

"Maybe they thought I had to be insane to go on provoking them like that. Or maybe they thought they could scare me into behaving, and they damn near did. They hang you in chains to the wall. Every night and morning you get whipped. The doctor stands by and says how many lashes for each one, and they pretend to think they can whip you into your senses, but they know better of course. They do it because they like to hear the screaming, and watch the poor chained things throw themselves around until their wrists bleed. Sometimes their bones are broken. I know all about it, Doctor."

"How long ago were you in the Bicêrte?"

"It was a year ago anyway."

"You would find things much changed if you saw it now."

"I don't see how it could be worse."

Florian started to tell him, then decided against it until he was sure the sister was actually there. "Is she at the Bicérte?"

"I never saw her there. No one would tell me."

"I can find out for you, if you wish."

"How?"

"I'm a consultant there."

One of *them*, then, and Ange Pitou sat up violently. Though the suddenness of his movement was like being struck over his wound, he would not show pain to the other. "I don't want anything from you. Give me my clothes and let me out of here."

"Really, I can't permit you to go out in this storm again. If you didn't want to become my patient, you should have picked another puddle to doze in. Please be reasonable."

"It's dangerous to cross me, Doctor."

Florian smiled as to a boasting child. "But I'm not trying to cross you. I only want you to trust me until tomorrow, when I may be able to give you good news concerning your sister."

"Do you think I would believe you if you did?"

"Why are you trying to offend me? I want to help you."

"But I've had your kind of help before. I told you, I've been in the Bicérte myself."

Florian stood up. "I'm not going to say any more until I know that she's there. Now go to sleep and let me get some sleep. I really think this has been the hardest day of my life." He smiled down into Pitou's set, angry face. "I give you my word," he said gently. "I never performed an embryotomy, and I never whipped an insane patient, nor ordered one whipped. Now go to sleep." He turned and went out, leaving the candles.

Ange Pitou lay quite a while, noticing the details of the comfortable room, telling himself he was only waiting for the doctor to fall asleep before he would collect his clothes and go. The medicine Florian had wanted him to drink remained untouched in its glass on the table. Pitou picked up the glass curiously. He sniffed its contents and liked the clean smell, so he tasted it with the end of his tongue. Immediately his mouth felt refreshed. "It's dangerous to cross me!" Ange Pitou said again, aloud. Then he drank the contents of the glass. The bed was a warm nest of comfort. Soon he fell asleep.

✻   ✻   ✻

Except on the seams, Ange Pitou's clothes were dried by morning.
Dr. Florian shook them out and brushed off the worst of the mud.
Such tatterdemalion garments he had never imagined. That's an
odd young man, he thought, you would think he'd be embarrassed
to appear before crowds dressed like that. He carried the clothes into
the next room where the singer was. Pitou was still asleep. Florian
did not disturb him; he had nothing more to say until he had seen
Dr. Pinel. He laid the clothes on a chair where Ange could find them
and went out.

"Try to keep him here until I get back," he said to Diane.

"Yes. I hope she's there, do you think she is?"

"It's impossible to say now, but I certainly hope so."

There was no look of mischief now; Diane's grey eyes were darkened with mourning for Pitou and his unfortunate sister. She had
a gift for appreciating the sufferings of others.

After Florian had gone, Diane laid a place for the singer, making
the table as attractive as possible. It was not long afterwards that
he came out, a raffish figure in his stained torn clothing, bareheaded
and brown. He looked at her with cold suspicion, balancing himself
lightly on the balls of his feet.

"I've kept breakfast warm for you," Diane said. "Please sit down
and I'll bring it. I'm the doctor's wife, and I know who you are,
Citizen. My husband has gone to find out what he can about your
sister. It's a horrible, horrible story! We're both so sorry for you.
Please sit down."

"I don't like doctors." His voice was harsh, its Norman accent decided.

"I know you don't," Diane said. "You will like my husband though,
when you know him. I'll bring your breakfast now."

When she came back with eggs, buttered bread, and a small bowl
of porridge, he was standing by the door, poised to go out. His watch-
ful dark eyes had not lost their look of suspicion. Diane said firmly,
"Citizen Pitou, no one can blame you for feeling as you do after
what happened. But the doctor wants to help you, don't you owe
it to yourself to at least hear what he has to say?" Pitou hesitated.
She pointed to the place at the table. He walked over and sat down.

He began eating noisily, his table manners as casual as his dress.
Diane sat across the table from him, her chin resting on her laced
fingers. She began telling him stories. She described the cruel necessity of amputation to a young girl who had been maimed by one
of the charlatans. There were similar cases she remembered and

21

related to him. After a while, he seemed to really be listening. Diane told him about the medical students, how they had refused to take advantage of the unwise laws that permitted untaught persons to practice; instead they submitted to hunger and cold in order to learn and Florian gave them gladly the only free evenings he had.

But then he stood up suddenly. "I'm going."

"All right," Diane said, making a helpless gesture. "I'm sorry you won't believe me."

"I don't know if I believe you or not. The people are waiting for me, that's why I'm going. I'll come back unless I'm being followed."

"Followed?" She lifted her eyebrows.

"You don't want *them* to find out I come here."

"Is that dangerous?"

"Yes," he said simply.

"All right, come back when you're not being followed. But the doctor will expect to find you here; after all, he's making a special trip for you. It's not his day at the Bicêrte."

"They're waiting for me," Ange said again.

"I should think you'd let them wait, this one time."

"No," he said, "I can't. They riot, you know."

"They do?" Diane said, amazed.

"The only times I haven't shown up were because I was in jail."

"How did you get out of jail?"

"The people make them let me go. That's why I can't be late, they'll think I'm in jail again and there will be another riot."

It sounded fantastic. Just the same, there had to be an explanation of some kind for his continued freedom. Suddenly Diane was aware of feeling deep alarm. She wished Charlot had never brought the singer here. She wondered if there was anything she could say to him that would help ward off the danger she felt threatened them because of having become involved with him.

She crossed over and put her hand lightly on his stained, torn sleeve. "The doctor didn't want you to know this until he could be sure your sister was really there. The Bicêrte is not at all like it was when you were there, in fact it is the one mental hospital in Europe where patients are being treated with kindness. They are not chained; they are not whipped. Dr. Pinel is mainly responsible, but Dr. Florian had a part in it too."

A little hope was mingled with the look of disbelief in his eyes. Diane said urgently, "My husband does much good. He helps people like your sister, he helps many people. He is incapable of

22

cruelty or selfishness. Don't let him become involved in anything
dangerous. Please!"

"I'll watch out for him. If you've told me the truth."

"It is the truth."

"If I think I'm being followed, I'll send someone else."

"Yes," she said. "If it really is dangerous for you to come here."
He nodded and went out. She could hear him running lightly down
the uncarpeted stairs. She moved to the window and looked down
on the street, and saw Ange Pitou emerge, agile, graceful in spite
of the ragamuffinly clothes. It was impossible to predict what he
might do. Had he believed her? A little way, maybe, but his wild
suspicious eyes remained in her memory as strong with foreboding
as a spoken threat.

III

As SUPERINTENDENT of the Bicêrte, Dr. Philippe Pinel had charge
of the largest community of insane persons in France. He was small
and insignificant-looking, with tan hair and beard, his skin badly
pitted from smallpox. Those who knew his story never ceased to
marvel at the hard courage concealed behind Pinel's timid, shrinking
appearance. This man, so shy that he could not ask the time of day
without stuttering, had defended himself before the terrible Revolutionary Tribune and come away victorious.

The little shy doctor had attracted the dislike of Marat, once a
physician himself, then a murdering demagogue, finally a victim to
well-deserved assassination. Dr. Marat could easily have had Dr.
Pinel killed, as he had Dr. Lavoisier; instead, it had amused him to
arrange Pinel's appointment to the Bicêrte. Dr. Pinel had never seen
the inside of an insane asylum before Dr. Marat's spite singled him
out for the charge of this one. Of course he knew supervised cruelty
was supposed to have a beneficial effect on disordered minds, but
that was one thing to read about, another to witness and to be responsible for its infliction. These horrible duties had nothing to do
with the healing art. No dog was ever beaten with such ferocity
and regularity as were these helpless beings. Their food was slops
poured into unwashed earthen plates set down on the filthy floor.
That Pinel's agonies on their behalf would greatly exceed anything he
might feel over his own impending death, Marat had known.

After his powerful enemy's death, Pinel petitioned to be relieved, but was ignored. It seemed he was doomed to spend his days in actions that were against every belief he owned. But then he rebelled. He ordered the beatings stopped; he began releasing the patients in lots of ten, and letting them go free into the corridors and the enclosed courtyard. He dismissed those doctors whom he believed to be sadistic or indifferent, replacing them with consultants, Florian for one.

The discharged doctors denounced Pinel on a charge of conspiring against the Republic through freeing insane persons and inciting them to murder the Deputies. His friends read in it his doom, but Pinel himself saw the chance to speak out in behalf of the tormented ones. Selfless devotion released his poor locked tongue on that one occasion only. Pinel, instead of stuttering and stammering as his habit was, spoke eloquently. If the jurymen were calloused to sudden death, they were not to the horrors he made them see vividly. And so he had saved himself, and what was more important to him, had won the right to administer the affairs of the Bicêrte in his own way, with humanity and love.

Dr. Florian watched Dr. Pinel going through an immense ledger for Angélique Pitou's name. He thought that if the patients continued to improve, Pinel's theories eventually would supplant the old cruel practices in force everywhere else. It was odd how he had found his life's work in the impossible circumstances where spite had placed him, and Florian, though without conventional religious belief, was aware of feeling veneration toward a grave and beautiful pattern that he glimpsed briefly. No trace was left of the weary bitterness that had possessed him last night. He felt renewed hope that some great work might be given to him also.

Dr. Pinel snapped the ledger shut and pushed it away. "No Angélique Pitou. No Pitou at all now, though there's a record that he was here, the brother. For two weeks, August a year ago. That was before the changeover." All this in a staccato stutter, while he peered at Florian over the tops of his spectacles.

"Then I'm glad I didn't tell him about you. It would have been shameful to raise his hopes but then have to tell him she isn't here after all. Can you find out where she is, do you think? Is there a chance of getting her transferred here?"

"Not much chance, no. On account of the brother's activities. No one in government would be interested in obliging him, quite the opposite, in fact. A very brave young man. What is he like?"

"He's hard," Dr. Florian said. "It's easy to imagine him becoming mean. But there's good in him, I think, and his concern over her is very real. He bears a violent dislike toward the profession, incidentally."

"Why?"

Florian told Pinel what Ange had said about his sister's history. Pinel shook his head. "There is so much of that sort of thing these days."

"Yes." Florian's thoughts jumped to his amputation case. He had seen her before coming here. She was feverish and in great pain. Her eyes haunted him with their look of absolute trust. If only there was some way to warn the people as he had warned her, too late, to refuse treatment by all but qualified men who could prove their qualifications. Pinel too was thoughtful, bunching his lower lip, tapping it.

"You're quite sure she wasn't married," he said.

"Why, no, in fact I imagine she is. Light ladies don't come from such backgrounds, bourgeois provincial I mean. Norman, I think, from the accent."

"Then she might be here after all."

"The husband's name, of course. How stupid of me. I'll find out and come back tomorrow."

"I would like you to see a patient now. She came to mind at once when you told me about the tragedy. Since they are twins, there could be a marked resemblance. Do you have time, Doctor?"

"Of course, Doctor."

They had to cross the men's ward to reach the women's side. The patients had become friendly under Pinel's regime, and the doctors were stopped many times. Pinel showed no impatience and felt none; these miracles of improvement gratified his heart. He thought that his charges seemed happier and better off than many people outside. He watched Dr. Florian closely, with approval. Florian had been a good choice for staff. Although he had not seen the Bicêrte as it had been, his patient sympathy seemed as endless as Pinel's own.

They entered the women's ward. It was tidier than the men's, because among the women were some in whom housewifely instincts had reasserted themselves as soon as the women were left to their bents. The most willing hands could not bring airiness or light into this cavern place, of course. But Pinel went on seeing in a double image, of what had been along with what he saw now. A chained madwoman is frightful. Her screams will make you believe in the

25

existence of terrors beyond knowledge. These women were delighted by Pinel's and Florian's unscheduled visit. Not all of them paid attention, of course. Some dreamed their lives away in private fantasies, but he could remember when even they had cowered and screamed at the sight of him, and with reason, too.

"She's in one of the cells," Dr. Pinel said. At one time, the cells had been reserved for the fortunate ones whose families had cared enough to bribe the doctors into giving them slightly better care. Pinel used the cells to isolate his violent cases who might hurt themselves or some others. The cell cases still had unusual care, though bribes were no longer taken.

They entered a cell. A woman was sitting bent over, and crooning to something she held in her arms. A veil of dark hair concealed her face. Her body seemed half-formed in the rough, loose garment of the institution.

"Speak to her, Doctor, using that name."

"Angélique," Dr. Florian said.

She lifted her face. The resemblance to Ange was unmistakable. She scrambled up. She had been handsome rather than pretty, but the large eyes glowed and her smile was sweet. She held out toward the men the bundle of dirty rags she had been cradling in her arms, then snatched it back, looking at them suspiciously.

"He is a beautiful child," Dr. Florian said, guessing everything.

"He is sleeping."

"I see that he is."

"But I must wake him soon, and nurse him."

"Yes," Florian said gently. "Of course."

"Will you let me hold him today, Angélique?" Dr. Pinel asked.

For a moment it seemed that she might; then she ran to the far end of the cell and crouched against the wall, peering at the men distrustfully from under her curtain of hair. The resemblance to Ange was much heightened by her look of ugly suspicion.

"Tomorrow, perhaps, you will permit it," Pinel said. The doctors withdrew.

Florian, genuinely impressed, said, "How did you guess that your patient was Pitou's sister?"

"I had imagined about her something very like the story you told me this morning. You see, while she was being mistreated, she screamed at anyone who approached her that her baby was being murdered. But when her own mistreatment stopped, she began this fantasy of the living child being in her arms. On the day she sur-

26

renders it to me, however briefly, I will know that trust has started in her again. Then she can come out of her cell and be with the others. I wish I could find out as much about all of them as you have been able to tell me about her. I have come to think that it helps. When you see their obsessed actions in terms of the experiences they have suffered, it seems to help them. Or help us, rather."

He cocked his head, thinking that over, and added, stuttering mildly, "Yes, it helps us. Notice that our reaction to her little bundle of rags was not astonished horror that she could be so ridiculously mistaken. Instead we felt that it was only by sad accident that the rags are not her baby as she believes. This was because we knew there had been a baby. I wish I could know all their histories. But no one except myself thinks it's important to know."

Dr. Florian left him feeling thoughtful. The advances Pinel was making in the science of treating disorders of the mind were as extreme as was the regression of medicine at large. The Revolution could be thanked for this much, because it was through Pinel's claim before the Tribune that the protagonists of the Rights of Man were permitting their insane comrades to endure unbearable oppression, that they had been won over to his ideas. No such deviation from old, classical methods would have been permitted in the King's time. Perhaps other good things would come into being as a result of the upheaval.

❖   ❖   ❖

A large crowd was waiting restlessly when Ange arrived. He came up to them singing. "I am fain to sing or satirize rascals, Septemberists, cheats, idlers, spies, and all the thievish gang that rule us!" His voice was powerful and shouting, and only incidentally musical. All of his songs started with that same line, although he seldom repeated himself otherwise. And Robespierre at least did not deserve the charge of being called thievish: he was the Incorruptible.

Composing as he went along, Ange walked his usual route, down the Rue de Coq to the Rue de L'Arbre-Sec. His delighted followers shoved and stumbled after him, trying to keep within range of his voice. When he had sung and talked four hours, he signed that he was done. They knew they could not keep him. That had been tried but he had turned sulky and morose. The mobs of Paris might rule the rulers, but Ange Pitou was his own man.

They dispersed unwillingly. Ange looked around him. A man reading a newspaper wakened his lively suspicion. He started in the direction of Florian's, but soon stopped and looked about him again. The man was close behind him. Ange angled off, the other following. He gave it up, and started toward his own lodgings on the Cité. But he was furious with disappointment. He wanted to hear for himself whether Florian had seen Angélique at the Bicêrte, and question him about the things his wife had mentioned. He paused, half resolved to go himself in spite of the agent. Diane's lovely, troubled face formed in memory; again she pleaded with him to be careful for Florian's sake. Either they were truly kind or he had let himself be taken in by them. Until he knew, he would keep his promise to her. Fidèle could go in his place. Though Robespierre's agents almost certainly knew that she lived with him, her goings and comings went unremarked by them so far as he knew.

Ange and Fidèle lived on the top floor of one of the narrow crowded houses on the Cité. The house and its companions stood out over the water on the narrow branch of the Seine. They were old buildings, drafty and damp. The room on the top floor was cold and very nearly bare.

Fidèle was not her real name; Ange had given her that name because he thought it expressed her better than her own, which was Marie-Rose. She liked her new name because Ange had given it to her. She was like some marvelous instrument on which he could play any tune he liked. Yet the instrument that was fine and true when he played on it could not inaugurate music of its own. His beliefs and convictions were the ideals she lived by, for she had none. She carried his standards bravely and she approved of everything he did, although she must know it would end in his being guillotined eventually. Fidèle was as though created by Ange.

She had been a colorless little being when he found her, wretched and shivering as an abandoned puppy and trying to sell her thin little body for money enough to eat. She had not known how to go about that, even. With so many girls engaged in the profession, it did not seem to him that this one had much chance of surviving. He had told her roughly to come with him and he would see that she was fed and housed anyway. She followed gratefully.

She would never be pretty. Her good features were her hair, abundant and copper colored, curling gently at the ends, and her eyes, a remarkably clear shade of green. Her little face was sharp and pointed, and her dainty bones poked at the skin of elbows and shoulderblades. She looked so fragile, you would think a good hug would break her in two. This proved not to be so. It never occurred to Ange to marry her. The safe conventional things of life had no meaning in these times. Why marry a woman today only to widow her tomorrow? They were happy as they were.

Her joy at seeing him made him realize, and not for the first time, how unfair it was for him to get drunk and fail to come home. Naturally she always imagined the worst. It occurred to Ange that he ought to make provision of some kind for her, before something desperate happened at last to him. It would not sweeten his last moments any to think of her sitting up here waiting, until starvation ended it for her. They sat on the floor crosslegged, and he told her about last night's adventures. Fidèle clapped her hands with joy at the idea that Angélique was not being mistreated after all.

Ange began drawing a diagram, explicit as to landmarks because Fidèle could not read; she would become lost unless he showed clearly just where she was to go. She studied it, nodding her head.

"Watch him closely," Ange said. "Ask a lot of questions. Don't let him put you off about anything."

"But why would he lie to you?"

"I don't trust doctors much. But *she* said it's the government's fault, and that may be, everything else is. Anyway, he's brave. Imagine anyone being brave enough to risk his life just to teach medical students!" It did not occur to Ange that teaching medicine might be a project as well worth the risk as was singing sedition on the streets.

"But why is it wrong for him to teach them?"

"Ah, it's this crazy government, they think it's unequal for one man to be licensed to practice and another not, so maybe they think it's unequal for one man to know more than another. But I guess that what's against the law is that they assemble to learn. Any kind of an assembly is seditious assembly. Ah, the things that go on. I don't know why people put up with it. It can't last much longer. Maybe I'll outlast Robespierre yet," Ange Pitou said.

Fidèle threw a shawl over her head and shoulders. Although the storm had passed, the weather remained sunless and cold. She looked at the diagram one more time, fixing it clearly in memory, then she slipped out.

It was a long walk. Though she had a little money, it did not occur to her to stop a fiacre. She never had ridden in one of those. It was growing late and Fidèle was very tired when she reached the Florians'. Her little sharp face was pinched with cold. Her bare legs were goosefleshed.

Ange had described the place carefully, the little portico, the long steep staircase, uncarpeted and dark, the doorway leading into their apartment. This must be the right place. Fidèle knocked timidly. The door opened almost at once. Diane, wearing a simple flowing dress belted tightly with a girdle of beaten gold, reminded the street waif of pictures of angels she had seen in the old days, in shop windows. Her shining hair, her face, smooth and lovely, and the large grey eyes filled with intelligence and understanding, moved Fidèle to awed admiration; she had never before spoken to a real lady.

Diane said kindly, "The doctor hasn't come in yet. Please come inside to wait. If you're ill, perhaps you should lie down."

"Ange sent me," Fidèle whispered huskily.

"Oh. I'm hoping we will have good news for Ange. Come in." Fidèle followed her, stepping with extreme care as though trying to save the floor from damage by her clumping shoes. Inside, she looked around with grave appreciation, drinking in the room's quiet beauty. Diane, wearing a little smile of friendliness, watched her understandingly. "Sit down, please. What is your name, my dear?"

"Fidèle," she whispered.

"What a pretty name that is!"

"It isn't my name really. Ange calls me that."

"I just finished making cocoa, I'll bring it in here. Excuse me." In the kitchen, she fixed a tray with the cocoa, sweetcakes, cups, and the serviettes. She took her time, wanting to give her queer little guest a chance to orient herself. But when Diane returned to the other room, she was startled to find Fidèle sitting primly on the floor, on her crossed legs.

Diane walked over with her free graceful stride, and sat on the floor too after putting the tray down carefully. It was the first time since her crawling days that Diane Florian had felt called on to sit on a floor. She poured cocoa and gave a cup to Fidèle, who drank it and ate cakes with the grave absorption of hunger. They did not talk any more until the tray was finished. The warm drink and the food stopped Fidèle's shivering.

Without seeming to watch her, Diane noticed every detail. Her dress, of coarse weave and badly worn, was an unattractive shade of grey. Her delicate bones showed plainly, as though she never got quite enough to eat, and her hands were not quite clean at the knuckles. Diane noticed that her shoes, with broken laces that had been tied together, were sizes large for her.

"Did you walk here?"

"Yes, Madame."

"Is it far?"

"Only from the Cité, Madame."

"But that's so far!" The girl looked down at her hands, then, seeing they were not clean, tried to hide them in her lap. Diane said quickly, "We'll try to find you a carriage to go back, though it's hard in this district." She wanted to add, "And you must take one of my cloaks," but was afraid of intruding too soon. Just the same, she was not going to let the poor little creature return as she had come. "What is it, Fidèle? Is there something you want to ask me?"

"No, Madame."

"You were looking at me very strangely."

Fidèle was now watching her own hands half hidden in her lap. "Ange didn't believe you this morning," she said, "about her not being chained and beaten any more."

"I don't know whether she is or not. If she's in the Bicêrte, she's not being mistreated in any way, but until Charlot comes home and tells us, we can't be sure that she's really there."

"Ange was at the Bicêrte. It wasn't like you said."

"No," Diane agreed. "My husband had no connection with it in those days, but Dr. Pinel has told him what it was like. It must have been horrible. But it's not like that any more."

"Ange wants proof."

"But how can I give you better proof than my word?" When Fidèle maintained a stubborn silence, Diane said more gently, "What kind of proof?"

"He doesn't trust you. He doesn't trust anyone but me."

"Are you saying you want to go to the Bicêrte and see for yourself?" Fidèle looked up. Her eyes were glowing with terror. "Perhaps it can be arranged," Diane said, "though Ange mustn't ask to go, not if he's watched as closely as he says. Do you want me to ask Charlot to take you?"

"No!"

"But you wanted proof. What other way is there?"

"I'd be afraid to go there with him!"

"Why?"

"He might never let me out!"

Diane laughed. "What a suspicious pair you are! Why would he want to do that? Why would we lie to you at all?"

"Ange hates doctors."

31

"I know, he told me. But don't you see, the man who hurt his sister was not a real doctor at all." She started to explain it again, but it seemed too hopeless. Fidèle was like some small, wary animal. Diane's feeling of this morning came back. While she had been talking to Ange, she had felt that her most sincere words were rendered meaningless by the inability of the listener to believe them. Then, with relief, she heard Charlot.

"The doctor is coming now. Perhaps you can believe him."

Florian opened the door and gave his floor-sitting wife an amazed stare. "This is Fidèle," Diane said quickly. "Ange sent her. We're glad you've come, because she can't believe me that the procedure at the Bicêrte has been changed, and she's afraid to go there with you because you might not let her out again."

"Good evening, Fidèle. Why didn't Ange come himself?"

"He was being followed," she whispered.

Florian's square-cut mouth twitched with amusement. "Was he? Does that happen often?"

"I think there's something to it, Charlot. He told me this morning it was dangerous for you if he came here." Diane could see he was not paying her full attention. He took off his coat and laid it on a chairback, then crossed the room and held his hands down to the girl. After a moment, she consented to letting him take her hands. He lifted her up. His thin face was intent and serious.

"I don't tell lies, Fidèle," he said. "I don't believe in lying to people. Do you tell lies often?"

"No, Doctor."

"When you tell the truth, do people sometimes not believe you?" She nodded. "How does it make you feel?" Pinpoints of light flickered in her green eyes. She was remembering a beating she had got as a child. Her work-wretched parent had struck her many heavy blows, until she confessed a fault she had not committed. But Florian was speaking again. "Do you know why Angélique became sick?"

"Because that doctor cut up her baby."

"Not really, no. It was because after that happened, she couldn't trust anybody. When she became convinced that all the world was her enemy, then she couldn't live in the world any more. When she heard the truth she thought she was hearing lies, and when kindness was shown her she thought evil was being planned, and so she became mad. You don't want to become like her." She dragged back in sudden terror, but he held her strongly and after a moment she submitted again. "It's true, Fidèle. However many times you have been hurt, you have to keep thinking that other human beings besides yourself can be loyal and truthful and fair. Otherwise, you may hurt yourself more than others could hurt you no matter what they did. Everything my wife and I have told you is true. Will you believe that?"

"Yes," she whispered.

"Will you help Ange believe it?"

"Yes."

He released her hands. His face relaxed and he smiled at her, his smile quick and warm. "Good. Angélique is there, I saw her myself. Dr. Pinel is handling her case, so Ange can be assured that she is having the best care. There has been remarkable improvement already. Dr. Pinel expects she will continue to improve. I intend to follow her case closely, and I'll be glad to answer questions about her at any time. Is there anything you want to ask me now?"

"Do they ever whip her?"

"Never," he said firmly.

"Isn't she chained up?

"Absolutely not. She is, however, confined to her cell. That is necessary because she might hurt herself or someone else if she had her freedom. Of course she will be happier when she can be with the others, and Dr. Pinel hopes that will come in time. Why does Ange think he's being followed? If they were that much interested in him, I should think they'd arrest him and save all that trouble."

"He's been arrested. Fourteen times." Fidèle said it with a pardonable pride and Dr. Florian, who had just given such eloquent expression to the necessity of putting credence in the words of others, exhibited amazement and disbelief. Everyone knew there was no way out of the revolutionary prisons except by way of the Conciergerie and thence to the guillotine.

"He explained it to me this morning," Diane said. "They riot until they get him back. The crowds, I mean."

"Is it possible?"

"Charlot, I wish you had never brought him here! He says it's dangerous to know him. But he promised me—and I guess he means to keep his word, since he sent her in his place."

Dr. Florian said slowly, "If Ange has that much influence with the crowds, he could do a great deal of good. I've been trying to think of some way to warn the people against the false doctors. Why

33

couldn't Ange do that? He's seen for himself the results of their bungling. Where does he live? I'll go at once."

"No, Charlot! Fidèle, make him understand! It's dangerous for you to go there."

"Yes," the street girl said slowly, "it's dangerous." She leaned against the wall, her arms drawn tightly together so that her chest looked narrower even than it was. "I like you," she said to the doctor. "Tell me what it is you want to say to Ange and then you won't have to go yourself."

He sketched the situation rapidly. She listened, nodding, her long copper-colored hair swinging. "The real doctors will have certificates of graduation from their schools," Florian said. "Tell the people to insist on seeing those before permitting any operation or accepting any medicament or course of treatment. If they can't find a private doctor who can show credentials of some kind, tell them the public hospitals are safe. That's all charity work except for occasional payments by the State which are too small to interest the adventurers. If Ange will do that, he will have done a great deal toward preventing other sad incidents."

"I'll tell him what you say."

"She walked here, Charlot. All the way from the Cité."

"I'll go down with her and see if I can't stop a carriage. Doesn't she have anything warmer than that shawl?"

"Just a moment." Diane went out and returned with a cloak that was warm and serviceable, that she had worn only a few times. "Don't be in any hurry to bring it back. I have another." She would have liked to make an outright gift of the cloak, but sensed that the loan of it would be easier to accept.

"Thank you very much, Madame," Fidèle said, making, but with the wrong leg, a stumbling little curtsy. Diane was less amused than touched. There was something reckless and brave about the girl, and the casual directness with which she had said to Florian, "I like you," had won the wife's heart.

Florian and Fidèle went out together. They walked several blocks before he succeeded in stopping a dilapidated old hack. "I never rode in one," she said uneasily.

"It won't be comfortable, but much less tiring than the long walk."

On the way back Florian met Legouvé, who lived in the district. He asked the medical student to follow the street singer for a day or two to see if Florian's words of warning were being passed on.

Legouvé promised to do this. Florian walked on home, full of hope that something had been accomplished toward warning the populace about the false doctors who maimed and slew them for profit under the protection of law.

TWO

The Medical Students

DR. PROSPERO CONTARINI thieved into Paris as guiltily as if he had been commissioned by his Duke to blow up the whole of the French Convention with an infernal machine concealed in his baggage. His baggage was small, innocent of everything but changes of body linen and a fine cheese, just in case the stories he had heard were true, that what Frenchmen had escaped the guillotine were starving. A search of his person was to be avoided, however, because he was traveling on a false passport and two more of them were sewn into his coat lining.

Dr. Contarini was associate professor of anatomy and clinical surgery at the University of Pavia. He was a mild-mannered, studious young man in love with University life, unmarried, the support of a large family of sisters and his mother. This was his first experience in derring-do, and he was not carrying it off well. He told himself that the next time he jumped and screamed because someone addressed an innocent remark, he would find himself in jail as a suspicious character. To be suspected was a capital offense in France, he knew. Just as he finished admonishing himself, a passing citizen told him he was blocking the way. He jumped and screamed, a sharp little eeeek! like a woman's on seeing a mouse. My word, he thought, this will never do! He hurried away in the direction he happened to be facing, the bag with the cheese in it slapping him smartly on his thin scholar's shank.

The addresses he had were for the Hôtel Dieu, the hospital where Florian had been connected at one time, and a residential address more than two years old. He decided on the residence first and stopped a carriage, an old creaking one drawn by a gaunt bay horse with a bony face and flopping underlip. Everything in Paris is sad, Dr. Contarini thought, giving the address to the melancholy driver. Everything in France is sad, he amended. The inns where the Italian doctor had stayed on his journey to the capital were dirty, the service was bad, the food unfit to eat, the prices outrageous, and every town of size had its public square in which a guillotine was func-

36

tioning with vicious efficiency. Fear like a choking fog penetrated everywhere. Sullen faces turned away from yours, denying your common humanity.

Would there be fearful changes in Charlot and Diane, after months of living like that? He had not heard from them since a brief note through smugglers' post two years ago, requesting him not to write again, since all foreign communication was interpreted as treasonable correspondence with the enemies of the Republic. He had not seen the Florians since a visit he had made to south France five years ago, on the eve of the Revolution. The throne was tottering then; royal heads sat uneasily on pale royal necks; but the three friends had guessed nothing of what was coming. All their indignation was focused on Florian's colleagues on the faculty of Montpellier school of medicine, who, out of envy, had compounded his disgrace. His license to practice in Hérault province had been revoked for all time as a result. His dismissal from the faculty had been couched in most brutal terms. Charlot's marriage was only a few weeks old at that time, and Dr. Contarini had wondered where Diane Florian ever had acquired so much spirit and faith. Charlot's own family had turned against him for the disgrace he had brought to their name, but not she.

By the time Dr. Contarini could carry the story back and arrangements had been made to include Pavia's most brilliant graduate on Pavia's present faculty, Charlot had carried his fight for reinstatement to Paris. There, while the medical faculty was making up its mind about him, he was allowed to treat the charity cases at the Hôtel Dieu. Diane had written, "If my husband is quite mad and murderous to boot, he is still fit to treat the penniless *canaille*, as you see. Needless to say, Charlot is determined that his poor despised patients shall receive better care than can be bought elsewhere for many louis." And no doubt they had.

Again Dr. Contarini had written, then Dr. Scarpa had; urging Dr. Florian to come to Italy where he was understood and appreciated. By then, Lafayette's gentlemanly Revolution had captured all free hearts and generous minds. Florian wrote enthusiastically that France was the threshold over which the rest of the world would pass into a new age of scientific enlightenment. By the time he realized his mistake, the borders were closed.

This idea of rescuing his friend from the *sans culottes* had been with Dr. Contarini for a long time. But he had no idea how to organize such an attempt, nor any assurance that Florian was still alive. Two months ago, an émigré doctor visiting Pavia mentioned having seen Florian a few weeks before. Dr. Scarpa, who had some amazing connections all over Europe, promptly borrowed a large sum from the moneylenders, and paved the way with gold and influence for a one-man raid into strange France. Dr. Scarpa had wanted to send a professional bravo. Dr. Contarini had claimed the task for himself, saying, "We were classmates. He's still my best friend. It's right that I should go." Dr. Scarpa had consented, but unwillingly. Many times since, Dr. Contarini had heartily wished that his chief had stood firm.

It seemed he had been in the fiacre a long time, where he was basting slowly in his own body juices. But finally it stopped, in a district so miserably poor that he could not imagine the Florians so much as stopping overnight, much less living there for two years. He left the vehicle, paying the driver exactly what he asked. I ought to be able to *buy* your horse for that sum, Dr. Contarini thought.

He stood for quite a while under the little portico, looking up and down the narrow, sweltering street. The door, standing ajar, revealed a small foyer and a staircase. Contarini was in no hurry to test his luck in coming here, being sure that he was going to be disappointed. He noticed a woman coming along the street toward him, carrying a heavy shopping basket with both hands. She looked exhausted and hotter even than he was, and he had an impulse to walk toward her and offer to carry the basket. So far he had escaped notice by minding his own business. He mounted the long staircase, his certainty deepening that the errand was useless. When he reached the landing there was only one door, so he knocked on that. There was no answer and no sound of movement inside. He deliberated between waiting here until someone did come or inquiring at the hospital. Since he did not know he was in easy walking distance of the hospital, he sat on the stair-landing to wait.

The woman with the market basket turned in. Dr. Contarini watched her climbing the stairs. In the dim light, she came close before he recognized Diane. "Come in," she said. Her voice was pleasant and unhurried. "The doctor will be home soon." He followed her, still stunned at seeing her like this. She set the basket down with a relieved sigh, and really looked at him. For a moment, her face registered nothing but astonishment. "Conte. *Conte!*" Then she was hugging him, and laughing and crying, and saying, "It can't be! How in the world—*Conte!*"

No one ever called him Conte but the Florians. It was an old pet name Charlot had bestowed on him in school days. He was so pleased at being called that again that he had to put Diane aside to get his handkerchief. He stood mopping his eyes and smiling at her foolishly.

"What are you doing in Paris! Don't you know it's dangerous for you to be here?" From an excess of emotion, her voice was almost scolding.

"I've come to save you; do you mind telling me what you're doing in those terrible clothes, carrying market baskets?"

"Well, I've been to market."

"What can Charlot be thinking of?"

"You don't understand, Conte. I have nice clothes, but I don't wear them where strangers can see me."

"Why can't your servant do the marketing?"

"Oh my dear! What servant?"

It was a little thing, and yet brought home the meaning of the Revolution as forcibly as the guillotines in the public squares had done. The necessity of masquerading in one's daily life must add up, in time, to unbearable vexation.

"What did you mean, 'save us'?"

"It's all arranged. I have passports for you. Dr. Scarpa arranged it. In my coat. The passports, I mean—look." He held out the coat, which had been hung over his arm, and showed her something was sewn in its lining.

"But where would we go?"

"To Italy with me, a place has been made for Charlot at the University."

For a little while, she allowed herself to dream. She stood holding his coat, her fingers moving caressingly over the flattish protuberance caused by the papers, and dreamed of living safely . . . of having servants again, and amusements, and most of all, the incredible joy of knowing that when Charlot went away in the morning, he would surely be back by night.

"I don't think he can go, Conte," she said.

"But of course he will, why wouldn't he?"

"You know him. He has responsibilities here."

"His first responsibility is to you."

"I don't know. Maybe. But—" She sighed plaintively. "They're coming tonight."

"The police, you mean!"

"Oh, no. Charlot's students." Her grey eyes lifted to his were filled

39

with renunciation. "I remember that night we thought he had been taken. They were with me, waiting too. I was so sorry for them. They have worked so hard—it means so much to them— There is no one else. If he did leave it to me, I couldn't say it."

"I don't understand, Diane. What couldn't you say?"

"That it would be right to abandon them."

"How many students does he have?"

"There are five of them."

He gave a short bark of laughter. "At Pavia, he would have fifty or a hundred to teach."

"But it wouldn't be the same, would it? You say, 'A place has been made for him,' but here, there is no one else. He's needed, Conte. So badly needed! It isn't only the students. There are so few real doctors left, but the people go right on falling sick or getting themselves hurt. I know how he feels, I know what his plans are. I don't think he'll go."

"What are his plans, Diane?"

"Robespierre can't last. Everyone feels that. He's overreached himself. The people are tired. Charlot had influential friends once. They're all in hiding now, as we are, but if the government falls, they'll come out. Some of them will become important again. Charlot has an idea that it might be his destiny to restore French medicine." She rubbed her forehead distractedly. "That sounds so vainglorious," she complained. "You'd have to live with it to understand. I don't think he can go."

"What about you? Do you want to go?"

"Ah, yes."

"Then you must help me convince him."

She shook her head. "He must decide himself. They trust him so. He gave his word to do everything he could toward seeing them placed in a real school, with facilities for dissection and experiment, under capable instruction. They believe he will do it someday. I believe that he will. I'll be very happy if he's willing to go to Italy. But I can't urge him, Conte, I can't!"

"You're incredible," he said, marveling.

"I've lived with him so many years. But it hasn't really been a long time, has it? It seems long because so much has happened. But I know how he thinks. Maybe he would give in if I begged him. I think he loves me very much. But if he were unhappy afterwards— A man like Charlot can't go against himself. The people who are

lucky enough to be loved by a man like that have no right to use his
love to try to change him."

"How long has he had these students, Diane?"

"Almost a year now."

"When does he find time for them?"

"They come here three nights a week."

"Here? At the apartment?" She nodded. "Three nights a week!"
She nodded again. "But you can't teach medicine piecemeal," Dr.
Contarini objected. "It requires steady application, and at least a
minimum of facilities. I know something about it. After all, I'm a
teacher myself."

"I know, Conte. He says the same thing."

"Let's be logical! If Charlot comes to Italy with me, five young
men who might possibly become doctors will be lost to the profession. But if he doesn't, a mind and talent that Dr. Scarpa calls
unique and invaluable may be destroyed at any moment." He looked
at her severely. "Diane. I risked my life to come here. A part of my
willingness was because Charlot is my friend, but more of it was
because I know that his life is more valuable than my own. I must
say this is not the reception I expected. I've gone in terror of my
life and the fear of not finding you, only to have you tell me blandly
that you prefer to stay where you are." His indignation made her
smile. "I don't see anything amusing about it," Dr. Contarini added,
somewhat sharply.

"But it's ridiculous."

"Very."

Diane made a little helpless gesture. "I have to start supper," she
said. "Whether we're going to Italy and be happy, or staying in
France and be conscientious, we have to eat. I don't know, Conte.
Let Charlot decide it. Whatever he says is all right with me."

        ✧   ✧   ✧

But Dr. Florian's decision, when he announced it, was not acceptable to his wife after all. First they ate. The food, though there was
no more than enough to fulfill the needs of their appetites, had
been seasoned skillfully. Dr. Contarini appreciated that, and much
else; he could see that it had taken loyalty and imagination on both
their parts to create this little oasis of warm charm in the heart of
troubled France. He admired them inordinately.

Florian he found more changed than Diane was. He seemed much older than he had been only five years ago. There was a sternness about him that Contarini did not remember having noticed before. His square-shaped mouth was firm to the point of hardness. It was almost an ascetic face, only occasionally relieved by the warm flashing smile that had always been his peculiar charm.

He listened attentively to everything Dr. Contarini had to say. He did not, as Diane had, reach any conclusion swiftly. He was obviously in close deliberation with himself, weighing pros and cons. Occasionally he asked questions. True to her word, Diane said nothing that would influence him one way or the other.

"Great things are afoot," Contarini was saying. "Dr. Spallanzani has joined our faculty. From Modena, you will remember, I know you're acquainted with his work. He's a tireless experimenter too, and Dr. Scarpa imagines you might do great things together. We're starting a real renaissance, Charlot, a new golden age, the sort of thing you hoped for in France, remember? But you were wrong, it was Pavia all the time." Briefly, Florian's dark eyes glowed with expectancy, but then he took back his look of sternly measuring one choice against another.

They finished eating, and Diane cleared the things away from the table. Still Charlot had not spoken. The students began coming. Legouvé and Monteil arrived together, Robert Lasné came practically on their heels, then Oliver Gris, then Jouvancy. Contarini studied them with deep interest. For these young men, Diane had been willing to renounce every temptation life can hold—personal safety, the companionship of her kind, amusements, recognition of her husband's extraordinary talents. They seemed callow and unattractive to command so much loyalty.

He realized they were in awe of himself, and wondered why. Their shy questions finally made him understand that it was because he had just come from Pavia. To them the University was a fabled place, impossible of attainment. Contarini guessed what wistful desire to return there had prompted Florian to tell them so much about it. He began to feel confident of the eventual decision.

The skeleton was produced. Its age, the silver wires that held it together, and the fact that a missing tibia had been replaced by a piece of carved wood, amused the Italian. Evidently this was the only equipment for study that they possessed. The students arranged themselves in a half circle, facing the doctors. Diane sat apart slightly, on the couch.

Dr. Florian said, "You were to have begun the study of the stomach, but that will keep." Diane giggled and he glanced at her sharply, but then smiled. "All right," he said, "the stomach won't keep, but I'll bring you another." It was Dr. Contarini's turn to side-glance sharply, but he read on his friend's closed, dark face that no final decision had been made yet.

"Our relationship necessarily has been subjective and indwelling," Dr. Florian was saying. "This opportunity of acquainting you with another mind capable of guiding you is too good to be missed. Also, I have been pushing you along fast, without any recapitulation. An evening devoted to summarizing what you know already would not be wasted. The paper you see in Dr. Contarini's hand lists subjects on which you have had instruction. One of Dr. Contarini's duties at the University of Pavia is to examine the new students and then place them. He will question you and comment on your answers." Florian left his chair and joined Diane on the couch as a signal they were on their own.

Dr. Contarini's only intention was to humor his friend. As he had said earlier medicine cannot be taught piecemeal, three nights a week. He began offhandedly, asking superficial questions that any intelligent layman could have answered. He read on their young faces their disappointment in him. Still without conviction, he deep-ened the quality of his interrogation. Then they began to assume personalities to him. Jouvancy, for instance, was quick and imagina-tive, while Robert Lasné's answers were plodding and badly ex-pressed. But that Lasné knew exactly what he wanted to say and that his knowledge was essentially correct, could not be doubted.

Awareness of Florian's true purpose dawned slowly. This was not, as he had claimed, a mere exercise. It was a duel on whose outcome his decision depended. If the students could demonstrate that they were capable of learning medicine from him under these adverse cir-cumstances, he would remain with them. But if Contarini, an expe-rienced teacher, could demonstrate that Florian had been deceiving himself in thinking so, he would give them up.

Dr. Contarini was frequently inadequate in his adult relation-ships, but the domination of the young came easily to him. And he could be sharp-tongued when he wished. His questions became tricky; his comments, when he trapped one of them, coldly sarcastic. He was deliberately being a bad teacher, by doing his best to put the students in a poor light. Forced into retreat by a nimble, trained mind no longer intent on anything but the besting of themselves, the young men fought doggedly without crying quarter. That the savagery of his attack was puzzling to them showed, and Contarini began to feel shame but Florian was worth it. He kept expecting Florian to interfere, but he did not.

Suddenly Dr. Contarini understood what Diane had meant when she talked about a man going against himself. He was doing that now and after all, he could not go on with it. He began to examine them coolly and fairly, in a sincere effort to measure their qualities of mind and the extent of their knowledge. He was amazed at how much they knew and how well they knew it and, though he was filled with sorrow at losing Florian to them, there was a kind of solemn joy, a reverence toward the insistent human spirit that will climb toward the light out of the darkest pits that malevolence can dig.

❉   ❉   ❉

The young men had just left them. Retreating footsteps could still be heard on the stairway. Dr. Florian looked at Dr. Contarini quizzically.

"I'm dazzled, Charlot. They have had the benefits of masterful teaching. I don't know another man who could have done it, except, perhaps, Dr. Scarpa."

"The quality of the teaching has had less to do with it than the fierceness of their will-to-learn."

"I imagine both were necessary in the achievement of this miracle. I would put all of them into second-year classes, without hesitation."

"Lasné too?"

"He makes a poor impression in comparison with the others, but yes, Lasné too."

"I'm glad to hear it. I get impatient with him, but then I find myself thinking that Dr. Pinel must have been much like him at that age."

"I know what this means, of course," Contarini said.

"Do you, Conte?"

"You won't give them up now."

"No."

"I don't know as I could abandon them either, if they were mine." He saw Diane watching her husband with shining eyes. His own feelings bewildered him. "I tried to spoil it for them," he said. "I tried to make them look stupid to you. Any teacher knows how."

"I was sure you wouldn't go on with it."

44

"Why didn't you stop me?" Florian smiled and shook his head. "Tell me," Dr. Contarini insisted.

"It was better this way. They would not have understood what you were doing, and so they would have had to think that I was protecting them from you because they were too weak."

"Well," Contarini said philosophically, "I seem to have come on a fool's errand. As Diane pointed out earlier today, there is something sublimely ridiculous about the rescuer on white horse who comes up at mad gallop, only to be told to go home again and stop bothering."

"I didn't say anything like that!" she protested.

"No, but you laughed at me."

Florian took her hand lightly. "Diane asks nothing of the world but to love it and laugh at it. I shall miss her laughing at me." He lifted the hand and kissed it.

She read the meaning that Contarini had missed in his words. She sat up, tense and frightened. "No, Charlot. Please!"

"It's the only thing to do."

"But why? Why? We're getting along all right. Nothing's happened, nothing's going to happen."

"You know I've always said that you must go if a way could be found."

"I won't do it, Charlot. I won't go without you."

"You must."

"You have no right to send me away from you! Not until you can say that you've stopped loving me, and you haven't, because I'd know."

"I can't permit you to stay in France when a way to leave it has been provided. That's final." His tone was almost cold. Only his eyes, and his mouth hard with hurt, gave him away that he was suffering as intensely as she was.

Dr. Contarini's embarrassment was acute. They had forgotten him, he knew, but the scene was too intimate to be observed by a third party. He thought about stealing out, but he was afraid. The less Paris saw of him, the more likely it was that he would get away from her alive. Then Charlot spoke to him. "When did you plan to leave, Conte?"

"As soon as possible."

"I suppose it's wise for her to travel lightly."

"Yes, we'll have to go horseback to the border," Contarini said.

"I won't go!"

"Be quiet, Diane. We'll discuss it later. I have a few thousand livres, enough for her for a year or two I should think. Can she stay with your mother?"

"Mother and the girls would be delighted to have her, of course, and there's plenty of room. But Charlot, have you really thought this out? While I assure you I can be trusted, it's decidedly irregular for us to go dashing about together. You can't so much as correspond with her, and it may be years before there's any decided change in the situation here. I don't like to be responsible for separating you."

"Yes, I've thought it out and I'm simply meeting all my obligations the best way I can. If she were yours, would you consent to her staying here when there was a way to escape?" He did not wait for any answer because none was necessary. He spoke to his wife gently. "I know it seems hard to go away and live with strangers. But I know Conte's mother and his sisters, and you won't be strangers long. They are gay and kind and loving, as you are." She started to speak, but he put his hand gently over her mouth. "No, my dear. Later if you must, but I can't bear much more. I'll come for her the first moment I can, Conte. If it is a long time, and her money runs out—"

He interrupted gruffly. "She is our most welcome guest. If you mean for her to pay for what little she eats, I'm only insulted."

"She will know how to be your guest without being your burden. What we have I want her to take, because I have income."

Contarini said, "If someone will show me where I'm to sleep, I think it would be a good idea to leave you two alone."

Diane rose promptly and led him to the extra bedroom. The street singer had been the last guest to use it. She had never got over being afraid of Ange's part in their lives even though he had been a marvel of circumspection. Fidèle came occasionally for reports on Angélique's progress. Angélique had left her cell and was mingling with the others, though she still defended her pitiful bundle of rags from everyone except Dr. Pinel and Dr. Florian. Neither Florian nor Diane had seen the street singer a second time, but the steady influx of the sick and injured to the Hôtel Dieu was a link, because Ange, once convinced by Fidèle of Florian's sincerity, warned his crowds regularly against the false doctors.

Diane turned the bed down for Dr. Contarini with brisk, hostess-like movements; pointed out the closet, gave him towels and soap. He felt awkward in her presence. He had brought her grave suffering, though that was unintentional. Finally he offered in stumbling words a half apology. "You know I never expected anything like this."

"I was so glad to see you," she said.

The reproach, though so gently spoken, hurt him. He did not know any answer to make, and made none. She left him, walking with quick free strides, her head high. Charlot seemed to be doing the only thing, and yet Dr. Contarini wondered if he were not doing the wrong thing.

        ✿   ✿   ✿

They lay side by side, their shoulders touching, and yet the loneliness and separateness they were feeling foretold what their feelings were going to be during the months, or years, ahead.

Diane said in a little voice, "I won't beg you any more, and I won't defy you, but this is a mistake, Charlot."

"I'm doing the best I know," he repeated.

"We've lived this way a long time. I have come to think that being together, and loving each other, kept us both safe. If you send me away, you won't be safe any more. Neither will I." He did not say anything. "We may never find each other again," she said.

"I'll come for you the first moment I can."

"But when will that be? You're so sure the Robespierre government is going to fall, but what makes you sure his successors are going to be any better? So far, every change has been for the worst."

"That's a reason for you to go, not a reason for keeping you."

"Something could happen to you here and I wouldn't know for months, or years. I don't see how I'm going to stand it."

"It is hard. I see that. Perhaps I'm asking too much."

"You are, indeed you are!"

"But either you must go alone with Conte, or I must give up my work here and go with you. It's your right to demand that I do." She was silent. "Speak up, Diane. Shall I go with you tomorrow?"

"I want to stay here with you."

"No."

She turned away and cried softly into her hands.

II

WHEN DIANE, in Italy, learned of the downfall and death of Robespierre and the end of the Terror, she began expecting Charlot to come. If she went out to ride or swim with the two Contarini girls who still lived home, she was impatient to get back. Neighbors dropped in and out of the house all the time; the sound of their knocking would make her heart pound. Then the Signora would shake her head and say in Italian, "The men punish us with their love. They can't help it, God made them that way."

Letters from him began coming finally, but they were uninformative, except as expressions of love and yearning. That the writer's caution was necessary was shown in the fact that none of them were without signs of having been tampered with. Dr. Contarini faithfully brought her what foreign intelligence he gleaned at the University. The new government was called the Directory. There were five Directors, and they kept changing with bewildering rapidity. He heard reports that society was coming back, and that people from those countries not at war with France were being allowed to come and go as in the old days before the Revolution. Diane could not go to Charlot because Italy, while not at war with France herself, belonged to Austria which was. She had no choice but to wait until he came for her, and none of his letters mentioned anything about that.

"I'm afraid things are worse there than we suppose," Conte said, when she gave him one of the letters to read. But though she tried to pin him down about that, he could not say just what had given him the impression.

In many ways, Diane's life was very happy. Pavia, called by the ancients The City of a Hundred Towers, lay some twenty miles south of Milan. In spite of its stout walls, it had been sacked three times, by Brennus and by Hannibal in classical times, and more recently by an Austrian division that had run wild and looted her before the commanders could regain control of their men. Scars from that time still showed and were pointed out to the visitor with gesticulations of horror, although already the ruins were mellowing into historical landmarks.

Diane's husband was still remembered kindly by many families from his year-of-practice among them, as was required by the University. She met people who had known him before she did, and she looked for the first times on scenes intimate in his memory; it made her feel oddly close to him. Walking along the narrow, ancient streets, smelling the characteristic odor that Charlot had described to her, of thyme and rosemary, verbena and orange blossoms, carried to them from the countryside on a soft wind, it would seem to her that all

48

she needed to do was turn quickly and she would see him, a younger, gayer Charlot. How had he ever resisted the temptation of returning here? When she thought of Paris she thought of its waiting, stifling darkness. Though the lanternposts were still standing, the lanterns never were lit any more. All France was like a giant lanternpost whose light had gone out.

An intense Francophobia existed among the Italians. Their sunny land had been conqueror's booty for a thousand years. The people were accustomed to foreign rule and had learned to live with it, but France they dreaded next to hellfire. Because of France's war with Austria, invasion was always a possibility. Diane attended church regularly with the Contarinis. While the priests and the people prayed to be delivered from the French, Diane prayed for Charlot.

❖   ❖   ❖

The first act of the new government involving the medical profession was the closing of the hospitals through cutting off funds for drugs and food and fuel. The homeless sick now had no place to go. Nothing in Robespierre's bloody record had been so base.

Dr. Florian and the other doctors stood around and watched the exodus, their faces tense and defeated. Some of the patients were barely able to crawl from their pallets. They would be dead by morning.

He applied for his visé into Italy. It was the only thing left to do; he could not appear to condone what this new government had done. If his application were refused, he was resolved to leave France by illegal means, though that would be hard since he had very little money. What he had, he paid as a bribe to an official in the visé office in the hope of getting the medical students out with him. If he could keep his promise to them of entering them in a real school capable of licensing them, he would have salvaged something out of these wasted years of lost effort. The blow had been too heavy to leave him with any feeling higher than relief that the fight was over, that he could now go to Diane with a clear conscience.

The day after the harrowing scene at the hospital, Ange Pitou made one of his visits. The street singer had begun coming to the apartment lately, sometimes with Fidèle, more often alone. He had come the first time on the night of Robespierre's fall, a wicker basket full of champagne bottles in either hand, and he had danced and sung, miming the execution which he had witnessed. Ange had

49

boasted then that his influence with the crowds of Paris was the cause of the downfall, and he had promised to harass the new government too unless it conducted itself in a way that pleased him.

When Florian told Ange what had happened, "What about the Bicêrte?" was his first response.

"I don't think that will be closed. Sick people are defenseless; when they're turned out, they simply die of exposure and lack of care. But the insane can be dangerous."

As soon as he had been reassured about Angélique, the singer turned mean. "So you're giving up your fight! Not I. I'll stay with it until they kill me."

"Yes, I'm giving up, I'm simply acknowledging that I'm beaten. The medical profession has received its death blow. Very few if any of the real doctors will remain now."

Ange said sullenly, "What's going to happen to us here? You told me to tell them to go to the real ones. Now you say they're all leaving."

"I can tell you what will happen. Endemic diseases will start up. The populace will begin dying in waves. Then, if it isn't too late, there will be proper legislation and the doctors will return."

"You can't go if I don't want you to," Ange said, eying him slyly.

"No? And why not?"

"It will take a month at least for your application to be acted on. Suppose I start putting it in my songs what your reason is for leaving. Paul Barras and those others won't like it. You'll be turned down."

"I suppose you are right, but since when have we become enemies?"

"We're not enemies, but I don't want you to go."

"We will be if you attempt to stop me!" Florian said sharply.

"Is Dr. Pinel going too?"

"I don't know. I haven't seen Pinel. Probably not, since the Bicêrte won't be included in the measure."

"I don't know him, though. I want you to stay."

"Because of Angélique, you mean." The singer nodded. "But then you're trying to penalize me because I tried to help you in the first place."

"I don't care. You're needed here."

"I can't stop you from executing your threat, Ange. But I can promise you that it will do you no good. You can't compel me to have any more to do with her, and you can't keep me from finding another way to get out."

"You'd get killed, trying that."

"I'll try just the same."

Both their faces were dark with anger. I deserve this for becoming his friend in the first place, Florian was thinking. I should have put him out that first night, when Monteil told me who he was. He's a troublemaker, he's without conscience.

But then Ange began to wheedle. "Will you stay if I can get your hospitals opened again?"

"How can you do that?"

"Will you stay if I can?"

Those moments watching while the sick crawled or stumbled into the bitter streets to die, had killed something in Florian. His feeling toward his dream now was without hope, and mocking. He was finished with France; he would be happy if he never saw her again. The idea of going to Diane had now taken hold of him with such power that any new delay seemed unbearable. But if the sacrifice of his own desires could buy only that, a place where the desperately ill could receive attention, he would have to make it.

"Yes," Florian said, "I'll stay if the hospitals open again. I don't think you can do it, though."

His duties at the Bicêrte were light and required very little time. With the Hôtel Dieu closed he had, for the first time since his graduation, plenty of leisure. In a mood of farewell, he visited what few places held good memories for him. He accepted invitations to go out into the new society that was beginning to form. Some friends from old days were becoming prominent, as he had imagined would happen. But they were in no mood for serious subjects, and neither was he now, he was merely marking time.

Twice he joined the crowds waiting for Ange. Though he was still angry at the singer for threatening him, he much enjoyed Ange's cleverness and his biting sarcasm. And Ange did what he could to get the hospitals reopened. He begged and commanded the people to demonstrate their displeasure until Barras and the other Directors gave in. But on this subject, he was swimming against the tide. People who were healthy enough to follow Ange around for hours were in no need of medical attentions for themselves. He could not whip up real interest because he could not make them see their own interests were involved. This selfishness was a widespread reaction to the end of the Terror, and Ange was too closely in tune with the crowds not to know that he was failing in his bid to force the Directory to rescind their order. He did not attempt to carry out his other threat, however.

Much of Florian's leisure time while he waited to hear about their visés, was spent with the students. They were wild with joy at the idea of entering the University. He drilled and examined them until he was satisfied that, in some subjects, they were ready for third-year classes. The money for their tuition was a problem, but no doubt he could arrange to pay that out of his own salary as an instructor. They were all he had to show for years of work and dreaming, and he was very proud of them. But he continued to warn them that they might not be allowed to leave after all. They were the right age for the Army.

One of the houses to which Florian went regularly was owned by an old friend who had been one of his first private patients in Paris. She was a widow, considerably older than he and somewhat influential; she was beginning to make herself felt again in the new society. She was obviously a little bit in love with him. Florian, accustomed to this emotional phenomenon in female patients, always had treated her advances with tact and courtesy. On one of her Thursdays, Florian learned that Carnot, one of the Directors, was also a guest.

He studied the great man from a distance. Carnot looked grizzled and kindly, not at all the sort of person who would want to pass a law callously condemning the homeless sick to die on the streets untended. His reputation was a good deal better than the reputations of his fellow Directors. It occurred to Florian that Carnot had the power to grant visés to the students. He asked his hostess to present him.

"I wish you would settle a minor mystery for me, Dr. Florian," Carnot said. "I'm told that in the past month more than a hundred members of your profession have applied to leave the country. Why this sudden hegira of physicians? Do you know?"

The grizzled old man looking at him with such kindness was one of the rulers of France. If he wished, he could reopen the medical schools as well as the hospitals; he could inaugurate legislation to force the false doctors out. No, Florian thought angrily, I'm through with all that. He answered with care, "I've requested a visé myself, Citizen-Director, and I hope very much that it will be granted. I've been offered a post on the faculty at the University of Pavia. It would mean a great deal to me to accept."

"And you want me to help you." Florian's sudden, charming smile answered him. The Director said, "But we have no desire to hold you here against your will. I see no reason for you to fear a refusal."

"But I've asked to take five young men with me. They are anxious to enter the University as students. It's their applications that I'm worried about."

"Army material, are they?"

"They're the right age," he admitted.

"Then I can tell you almost certainly that they will not be allowed to go. With three wars on our borders, this is not the time to send our young men out of the country to study. I should think that would be obvious to you." He had spoken sharply, and finishing, made a curt gesture of dismissal.

"They are the only medical students in France. It would be criminal folly to force them into the Army." Carnot swung around, startled and displeased. Florian met his glance firmly, and after a moment, the old man softened.

"That was a bold speech, Dr. Florian. But I see that you realize it yourself. You may speak to me without fear, but first, perhaps our hostess will be kind enough to show us to a room where we can talk without being overheard."

Fluttering with excitement, she took them into her own apartment where a warm fire was going and there were comfortable chairs. Carnot indicated that she should leave them, then said to Florian, "I have an idea that your flash of animosity toward myself had its source in our recent measure depriving the hospitals. I want you to know that I had nothing to do with that, it was passed over my objections in fact. Our government is very short of money and some of us have luxurious tastes." His mouth pulling down wryly, he added, "My colleagues felt that the Luxembourg Palace ought to be restored and redecorated so that our sittings might be held in surroundings befitting our power and importance. That's where your hospital money is going."

"Truly, Citizen-Director, it was not from animosity that I spoke, but because I need your help."

"I don't think you're going to win my consent as far as the young men are concerned, but I'm willing to listen to you."

"That's all I ask, that you will permit me to present their case."

"Very well, do so."

Carnot listened to the story thoughtfully, fingering his fringe of beard. When Florian told him how the students had acquitted themselves before Dr. Contarini, he smiled with warm approbation. "They are remarkably determined. I begin to understand your indignation on their behalf. Suppose we compromise. Select the two most promising of the students and I'll see to it that they get passports, but I'll conscript the others. No? You're not satisfied?"

Florian was imagining himself with them, telling them that. Three young faces were naked and hurt, two others glorified. It was so unfair. "It's unfair," he said.

"It is, isn't it? Most compromises are. But it's the best bargain I can make, and I'm humoring you as it is. It isn't medical students we need these days, but soldiers."

"That simply isn't true, Citizen-Director. One day you'll find to your cost that my five young men would have been more valuable than five battalions. But then it will be too late. When medical knowledge has been eradicated, one epidemic is going to follow another until the populace has been wiped out. That will be the end of your Revolution. It also will be the end of France."

"There's no shortage of doctors, surely?"

"There's no shortage of medical mountebanks, you mean. From the first days of the Revolution, unlicensed, untaught men have been permitted to practice. Their numbers multiply every day; it's an easy living for them. Most of my work these past five years has been correcting blunders made by them. Often it's too late."

"Can this be true? Why hasn't it been called to my attention before?"

Florian said angrily, "Because the real doctors left France long ago. The handful of us who are left are on the point of going. One piece of legislation follows another to the detriment of the profession, and your order closing the hospitals was the death blow. We're finished with France. We're sick at heart. When you're driven to reforming the laws, maybe the doctors will come back. Maybe they'll come back in time. Maybe they won't."

"You're an angry man, Dr. Florian."

"I told you. I'm sick at heart."

"I should think love of your country would persuade you to stay here, if things are as bad as you say."

"For years I've been telling myself the same thing. Now I'm tired. I want a measure of peace and security, and some personal happiness."

"As all men do, and no one should blame you. You've given me much to think about, Doctor. I wish you weren't leaving because we

54

might have accomplished a great deal together. Certainly I can do nothing toward restoring the medical profession if the doctors themselves refuse to help me." Florian looked at him. Carnot met the glance smilingly. "Surely you didn't think that I'd let you convince me of the danger, but then do nothing about it?"

"Have I convinced you?"

"I'll make an investigation, of course. Do you mind telling me something about yourself? Your education, your background—or are you so determined on going that further talk between us is useless?"

"I don't know! I thought I was. And yet I've dreamed of nothing else all these years but an opportunity coming finally, of doing something toward re-establishing French medicine. If you are planning anything of the kind, I would like to have a part in it."

"That's up to you."

"There are other considerations."

"Do you care to confide them to me?"

"My wife is in Italy. I miss her very much, but I don't want to bring her back here if there's going to be further trouble, as many people seem to think."

"Our government is not a completely stable one," Carnot admitted.

"Diane was with me through most of the Terror. I don't want her to have to go through any more."

The Director said curiously, "How did you get her out? The borders were closed then."

"Friends of mine on the faculty at Pavia arranged about false passports and bribed the border guards. I was supposed to have gone too."

"They must think a great deal of you at Pavia. And why didn't you go when your wife did?"

"I had my students, and as I told you, this idea of serving the cause of French medicine."

"Which you have given up since."

Florian said tightly, "We had to stand by and watch our patients stumble off to die. Nothing I have ever experienced caused such hopelessness and bitterness of spirit as that."

"I can imagine your feelings. I would have shared them, had I been compelled to witness it. But we haven't settled the matter of your students. As I remember, you refused compromise and now I think you were right. If I see to it that they are allowed to leave

55

France and finish their studies, could they be trusted to return here when they were graduate doctors?"

"I think they would make any bargain. I think they would promise you an arm or a leg to be allowed to go to a school capable of licensing them."

Carnot said pleasantly, "But I have no use for their arms or legs. Five graduate doctors are worth bargaining for, perhaps. What about their tuition?"

"I planned to pay it out of my salary as an instructor."

"Is Pavia an exceptional medical college?"

"The best in Europe, Citizen-Director."

"Did you graduate there?"

"Yes, and then from Leyden."

"In Holland, isn't it?"

"Yes, Citizen-Director."

"Was it necessary to go to two schools?"

"Dr. Scarpa particularly wanted me to go to Leyden. He has, and had then, the chair of anatomy at Pavia. He's unquestionably the finest anatomist in Europe."

"I want to know why he considered it necessary for you to graduate from two schools." Florian flushed, and looked at the toes of his shoes. "Is it modesty that prevents you from answering me, Dr. Florian?"

"Dr. Scarpa was exceptionally kind to me."

"In short, he thought you were an exceptional student who ought to have an exceptional education." Florian's flush deepened. Carnot said, "You must learn to speak out for yourself. I don't like boasters either, but if I'm to make up my mind about you correctly I must be trusted with the facts. Would these young men of yours be capable of instructing others after they were graduated from Pavia? Or would they be required to take two degrees also."

"Oh no, it's unusual to do that. Yes, they'd be qualified to teach."

"How many years does it take to make a doctor?"

"Five years usually, that includes the year-of-practice. But I think mine could do it all in three years."

"Very well. Their expenses and tuition will be paid out of the public funds. Make up an estimate of what the whole thing will cost. If the entire bill is paid at once, there won't be a chance of another turn of fortune robbing them before they have finished. Then send them to me, I want to see them for myself, and I want to be assured they are willing to return to France."

When Florian tried to speak he was choked with emotion. He was imagining their young faces when they heard his news. Carnot smiled understandingly. "There is no need to thank me," he said. "You and your young men have earned every help I can give you. We will consider their education as our first move in this business of restoring the profession. But we have come to no decision about you. Are you going with your young men or staying here to help me?"

"Whatever you command, Citizen-Director."

"I don't want to command you. You have rendered a considerable service to the nation already. If your heart is set on going, it's only right that you be allowed to."

"If I can help, of course I want to stay."

"Good. Let me tell you what I have in mind. As you may know, I'm Minister of War. I have very little to do with the affairs of the interior. Paul Barras is Minister of the Interior. He's been after me to appoint his pet general to the command of the Army of Italy. While I think the young man has great talent, I've held back because I don't want Barras meddling with the Armies. However, I will consent to Bonaparte for the Army of Italy if Barras will consent to the appointment of a Medical Inspector. It will be necessary to investigate your background, of course. If you have been candid with me, as I believe you have, the post is yours if you want it. It will carry an annual salary of six thousand livres a year."

"Of course I want it!" Florian said, flushing with joy. "Six thousand livres a year is too much, however. I can get along on much less and if your government is in such financial straits as to have to close the hospitals, you can't afford to pay such salaries. Two thousand livres a year is more than enough; in fact, half that sum is sufficient."

"You're very refreshing, Dr. Florian," Carnot murmured, then said, "I have an idea we're the only two persons in Paris who are not primarily engaged in lining our own pockets." Florian laughed. "But more of that later," Carnot said. "The Medical Inspector will be required to visit all the principal cities of France and make recommendations for each. He will interview the various doctors, weeding out the false ones, naming those qualified to act as instructors, to staff the hospitals, or to treat patients in private practice. I will require cost estimates for each school and hospital, both the actual reopening and maintenance afterwards. However, it is only fair to say that I'm powerless at this point to do any more than that."

"I don't ask more than that. Just to get the schools and the hospitals reopened, and the practice limited to qualified men."

"But you don't understand me. At the present time I can't force your legislation through. Paul Barras and I are involved in a duel for power. It would only weaken my position to start measures and have them fail. I would like to promise you that as fast as you can get the facts and figures to me, action will be taken, but I can't make promises of that kind until there is an outcome of some sort between Barras and me."

"I see."

"Do you still want the post? I assure you that much groundwork is necessary before anything can be done. On the other hand, you might think this is too speculative by far, and I wouldn't blame you if you did."

"I am disappointed. I thought we could start at once."

Carnot said, "I want to spend the revenues of the nation in bringing our wars to successful conclusion, and in reforming the affairs of the interior. Paul Barras wants the money diverted into his own pocket. Since he's willing for the other Directors to enrich themselves at public expense, he has dangerous influence. If you accept my offer, you may indeed fulfill your dream of restoring French medicine. But if he defeats me, nothing will come of it and your work will have been wasted. Do you want time to make your decision?"

"No," Florian said, "you've been more than fair, you have promised all you can. I'll stay of course."

"What about your wife? Do you want me to arrange to bring her back here?"

"What is your sincere opinion about that?"

"My sincere opinion, yes." He looked thoughtful, stroking his beard. "My wife is here," he said. "A minute please, Dr. Florian. When it became evident that Barras and I were involved in a death struggle, I made very close arrangements. Very close, yes. Everything is mapped out. There is very little chance of either of us being taken. Since you and the Citizeness Florian would not be in the same danger, it would be futile to lay such elaborate plans. You wanted my sincere opinion. In your place I would continue the arrangement you now have, until Barras has been ousted, or I have. Either way, it ought not to take long."

"All right," Florian said. "It's good advice, I know." Diane's words returned hauntingly. "We may never find each other again," she had said. He frowned into the fire. He did not realize how naked with longing his face was but Carnot, watching him, shook his head once in a little gesture of commiseration.

But Florian's feeling of loss drained away. Something great and good had been offered him. If his meeting with Carnot was to result in all the old man had promised, Charlot Florian would have performed services to his profession as great as any physician in history short of Hippocrates himself. He shivered. His joy was so deep, it was like being afraid, or being cold.

III

THE MEDICAL STUDENTS arrived in Pavia. Their young faces were transfigured; there was a kind of glory about them. Dr. Contarini met them and took them around, and Dr. Scarpa himself interviewed them. Scarpa was fascinated by the sufferings they had endured, the faith they had shown, to earn this day. He invited all of them into his classes; an exceptional honor. He was much moved by the idea that Charlot Florian had sent them to him.

The students were burdened with messages for Diane. Dr. Contarini took them home with him, and they were closeted with her for an entire afternoon. All the things Florian had not dared write her because of the censorship, he had confided to them. She heard for the first time of his meeting with Carnot, his new title, his important duties. Dr. Charlot Florian, Medical Inspector for the French Republic. She felt drowning in pride of him. The investigation of himself had been a thorough one and that old trouble at Montpellier had come to light, but Carnot had been quick to see there was more credit in it than damage. Diane was filled with love and respect toward a man she had never seen.

She found it hard to resign herself to remaining in Italy. Charlot had explained carefully to the students, who had memorized his explanations: the struggle for power with Paul Barras, the fact that he was seldom in Paris, the assurance that this phase of affairs would end soon. Loyally, she fought down her feeling of hurt that he consented to their separation when the turn of affairs had made reunion possible.

She was so happy for the students that she cried a little after they were gone. Some of the wonder and awe they felt at really being here, transferred itself to her. Charlot had promised to see them entered someday in a real college. He had kept his promise magnificently, despite insurmountable odds. Because of him, Dr. Lasné and Dr. Jouvancy, Dr. Gris, Dr. Monteil, and Dr. Legouvé would exist. It was almost an act of creation. No wonder she cried, remembering the night they had sat with her when Charlot was so late and they had supposed he was taken. They are like grown sons of ours, Diane thought today as she had thought then.

❧   ❧   ❧

Ange Pitou skipped along between his captors, and was laughing. So he was being arrested again! This new government was supposed to stand for no more indiscriminate denunciations, no more guillotinings, no more arrests of innocent persons, but the new government, like the old, went right on arresting Ange Pitou. This was the fifteenth time for him. But the new government would not be able to hold him either. If they did not know that yet they would learn it quickly. He skipped along between two burly, heavily-armed men, trilling a note occasionally, so that passersby would know him and pass the word around that Ange was on his way to prison again.

They were taking him to the Luxembourg. He had been held in that prison before and had seen with his own eyes the wreck France's government had made of one of France's finest palaces. The gardens were ruined, the ancient trees uprooted, and little spindly Liberty trees planted in their place; the land was plowed and planted to corn, to feed patriots. The expensive furnishings had been moved out on the streets and abandoned, and the citizens had carted them away to their hovel-homes, to sleep on or sit on, or to burn as fuel in their empty coal grates. Nothing remained of the Luxembourg but great bare rooms with scarred floors, their painted ceilings dirtied, their chandeliers smashed, the tapestries hanging in ragged strips, and everywhere, prisoners sitting or lying. He fully expected to see those scenes again. He had honestly forgotten his song about how Robespierre the blood-drinker had asked no recompense of the State he ruled beyond frequent changes of linen and money to pay his board bill at the humble carpenter's where he had lived. But the five kings had to have a palace to live in, the song went: so the Luxembourg was being restored to the nation as fine as ever, but at the cost of the hospitals. That was the gist of his song, but he had forgotten and was amazed when the great door opened and showed him a palace again.

Royalist Ange could not stop a thrill of joy and wonder. It was as if between these walls the Revolution had been erased. Whose had been the good taste that had planned these magnificent decorations, as fine as any to be seen in the King's time? Then he remembered that one of them, Paul Barras, was nobly born.

Ange was led past the Salle d'Attente, the Salle du Trône, and the Grande Galerie, where painters were still working to restore the ruined works of Rubens. He was taken up the grand staircase that swooped down with a dancer's grace, and then into an apartment where he was left alone. But he was sure the door was being guarded.

He waited. He was not in the least afraid. All of this was most unusual, but the darling of the Paris crowds was safe anywhere in Paris. He studied his surroundings. Hangings, curtains, and the sofa were in crimson damask with a wide gold border. One huge chandelier, a masterpiece of glittering crystal, hung in the center of the room, and smaller ones that were clustered near the great fireplace dazzled and flashed from the light of the leaping flames. It was a real wood fire, too.

The doors of the apartment were full-length mirrors of fine quality. Ange could see himself sitting on the edge of a brocade chair. Though raggedly dressed, he looked youthful and handsome, he thought. He left the chair and posed before the mirrors, throwing back his head as if to sing, then making the famous grimaces. No wonder they laugh and applaud me! Ange thought, wholly satisfied. Little Ange Pitou from Normandy, he thought, who was in a seminary only a few years ago. Behold me now! I am about to have audience with a Director of France, in a palace where the King used to live. But I deserve my little honors, he thought. It requires talent and courage to speak your mind as I do. What does the Directory want of me? Do they want to offer me a place in their government? It would make them many friends if I consented. But I won't consent, no, not I. Ange Pitou cannot be bought with honors and money, no, not Ange Pitou. Instead I will sing it out on the streets tomorrow, how they tried to bribe me and I could not be bought. He grimaced again, bowing, and his hands flew out in a gesture of repudiating all this. He heard a low chuckle. He turned quickly.

A huge man had come into the room, but moving so lightly that Ange had not heard him. In his coat of white satin thickly embroidered with gold, he seemed overpoweringly handsome and important. Ange smiled diffidently, less afraid than filled with admiration.

"You are Ange Pitou." He bowed. "I am the Director Barras." Ange bowed again, lower. "I used sometimes to follow you and listen to your songs. I thought you were most amusing. Why have I ceased to find you amusing, I wonder?"

"I am sorry to hear that, Citizen-Director, but the people like me as well as ever."

"I think you give them too much of the same thing. Times have changed, but your songs are the same. France has a respectable government, yet you sing as if the blood-drinkers were still in power."

"Not blood-drinkers. Not you, Citizen. You drink gold," Ange said boldly.

Barras smiled, not in the least offended. "But I'm generous about sharing it. How much do you want to sing as I tell you?"

"My crowds give me money enough to eat all I can hold, and drink more than I should. What would I do with more money? And I couldn't sing as I was told, Citizen-Director. The music would fly out of my head."

"You can't know that until you have tried."

"No," Ange said, "I couldn't, truly."

"But the *Réveil d'Epiménide* was your song."

"But I was not the truthteller then." To Ange, the retort was eminently logical. Barras only smiled as though he thought it naive. "My songs are all I have," Ange said. "Truly, Citizen-Director, I couldn't do as you ask. It would kill me inside."

"I see." Barras walked away from Ange and pulled a bell cord. The two burly men who had arrested him came in promptly. "I see," Barras said again, watching Ange from across the room. "Your mind is made up, I take it. And so is mine. One of us will have to give in. I expect it will be you who gives in." He sat down on the brocade chair Ange had used. "Proceed," he said calmly to the men.

*   *   *

The Medical Inspector for the French Republic was in Paris for the first time since his appointment. He had been as far south as the Gironde, visiting all the larger cities, scrutinizing the hospital buildings and interviewing city officials and members of the profession. He had planned a longer trip that would end at Montpellier, but events in Italy had brought him back filled with alarm for Diane's safety.

Until recently, the Army of Italy had done nothing more than engage in occasional border skirmishes. While Generals Pichegru and Moreau waged hard war on the Rhine, the other commander sat tight, watching his ragtag bobtail Army dissolve into a band of chicken and pig raiders. The Army of Italy was a national joke. But then had come Bonaparte's appointment as commander. Through some miracle of leadership, the twenty-six-year-old general had transformed a band of ragamuffins into a fighting Army, had swept them with him into the rich Po valley. Montenotte, Arcole, Rivoli, Lodi, the victories followed each other so swiftly that while the cities of France were celebrating one of them, another was being made. The couriers could not ride fast enough to keep up with the victories of Bonaparte. Florian remembered Carnot having said that he would give in to Barras about appointing Bonaparte if Barras would give in to him about Florian. It was a shock to realize that his ambitions for the medical profession had motivated all that blood and death and clangor . . . it might be Diane's death that he had arranged that day. Milan had been occupied; that meant that Pavia, only twenty miles away, was in his hands or would be.

The temptation to simply continue south and join Diane had been extreme, but common sense told Florian that the Minister of War could do a great deal more toward insuring her safety than could an absconding Medical Inspector. Without stopping at the apartment to change his travel-stained clothing, he hurried to the Petite Luxembourg where all the Directors except Barras were housed. Barras had an apartment in the Palace itself. It crossed Florian's mind that the little fact might be a straw on the wind as to which of them had forged ahead in the struggle for power. Or it might merely mean that such things mattered a great deal to Barras, but very little to Carnot.

After a considerable wait, the Director Carnot's secretary returned and informed Dr. Florian that he would be received the next morning at ten o'clock. "He said to tell you there is nothing to worry about; the matter that concerns you has been taken care of," the secretary reported. So the Minister of War had remembered without being prodded that Diane Florian was in the theater of war. Humble gratitude toward the kindly old man filled Florian.

His mind eased, he went to the apartment for the bath and change he needed badly and then to the Bicêrte to see Dr. Pinel. On his way there, he passed the closed and bolted doors of the Hôtel Dieu. That bitter scene of exodus returned, but its memory moved him to determination and hope rather than despair.

As Medical Inspector, Florian now outranked his old superior, but Dr. Pinel did not show or feel any resentment. The two doctors talked a long time. Pinel was excited about some experiments he was making in what he called "hand-Hygeia." To what extent was possible, he reproduced life outside but on a small scale, giving the inmates light tasks to do, praising them warmly for their efforts however unsuccessful. Florian went on-rounds with Pinel and saw for himself how diligently they worked at basket-weaving and bead-stringing.

"But where is Angélique? I don't see her anywhere."

"I would have forgotten to tell you," Pinel said. "She died in her sleep several days ago. The autopsy disclosed a badly damaged heart. I think she went quickly, without any pain. Will you let the brother know?"

Florian had no idea where Ange lived even, except that it was somewhere on the Cité. "I'll find some way to let him know," he promised.

The second time he returned to the apartment he saw someone was sitting on the staircase. The light was too dim to see clearly, but he thought he recognized Fidèle. When he came nearer, he saw that it was she, a forlorn little being in the same ugly clothes she had been wearing the first time he saw her. Her presence relieved him of the necessity of hunting for Ange. But all of her old suspicion of him was back in her eyes and on her face. "Are you really Ange's friend?" she asked challengingly.

"Why do you ask that?"

She did not answer; she waited for him to answer her. Were they friends? It was a poor brand of friendship Ange had shown that day he threatened to keep Florian from getting his visé. Florian had never trusted him much since. "Yes," he said finally, "we're friends."

"He's been hurt, Doctor. Will you come?"

"Of course. How badly is he hurt?"

"I don't know, but he's crying from pain."

"What kind of accident was it?"

"I don't know that either."

"I'll have to get some things I may need, come along." She followed obediently. Inside, she looked around at the litter his halfway unpacking had made. "Have you been away, Doctor?"

"I got back just a few hours ago." He was calling to her from the next room, where he was packing some powders and instruments in the smaller of two boxes with handles that he kept for this purpose. "Did Ange send for me, Fidèle?"

The question embarrassed her. Florian was the only real doctor she knew and she certainly did not want one of the charlatans attending Ange, hurting him perhaps more than he was already hurt. But when she mentioned going for Florian, Ange had said, "Get someone else. I don't want him. He wouldn't come anyway. He's grown too important to bother with me and he's hand-in-glove with *them,* now." All of this accompanied by wrenching sobs of pain, but as far as Fidèle could see, Florian was the same as always, courteous and kind, willing for them to make demands on his time. He came out with his box. "Did he send for me?" he repeated.

"No, Doctor."

"I was going to try to find him. There is something I must tell him, but if he's been badly hurt, today would not be a good time, perhaps."

"Please don't say anything to make him feel worse!"

"I won't. You can trust me."

The times of walking along the streets looking for an infrequent public hack were over for Florian. The Medical Inspector had his own carriage and driver and, on his trips, a detail of armed outriders protected him from the highwaymen that infested the provinces. Fidèle was so awed by the smart carriage and its handsome team of four matched greys that it was with difficulty he could persuade her to enter it. She sat holding her hands tightly, and trying to make herself small in a corner. Florian began questioning her and talking to her, trying to put her at ease, and by the time they were rolling across the bridge of the narrow branch of the river she was beginning to enjoy her ride.

The room she shared with Ange was on the top floor of an old building. Ange was lying on a mattress in a place as nearly safe from drafts as could be found, and blankets were piled over him, yet he was shivering with cold. A girl about Fidèle's age had been sitting tailor-fashion on the floor. She rose as they entered. Her black hair looked as if she clipped it herself, with fingernail scissors. "He acts just like he did when you left," she reported to Fidèle.

"Hullo, Ange," Florian said, going over.

"Is that you, Dr. Florian?"

"Yes."

"I told her not to bother you. I don't need a doctor anyway."

"It isn't a bother, Ange. What happened to you?"

He grimaced. "I have an employer now. I don't sing my own songs any more, I sing what I'm told to sing. They even tried rhyme!" He laughed harshly, and as he did, tears spurted. He stopped the tears at once, the laughter too. " 'France has a stable government at

65

last. Bloodshed and suffering are in the past.' They think I can set that to music!"

Florian said soothingly, "It would be hard, but if Carnot gets his way, your new rhyme will become a reality."

"I heard you'd sold out to him."

"Sold out to him," Florian repeated.

"Fancy title, and fancy salary to go with it, I heard. Don't talk to me about Carnot, I don't want to hear about it. I've had all of the Directory I can stand, for one day."

"What did happen, Ange?"

"I had an interview with your friend's confrère, that's all."

"Who do you mean?"

"Paul Barras, of course, who else makes a practice of beating up private citizens in crimson-damask apartments? First he tried to bribe me. Then he called his thugs in. They beat me terribly. They beat me until I was crawling around trying to get away. He sat in a chair and watched. He was wearing white satin breeches and a satin coat with gold embroidery. Every place I touch, I hurt, and there isn't a mark on me."

"I had better examine you."

"You won't find anything."

"An examination would be wise." He sent the girls out. He uncovered Ange and examined the stripped body with his sensitive fingertips. Nothing so obvious as broken bones were to be found, but Florian could tell the beating had been a thorough one, skillfully administered to draw out every reaction to pain. The signs of internal rupture were not present, but that was hard to detect; the possibility remained. He told Ange the symptoms to watch for. "If anything like that happens, send Fidèle after me at once. I'll be in Paris a week at least, that's time for it to show up if it's going to. Rest is what you need now. I'll give you something to help you sleep."

"What am I going to do!" Ange groaned.

"Judging by what's happened already, it would be best to give in to him. But you don't have to make up your mind for a few days. No one could expect you to do any singing of any kind for a while."

Ange's hatred of authority was as much a part of him as his gift. Florian's appointment had seemed to put the doctor on the side of authority, thus Ange's former liking had been turned to antipathy and distrust. But he could not fail to notice what Fidèle had noticed earlier: Florian was unchanged by good fortune. He was as gentle and considerate as ever. And he possessed another quality that Ange admired though he had none: it was stability, of emotions, of ethics, of judgment. Ange did not want to be left with his problem, with only little, loyal Fidèle to help him. "Please hear the rest, Doctor. Please advise me. It will kill me if I have to sing as Barras tells me."

"Go ahead, Ange. If you think I can help." The singer's unaccustomed humility had touched him.

"I didn't give in to the beating," Ange said. Florian felt a flash of admiration. "I crawled around at his feet, and I even tried to crowd in behind his chair, but I didn't give in. Then he played another card he was holding. He called them off me and sent them out, and he said, 'Where is the Citizeness Angélique Pitou Brossard these days?'" Florian started, remembering what Pinel had told him earlier. "I was trying to stand up," Ange went on, "I didn't even answer him. 'Isn't she in the Bicêrte, confined as mad?' If he knew there wasn't any point lying, so I said she was. He said, 'Have you happened to hear about the noble experiment of Dr. Philippe Pinel?' My wits weren't working any too well, I said yes, I had. 'Now I wonder where you could have learned about that. Were you happy for your sister when you heard about Dr. Pinel?' I said of course, I'm not a monster. 'Well, good, so you are not a monster. Very well, Citizen Pitou. Will you sing songs for me on the streets? Or shall I command Dr. Pinel to make an end to his experiment, and restore the treatment of the insane that is being used at our other institutions?'"

Florian said quickly, "You must not let him interfere with Dr. Pinel's work!"

"Am I really supposed to start singing that France has a stable government at last, after a taste like I got of his good government?"

"What else can you do? What are your songs, compared to so much suffering?"

Ange rolled slightly on the mattress to stare into Florian's face. His wild-animal eyes were hot and demanding. "Suppose it was you. Suppose Barras wanted you to do something for him. First he offered you gold, then he had you beaten, finally he promised to hurt someone you loved and a lot of other people too unless you did what he wanted. Suppose what he wanted was that you deliberately murder someone during a surgical operation. Would you do it?"

"No!"

"My songs are my profession, Doctor. They are myself."

"I spoke too quickly, Ange. Let me think about it."

"It isn't Dr. Pinel's work that stops me. I have my own work," Ange said. "And it isn't the other insane, either, because they don't suffer any more from beatings than I do. It's Angélique. We're twins, you know. Sometimes twins seem to know what is happening to each other without having to be told. Suppose Angélique understood that I had decided she should be chained up again, and beaten, so that I might go free? Does that sound odd to you, Dr. Florian?"

"I think I understand how you feel. Let me think it over, Ange."

Since Barras knew of the sister's existence at all, he also knew that it had been terminated. He had tricked Ange. Florian could expose the trick, but that would send the singer tilting crazily against power. His crowds might or might not be able to save Ange from Guiana. Deportation was the practice now, instead of the guillotine, and some said Guiana was the more extreme punishment. But Ange was a brave man, a daring one. He had not given in to beating or threat, it had meant that much to him to live, or die, free. As far as Ange was concerned, the act of a friend would be to tell him the truth and let him take his own chances in his own way.

There was Pinel. If Ange were allowed to continue in his old freebooter's ways, it might cost Dr. Pinel the fruits of his life's work and bring misery down on helpless human beings. Posterity would take the end of the Bicêrte experiment to mean that it had been proved a failure. In that case, the experiment would have retarded, rather than advanced, the treatment of disordered mentalities. That was a high ransom for one man's rights.

Dr. Florian wondered if Carnot could be persuaded to stop Barras from carrying out his threat. But Carnot was not ready yet for a test of power. As indignant as he had been about the closing of the hospitals, he had not moved against Barras to get them reopened. Either he was overcautious, or he knew how delicate his situation was; probably the latter. Even if Florian could persuade him to interfere, and then it resulted in a victory for Barras, everything was lost. The scales had tipped very far away from Ange.

"Ange, you can't give your sister up to that kind of treatment again. It would be horrible, far worse than changing your songs to suit Paul Barras." The half lie of withholding information came easily to him. As early as Hippocrates, the physician was being advised to hold his own counsel before patients. This was not a medical matter, of course. "I know how you feel," Florian said, "and I'm sorry for you. But you have no other choice."

"All right, Doctor," Ange said. "I guess you know best." His trained, resonant voice was peculiarly flat and dead. Florian got up and went out. He had done the only thing, yet his remorse was strong. Ange had been thinking of no one but himself, had cared about nothing but his own desires, just the same, he had put himself in his doctor's hands; he had trusted a false friend. Florian had sold him to Paul Barras, for Pinel's sake, and for the sake of the insane population today and in the future. If he knew he would hate me, and I deserve his hatred, the doctor thought. He wished with all his heart that none of it had ever happened.

❖   ❖   ❖

The interview with Carnot was brief. He looked tired and worried, and though he was as gracious as before it was plain that his thoughts were elsewhere. There was no opportunity to mention Ange, nor would it have done any good. The man was obviously overburdened already.

"At the start of the campaign General Berthier, who is Bonaparte's Chief of Staff, was requested to receive your wife with every civility and to extend every protection, if that became necessary. The Citizeness Florian has been informed of her privileges. I hope you are satisfied with me, I did the best I could for you. I'm sorry now I didn't advise you differently about letting her return here."

"I'm deeply grateful to you, Citizen-Director. Does the protection include the Italian family with whom she's staying?"

"It does not, Dr. Florian. Should it have?"

It was unfair to press Carnot. Florian had the feeling that another demand on him, however trivial, might cause him to cry out in actual pain. The doctor said diffidently, "They have been extremely kind to both of us."

"But there is no reason to suppose that anyone will need special protection. The Italian cities are surrendering without a show of resistance. Anyway, Bonaparte is the last man on earth to make war on civilians. So far at least, he has limited his atrocities to shooting Army contractors and his own men. If you don't mind, Dr. Florian, we won't go into the subject of your findings today. My calendar is crowded." Florian bowed and withdrew.

Carnot had not volunteered any information about how affairs were shaping between himself and Paul Barras. But Carnot was the Organizer of Victories after all; he had performed great services for his country; Barras had done nothing but loot her.

IV

"I do not make war on the Italian people. My fight is with your Austrian oppressors. You have nothing to fear from me." Words, only words, some said, but Bonaparte lived up to his words. Diane saw unwilling respect for him grow in the people around her. After months of hearing nothing but blame and hatred of her country, she could not stop a small pleasure at seeing France represented in so excellent a light. Many said his troops would get out of hand, as had happened years ago when the Austrians invaded Italy. But the young commander's discipline remained flawless. Not a single incident happened to touch off flammable minds.

Then he left north Italy, with sharp words. "If you are going to fight me, do it now. I will make a terrible example of that city or province that has accepted me but then betrays me." It was plain to anyone that his threats were dictated by the fact that the garrisons he left in the conquered cities were pitifully inadequate. Too many victories had wasted his Army away.

Bonaparte and the main troops continued toward the Republic of Venice. In Pavia, there was news of new victories, then rumors of reverses. One of the Contarini girls came to the house late one night, and was closeted with her mother for hours in the room that adjoined Diane's. Sounds of her sobbing punctuated their anxious exchanges. Diane was not consciously trying to listen, but her command of the Milano dialect had become excellent after months of living among them. She heard the distracted wife confessing that her husband was a ringleader in an uprising that was being planned.

The French garrison in Pavia was less than a hundred men. They were going to be massacred. What was worse, nearly fifty wounded French soldiers under the care of an Army doctor were in the hospital. Their murders were being planned too. The women in the next room mourned together. They knew this was wrong, and they knew also that it was unwise. A terrible reprisal had been promised. But they were women, they could do nothing. Diane too was a woman but she was also the wife of a doctor. Charlot would never permit silence about an insurrection that involved the slaughter of bedfast men.

Diane thought about going to the next room and demanding of mother and daughter that they take her to the leaders. She would reason with them, she would point out the futility of what they were planning, the sure retribution, and especially, the ugliness of breaking their word to Bonaparte now that his back was turned. But the soft mourning noises reminded her again that she was only a woman. Men would listen to her with hard shut eyes, then push her counsel aside.

Her next plan was to warn the Army doctor. But he could do nothing unless the captain of the garrison helped him, and although the injured men were her first concern, the others ought to be warned too. And then she saw clearly a way to save the soldiers and the city too.

She made a small light and dressed quickly by it. The riding habit of green velvet she was donning had been given to her by the weeping wife in the next room whose time was too filled with babies to think of using it. Diane left the house with deliberate quiet. She did not like the idea that she was being stealthy, but told herself again this was the only thing to do. Her little riding mare, a gift from Conte, was stabled with the other horses barely a block away. There was no need to carry a light, the moon was full.

Now that she knew what was being planned, Diane could feel the tenseness lacing the quiet town. She noticed lights burning late and low in the houses. And yet Pavia bathed in moonlight seemed the very center of human innocence. She knew how kind its people were, how simple and good. These terrible wars, she thought, they make us act as God never intended us to do. She had heard His Name called out again and again in the churches, but coupled with prayers asking for hellfire and damnation on the French. How did God feel when some of His children prayed to Him to destroy some others? The little brown mare rapped her dainty feet sharply and quickly on the cobblestones, rat-a-tat-tat, like the start of a riffle of drums. The air was soft, and carried its scent of thyme and verbena, and the stars were large and low. Charlot seemed to be walking at Diane's stirrup and encouraging her.

If she could help it, she would not tell the captain of the garrison that there were actual plans. Then all taint of treachery would be removed from her action. Just let me save this peace and this city, she prayed, and those brave men.

The garrison was in an unused building fronting on the public square. Her everready appreciation of the ridiculous prompted a small sorrowful chuckling. A garrison that can be lodged in a single building that others have abandoned as useless! She rode up to it and was challenged sharply.

"I am a French citizeness. I must see your captain at once. I have important intelligence." Now she could see his face. He looked to be no older than one of the medical students.

Remembering them shocked her anew. Suppose she had not overheard those few broken sentences, suppose the revolt had occurred, and Bonaparte followed his threat of giving the city to the sword. The University would be pulled down too. It was the crown, the jewel, the finest thing in Italy, but the hotheads had never spared a thought in its direction. They had risked its destruction for the pleasure of murdering a few Frenchmen. "At once!" she repeated, "it's important."

He was startled, but polite. He conducted her with as much élan as if this were Headquarters itself. But he had to keep calling out warnings that a lady was with him, and as it was she caught glimpses of pink human flesh streaking toward shelter.

The captain was as young and tender-faced as his sentry. He was trying valiantly to raise a beard. Again she was reminded of the medical students. Diane said urgently, "I am the Citizeness Florian, my husband is the Medical Inspector for the Republic. Citizen-Captain, you must leave Pavia at once with your injured men. The people are very excited. There might be trouble, serious trouble."

"A soldier does not run away from that possibility, Citizeness."

She saw she had been naive to think she could hide the facts. Imagine Legouvé or Lasné or Monteil wanting to quit because Charlot told them that medicine was hard. She could not stop herself from thinking that she knew this uniformed boy well, his hopes, his mistakes, his hundred little gaucheries. Though he looked at her so hungrily, there was no insult to her in his attitude.

Diane said, "I overheard plans being laid to massacre yourself and your men. Even your injured soldiers in the hospital are going to be killed, unless you go at once."

A look of infinite sadness crossed his boyish face. "But my orders are to stay here, Citizeness."

"Surely your commander wouldn't want you to stay under the circumstances?"

"He would want me to obey my orders. What are you doing in Italy, Citizeness?"

"I'm visiting friends," Diane said, somewhat awkwardly.

"You picked a strange time to go visiting."

"I came here some time ago, during the Terror. Are you doubting my story? Please don't!"

"Far from it, I was wondering how the Medical Inspector endured the separation."

"Oh." She tried not to laugh; indeed, she did not feel like laughing. He was puerile and yet a veteran, and in his eyes was all knowledge and all need to know. Diane met those puzzling eyes with her own, direct and friendly, and said, "He thought I would be safer here. It was a mistake. Men make mistakes easily where women are concerned."

"I suppose so. I wouldn't know." He looked away.

The breaking-apart of their glances gave her a chance to notice how Spartan his room was. There was nothing in it but the necessities and his pallet. The commander of the Pavia garrison commanded less than a hundred men, but a commode.

"I don't see any objection to moving the wounded men out," he said slowly.

"There are too few of you to put up any defense. Surely you realize that!"

"Oh, yes. I realize that."

"Your General won't have supposed that anything like this was going to happen."

"Of course he did. We don't have men enough to garrison the towns, Citizeness. Don't you understand? We're trying to hold Italy, but we don't have the men."

"Then your duty is to save yourselves."

"You don't understand." He was being as patient with her as though she were the child, not himself. "If Pavia revolts, he will make an example of Pavia, and that will deter the other cities. Once the Italians understand that he means what he says, there won't be any more trouble. But if I withdrew and the word got around that I was frightened away, all the cities would rise up." He said slowly, "I'm not saying that I'm happy over the idea that I and my men are going to be the ones sacrificed, but there's simply no help for it."

He could not be twenty years old yet. He had all his life before him. He stood there, calmly and sadly, and exchanged glance for glance with death. "Your General asks too much!" Diane said.

His eyes came around to her. There was nothing fanatic about him. His voice was soft when he said, "Yes, he exacts a great deal. I don't expect you to understand when I tell you that we are glad to give it."

It was no use. He was a stubborn child. She turned away, her eyes filling with tears.

"If you will wait in the next room, Citizeness, I want to give you something. It will take only a moment."

"I love this city," she said, her voice rough from emotion. "You want to kill it. The University is worth more than all the wars that ever will be fought. I suppose that will be pulled down too. You and your dead will have a monument to be proud of, Citizen-Captain. An immense rubble under which the enlightenment of centuries will be buried."

"I'm sorry," he said. "I wish things were different. But they were warned."

Her head down, her shoulders shaking, she started away. He moved quickly, and took her arm. She paid no attention to where he was taking her, blind with grief. He left her in an anteroom that contained but one chair. He returned in seconds, with a paper.

"If they do revolt, you may have some use for this." With delicate, respectful fingers, he stowed the paper away into a pocket of the green riding habit. "I will evacuate our wounded tonight. You have saved their lives, anyway. The Republic is grateful."

On her way out, he gallantly at her side, she saw more of his soldiers. All were children or greybeards. The expendable, left here like tethered lambs to attract death to themselves, and so give their commander an excuse for more killings. Dread and hatred of Bonaparte began in Diane; she was ashamed that she had ever admired him.

❖   ❖   ❖

The sun fell down on Pavia sweetly, and a soft wind carried the familiar scent of lemon and olive groves and the tang of herb gardens. The public square was jammed as though for a fête, but it was armed cavalrymen who held closed the four broad avenues and six narrow streets leading into the square. The people were stunned and silent, gazing wretchedly on the bodies of their murdered officials. They were not trying to escape and their own anger was worn out. They felt nothing but an odd childlike hurt, that it was going to happen to them exactly as had been promised. This fact lent to the horrible proceedings a tinge of necessity, of predestination, and so they were not angry at all, only hurt.

A little apart from everyone else were the survivors of what had been the French garrison. Four men only were left to bear witness against the town councillors, and the priests, and the people of Pavia. Two of these were wounded and all were unbelievably dirty and very nearly starved, from hiding out so many days in cellars and garbage pits, as miserable, as hard to kill, as rats. Near them, on his white horse, somewhat to the front of his adjutants and officers, was General Bonaparte. He seemed indifferent to the good target he made. He was holding a big watch of chased gold which swung slightly from his hand, striking back darts of pure golden light. At ten minutes to noon exactly, he lowered the watch as a signal to the cavalrymen. They pulled their horses away from the street openings. All of this was being done with the precision of a military review, and that more than anything else struck terror in civilian hearts.

The men and women of Pavia, dragging their crying children by the hands, jostled each other at the mouths of the four broad avenues and six narrow streets. All that prevented a panic in which they would have fought each other to be first was the assurance that the death behind them would not be unleashed until noon exactly. He had said so, and he kept his word.

* * *

The University had been declared out-of-bounds to pillagers. Its faculty and its several hundred students were told they would not be molested as long as they remained in their anterium and amphitheaters and the library with its hundred and twenty thousand great books. But some married men and those with families had chosen to take their chances outside with their loved ones. Shortly before noon, the gates were closed and a guard was mounted. It was now too late for Dr. Contarini to follow their bold example.

He stayed close by Dr. Scarpa, whose seeming assurance that all was well if the University was spared was calming, but then Scarpa had no kin in the doomed city. When the terror outside was only two hours old, it seemed to have been going on forever. Occasionally the sound of a scream, or a shattering, or a shot, reached to this quiet place, or a spiral of smoke stained the pure arch of sky. But there was no real danger of a holocaust since most of Pavia's buildings were of stone, and the avengers themselves would be against the early, total destruction of their plaything.

At the University it might have been merely another day, except no one was studying. Students and masters alike wandered around through the botanical gardens and in the museums. Dr. Contarini thought he could read his own feelings on most faces he saw, as if others besides himself felt that they perpetrated the villainy by mere reason of being safe from it.

"—doubt it was ever done before," Dr. Scarpa was saying. He poked with his walking stick at some dried lichen disfiguring the wall. "The sack of cities is as old as warfare, of course. Barbarians and moderns too have held it out as a prize for their armies to fight for. And then as often as not the commander couldn't stop it if he tried. But as a punitive measure, I do believe it's unheard of. Oddly cold-blooded."

Contarini wished that Scarpa would stop talking about it. But he would go mad with loneliness and guilt if they separated. He mumbled something about the French having become so depraved during their Revolution that human standards hardly applied to them.

"I suppose that's it," Scarpa agreed, shoving the stick underarm with a graceful dandified gesture. "Odd that a man like him would choose to spare a place like this, however. I'm getting warm. Why don't we rest in the anterium? It's always cool there."

Contarini said with a flash of bitterness, "It must be fine to care as little as you do about what's going on out there."

"My dear boy. Is that what you really think of me?" He stopped walking, and turned his pale long studious face. "I am sick at heart," he said.

It had been a foolish remark. Contarini was ashamed of having made it. He did not say anything.

"Naturally I'm grateful," Scarpa said, starting out again. "I'm old and frail to be running like a rabbit before a pack of murderous hounds. But even more than this worn-out life of mine that has had its great climax, when I was asked here to reorganize the anatomy department, I'm trying to say, the work is done and is being allowed to remain. It is horrifying to think that a man so young and unprincipled wields the power to destroy or save the efforts of others. Don't you find it so?"

"There they are," Dr. Contarini interrupted. He indicated with a motion of his head where Dr. Scarpa was to look. "Always together, poor young men. No one else will have anything to do with them."

"Their University life has been a great disappointment to them, I'm afraid. However they are doing excellent work." Scarpa sighed. "I shall never forget that first day they came to us. The awe and wonder with which they regarded us, like newcomers into heaven, so to speak. Charlot would be disappointed if he knew how difficult things are for them."

"They have suffered more from their country than anyone else. You would think the other students would take that into account."

"But only moments ago, we ourselves were talking about the depravity of everything French. We can't expect young hotheads to be wise when old, knowledge-stuffed heads like my own are so quick to condemn. Should we ask them to come along with us? This is a difficult day for them, too."

"I want to ask you something."

"Yes, Prospero?"

"Should I have taken my chances outside?"

"You asked me that before. I told you each man should make his own choice. How can one man answer for another on a thing like that?"

"What would you have done in my place?"

"How can I answer that either? I have never been in your place."

They had forgotten Dr. Florian's five young men. They walked along a dim, vaulted corridor that was said to be as ancient as the University charter was, and that had come from Charlemagne. For a moment they were alone in the cool and the quiet, then a student, running, came from the direction of the anterium.

"Dr. Scarpa—quickly—the French are here!"

"Quickly, what?" Scarpa said reasonably. But he had turned ashen. The student, not answering, ran back along the corridor. "I think we may as well meet them," Scarpa said, continuing his slow pace. "I see no hope for us in flight. Perhaps if we remind them that their General specifically ordered that the University not be entered—"

"He may have rescinded his order!" Contarini interrupted.

"But that would be odder than giving it in the first place. No, he's lost control after all. I never did think he could do it. Letting the genie out of the bottle is easy enough, getting him back in again is something else. I fancy you'll see Pavia pillaged for a week instead of twenty-four hours. Aren't you coming, Prospero?"

"Yes," Contarini said desperately. In Dr. Scarpa's reaction to the present danger, he read a true answer to the question he had just put. Scarpa in Contarini's place would have been outside these safe walls, doing the best he could for his loved ones, though unarmed probably except for his cane. We never know what we are until our chance comes to measure ourselves, Contarini thought. Now I know what I am, and what Scarpa is: why his name will be kept alive like

Ramazzini's and Belluno's and Folli's, and mine not. As soon as he had decided he was not of much account and never would become great and famous, he lost the larger part of his fear and went along steadily.

Though roofless, the anterium was shaded by the overhang of college buildings and was cool and comfortable. Students received their visitors in it on fine days, when their cell-like rooms would have been stuffy and uncomfortable. Contarini was so full of a picture of hard-faced ravening soldiers with their swords out that he was a moment adjusting to the fact that the place was occupied by a dozen high-echelon French officers waiting courteously for someone to receive them.

One of these was more plainly dressed than the others, thin-faced, lank-haired, ridiculously young. Neither Scarpa nor Contarini had ever seen him before; both knew at once who he was. Even in the confusion of meeting him unexpectedly, the clinicians did not fail to notice that he was a worn-down human being for whom bed rest and an egg-meat-and-milk diet ought to be prescribed. He looked exhausted.

Scarpa walked forward fearlessly. "Welcome, General Bonaparte. The University is honored. And very grateful."

"Thank you. Honor and gratitude both are unusual in Italy."

Scarpa did not let himself show dismay. He said carefully, "It has been my experience that an anger as profound as yours inevitably is rooted in a misunderstanding."

"So." He smiled unpleasantly. "Pavia is paying a rather high price for letting herself be misunderstood."

"Yes," Scarpa said. "My friend and I were discussing that a moment ago. Is there another case in all history where a city was sacked as punishment? I don't recall one. The Roman system of decimation is the severest punishment against a city that I seem to remember. It was, of course, lenient compared to this. Or does it distress you to talk about it, General?"

"I'm not accustomed to accepting the comments of nameless strangers."

"My name is Antonio Scarpa, of the Anatomical College and the College of Clinical Surgery. And my young associate here is Dr. Contarini."

"I have heard about you, Scarpa." A note of warm approval changed his harsh bitter way of speaking. Scarpa's face colored. He could not help but feel gratification; at the same time he wondered if the compliment to himself was mere cunning, intended to advance some unguessable aim. It was so unlikely that a twenty-six-year-old foreign General knew or cared about the work of Antonio Scarpa.

Then Bonaparte said, "You and Morgagni and Spallanzani can be thanked for restoring the eminence Salerno once brought to Italian medicine."

His flush deepened. This man knew what he was talking about. "You're very kind," Scarpa murmured, then felt surprise at his use of that word.

"I read *De sedibus* while I was in garrison at Auxonne. I was delighted to see evidence that medicine was advancing far beyond charlatanism. Which of your faculty was it that came before the town councillors to try to prevent the uprising?"

Scarpa was a moment containing the question, in his astonishment over *De sedibus*. "Giovanni Rasori, General," he said finally. "He's very partial to you and to the French Revolution, and around here we're accustomed to him running about announcing another victory as though—my word."

Amused, Bonaparte finished it. "As though that were good news instead of bad, you mean."

"I'm not usually so tactless, General."

"But I'm pleased to hear that one man in Italy can believe that my intentions are good."

"I doubt that Rasori himself will believe it after today." Contarini heard himself saying it. His hand flew to his mouth, his eyes widened with horror.

Bonaparte dealt him a severe glance that changed back to amusement. "The opening was perfect, of course. Don't do it again." He began to introduce his officers. All but one were young, some as young as he. The exception was General Berthier, the Chief of Staff, middle-aged, squat, florid, with thin pinkish hair and a nervous habit of gnawing his fingernails. Marmont, Junot, LeClerc, Murat, and the others, were handsome and guileless looking, their exploits on the battlefield hard to believe, since they more closely resembled a group of huge children who have been promised a picnic but led into a classroom instead. Their commander's youth seemed ancient and civilized, contrasted to theirs.

"Whose permission do we ask to see the numismatic collection and the library, and the museum of natural history?"

"I wouldn't think you'd find it necessary to ask anyone's, General, but may we conduct you? Dr. Spallanzani, whom you mentioned earlier, has the chair of natural history, so the museum of course is in his charge," Scarpa said, as they walked down the flagged corridor. "Though I don't believe we'll find him in his usual haunts today. There is very little work of any kind being done, I'm afraid."

"There isn't time to waste when one is preparing for his profession."

Scarpa said coolly, "That's somewhat draconian, under the circumstances. Many of the students, and some of the faculty, have their families in the city."

"But you don't?"

"Thank God, I do not. I believe I have heard you have a rather large family of brothers and sisters yourself. I doubt you would have applied yourself to *De sedibus* did you find them in circumstances like ours."

"I doubt it too," Bonaparte said, his voice a warning to let it drop.

After all, Lazzaro Spallanzani was puttering around in his museum. He was nearly seventy years old; his wife and close kinsmen were dead. Scarpa was sorry to find Spallanzani there, because lately he had exhibited the first signs of senility and was capable of saying almost anything. Without paying the slightest attention to the Army people, the gentle giant said to Scarpa, "I got it back again this morning."

"This is Dr. Spallanzani, General. Please don't encourage him to tell you about his experiments. You might find them distasteful."

Spallanzani said amiably, "No more than some of yours, I'm sure. Did you say he was a General? He's too young."

"It's General Bonaparte, Doctor."

"No! Really? What a commotion you've been causing, young man!" He peered at Bonaparte from watering faded eyes. "You're joking, Scarpa. He doesn't have his beard yet."

"He hasn't had time to grow one," Bonaparte said good-humoredly. "What sort of experiments? Tell me."

"Well sir, every night for a month I've been swallowing my money pouch, the little one with no sharp edges. Without fail I recover it two days later, in plenty of time to swallow it again that night. Here it is," Spallanzani said, holding something out in his blunt-tipped wrinkled paw. It was as he had described, a small pouch of soft leather that looked to have been recently washed.

"But why do you swallow it?"

"To get it back, of course."

"Please let me explain, General," Dr. Scarpa said. "Dr. Spallanzani is demonstrating one of the pernicious fallacies of Galen, who believed the liver will accept for digestion anything that is taken into the stomach. The recovery every other day of his money pouch signalizes that the stomach casts out in excreta anything that cannot be assimilated, and that the process requires two days."

Bonaparte remarked to his officers, "Now we'll know what to do with an enemy courier who swallows his papers. Two days, though!" He said to Spallanzani, "We had one like that last week. Usually our doctors can persuade him to cast it up, but not that time."

"Well, you see it had left the stomach. Just like my money pouch. If the emetic won't work, try a cathartic. Do you want to see my frogs?"

Scarpa said frantically, "No, not your frogs, for God's sake, Doctor. He's not a medical student, why would he want to see those?"

"Oh, well," the old man said, hurt. "I'll just go on about my business then."

"We'll look at the frogs now," Bonaparte said.

When the sulking aides and officers understood what Spallanzani was trying to prove with his wax-coated amphibians, they began to snicker and hoot. "Gentlemen, this isn't a barracks." But Bonaparte was too diverted to be convincing, and they went on winking and grinning at each other. Contarini whispered to Scarpa, "That saturnalia out there is four hours old. And they joke about frogs and money pouches!"

"I know. It's hard to bear."

"What kind of man is he anyway?"

"Certainly not what I expected. Atrocities are not usually committed by men of scientific bent."

"I think we ought to be doing something more than letting him drag us around on a sightseeing tour."

"I'll try again. But don't let's be noticed whispering together. No one enjoys a conspiracy against himself." Contarini withdrew a little.

Dr. Spallanzani was now exhibiting his bone. It was huge, a survival of prehistoric times. He traced with a wrinkled forefinger the lines of a fracture, partially reset. "By accident, young man? An accidental jostling by others of his kind? Or by prehistoric man, who found him injured, helpless, a prey to all that crept or flew or galloped, and had pity, and attempted to mend with his clumsy half-found hands this hurt thing that had fallen his way. Which, young man? Ask yourself that before you decide to come here. Every man lives to the right or left of this bone, young man. A man to the left of this bone has no business with the art of Hippocrates."

Really, Contarini thought. He gets worse every week.

"I think I love this bone, young man. Because it means that someone cared enough to try to relieve a hurt thing, even before mankind knew it had a conscience. Perhaps this bone in my hands is the work of the very first doctor. Or else it was an accident. He could have pushed against a rock, I suppose, or been jostled in the herd. In that case, I have built my life on a comicality."

"No," Bonaparte said. "I'm sure someone tried to help him."

"Well, that's the comment I like to hear, it helps put you on the right side of my bone. Study hard and live to help others and you'll never regret it, I promise you that."

Was old Spallanzani really so confused with age that he could not distinguish between Pavia's murderer and a first-year medical student? Or was he being more subtle than Scarpa himself? If I were standing where that pale hot-eyed boy is, Dr. Contarini thought, and I was looking at Spallanzani's boring old bone that all of us have become sick of hearing about, but I was hearing it for the first time, and I had on my conscience what he does—I'd burst into tears, or start praying.

Scarpa interposed softly, "Dr. Spallanzani occupied the chairs of logic and metaphysics at both Reggio and Modena before he came to us. Are you interested in those subjects, General?"

"I'm interested in everything," he said simply.

"An idea has been teasing me along the lines of Dr. Spallanzani's specialty. Do I have your permission to submit it to him?"

Perhaps Scarpa's extreme care made him an object of suspicion. Bonaparte looked at him hard, then made a slight negative motion. "A lot of that stuff has gone right out of my head," Spallanzani was saying. "For some reason I've come to like what I can see better than what I can fancy. I suppose all that dreamery about angels on needlepoints properly belongs to the young. But give us your question, Scarpa, I'll do the best I can with it."

He took a sharp breath and said, "A small Army lacking in everything embarks on a career of conquest, and succeeds."

"But that's so unlikely."

"Well, their leader is a man of genius, Doctor. Please accept the original premise, we'll get nowhere if you don't. The victories of this Army are responsible for putting the home government on its feet, both as to popular opinion, and financially. A treasury of gold is poured back into empty coffers through the victories of this Army.

But victory can be costly too. Small to begin with, this Army continues to diminish."

Only Spallanzani seemed unaware of the charged atmosphere. Contarini found himself breathing in shallow gasps. Scarpa talked faster and faster, as though fearful his time was running out. The aides and officers were narrow-eyed and tense. Bonaparte, negligently leaning against the glass case containing the bone, gave the impression of being the source of all danger.

"The enemy, which is large and powerful, continues to throw ever-larger fresh armies into the field. The home government that has profited by the victories is appealed to again and again for replacements. None is forthcoming, not so much as a single division is sent, yet replacements are easily available."

"That's enough, Scarpa."

"Enough of what? I think it's an interesting story," Spallanzani said.

"I wish the General would give me leave to finish it."

Spallanzani said, "Young man, there can't be closed-off territories in the war of ideas or the whole thing falls apart. You may as well learn that right now. Go on, Scarpa, let's hear the rest."

The officers looked incredulous. Bonaparte smiled slightly. He neither gave his permission nor reiterated his prohibition and, after a moment, Scarpa resumed.

"Obviously, no conquest of town or province will amount to much unless the conquered territory can be held. Otherwise your conqueror remains master of the ground he stands on only. In order to hold what has been won, troops must be detached from the main body as garrisons. But the commander wants to move on to other conquests."

"Quite a problem," Spallanzani said. "Out of my field, though. Submit it to the College of Mathematics, they'll tell you it can't be done."

"Two choices exist. Either garrison the towns sufficiently, or garrison them with twenty-five or fifty or a hundred men insufficient to the purpose, taking your chance that the townsfolk will be spiritless enough to accept dominion by a minority of interlopers. Do you see any other way out?"

"No," Spallanzani said.

"Do you, Dr. Contarini?"

"No."

"General Bonaparte?"

"You're doing this at your risk, Scarpa."

"Would you gentlemen care to comment on the military aspects of this situation?"

"It's plain hell, Professor," one of the officers said. His chief glanced at him and he subsided, looking alarmed.

"The commander in my tale decided to weaken his main Army as little as possible in order to continue the conquests. He did so in full knowledge that he risked the lives of the men he left behind, through revolt of some or all of the insufficiently garrisoned cities."

"Now wait a minute," Spallanzani said. "Maybe he didn't realize that. After all, the towns had been conquered, hadn't they? Some sort of pact or treaty had been made, hadn't it? Maybe he simply trusted their word."

"I don't think so. He was a man of genius, he understood human nature. I think he must have known what would happen."

Bonaparte said coolly, "Did he do anything at all to avert that? For instance, did he make it plain that reprisal would be swift and extreme? If he didn't, he deserves to lose his command."

"Oh yes, he did that!" Scarpa said, not quite able to control the tremor in his voice. "He threatened the conquered cities with the worst punishment imaginable. But then he went away. Very far away, into another country. And there were just the little garrisons, twenty-five and fifty and a hundred men, in cities that had had a proud history, among people in whom the spark of courage had never been wholly extinguished although their misfortunes were as numerous as they were long."

"Did they all revolt?" Spallanzani asked.

"So far in my tale, only one. When he found time, he came back, as he had promised to do. The survivors told him that the priests and the city officials had incited the people. They were collected up and killed."

"He would have to do that, I suppose."

"Should he have gone any further?"

"Punished more people, you mean?"

"Punished all the people, yes."

"I wouldn't think so. Why would he want to? It's human nature to shake off a yoke that rests lightly, and the reason we're not the domesticated creatures of some other form of life, I imagine. No, he should have punished the guiltiest and forgiven the rest, I would say."

"He put the city to sack," Scarpa said.

Spallanzani looked shocked. "Surely not, Doctor! Probably he couldn't help that. Remember when the Austrians were here, not so many years ago. But I don't think any civilized human being of modern times would do a thing like that deliberately."

Scarpa turned his strained face and said, "What do you think, General?"

"I think you forgot to mention what threat it was that he made when he left his inferior garrisons and marched out of the country."

"Yes. Perhaps I did. Yes. That was the threat. That if any of the cities revolted, they would be put to the sword. Yes, I did fail to mention that."

Spallanzani looked at him quizzically. "Puts another complexion on things, doesn't it? You ought to know by now that all the facts are supposed to be in before the speculations start. Well now, I don't know. That's hard. He said he would and then he did, is that it?"

"Exactly."

"There was no element of the troops breaking discipline because they knew the threat had been made?"

"No. Definitely not."

"Well," old Spallanzani said, shrugging, "I think myself it would have been enough to shoot those who provoked the riot. That's what I'd do, I'm sure. Not that there isn't a certain virtue in keeping your word no matter what it was that you swore to. Perhaps he's sorry now he ever made a vow like that. I'm sure I would be." Bonaparte's was a face without expression.

Scarpa said, "But what I really wanted, Doctor, was that you assign the moral guilt for us. Obviously it belongs somewhere. This was not an accident of nature. It was the work of a man. Or of men. You appear to have exculpated the commander already, by saying he felt he had to keep his word. Whose, then, was the guilt, Dr. Spallanzani? The townspeople who had to bear the awful punishment, was the guilt theirs?"

He answered almost carelessly. "Oh no, whoever the men were who refused him the troops he needed, there's where the moral guilt is."

During the long silence, Scarpa drew lines on the floor with his cane, Spallanzani gazed around innocently, Bonaparte leaned against the case and was devoid of expression. "That was prettily argued, Dr. Scarpa," he said finally. "You were continually warned, yet you chose to denounce the government of France in the presence of my officers and myself. What do you expect me to do?"

"I had hoped that a new understanding of causes might dispose you to mercy. If it doesn't—well, I had to try."

"A man as precariously placed as I am had better temper his mercy with a little justice."

"You provided the temptation yourself. It would be justice as well as mercy to alleviate somewhat the consequences of our having fallen into it."

"Scarpa, you're under arrest. Go to your quarters and remain there. You others, hear this. I've been patient with you so far, but the next man who questions my orders is going to get himself shot."

Dr. Contarini was not aware of coming to any decision. He simply left his safe place in the background and walked up, saying, "I ask permission to leave the University. My mother is out there, and my sister. I can't stand it any more."

Scarpa, on his way out, hesitated and looked around. Bonaparte was watching Contarini almost shyly. Then his head drooped. He sounded ashamed when he said, "Certainly you may go. I realize what you're feeling."

"If you do, how can you let it go on?" When he did not look up, Contarini tried to come closer. An officer shouldered him back with unnecessary roughness.

"Go on now. He said you could go. Don't bother him about it."

Contarini began to shout. "Don't bother him! What kind of monsters are you?" He tried to dodge around. A blond officer jumped forward to help. The doctor wrestled with the two of them. Bonaparte stood quietly, his head down so no one could see his face. Scarpa lingered at the doorway, and Spallanzani watched everything from candid eyes as round and innocent as a child's.

The blond officer said through his teeth, "Shut up, now, before I shut you up for good. Leave him alone. He feels bad enough as it is."

He went on yelling. "Stop it, General, for God's sake! How can a civilized man do a thing like this? Stop it and we'll do anything. Anything you want. Just stop it." Then a pistol was shoved against his stomach. Contarini stared down at swarthy hand with lethal metal fingertip; his flesh crawled away from the jabbing touch; his madness drained out.

"Marmont—LeClerc—Let him alone." The voice did not sound like Bonaparte's. It was a weary voice, and almost uncertain. The pistol disappeared. The officers relinquished their savage grips. Contarini had an odd feeling that everyone in the room had left it except himself and the youthful figure by the glass case standing quietly with bent head.

He walked up. "If you give the order to have it stopped, they'll obey you. You know they will."

"My mind is made up." The words themselves were definite, but were spoken as though the man were dreaming. Then he lifted his head. The effort of doing it seemed barely within the reach of his strength. A thrill of fear shot through Contarini. The face was white and drawn and sick and there was no youth left in it.

"You didn't have to conspire among yourselves to tell me that my treatment of Pavia is a crime. I know it. You didn't have to point out that I myself am to blame. I know that. It was a mistake in judgment."

The blond officer moved up and stood near him. It was unobtrusively done, and the doctors did not realize at first that the officer was supporting him. "I never committed a crime before," the dreamer's voice said. "I thought I could frighten you. I underestimated you. It was a mistake in judgment. When a man like myself gives his word, he has no choice but to keep it."

Scarpa said softly from the doorway, "General, you're not well. You ought to lie down. Sit down anyway."

"I hate this more than you do, more than any other man could. If I let Pavia off, they will begin saying in Brescia and Vicenza and Modena that there is nothing to fear, that I make empty threats. No one ever tried to test me before. I had begun to think that men were easily frightened."

He was leaning frankly on his officer. His low voice had no intonation, he did not make a single gesture. He was like a statue speaking. "The fear that I might sack Pavia was as good as two thousand fresh troops at my back. The fact that I have sacked it, what is that?—a mere outrage, a commonplace atrocity fit for barbarians. I, to make war on civilians and women. I who hate mobs, to turn my Army into a looting beastly mob of rapists and butchering thieves. Why do you think I slunk in here? To bully and frighten you, perhaps? No. Because here is order, and contemplation, and virtue, the things I believed I lived by. And out there is the work of my hands."

"Let me send them away, General."

"Yes."

"Get out," the blond officer said coldly.

For quite a while, nothing was said among the doctors standing at the far end of the hallway, in the arching gloom, away from that closed door. Contarini was first to speak. "Was that clinical?"

"I don't know," Scarpa said.

"The change was complete. Face, voice, manner. And the way that officer hurried up, as if he'd been through it before."

"Were you thinking of incipient epilepsy?"

"That, or I even wondered—catalepsy?"

"I never knew one of them to talk."

"He's not sick," Spallanzani said. "He's just worn out." The others looked at him coldly. They felt that metaphysics and natural history made a poor background for diagnosis. "No, really," the gentle giant said. "I never saw a man hold a tighter rein on himself. We thought he hadn't seen through to the true causes, but we were wrong, he knew all the time. You and me, Scarpa, he could fend off with his authority. But he couldn't do that to Contarini here, because he couldn't keep from putting himself in Contarini's place. Though he has the power to stop what's going on out there, he doesn't dare use it. Don't you see how he found himself in an impossible position? His officers know it. It's a good sign in a man to make himself loved like that."

The door of the museum opened and the blond officer came out. He looked up and down the corridor until his eyes adjusted to the dim light. He saw them and came over. Scarpa said, "Is he feeling any better? Did you get him to lie down?" The officer compressed his lips, ignoring the question. Scarpa said, "We are doctors, it's our business to alleviate pain or distress. Please trust me. You touched him, was there any muscular rigidity?"

"See here. Aren't you supposed to be in your quarters under arrest?"

"Yes. What's going to happen to me, do you know?"

"He was just making a gesture. He'll conveniently forget about you if you keep out of sight."

"Really? Are you sure?"

"No one, ever, is quite sure around Bonaparte, but I think that's what he was doing."

"Then I'll go in a minute. But I wish you would answer my questions, because if he's ill perhaps we can help him."

The officer said brusquely, "He's all right. He's been going without enough rest for months and he was awake all night over this sorry business. Then this shouting fool who calls himself a doctor comes at him bellowing about monsters." He looked at Contarini hard.

"Well? Do you want me to take you through the guard? Or were you bluffing? We said you were, but he's convinced you meant it."

Far more than the officer realized, his few words recreated in the doctors' imaginations what had been happening in that closed room. Bonaparte, sick with shame, his atrocious act brought home to him during that swift moment of identifying himself with Contarini, and the officers, loving him, wanting to spare him, broad in their assurances that it had been mere histrionics. As far as his mother and sisters were concerned, Dr. Contarini would be throwing his life away if he accepted the challenge. He never could find them now; he could do them no good if he did. But Contarini too found himself in an impossible position, because if he backed down, his cowardice would absolve the other.

"I wasn't bluffing," Contarini said. His voice was level and quiet, but his eyes were glowing with terror. He saw in the officer's angry bafflement that he had read the situation correctly. You won't forget me soon, General Bonaparte, Contarini thought to himself. He went out with the officer.

THREE

The Bonnet Rouge

"CONTE IS DEAD," Diane said again, almost listlessly. Charlot Florian tightened his arms around her but did not try to speak. Let her talk it out, he thought. His heart was heavy with anger and sorrow. He had sent her to Pavia because he wanted her safe and happy. Instead she had witnessed sights worse than anything at the height of the Terror. "Cut down on the street like a mad dog, right outside the University," Diane said. "So useless, such a waste. They were with me all the time."

He had heard her story before so he knew what was meant. Conte's mother and sisters had been saved by her, and she had tried to save the sons-in-law too. But the men had not been allowed to stay. "What's happened to the world, Charlot?" she asked. "It's all weeping and death. That captain was only a boy. I told him exactly what he was doing. I loved Pavia, Charlot. I'm glad you didn't have to see her, afterwards."

"I know, my darling."

"Are we French damned? Whatever we touch, whatever touches us, is poisoned, pulled down, destroyed. That paper was so terribly sad. He didn't actually say it, but 'We who are about to die salute you,' it was like that. He was such a boy, he wasn't any older than the students. I didn't look at it that night, I was so upset, then I forgot I had it. When we heard what Bonaparte was going to do, I didn't know how to act. I knew I could claim protection for myself, but I couldn't just walk away from the Signora and her daughters and save myself, could I? Could I, Charlot?"

"You didn't have to, dear. You did save them, you know."

"I remembered the captain had put something in my pocket. They were about to start out for the square then. Everyone had to go to the square, you understand, and watch while the priests and the city officials were killed."

"Yes. It was horrible."

"The Signora kept begging me to go to Headquarters and save myself. I couldn't make up my mind to do it. I would have in the end, I suppose. Nobody lets himself be killed if he can stop it, does he? Except Conte. Why, Charlot? Why did he do it? His mother told us she'd made him promise that he wouldn't leave the University. Why did he do it after he promised her? He knew there was nothing he could do. Ah, why couldn't I have thought of that paper before! If Conte had known about it, he'd have known they were going to be all right. He'd be alive now if I'd looked at that paper earlier."

"Try not to think about it, my darling. He wouldn't want you to grieve like this." He tried to hide from her how he himself felt.

"It said I had saved the lives of fifty injured soldiers of France. 'My General will know how to express the gratitude that we of the garrison can only feel'—he was a boy. They were all boys and old men. Why did Conte break his promise to his mother? He must have known there wasn't anything he could do."

"It would be hard to act otherwise. You don't think I'd have stayed in the University if you were out there, surely."

"But they were with me. They were safe."

"Conte didn't know that, dear."

"I killed him, Charlot."

"You know that's not true. You have suffered enough, you must not start making things up to torment yourself about. Forgetting about that paper was a sad mischance that could have happened to anyone."

She turned in his arms, pressing herself against him fiercely. "Don't ever, ever send me away from you again! Promise me!"

"I never will, my darling. I do promise. I admit I was wrong."

The fierce hurt to her would pass away. Someday all this would be a sad memory, returning rarely to trouble her. Meanwhile he could only do his best to try to bring her back into his ordered world of service to others, of building slowly to a future in which the emphasis would be on healing, not devastation.

In the Medical Inspector's handsome carriage flanked by outriders, Diane and Charlot rode through the towns of France toward Paris. Advised by Carnot that she was being sent back, he had met the Army train with its wagonloads of pelf and captured Austrian standards at the border. The French towns were ablaze with excitement. There were illuminations every night, and ceremonies and rejoicings. At last the people had a national hero whom they could cheer unreservedly, a soldier whose name was synonymous with victory and whose bulletins now began to speak of peace becoming more possible. Bonaparte was like the sun; his rays fell everywhere. But Diane turned her face away, and her accurate knowledge of him was a sick dread back of her eyes. She had looked on his handiwork, she knew him for what he was, her attitude said.

The Florians were in south France when the long duel between Barras and Carnot ended finally. The doctor did not hear the news about that; it was a palace revolution and lost sight of in the enthusiasm generated by the victories.

❖ ❖ ❖

Ange had become tired and apathetic. His vitality that had drawn others relentlessly merely flickered now, a flame about to go out. The crowds that had followed him were much diminished and as apathetic as he. Only when he sang of the victories in Italy was there any real response and that was directed toward the hero of Arcole and Lodi. The truthteller, he had called himself, but now every day he sang lies.

Fidèle had liked to follow him around and applaud him, but he asked her not to do that any more. She was glad not to because she loved him. Times of watching Ange walk the streets singing praises of the Directory while tears of weakness gathered in his eyes and spilled down his brown cheeks, were like blows raining down on her heart. Fidèle knew he would rather die than live as he was doing; she knew the long hot passing days destroyed him in a way more final than even death could. Where Ange was concerned, Fidèle was very wise.

On the seventeenth of Fructidor, Ange was met at the west gate of the church by one of Barras' personal guards. He was commanded to stay off the streets for a few days. Unbearably provoked by his curiosity, he prowled disobediently, collecting bits of information until the blatant wrongdoing finally became clear to him. Deeply thoughtful, he returned to the place on the Cité and told Fidèle what he had learned. It was simply a purge, he told her, Barras was ridding himself of his enemies and those who had annoyed him under a convenient cloak of conspiracy against the government.

Though Carnot himself had escaped arrest and was in flight, Barthélemy, the Director who had supported his ideas, was under arrest and so was Charles Pichegru, the conqueror of Holland, now charged with selling himself to the foe. Generals Willot and Imbert-Colomes, sundry other notables, a great many deputies, and a long

list of journalists, judges and priests were being held. The talk was
that they would be deported to Guiana where, everyone knew, no
one survived and no one escaped.

Fidèle and Ange talked all night. She understood perfectly that
he was making the only possible choice, that Barras had tried the
truthteller too far when he arranged Fructidor. Though Ange had
not forgotten about his sister, he had convinced himself that she
would prefer to be chained and beaten every day rather than consent to his silence now.

The next morning, they went hand-in-hand to the old rendezvous.
He wanted her with him and she wanted to come. A desultory crowd
of not more than twenty persons was waiting. Fidèle could remember when they had attended him by the hundreds. He strode up,
his face convulsed with wrath, blaring out the old words so much
more appropriate to the Directors than to Robespierre. "I am fain to
sing or satirize rascals, Septemberists, cheats, idlers, spies, and all
the thievish gang that rule us!"

His powerful voice rolling out imprecations, he gathered up his
crowds quickly. Slapping his bottom to show his opinion of how
France was governed, grimacing horribly as he recited the names
of the Directors who were left as though each was a word of unspeak-
able filth, he told and retold the facts behind the purge. He sang and
talked for hours without ever seeming to repeat himself. Ange, his
crowds about him, roared up the streets. And Fidèle followed in her
broken shoes that were sizes large for her, and her little pointed
face was stern with joy. Ange had come back. The truthteller had
come back.

*   *   *

The Florians arrived outside Paris in late evening after the barriers
had been closed. Dr. Florian showed his pass permitting him to go
anywhere at any time, and signed by Carnot himself. The guard
shoved it back surlily. "It's all right, I suppose, but you'd better get
that changed, Citizen." He was puzzled by the remark, but did not
question the guard because he was anxious to get Diane home
where she could rest.

They found Fidèle sitting on the same stairtread where she had
waited for him the day of Ange's beating by Barras' thugs. Fidèle
told them the news and said that Ange had been taken. Diane took
the little forlorn figure in her arms and felt delicate bones under her

hands, reminding her of a time she had held a hurt bird. "He'll be all right, Fidèle. He's been in trouble so many times, but he always gets out."

"It's different this time," Fidèle said.

"My God," Florian said softly, "this is the end of everything." There was not going to be any reopening of medical schools and hospitals, no sane restrictions to guard the populace against assassins disguised as doctors. That dream was finished. He was hardly paying attention to Fidèle in his effort to comprehend the full extent of the disaster.

Diane was still assuming he had power and importance and said, "Charlot won't let anything happen to Ange. Sit down, Fidèle, you look worn out! How long have you been waiting down there?"

"Two days now." Diane looked at her wonderingly. "There didn't seem any other place to go," Fidèle said. "I knew the doctor would come back someday."

"But my dear! How did you eat?"

"I bought things from the street vendors." She turned to Florian. Her little sharp face was infinitely appealing. "Will you help us, Doctor?"

"Of course he will," Diane said.

"But what can I do, Fidèle? How long ago did this happen?"

"Three days ago, Doctor." She told a few more details. He listened as attentively as he could, but was stunned from the force of the blow to his hopes.

"Ange will be all right," he said, "his crowds will watch out for him. This isn't the first time, remember."

"It's different this time," she repeated.

"Why would it be different, Fidèle?" Florian said, immensely weary, immensely patient.

"They haven't followed him for a long time, Doctor. They followed him that day, but Ange told me himself they wouldn't try to save him this time. He's lost them."

Diane was surprised and curious but Florian already knew what was coming. Why hadn't he realized what would happen? His decision on the day of the beating had done so much more to Ange than merely change the singer's songs. It had broken his safety. Singing lies every day, of course he had lost his hold on the crowds. One day of truthtelling would not re-establish the rapport, if, indeed, it ever could be re-established. Fashions changed swiftly in Paris. Ange had let himself go out-of-fashion in order to save his sister who was dead anyway and beyond feeling pain. Guilt over that day lashed the doctor. What had he done? He had betrayed a man who trusted him, betrayed him, it now seemed, to his death.

He repeated her words wonderingly. "Ange knew they wouldn't try to save him." She nodded, her long copper-colored hair swinging. "Why didn't you stop him, then?"

"He had to do it, Doctor, he is the truthteller."

"Ah, my God, I can't help you," he groaned. "If Carnot is gone, I have no influence left either. Fidèle——" He started to tell her. But she was suffering enough already. As doctors have had to do throughout their history, he concealed his action, not to save himself pain (it would have relieved him to tell it) but to save her.

   ❋   ❋   ❋

Fidèle lay awake a long time in the strange bed that was so soft, in the strange room where Ange had slept on the night he first met Dr. Florian. "You shall stay with us as long as you like. Forever, if you like," the doctor had told Fidèle, and something dark and stern on his face had made her wonder. Why did he suffer so for Ange and Fidèle? He had always been kind to them, but not close.

Ange, where are you now, what are you suffering? What is being done to you? Her whole being tried helplessly to follow him down whatever dark passages he was being compelled to traverse. Ange— his name always had meant gaiety, and excitement, and courage, but now it was the syllable of despair. Ange was the name of the flame. Ange was courage and fury, was buffoonery, wit, and even coarseness. Ange was the sharpness of the knife, the humiliation of the lash, the laughing sneering devil-face of misfortune grandly tempted and splendidly borne. Ange was the revolt against revolt; Ange held up the mirror of convention only to smash it. And Ange had disappeared forever into the maw of Paul Barras' misgovern-ment. Admit it, admit you will never see him again. There is life to come to terms with, and the Florians, who made such generous terms. If Ange were here, what would he say she should do? He would tell her to go with them, taking every bit of the protection they offered with such puzzling generosity. America was so very far away, a land teeming with scalping Indians, what would happen to a Paris street girl in a place like that? But Dr. Florian was the kind of man who creates security around him. Even in America, she would be safe with him and Diane. "I'm through with France," Dr.

Florian had told them. "I said it once before, but then I let Carnot convince me otherwise. But Italy is not far enough away, Diane's experiences prove that. We're going to the United States. Fidèle too, if she wishes."

Left by herself in Paris, Fidèle would starve to death. But if she went to America with the Florians, it would seem to erase Ange from the boulevards forever, since no eyes would remain to look on old haunts of his in loving hope that he would return to them one day. If she went to a new life, would she not be putting the final period to their life together? But no one escapes Guiana, no one survives it, Fidèle told herself. She wept quietly into the strange pillow that was so soft.

❋　　　❋　　　❋

Diane said, "What happened in there, Charlot?"

"What do you mean?"

"My dear, I have lived with you for years. A few months' separation hasn't made strangers of us. You were suffering terribly about something, what was it?"

He turned gratefully. "I don't want to burden you with it. But I do want to unburden myself." He told her the whole thing. When he had finished, she simply lay there without comment. "What are you thinking?" he asked finally.

"Of them. When we first met them." She lifted herself on her elbow and looked at him, her glance sweet and firm. "I don't want to hurt you, Charlot."

"Go on," he said grimly.

"I was thinking of how suspicious both of them were of us and how we begged them to trust us. I was remembering that little speech you made her the first night she came here. You told her you didn't lie and you wouldn't lie. Is there anything you can do to help him?"

"No. Nothing. I wish there were. Are you ashamed of me, Diane?"

"I never could be that. I wish we never had met them. I knew from the first that he would do something terrible to us. But I didn't know that we would do it to him."

"You keep saying 'we.' You have done nothing."

"Don't take my half away, Charlot. You promised me you'd never send me away from you again. Don't begin doing it so soon."

"Diane, when I did that to Ange, it was the best I knew."

"I know that. Don't worry about it. Perhaps God will understand."

But he did not have her faith in God; and also, he had to stand on his own actions. Doctors do.

✻   ✻   ✻

He still had connections enough to find out accurately what was happening to Fructidor's victims. In lots of forty, the several hundred arrested persons were being transported across the half of France in iron cages on wheels, open to the weather. Arrived at Rochefort, they were being thrown into dungeons to wait for the whole of the condemned lot to be assembled. This time, Barras was going to be sure of his vengeance. He was taking no chances that, as had happened in the past, a British vessel would stop the prison ship and take the condemned men aboard, releasing them later in those countries where the ships touched. A fleet of French warships had been ordered to accompany the prison fleet when it sailed from Rochefort.

Florian heard stories of brutal guards who encouraged the ignorant crowds to pelt the victims with rotten fruit, spoiled fish, and eggs. Proud, free, careless Ange—his heart surely would break under the indignities. Ange had endured bravely the beating Paul Barras had ordered for him, but Ange could not endure much of that.

He told Diane what he had learned, leaving it to her judgment how much Fidèle should be told. Diane told Fidèle everything, but then went on to talk in a lively fashion of what life in America would be like, of the happiness the three of them would find there. Once she had heard and accepted Charlot's story, she had accepted their lifelong obligation to Fidèle. Caring for her was all they could do toward righting the grave wrong they had done toward the luckless pair.

II

ANGE PITOU stood stoically under the hail of rotted fish and vegetables. Nearly his only emotion was selfless pity for those in the cart with him who were old and venerable, unused to violence and not able to understand why the raving crowd exhibited so much glee at the sight of their sufferings. Three of the forty persons in the cart were sick. He felt a profound indignation on their behalf, and contempt of the frenzied stupid crowd.

97

He had always loved crowds. Ange had loved them, and they him: a leaping as from flame to shavings and a common burning in protest of wrongs. But these crowds were different, or else Ange himself had changed. These crowds were malevolent and silly. Or his ability to feel out the people, and then express their thoughts, was gone from him. He was not sure which it was and did not much care; the result was the same, that he was as indifferent to this crowd as it was hateful toward him and the others. All his emotions were directed toward the old men in the cart and the sick ones.

When one of these would fall down from exhaustion, Ange would bend as far as the crush allowed and whisper fiercely, "Don't give up. The law protects you. You're not fit to be sent there." Somehow his old secret of spark to tinder was preserved in little ways like these because the fallen one, a deputy, a hoary journalist, a judge wise in years and decisions, would feel that crude strength lifting him up, even though the only aid he could give was his words, or sometimes a hand held down.

The law he mentioned was one that Carnot had sponsored, and provided for physical examinations before the victims of the Directory's fury could be shipped away to Guiana. Now that Carnot himself was in flight, the law might not be in force any more. But the old men would die of terror and shame unless someone gave them a little hope.

Ange decided that the demonstrations against the prisoners were too ugly to be wholly spontaneous. Agents of Barras must have preceded the carts and paid good money to buy such frenzies of cruel rage. He wiped a blob of saliva from his face and thought that, while every mouth contains spittle, a brain is required to tell you in which direction you should eject it. His Paris crowds had been a lot smarter.

Many things afflicted the prisoners. They were not fed properly or regularly. Whatever clothes they had been wearing at the time of their arrest they were wearing still, and some suffered very much from the heaviness of official robes under the beating sunlight. The cart was always parked out where there was no shade by daytime and no shelter by night, and was left unguarded while the escort stuffed themselves with food and wine and made abrupt brutal advances toward the chambermaids. The prisoners were chained together, and those on the outside were chained to the bars of the cart, so it was not necessary to keep a guard on them.

As night came down, the furious shrieking men of the towns, and their women and children, would tire of the sport of bear-baiting human beings and would go to their homes, satiated. The stars of the sky were quiet and kind, and Ange watched each one come out. The others in the cart slept. It was too bad they could not sleep in the daytime as he did, in the jolting burn-hot daytime or with the paid crowds milling around, but they could not, and so exhaustion prevented them from watching the loveliness of night with him.

I had my cause, Ange thought, and I fought as long and hard as I could. I had my friends and my woman. A lot of men go down to death without ever having had as much. Look at the countryside of France, bathed in the light of the late-harvest moon! Was there ever a sight so purple and silver, and the blazes on the stock I see over there blue-silver, as I remember from my childhood in Normandy? It is important to me that I have partaken of every sunset and every dawn that occurred while I occurred. After all, I am a lucky man.

❂   ❂   ❂

By the time Florian arrived home, the contagion of terror had swept Diane as well. She tried to tell herself that Fidèle had lived so long with the outlaw Pitou that it was natural in her to distrust an official visit. Diane herself ought to show more sense. After all, officials of the Directorial government were liable to the same ills of the flesh as other men. Perhaps this one wanted relief from a persistent headache or an upset stomach. Or his coming might mean that Dr. Florian was wanted as a consultant on some important case. It even crossed her mind that the new Directors, Douai and François de Neufchâteau, had found among Carnot's papers the plans and estimates for reopening medical schools and hospitals and were interested in going on with it. But when she advanced these theories, Fidèle looked at her as though Diane was a naive child. "They're coming to arrest him! I know it!" she kept saying.

Florian received their excited recitation of the news with lifted eyebrows. "Diane, for heaven's sake! I thought you had more sense." He began listing the very things she had already thought of as more probable than his arrest, since he had done nothing to incur arrest. Then he said more gently, "I shouldn't have scolded you. What happened at Pavia was enough to break anyone's trust in men of affairs." She smiled at him gratefully. Even Fidèle seemed convinced now.

The official came back shortly afterwards. He said to Florian, "You are to start at once for Rochefort, where you will examine for physical fitness the prisoners on the *Bonnet Rouge*."

Florian asked to see his credentials. They were in order. He asked him to repeat the directive. It remained the same. He burst out angrily, "But that's nonsensical! There are capable doctors in Rochefort, surely? What is the matter with the ship's doctor on the *Bonnet Rouge* that he can't examine them?"

Fidèle touched his arm, saying, "Please go, Doctor. Please!"

"The order is from the Executive Directory, Dr. Florian."

"It's the most inefficient thing I ever heard of. It would make a little sense if I'd been appointed to examine the whole lot, but one shipload! I have my patients, they're sick, they depend on me. I don't have time to be running damn fool errands for the Executive Directory or anyone else."

"Please!" Fidèle whispered desperately.

"Am I to understand that you refuse your appointment?"

"I don't know whether I refuse it or not. I'm certainly going to look into it."

"Well, that's your privilege, of course. In your shoes, I'd do what I was told." He bowed insolently and went out.

Diane, looking white and strained, said, "Do you think you can get out of it?"

"I'm almost sure I can. The whole thing is ridiculous." He mentioned some important names, but then he noticed Fidèle. She looked as if each name he used was another whip to cut her flesh. "What is it, my poor child? Why do you want so much for me to go?"

"Maybe Ange will be on that boat," she whispered huskily.

He had not even thought of that possibility. "It would be a most remarkable coincidence. There may be a dozen or more prison ships. It's most improbable that I'd find Ange on that particular one."

"But it could happen," she pleaded.

"But Fidèle, if he were we couldn't exchange more than a few words. What purpose would be served?"

"If he is on that ship—"

"Go on," Florian said.

"You mean Charlot could declare him unfit. Is that it, Fidèle?" Diane said. "But he couldn't do that, dear."

"That time I examined him, I found nothing to indicate he won't live for a hundred years," Florian said.

Fidèle said insistently, her hands clasped, "But you could say he wasn't. You're the doctor, and you could say it!" Such an idea would never have occurred to him. He felt simple astonishment. She went on, "The law says they can't send him there if a doctor dismisses him. They would have to bring him back to Paris. He would be in prison, but there would be some chance of getting him out some-day. If he goes to Guiana, he'll die! You know it!"

But wouldn't that be a violation of medical responsibility? To ex-cuse a man in good health might be as damnable, ethically speaking, as to pass one who was not. He hesitated, biting his lip. But then she slipped down on her knees. Her little warm, soiled hands tugged at his. "Ah, please. Please!"

Florian's eyes met Diane's over Fidèle's bowed head. Husband and wife both were thinking that the pathetic, ignorant pair had been asked to trust him but then he had lied to them. That Ange was in this danger was because of what Florian had done. "Ah, don't," he said helplessly, "please don't." He tried to lift her but she clung to his knees. "I'll go," he said, "I'll do anything you want me to." He felt her tears on his hands. "I don't think he'll be on that ship. But I'll go."

❖　　　❖　　　❖

The medical box was heavy. Hippocrates had written that the doc-tor about to go on a short journey should prepare—"as for a long Voyage, not knowing the Encounters and Adventures that may be in store for him, and it being better to go overpacked than to find a necessary Instrument wanting." So the box contained a varied supply of powders, his surgical instruments, a fever gauge he had constructed on the model of one used by Sanctorius, and his Leeu-wenhoek microscope. It was a real task to get Dr. Florian and his heavy box over the side of the ship.

The *Bonnet Rouge* did not look seaworthy, and he found her badly kept. The sailors seemed lackluster and sullen. The captain and his first officer struck Florian as shifty-eyed men who seemed unfit for command of any sort.

"You'll find lanterns and everything else you need down there, Doctor," the captain said.

Mindful of ethics, Dr. Florian suggested that the ship's doctor be invited to accompany him. But Dr. Keroual had been put off at Île d'Oléron a few leagues out to see to the medical needs of several hundred priests immolated there, Florian was told. The ship would pick Keroual up after the sailing. He thought again that it would have made a little sense if they had appointed him to go to Île d'Oléron instead. But no, they must send the ship's doctor there, and bring Florian all the way from Paris to examine the men on his ship.

Sailors opened the hatchway for him. Florian started into the dark stench of the hold with his box. In a space none too large for twenty men, nearly a hundred must be crammed. They were chained too, he could tell from hearing chains clanking. That was an unnecessary cruelty; they were certainly unarmed, and the ladder of rotten rope by which he had descended could not accommodate more than one man at a time.

He did not know quite how to behave. The feeling of apologetic embarrassment was new to him, and disagreeable, but he realized that his appearance here to tap backs and examine throats was backed by the weight of that same authority that had condemned them. It would seem to them that he approved of the monstrous injustice being done them. "I am Dr. Florian. I have been appointed to examine you for fitness."

A voice flashed out gaily from shadows too deep for his light-accustomed eyes to see faces. "Hullo, Doctor! I thought it was you. So my luck hasn't run out after all." It was Ange Pitou's voice. It had seemed so unlikely, but the instinct of Fidèle's loyal heart had been more accurate than Florian's knowledge of mathematical probabilities. Before he could gather his wits and answer, Ange was saying cheerfully, "How in the world did you arrange this? I'm eternally grateful, I can tell you. I'd given up all hope of being rescued."

The doctor's square-cut mouth tightened with anger. It was bad enough to be compelled to violate medical responsibility for the singer's sake, without having it thrown in the faces of the other condemned, most of whom he would have to pass. Though he could not see anything, he could feel the indignation toward himself that must be written on all their hidden faces. But Pitou would not be here except for you, Florian told himself.

He knew it was dangerous to release Ange. If he were found out, his action almost certainly would prevent him from getting visés to America, if there were not worse retaliation. Paul Barras appeared to have a particular grudge against the singer. He might go so far as to order an examination by another doctor, who would find a man in perfect physical condition. Then Florian would be required to explain himself and there would be no explanation to make.

He found the lanterns and was lighting them, thinking, yes, it's dangerous, but I'll have to take the chance. I owe him that much. "I don't know how it happened, Ange," he said finally. "I was appointed, that's all I know about it." There were five lanterns, but not fuel enough to keep one going for any length of time.

"The odd thing is, we were examined once already, in the prison at Rochefort," Ange said.

"Yes, that is odd, but then nothing that this government does can surprise me now. I have never seen so much bungling in high places. Robespierre seemed irrational a good part of the time, but he was a miracle of clarity compared to what goes on these days." His voice fell away before the realization of how safe it was to speak before them with such candor, because like dead men, they could not tell tales. Embarrassment amounting to agony claimed him. This was hellish work for a healer!

When the five lanterns were going, he could see Ange and the others. They were lying on the floor of the hold, partially immersed in dirty cold water, and the same long leg-chain bound them all. My God, he thought, Guiana won't have a chance to kill them. They'll die before they get there. He was half conscious of a rattling and slapping above deck, but in his concern over the prisoners, paid no attention. He decided to leave the examination of Ange until later. If he had an opportunity to excuse one or two of the others, it would not seem so obvious when he excused the singer. But then, if they had been examined already, it was not likely that even this small shield would be granted as concealment of his action of ugly favoritism.

Inwardly shrinking back, he approached one of them, a brawny young giant. Florian's examination, though swift, was thorough. "I'm sorry, friend," he said gently. The man turned his head away, not speaking. Florian began to sweat in the chill damp hold. This was the hardest thing he had ever done.

To the eighth man he said, "How old are you?"

"Sixty-three, Doctor."

"I will recommend you unfit because of age."

"Thank you, Doctor! Thank you!"

"Don't," Florian said, touching his naked thin shoulder. "I wish I dared do the same for the lot of you." His voice throbbed with sincerity, and when he had to say to the next man, "I'm sorry," a pair of hopeless eyes consented to meet his, almost with sympathy.

The seventeenth man whispered to him, "I have two thousand

livres buried at the foot of a tree in my garden. Pronounce me unfit, and I'll tell you where to dig."

Florian said in his natural voice, "But you are unfit. You don't have to pay me to say so." He had heard the characteristic snoring sound of a pussy thorax.

The fiftieth man said to him, "You are being much too thorough, Doctor."

"Believe me, my only fear is that I might not be thorough enough."

"Are you really so anxious to see Guiana for yourself? This ship lifted anchor half an hour ago."

He was stunned. Fearful thoughts pressed down. The Executive Directory, so vengeful, so careless. But he had done nothing to attract their vengeance, and no carelessness could go as far as that. "You must be mistaken."

"I've been in the holds of ships before. Can't you feel the difference? The wood seems to move under you."

"It doesn't feel different to me."

"Look at the light from the portholes." To him, the same watery light. "A ship at anchor, the light flickers. A ship asail, the flickers are quickened and much wider."

Florian fought off his feeling of panic. "I imagine I'm to be let off at the Île d'Oléron when they pick up your ship's doctor, and then sent back by smallboat. How long has that been festering like this?"

"Were you told this ship stopped at Île d'Oléron?"

"Yes. Try not to jerk away, this won't hurt you."

"Now who would tell you such lies? The ship's doctor was leaning over the rail drunk a few hours ago. I saw him myself when we were brought over. And I know this ship, she doesn't stop at Île d'Oléron or any place else, it's a straight run to Martinique unless there are special orders to Guiana."

"You must be mistaken!"

"The ship's doctor is Bénigne Keroual whom I have seen a dozen times drunk in port, and I saw him again at Rochefort, and again a few hours ago on this ship, with his head over the rail."

"It isn't possible," Florian said. But truth has a ring of its own. You learn in time to identify it. Hippocrates had written, "The physician should keep aware of the fact that patients often lie." So you trained your ear to the little sub-sounds of the human voice. An innocent lie of embarrassment from the patient can mean the failure of a treatment; the truth he told you that you didn't reckon on could mean his death. The doctor had learned to test men's words as some others test their coins, and this man's words rang true.

"Who hates you so, Doctor?"

"No one," Florian said mechanically. But was it true?—there were families of patients who had died under his care; there were crippled men who might believe that another physician could have saved the sight of their eyes or the use of hands or legs. No enemies? Every doctor has enemies. And there was his connection with Carnot. Perhaps the other Directors so feared and hated Carnot that they wanted to rid themselves of all his friends and supporters. He felt the deep inward sinking of true terror. Diane! He heard with astonishment the groan that burst from him.

The condemned man spoke to him with wry kindness. "Perhaps it's as you say, a mistake. Or they were in such a hurry, perhaps they decided you wouldn't mind a sea voyage to Martinique and back."

He seized on that with the illogical hope of the despairing. The self-important minions of the Directory might indeed feel that a mere doctor's convenience, and the health of his patients, could be set aside without so much as consulting him. Perhaps when his work was done, he would be brought out of the fetid hold and given a cabin to himself, apologies . . . Immediately he was aware of feeling shame over this growing picture of personal comfort. A fresh sea voyage for the tired doctor, while beneath him, a man more than sixty years old and another gravely ill of a pulmonary disturbance lay in chains on the soaked floor of the hold.

Mechanically Florian moved on to the next man. It required only the briefest examination to tell him the man was dead. Had a doctor in Rochefort really pronounced the dead man as fit for exile in a place that was notorious for killing the strong and the young? Had any man taken the holy oath, yet done this? He stared down at the dead thing in gyves, and the words formed on his lips—"I swear by Apollo the physician, and Aesculapius and Hygeia and Panacea and all the gods and goddesses—" because he had to know that he was still Florian and still true, though all the world was mad.

❖   ❖   ❖

The hatchway was pushed back. A man's head showed in the opening many feet above them. Florian began to climb the rope ladder toward the blistering beauty of sky and sunlight. He left his box where it was, on the floor of the hold. The things in that could be sent for or replaced. All he wanted was to get out.

"Don't climb any higher," the sailor said. "I'll knock you on the head as soon as I can reach you." The astonished doctor stopped climbing.

"There's been a mistake!" he said. He was convinced by now and said angrily, "I was brought here to examine the men for fitness. Nearly ten I have seen are definitely unfit and ought to be sent back with me. And one of them is dead."

"You got a dead one down there already?"

"He died before I saw him."

"How did you slip your chains?"

"I never was in chains. I just finished telling you, it's a mistake. I'm a physician, I was brought here from Paris to examine the men."

"They were examined in Rochefort."

"So they told me, but I was brought here to do it just the same." He started climbing again.

"I mean it!" the man said sharply. He produced an iron bar with a wicked hook at its end. "You come any higher, you get this, right in your face. Well, if you're out of chains, that's less work for me. Stand down for the water bucket. Stand down, I said!"

Florian shouted at him. "Will you please tell your captain that the Medical Inspector for the French Republic is down here?"

One of the prisoners called out weakly. "Please let him put the water down, Doctor."

Florian, ashamed, left the ladder. "All right, lower your bucket, but for God's sake remember to tell them up there that I'm still down here." He caught the dirty, rust-crusted pail and untied the unfamiliar knot with the ease born of practice in tying ligatures. The rope was withdrawn. The hatchway slammed shut, cutting off the light.

The lanterns had burned out long before this. Florian found his way over the foul floor by the pale washed light from the high portholes. He went from man to man, tending their thirst from a corroded dipper. Diane, Diane. . . . He gave them water, thinking of no one but her. He did not take any of the water for himself, there was so little of it to divide among nearly a hundred men. Anyway, it smelled dank. This ship had been in port a night ago, yet could not provide fresh water for drinking purposes. When the pail was empty, he put it down beside the rope ladder.

If he were going to be rescued, he did not want to get his clothes fouled. He decided to stand up as long as he could. He went over to where Ange was hunkered down, his chin resting on his crossed forearms.

"Sit," Ange said, "it isn't so bad. Your butt gets numb after a while."

"I'm still hoping it's a mistake."

"Hope is pleasant, though you can't eat it of course, or sit on it even. If you want my opinion, you're in it with the rest of us. I'm sorry for you. I'm even sorry for myself. I was so sure that I was going to be rescued after all. You were going to excuse me, weren't you?"

"I wish you'd stop talking about it. How do you think it makes the rest of them feel? Yes, I was going to excuse you, I owe you that much."

"You do? Why?"

"It's largely my fault that you're here."

"Well," Ange said, "that's a relief to my conscience, because it's largely *my* fault that *you're* here. That last day I sang, I was so angry, I told everything I knew that was against Barras. I told the people what you'd said was going to happen to them, the epidemics until they were wiped out. I think I used your name a time or two. It's too bad your name is so easy to rhyme, because if it hadn't been, I wouldn't have used it maybe. You've always been good to me. When I'm angry, I don't show very good sense."

Florian touched his shoulder lightly, thinking that what Ange had done out of deep emotion might or might not have been the main factor in Florian's being here, but that his deliberate betrayal of the singer's trust, for Pinel's sake and the sake of the insane, had had everything to do with Ange's plight.

"Aren't you angry with me, Doctor?"

"No, Ange. I have a confession to make myself. But let's not talk any more now. I can't seem to keep my mind on what we're saying." His mind was filled with a picture of Diane, serenely waiting, believing he would be on his way to her, while every hour that passed was putting leagues of depthless ocean waters between them. Even if this were a mistake, even if there had been no malevolent intention toward him, it would be weeks before he could complete the voyage to Martinique and back. She would think he had been killed by highwaymen. He put his hand to his eyes, and it came away wet.

He said tonelessly, "Don't worry about Fidèle, Ange. She's with Diane."

"So you took her in too." Ange said gruffly, "I don't know why you're so kind to us. I never have figured that out."

"Ah, don't, Ange," Florian said helplessly, and turned and walked away. I'll have to tell him, he thought, but not now, please not now, I can't bear any more. Diane, Diane. . . . His heart beat in two syllables, his whole being pulsed to her name.

III

THE PRISON FLEET was out four days from Rochefort before Bénigne Keroual, ship's doctor on the *Bonnet Rouge,* accepted the fact that further drunkenness was a physical impossibility. He would have to become completely sober before his system would tolerate more alcohol. He would rather be condemned to a flogging and unless he had behaved better than usual during the past eight days of walking unconsciousness, he deserved one.

The fifteen ships sailed steadily toward French Guiana over a quiet sea. Seen as a whole, the fleet was impressive. White sails flashed like gull wings, trim bows cut into the immeasurable waste of the Atlantic economically and persistently. The escort ships were well-built, well-kept, well-manned. The eight prison ships sailed in the center of the formation. Their decks were green with slime, their rigging tangled. They rolled and stumbled along, holding their course only because the trim escort ships were herding them.

The indifference of officers and sailors on the prison ships was, in part at least, defensive. They knew that the prisoners belowdeck were innocent men against whom no charge could be lodged except that of opposing in legal ways the unscrupulous and opportunistic government that called itself the French Directory. The prisoners were deputies who had demanded better laws, or judges who had upheld just decisions, or journalists who had written boldly against profiteering and corruption, or priests who had loved God better than the State. These were the men France had cast up.

Attempts at colonizing Guiana had been made by the French kings; to the French Directory was reserved the dubious honor of inaugurating a penal system there. Almost from the first, the Directory had rid itself of enemies by this new, savage method. Merchant ships bound for Haiti or Martinique would receive sealed orders to stop at Cayenne harbor and let off a dozen or more chained unfortunates. The merchant captains had responded by seeking out British warships to whom they could surrender themselves. When the deportees had been taken aboard the other ship, the captured

French vessel would be allowed to escape. It was a civilized and generous arrangement of the kind that seems to spring up wherever there is ruthless oppression. But nothing like that would be allowed to happen this time, since the task of getting the eight hundred odd deportees to Guiana had been entrusted to the French Navy. The Navy's pride was of a different order than the merchantmen's, and the Navy was prepared to fight. So the mute indignant sailors on the merchant ships became more sloppy every day. And Bénigne Keroual stayed drunk.

Keroual was a tubby little man in his early fifties, with a broad, good-natured face and a friendly eye seldom in focus. There was no meanness in him, only a raging appetite for the draught that quenches memory. The pattern of his sprees was always the same. His drinking would begin in self-disgust, when some evil misdemeanor committed during a former drunkenness either floated back into his memory, or was reported to him, or else was recognized by its repercussions. In his misery he would pour drinks and when the liquor began to take effect, he would be presented with the warming thought that it was not too late for him to become the good doctor he wanted to be. It would seem to him that all he had to do to become a good doctor was to have another drink and yet another, in order to sustain the passion and refuel the dream. Then he would lose consciousness. Even though he would be walking around, or sitting and pouring drinks, he would be unconscious. He would go about like a zombi prescribing medicines, even wielding the knife sometimes with a hand astonishingly steady. His ruling thought would be to finish whatever the task was, in order to get back to his bottle.

Of all the loneliness and terror that life can hold, there was nothing quite like Dr. Keroual's when he wakened to the realization that he had been drunk again after all.

*　　　*　　　*

The prisoners had no other occupation than their bitter thoughts and their conversations with each other. All around Florian, voices broken and sad, or voices hard with determination to make the best of things, murmured out the secrets of other hearts. By now he had relinquished the hope that his being here was a mistake, but he was compelled to realize that his sufferings were no greater than the sufferings of others, nor had any special injustice been done him. They were all as innocent of misdoing as he was.

Not the least of his mental torments was his feeling that he had played the fool. Twice he had had the opportunity to leave France and twice refused it, hugging his dream of performing great services. Dr. Contarini had risked his life to rescue his friend. Florian's obligation to the medical students had held him back that time. But later, when Carnot had arranged visés for them and paid their tuitions at the University, what folly of self-delusion had kept him from going? The Director had been candid to the point of indiscretion in his warnings of what might happen. To Florian now, his actions and sacrifices looked like the mock-heroism of the born dupe.

Medical Inspector of the French Republic . . . he had fallen into a glittering trap. What good to him now was that high-sounding title, or his handsome salary of six thousand livres a year? No doubt Barras was collecting that for himself, the post of Medical Inspector having been abolished at the moment the person of the Medical Inspector entered the hold of the *Bonnet Rouge*. He remembered the bargain Carnot had made with Barras in order to create this poor dupe of a Medical Inspector, his consent to the appointment of Bonaparte as commander of the Army of Italy. And the massacre Bonaparte had ordered at Pavia had claimed, along with several hundred other lives, the life of that same Dr. Contarini who had risked life for Florian's sake.

The design was impossibly twisted, and impenetrable. He remembered having felt at one time veneration toward a beautiful pattern whose outline he believed he had glimpsed briefly. Sitting in the cold soiled bilgewater, his butt numb as Ange had promised would happen once he consented to sit, he tried to recall what had inspired his moment of faith. Except for Diane's love he could not think of a single experience of his since the first days of the Revolution that deserved to prompt faith. He gave up trying to remember; no past joy would provide consolation now.

His own thoughts were poisoning him. Florian got up and picked his way carefully over recumbent forms like so many watersoaked logs, to where Ange, toward the end of the leg-chain, brooded too. At least I've been spared the chain, Florian thought.

Ange looked up at the doctor. His swarthy face broke into a smile of remarkable sweetness. His vital, animal magnetism reached out. "I've been hoping you'd come over," he said, almost shyly.

"It takes a while to accept anything like this. I've been thinking over my whole past life. I suppose you went through that too, when it first happened."

"The past seems a waste of time to me."

"Not when your today is this, and Guiana is your tomorrow."

"There's something to that," the singer agreed. "Still, maybe it won't be so bad. I've always said that I could be happy anywhere. Very likely, I can be happy on Guiana too. Anyhow I've made up my mind to try."

"That's brave, and philosophical too. I wish I had your ability to adapt myself, but I'm much afraid that I don't."

"I had two big worries when they chained me up. You took one of them away when you told me Fidèle was going to be all right."

"Diane has a gift for friendship," Florian said, "and she was herself so long a time the guest of strangers, she will understand all the problems of guesthood. What was your other worry? Or do you prefer to keep it to yourself? There is nothing I can do to help you, God knows."

"It's Angélique," Ange said.

He had not a shadow of excuse for putting it off another time. Sitting, hugging his knees, Florian said, "I told you I had a confession to make. It concerns her. Angélique is dead."

Ange said in a terrible voice, "Did Paul Barras have her killed because of what I did?"

"No, no. She died of natural causes weeks before that. In fact she had been dead some days before your interview with Barras, so you can be assured he had nothing to do with it. This is the hard part to say, Ange. I knew it that day I saw you."

Ange said slowly, "You mean you knew she was dead when you came with Fidèle?"

"Yes. I had just learned about it, and I was going to try to find you and tell you. But when I got home, she was waiting for me and said you'd been hurt."

The singer cried out, "But why didn't you tell me?"

"I wanted to protect Dr. Pinel and his patients. If you will remember, you told me yourself that only Angélique stood in the way of your disobeying. Ange, I did not know then how grave the wrong was that I did you, but I can't honestly say if I had known I would have decided differently. The Bicêrte experiment is the one good thing so far to have come out of the Revolution. I couldn't permit him to interfere with that."

Ange said slowly, "I let you decide for me. Because I trusted you."

"I remember."

"And you sat there with your black lie hidden behind your face of a friend and told me I couldn't give my sister up to that kind of treatment again."

"I know. I remember."

"I didn't want to like you. I hated doctors. I knew what doctors were like. But you kept after me until I trusted you. I sang on the streets what you told me to say. I told Fidèle you were the one man since Pascal that I'd loved. All the time, you were like the rest of them. You harmed me as cruelly as that surgeon harmed Angélique, as I should have known you would. It's your fault that I lost the crowds. It's your fault that I'm here."

"All that is true," Florian said, suffering.

"I have just one thing to say to you, Dr. Florian. Keep out of my way. If I weren't chained, I would kill you."

"I won't attempt to plead with you now." He stood up. He spoke in a very gentle voice. "You're too shocked and angry to appreciate my motives, and perhaps I expect too much when I hope that you will try. I'm still your friend, Ange. But I'll keep out of your way, as you ask; since you're chained and I'm not, it's your right to insist on that much. Though this is a poor time for breaking friendships."

Brooding darkly, sunk in himself, the singer made no reply.

✿   ✿   ✿

The cabin-boy on the *Bonnet Rouge* very nearly loved Dr. Keroual. Though depraved and dissolute, the tubby ship's doctor was the kindest human being the boy had ever known. So when he learned that Keroual was lashing himself over his neglect of the miserable human freight in the hold of the ship, the boy told him quickly that they had to tend them a man who called himself the Medical Inspector for the Republic. At once, Keroual was afire to go down there and see for himself. A real doctor, among that cargo of damned souls? Could it be someone he had known during his student days? The other doctor might be someone he could talk to about his ambitions, a being who would understand him, even help him perhaps. He struggled to get out of the bunk.

The crew watched incuriously as he plunged and fell along the decks. They were used to their doctor's ways. He was a part of what you put up with on this hell ship. They knew better than to fall sick during a voyage and come under the mindless hands of Keroual.

When he was seen kneeling at the hatchway, plucking at it help-

lessly as a dying man does at his bedclothes, one of the sailors came
forward to help. In spite of himself, Keroual was liked.

He began his descent by a ladder of rotten rope, but he missed
his footing and fell heavily, crashing into chained men unable to get
out of his way. He was furious at presenting himself so clumsily, and
because the floor of the hold was inches deep in filth and muddy
water. The smell was awful to a man in his state.

He became aware of a muttering from them. He could see nothing, nothing at all, but evidently they could see him. He felt their
anger, direct and hard, yet he was sure he had had nothing to do
with any of them before. Puzzlement turned to fright and a sensation
that they were converging on him in the dark. Then a voice flashed
out, quick and authoritative. "Go back, Doctor. At once! You're not
safe here."

Bewildered but obedient, he scrambled a little way up the swaying ladder and hung there. "What's the matter with you? I'm not
your enemy. I'm a physician. I want to help you." A yell of wild
laughter answered him. He realized it was no use. He finished climbing, and pounded on the hatchway until it was pulled back for him.

His rejection by men so desperate hurt him in some new, final
way, and Keroual proceeded to do what he knew better than do.
He compelled his system to accept more liquor days before he was
ready and as always happened when he tried that, drunkenness
passed rapidly into real illness.

❖   ❖   ❖

Keroual's cabin door opened. A gaunt, fine-drawn man carrying a
large box strode in. He was unimaginably filthy. "Are you ill, Doctor?
What is the trouble?" Keroual believed he recognized the voice that
had ordered him out of the hold four days before.

"It's my stomach," he said. "For God's sake, do something."

"I'll see if you have fever." He lifted out a complicated arrangement involving tubes and bowls for water, and a bulb which he indicated Keroual should put into his mouth.

"Is that a fever gauge? I never saw one before."

"I built it after the model by Sanctorius, but I plugged one end,
which makes it quicker and more accurate. Please take the bulb
into your mouth, Doctor." Keroual obeyed him.

For quite a while, the sick man lay there breathing with difficulty because of the size of the bulb. The other doctor wandered

around in the cabin, looking out of its portholes and noticing each furnishing and comfort within. His keen dark face was wistful. He would be handsome if he were allowed to bathe and shave, Keroual thought.

Finally the ship's doctor was allowed to push the bulb out of his mouth. The changed position of the water in the bowls indicated a slight temperature that was not hazardous, the other said. "I'll give you a stomachic. There's very little more I can do for you."

"What is your name, Doctor?"

"I am Dr. Florian, Dr. Keroual."

"You didn't study at Montpellier by any chance, did you?"

"No. I studied at Pavia and Leyden. But I taught at Montpellier for a year. Did you study there?"

"Bordeu was one of my teachers. Barthez was a classmate of mine."

"Those were great days at Montpellier. But then you must have studied at the same time as Dr. Pinel."

"Philippe Pinel? Do you know Philippe?"

"I was one of his staff consultants at the Bicêrte."

"That's an insane asylum, isn't it? Somehow I can't imagine Philippe Pinel in work like that. He had to give up his surgery classes, he was so softhearted."

Dr. Florian handed Dr. Keroual the dose he had prepared. The older doctor, tasting it, believed he recognized the root of the *Jateorhica palmata* as an ingredient, but some other tastes were unfamiliar to him. For a moment, the effort of swallowing made him sicker than ever, but the medicament stayed down. Then he began to feel somewhat better.

Dr. Florian replaced the things in the box and closed it. He stood awkwardly, his hands hanging at his sides, his dark eyes probing his sick colleague's face. It had always been hard for Dr. Florian to ask favors and particularly it was hard while he was giving treatment. The little stout man was a doctor, of course.

Before Florian could find words to express his request, Dr. Keroual said, "I'm distressed to find a colleague in such a plight. Is there anything I can do to help you, I wonder?"

The old charming smile flashed out from behind dirt and beard stubble. "Indeed there is. If you would please question the captain about me. I'm still not completely convinced that all of this isn't a ridiculous mistake." He related the details of his odd incarceration.

Keroual was astounded. "Of course it was a mistake! I'll talk to the captain today. You'll be released at once."

"I hope you're right, but there is a very good chance that I was deliberately tricked aboard. You see, when I began my examinations, the men told me that they had been examined already, in the prison at Rochefort."

"That is strange. You were appointed to do it, but they had been examined before you got there? That's very strange. You're quite sure they had been examined the other time?"

"Don't you remember, Dr. Keroual?"

"Should I remember?" Keroual said carefully.

"They told me it was you."

He closed his eyes. "Quite possibly they were right. I don't remember." He roused himself and said, "Why were they so angry when I went down there?" Florian looked at him but did not speak. "You may as well tell me," Keroual said petulantly.

"I don't want to seem critical, Doctor. I'm afraid you passed as fit men who were not. One of them died only hours after he was taken aboard. Three have died since, and others were too old or in frail health. You would have been perfectly justified in excusing many of them, but you seem to have passed the whole lot."

Keroual's face worked. "I was drunk," he said. "I don't even remember." He wiped away the too-easy tears with his fat little hands. "You must despise me!" he said.

"Of course I don't despise you. You're disturbed and ill. I wish I could help you."

"You have a remarkable gift, Dr. Florian. A gift for sincerity and kindness." He dragged himself up on the bunk and looked at the younger man owlishly, his tears still dripping. "You give me a purpose in life," Dr. Keroual said. "I am going to help you, Dr. Florian." Florian smiled wistfully. "If it's a mistake you'll be released today," Keroual said, "but if it was not, I am going to find out what secret forces were at work to put you here. I am going to force them to reverse themselves. There is always a way, if someone will just try hard enough."

"Whoever was responsible is powerful and unscrupulous. You may come to harm yourself."

He ignored the warning. "A three months' leave is due me when we get back to France. I had intended to spend the time as I always do, drinking in taverns, recovering in brothels. But now I have a purpose in life, the rescue of yourself. I shall remain sober until that is accomplished," Bénigne Keroual said.

IV

"NAUGHT SHOULD be betrayed of what may happen or of what may eventually threaten, because many patients have been driven in this way to extreme measures." The aphorism had been impressed on Florian from his student days, until it had become a part of him. He returned to the hold of the ship with the picture Keroual had drawn mercilessly clear in his mind, but he was resolved not to tell the others what lay ahead. He had no intention of adding to their sufferings.

Ange was singing again when Florian crawled back into the hold, so he was spared for the time the inevitable questionings by the others. He was glad for this respite, which gave him a chance to go over all the things he had been told.

A part of his mind was appreciating Ange's artistry. For these homesick, wretched beings, his voice was no blaring trumpet calling them to arms and indignation, but a soft musical whispering, nostalgic and melancholy. Through Ange, all the men in the hold of the *Bonnet Rouge* had drawn close: the singer sometimes put their private dramas into song, and then they seemed to share their very heartbeats with their fellows.

Florian moved quietly among the chained men, trying not to interrupt their eager listening, until he found his own place beside his new friends, Father Roger and Michel Fleures. The priest clasped his hand briefly; the journalist shook his head in a gesture of affectionate commiseration. Florian's mysterious summons to go above had given his friends hope that he was going to escape the common fate after all. Their generosity toward himself lifted his spirits. Surely, he thought, as long as we remain capable of caring about what happens to each other it won't be like Dr. Keroual said.

"There never was devised a crueler penal system than the *guillotine sèche*, which is the name we who know about it have given to Guiana," Dr. Keroual had said. "Let me tell you about the life there. It is better that you know beforehand what you're going to face. In fact, I have good reason for wanting you to know. You see, I know what happens to men who are condemned to Guiana. The fortunate ones die quickly. The others die in mind and spirit. I don't want that to happen to you, Dr. Florian. Can you believe that I am going to help you?"

"I believe you will try."

"Your trust in me is going to be your only safeguard against going to pieces. Please really try to feel it. I swear I will do my part."

"All right, Dr. Keroual," Florian had said, and a confused, faithless sort of faith actually began to grow in him. The bombastic little inebriate was a slender reed for hope to lean on, but better than nothing at all. Ange was singing now of the boulevards of Paris when the chestnut trees came to leaf. A hundred hearts ached for that sight again.

"Some fifty miles west of Cayenne is a little fever-ridden Indian village of grass huts and narrow weed-choked paths filled with old refuse. It is called Sinnamarie. Have you heard that name before?"

"No, Dr. Keroual."

"You will come to know it as another word for Gehenna. Sinnamarie was uninhabited for years because the Indians considered it an unlucky place, which indeed it is. Three years ago, after Thermidor, a hundred and fifty-three friends of Robespierre's were sent there. I don't know how many of them you will find alive; at most a dozen, I should think. And in the years since, others have been sent in small lots, though few of them ever arrived there."

"Is it the climate, Dr. Keroual?"

"The climate is the unhealthiest in the world. But there are other factors. All manner of creeping, crawling, flying things abound, many of them poisonous to man. The jungle, where you will be required to find your food, has as many dangerous fruits and growths as it has of those that are safe to eat. Your hunting parties will be stalked by beasts and giant howling red monkeys. It is easy to lose your way and wander in the jungle until weakness brings you down as the prey of army ants, giant ants whose jaws can tear the flesh from a man's frame in minutes, and who subsist only on living food."

"Is it really expected of us to forage in the jungle?" Florian had asked incredulously. "Surely some simple diet is issued in the prison? What would keep us from escaping, if we were at liberty to be chased by red monkeys and monster ants?"

Ange was singing of women, the women the prisoners loved, who loved them. My woman has copper hair and green eyes, Ange sang, and she is as small as a child. But others of you love women with raven hair, or hair of gold; eyes grey, eyes black, eyes brown; large-breasted women, narrow-waisted women, all of our women are beautiful; we will never see them again. Florian's eyes filled with tears. In spite of his emotion, some detached part of his mind was marveling at the curative powers of art. Though Ange's songs lacerated the

117

heart, they consoled also. It is because he makes us realize that our sufferings are shared. No one of us is alone, the doctor thought.

"You will be marched into Cayenne in gyves," Keroual had said. "You will be let stay there a night, maybe two, in overcrowded native huts. But first there will be a little ceremony. The captain of the ship will turn you over to the Governor, and in the name of the Republic, he will wash his hands of you. He will tell you that your country has no further interest in your fate. The Governor, accepting charge of you, will make a similar speech. He too will wash his hands of you, and he will advise you to forget that you are men. You will last longer, and suffer less, if you will forget that you were men, he will tell you, and that is good advice, Dr. Florian, for the others. But I don't want you to believe the Governor, Dr. Florian, I don't want you to listen to what he's saying. I see in you the one chance Bénigne Keroual has to justify his existence. If I save you, I shall after all have given a good doctor to the world."

Ange was singing of mothers. "Our mothers are beautiful too. Mine is dead, but she was beautiful when living and the little headstone on her grave is damp with the tears she weeps out of heaven for the fate of her son. But some of us left living mothers, to weep their tears for us in this world. I think it must be hard to be the mothers of sons so unlucky as we."

Keroual had said, "In a day or two, at the Governor's convenience, you will be marched out of Cayenne still in gyves, along the coast, to the split of the Kourour River, which is deep enough and wide enough to prevent you from crossing back. There will be boats to ferry you across, but these will be taken away and you won't see them again, ever. It will have been explained to you that if you are seen out of the confines of Sinnamarie, you will unhesitatingly be shot down, as though you really were the beasts you will come to resemble. This prohibition will not prevent you from hunting food in the jungle, because of white men only the men of Sinnamarie are desperate enough to venture out in it. You will be strictly forbidden to trade with Indians. This prohibition also amounts to nothing, because nothing will be left you or given you that can be used in trade. The Indians are by far the more skilled at finding food and valuables in your common area of search. They are, incidentally, dirty, slovenly, beggared, but not hostile."

"Then we really do have considerable liberty."

"You have all the liberty in the world, Dr. Florian. But what it amounts to, you have the liberty to rot. You will find that the sternest punitive disciplines would be welcomed in the place of what has been decreed for you. Life in Sinnamarie is exactly like life in a leper colony. There is nothing, no hope, no work for the hands or the mind, nothing, no way. It is Limbo."

"Still, if we work together, and pool our common talents——"

"You're not taking the climate into account, nor the fact that you are Europeans, with a long background of civilization. I beg of you, Dr. Florian, don't get up false hopes that will only increase your despair when you realize the truth. Constant soaking rains will destroy your clothing, but no new clothes will be issued. No clothes, no food, no medicine ever is sent to Sinnamarie, because the men who are there were taken there to die, and the sooner it's over the better satisfied the government will be. Do you see how it might be better to be in a prison, where at least some acknowledgment is made that you are living and human? I tell you, Doctor, a day will come when you would be grateful for the lash, because of the implicit compliment to yourself in the fact that there would be another human being at the other end of it."

Ange's voice dropped away into a soft humming, unbelievably sweet and sad, and then stopped altogether. For many minutes, the men rested quietly under the spell he had woven for them. There was no sound but the monotonous slap-slap of the sea against the sides of the ship. There must be some way to fight Guiana, Dr. Florian thought. "I don't know how long my mission of saving you will take me," Dr. Keroual had said. "It may be weeks, or years. But never stop believing that I will come in time. It isn't the climate that breaks the men, nor yet the beasts and the fevers; it's themselves, because they have no hope. Believe in me, Dr. Florian, and I will surely do my part." And he had poured onto the floor the contents of a bottle of brandy nearly half full.

*   *   *

Dr. Keroual faced the captain of the *Bonnet Rouge* in the latter's cabin. The captain said, "I heard that you had him brought up. Don't do it again. It was all right that one time, I suppose, if you were really sick."

"Won't you tell me what happened? Why wasn't he arrested, like the others?"

"I will tell you what I know. It isn't much. I was informed that the Medical Inspector of the French Republic would call on my ship, and ask to go into the hold and examine the prisoners. I was to show him every courtesy, as befitted his position. Once the hatchway had been put down, I was to forget that I had ever seen the Medical Inspector. And I intend to forget it, Dr. Keroual, and I advise you to do the same."

Keroual went away thoughtfully. He realized he had taken on a very large task, a dangerous one. It did not alter his decision but he wished he had not been so hasty in his renunciation of the bottle, because it seemed to him that a good stiff drink was just what he needed to clarify his thoughts and bolster his courage.

❋   ❋   ❋

All of the men in the hold of the *Bonnet Rouge* were the friends of all the others, but there were special friendships, like that of Dr. Florian with Father Roger and Michel Fleures. Ironically enough, the deportation of Fleures was occasioned by a series of articles the journalist had written condemning the Guiana system and appealing for a halt to the cruel practice. He was very young and no larger than a boy, but clever, and he owned a wealth of superficial information on many varied subjects. Father Roger, the Jesuit priest, had a keen developed mind similar in its processes to Florian's own. The doctor was impressed that the paths of faith and science could parallel each other so closely.

Ange alone made no special friends; by turns he was morose toward everyone, or his heart spoke out to them all. His animosity toward Florian, and Florian's acquiescence, were noticeable in the shared closeness of the little community, but no one questioned either of them about it.

Florian became as acquainted with the inkstained flurries of journalism and the matins and retreats of the priesthood as he was with anatomy or the Drug List. His intimacy with Father Roger and Fleures was not conducive to the keeping of secrets. He found himself telling them what Keroual had said. It was not at all impossible to have a private conversation, because as soon as men were noticed with their heads together their neighbors on the leg-chain struck up other conversations, as a courtesy. He gave a full account, omitting nothing except Keroual's promise to rescue him. It seemed inappropriate to paint such horrors, then announce calmly that he alone stood a chance of escaping them. And also Keroual had promised to send for him another time, but had not done so. Perhaps he had decided for his own sake to put the condemned doctor out of his thoughts.

Some of what Florian told them, Fleures was able to confirm to the extent of having heard the same thing in his newspaper office. The trained imaginations of the priest and the journalist easily comprehended what awful danger to human spirit life on Guiana was going to be. As recognition began, the quick would steal from the slow ones; the strong would take by force from those weaker, until both physical and moral strength had been exhausted. Eventually all would succumb to the jungle.

Florian said, "The only chance I see for us is that we submit ourselves voluntarily to a strong leader. If we're banded together in a community in which all serve and all benefit, in spite of the Governor we may remain men."

Father Roger said, "I believe it's a good plan. But I think you'll find it won't be acceptable to them for some little time. There has been so much authority in their lives, and of a hateful nature. At first they will welcome their freedom."

"I imagine you're right about that." Florian was impressed again at the priest's understanding of human nature.

"Also, your plan requires a leader of great ability, insight and strength of character."

Michel Fleures said, "I'm sure I heard that Barthélemy is being deported with us. He's an ex-Director, maybe he would do."

Florian grimaced. Father Roger said sharply, "There is only one thing to be said in favor of our exile. And that is that we need never have anything to do with the French Directory again."

FOUR

Sinnamarie

THEIR FIRST SIGHT of the most dreaded place on earth was not terrifying. To men immured for seven weeks in a crowded cage below sea level, the beauty of sunlight was shocking, the gift of fresh air glorious. All but Florian still gyved, they were allowed to leave the hold before the docking. Their dark-filled eyes were useless for seeing and, too anxious to wait, they kept trying to force sight. Finally they could make out a row of armed sailors with weapons ready, and behind them, the blank and beautiful waste of water, and ahead, the whitecaps and the big breakers. Seven other prison hulks were sailing in with them, but the escort of smart cruisers was drawing off, their work done.

Dr. Florian, Father Roger and Fleures were together as always. Ange Pitou was a lonely figure nearly at the end of the leg-chain. He who had refused his intimacy was the one left out of this joyous moment of sharing with one's friends the delight of seeing land again. Dr. Florian acknowledged to himself that he, more than Paul Barras even, was responsible for Ange's renewed distrust of the world.

The prisoners saw three islands, green and studded with palms, lifting themselves out of the spray-topped waters. Little Fleures named them for those nearest him, Royale and Saint Joseph and the Devil's, and explained how they had become the sanctuary for colonists sent here by Louis XIV, but who had found life on the mainland intolerable. The islands slipped by.

The prison ships, in file and tacking cautiously, entered the wide mouth of the Cayenne River. The land-hungry prisoners could see the city itself, occupying nearly a mile of beach land. South, west and east of Cayenne, the rain-forests stood, a waving mass of pure greenish shades. The marketplace was by the pier, nearly at water's edge. Brightly dressed figures crowded there, staring out to sea. It seemed to the lonely men that they were being welcomed.

While the others were counting every visible detail on the land, Dr. Florian's principal attention remained with the ship. This was the last chance for Dr. Keroual to make some sign. A mere wave of

the hand, or a smile, would give Florian a thread of hope to spin behind him when he entered the dark jungle maze. But he did not see
Dr. Keroual until the actual disembarking, when he passed within
inches of him. Keroual's eyes rested directly on Florian, but without
recognition. He was hopelessly drunk. The little bud of faith in him
withered and fell away.

Everything that happened afterwards was exact to Keroual's description. The *Bonnet Rouge* had been the fifth ship to dock. The
men on the pier were the Governor, the commander of the garrison,
and soldiers who participated briefly and gracelessly in the ceremony
of accepting the prisoners from the ships' captains. The speeches
were as Keroual had said they would be, even to the detail of their
being advised to forget that they had been men. Then the condemned were paraded before two low-grade field officers whose
duty was to make sure they retained nothing that might have trading
value with the wretched Indian population. When it was Florian's
turn, the officer signaled for him to lay down his box and go on
without it.

"It's my medical box, Lieutenant," Florian said. "From all I've
heard, we'll need it where we're going. Don't you think I might keep
it?"

He hesitated, a look of respect crossing his hard young face. "Open
it," he said finally. Florian unstrapped the box and lifted back its
lid. The officer peered inside, then blackened. "What are all those
knives for?"

"They are surgical instruments, lances and probes and scalpels."

"I'll have to confiscate those." He nodded to a soldier, who began
lifting them out until they made a small heap. Florian did not try to
save them, though they were fine surgical instruments and he was
sure to need them. What few of them were without sharp edges or
points were left in the box.

"What's that thing?" the officer said, pointing.

"My Leeuwenhoek. It's a microscope. Sometimes we are able to
see important phenomena not observable to the naked eye. I wish
you'd let me keep it."

"And what's that?"

"A water thermometer, to gauge the height of a fever."

"You'll need that too, in Sinnamarie. And the jars and bottles,
what are they?"

"Herbs and spices and drugs that we have found effective in certain treatments, Lieutenant."

"I'll probably get in trouble over this. Don't flaunt the damn box around any more than you must."

"I'll do my best. And thank you."

"I'm sorry about the knives. Really, I couldn't have let those go through."

"I'm sorry too, but I quite understand. You've been very humane as it is."

"I'm an officer," he said, "not an executioner." He turned away to the next man and Florian moved on, trying to carry the big wooden box inconspicuously.

After each examination of twenty men, those were marched away from the pier under a guard. In the time consumed over the medical box, Florian had become separated from Father Roger and Michel Fleures. In fact none of the other men in his party had crossed over on the *Bonnet Rouge*. He felt lonely among the strangers, all of whom seemed to know each other and none of whom spoke to him.

Now the prisoners could see that the city's beautiful appearance from a distance was a lie. It was incredibly dirty and of fantastic construction. The low houses were built of wood or, occasionally, grass. Weeds choked the streets. An attempt to drain Cayenne through a system of ditches had resulted in the inhabitants throwing their garbage there, so that Cayenne did not smell very much better than the holds of the prison ships. The longer they walked, the more depressing it all became. And Dr. Keroual had said that Sinnamarie was much worse!

One other man in the party besides Florian was out of chains. He was a barrel-chested man in his early forties, prematurely grey. His clothes were neat and he had a fine proud carriage. From his expression, he believed all this to be a boring interlude interrupting his more important affairs. Although he noticed Florian watching him, he did not smile or speak. He was curious about the box though. His eyes kept turning to it.

They were driven like cattle into one of the low wooden houses that was backed against the rain-forest. It was unfurnished, and yet the crowding was as bad as on shipboard. They heard the outside bolt being drawn on them and Florian, who had been shoved to a place near the fly-specked stationary window, could see their little guard of five men marching briskly toward the pier.

"I'm going to break the glass out of that window." The big man in clean clothes spoke as if another's opinion would not be of the slightest interest to him. But then he added with a minimum of courtesy, "We'll stifle in here."

"Go ahead, General," someone said.

He clenched a fist that was brutally large and fleshy. As he lifted his arm, Florian said quickly, "Don't. No sense ripping your hand to pieces. I'll unpack my box and we can push the glass out with that."

"A good idea, since it will end my curiosity as to what the devil you have in there."

"It's a medical box," Florian said. He lifted out the Leeuwenhoek and the thermometer and handed the thin glass bottles to the nearest man. Dried plant roots and the powders in wooden boxes, he left where they were. A quick shove removed all of the window except a few jagged shards. These he knocked away with precise short strokes. The space made would accommodate a man's head, no more. The outside air moved in sluggishly; it was heavy and soggy, nearly as hard to breathe as the close air in the hut.

"You're a doctor, I take it. But I'm surprised they let you keep that box."

"The lieutenant was humane enough to realize how grave our need of it would be. Yes, I am Dr. Charlot Florian, formerly the Medical Inspector for the Republic." His words were tinged with a self-mockery that the other at once adopted.

"General Charles Pichegru, formerly commander of the Army of the Rhine."

Pichegru was a famous name in France, the name of a bold soldier, many times a victor, and one of the Revolution's greats. Barras had accused him of conspiring with his country's enemies, Florian remembered. There had been published excerpts of letters dictated by the General from his headquarters at Altkirch. More than likely, the letters were outright forgeries, or else the damaging paragraphs would have been innocent enough in context. Florian held out his hand.

The other pushed it aside brusquely. "Are you sure you want to do that? I was caught red-handed trying to sell out to the enemy."

"I am sure you believed you had a good reason," the doctor said gently.

"I had five good reasons. They call themselves a Directory."

The other men in the hut laughed. Not one seemed to feel any condemnation of the self-acknowledged traitor. "Your reasons are certainly convincing, General," Florian said drily.

Pichegru produced his snuffbox, an ornate bauble that looked to be solid gold, and offered it, opened, to Florian. Evidently he wanted to atone for having refused the handshake. Florian, though not a user, accepted a pinch. "I see that they let you keep a box too, General."

Again he was answered in mocking parody of earlier words of his own. "The lieutenant was humane enough to realize how grave my need of snuff would be." Florian realized how the youthful officer could not have compelled himself to rifle the pockets of the great, fallen commander.

He leaned against the wall and looked at the doctor from his cool, light-blue eyes. "So we have a doctor. Are you one of the real ones? But of course you are, or you wouldn't be here. That's Barras' idea of serving the country. Keep all the rascals like himself in clover at Paris, and ship out the useful ones to die. If you had been one of the medical mountebanks, you'd be safe at home now and piling up a fortune. Yes, it's quite a little experiment we'll be making here in civilization-building. At the risk of seeming to include myself in such a bright company, I will say that the eight hundred odd men who were landed at Cayenne harbor today were the flower of France."

A pleased murmuring from the other men in the hut answered him. Florian did not make any answer because none occurred to him. The General went on, "We're nearly all of us professional men. It will be interesting to see what our trainings and talents will do toward helping us to a happy life amidst red monkeys and crocodiles." So he had heard some stories too. "Did you know we have a bona-fide Director of France with us? Barthélemy I mean. He and Carnot were the ones who cared a little bit what happened to the country, so they got the shove. Carnot got away, but Barthélemy was on the same ship I was. Not a bad fellow if you don't mind a whiner. And speaking of your medical box and my snuff box, I give you one guess as to what Barthélemy was allowed to bring."

"I'm sure that any guess of mine would be wasted, General."

"A mistress," another of the men said promptly. "That's what they all traffic in, isn't it?"

"That isn't the answer, and yet it isn't too wide of the mark either. Barthélemy's little possession is even more baffling. He brought his valet."

"Surely you're joking!" Florian said.

"I am not joking. The man's name is Letellier, and he combs the Director's hair and brushes out his clothes. And when Barthélemy is in a mood to do you a favor, he offers Letellier's services. I ought to know as he's been combing my hair for a week now." He looked around him sardonically and said, "I hope you don't imagine that Barthélemy and I put up with what you fellows did. Not at all. We had cabins to ourselves, and decent meals with wine on our table. And we promenaded the deck whenever we had a mind to. You see for yourselves that your earnest efforts to do right were more serious offenses by far than my treachery."

No one said anything. There was no laughter this time. Florian wondered why General Pichegru seemed to want to provoke him and these others to anger.

He dominated the room completely. "Quite a little experiment!" he said again. "There's Barthélemy to govern us, and there's General Willot and myself to train troops, and you, Dr. Florian, can open a hospital and dispensary out of your medical box. And there's half a hundred journalists and scribblers of all kinds. We can have a little newspaper, though there's no presses or paper of course. But we can use the town crier system if we find palm leaves hard to write on.

"That's not to mention the priests, who will be busy shriving us though there'll be scant need for their gentler offices. Perhaps they will want to build a church out of palm thatch. Would you help them in that case, Dr. Florian? And there are lawyers to argue our little disputes, and judges to rule on them. And a hundred or more ex-Deputies. They can pass laws for the ex-Director Barthélemy to override himself the while he shoves them down the throats of the rest of you, with the help of mine and Willot's Army. No reason for any of us not to be busy. But I don't amuse you, Dr. Florian."

"No," he agreed, "I'm not much amused."

"Perhaps you find my levity unbecoming."

"It's not that, General, but rather that you seem to have been thinking along the same lines I have. Except that you think it natural to accept Barthélemy's leadership on Guiana because he was one of our rulers in France. But then we were so badly ruled, that's hardly a recommendation."

"I don't believe I know what you're talking about."

"Your plan of close cooperation among us all, each man fulfilling his role in the community according to his qualifications. A priest who is with us, Father Roger, and a journalist, Michel Fleures, and I, have talked about this before. We were hoping there would be a natural leader among us who would take the whole thing in hand. I don't think Barthélemy will do and I imagine you yourself might be the right man. You're experienced in organization and command,

and—What is it, General?" The light-blue eyes were as cold as frost.

"Don't count on me for anything of that nature, Dr. Florian. I had very little to do with the rest of you on the way out here, and I shall continue to behave in the same way." He gestured and the others crowded back to make room for him, and he walked to the far end of the hut where he remained leaning against the wall, alone.

Dr. Florian was astonished at the sharpness of the rebuff. He could not imagine what he could have done to have incurred it.

*   *   *

Again exactly as Bénigne Keroual had foretold, it happened to them. Their stopover at Cayenne was two days long. Then they were marched down the coast, chained together by the wrists. At the split of the Kourour, the gyves were struck off. Boats that had been packed by the prisoners were put down in the water. The boats could hold eight persons. Six prisoners, two of them rowing, and two guards with rifles resting on their forearms but pointed into the boat, to go over; then the guards put their rifles down and rowed back for the next load.

The work of ferrying several hundred men in lots of six, in nine boats, took the better part of a day. Those who had been landed had been told not to leave until all were across. As soon as the men landed, they knelt on the ooze and bathed themselves as best they could without soap. The waters of the Kourour were muddy and yellow and the men looked no cleaner after bathing, but they did feel better.

Florian and Fleures and Father Roger were among the first to cross. After they bathed, they sat in thronelike seats made by the flaring roots of a jungle giant and watched their fellows arriving. When Ange Pitou was landed, he began clowning and singing. Everyone watched Ange and followed the words of his song. It felt good to be out of chains, free.

It was nearly nightfall when the soldiers recrossed the river for the last time and marched back toward Cayenne carrying the boats. The outcasts turned their faces toward the unknown. But they were in high spirits. Even Dr. Florian felt Dr. Keroual's warnings slip away into meaninglessness. The camaraderie among the men gave him new heart.

There was a path of sorts, easy to follow though difficult to walk on. Sinnamarie was not far away. But when they came there, a shocked silence fell. The village seemed lifeless and deserted. Open as it was on all sides to the encroaching jungle, there was no protection from preying forest beasts. The men could see how every effort to keep the village neat and livable had stopped months, or years, ago. They advanced cautiously.

Sinnamarie was not entirely abandoned. In time they found a few living creatures that resembled men. Naked, emaciated beings, some of whom were dull and listless, the others shrill with hysterical joy at seeing new faces. Judging by the fact that these had survived what had killed their fellows, they had been the fit and strong only as long ago as Thermidor. The newcomers fell into awed silence. They could read their own futures in these bodies so miserably thin that an anatomist could have studied them with profit. Even the skin of the survivors was strange, so bitten and lacerated and roughened that it might have been the outer envelope of another, lower form of life.

The French of the survivors was like some new, base dialect. They had stopped talking among themselves long ago, because nothing remained to say. Now they had nearly forgotten speech as a method of communication. With difficulty the newcomers learned that no food was stored in Sinnamarie, or had been for a long time. If they were hungry, they would have to go out in the jungle and hunt. No one was that hungry, it turned out. There was no water in the village either. If they wanted water to drink, there was a fresh spring several kilometers away. Several kilometers into the jungle, however —the newcomers added thirst to hunger in a growing list of discomforts.

This is the sort of thing we must fight against happening to us, Dr. Florian thought. Plans to store food, to develop a spring in the village, revolved in his head. But the grass huts falling away into dirt-filled rubble would hardly do for storage places. Anything left in them would spoil from dampness, unless it was eaten first by swarming vermin. In all of Sinnamarie there was only one wooden building. It was quite large, low, oblong, with two windows both innocent of glass or shutters. But it would do for a hospital.

Father Roger, walking with him, remarked that the building was large enough to hold Masses. We can work that out, Florian thought; the building can be partitioned, maybe. While he was watching, the sixteen notables and the valet entered the wooden building en masse and did not come out again. Evidently they intended to appropriate it for their own use, and no one disputed it with them: the place was too strange, the men too worn out from the long march and the alternations of emotion, to care much about anything. They divided themselves around in the grass huts according to the friendships that had been made during the crossing. Dr. Florian, Father Roger and Michel Fleures took one of the smaller huts in the last stages of ruin.

They curled up in that partial shelter and tried to sleep. But vermin swarmed over them and armies of mosquitoes sang and darted and stung. They did not talk much, their hearts were too full. This was Sinnamarie, their only home now. This was the life they had been condemned to lead.

By now, Diane's uncertainty about what could have been keeping him would have turned into bitter conviction that he was dead. He concentrated on her fiercely, as though in some way he could communicate with her through sheer force of will and desire. Hungry, thirsty, tormented by pests, he lay there and thought about Diane until her love gave him the gift of sleep, and he slept.

II

RAIN WAKENED THEM, falling into the interiors of the grass huts with the same force as outside. The men fled their huts. The beginning dawn showed them the confused, distracted faces of their comrades. The fall of rain was heavy but did not relieve the muggy heat. Steam rose from their drenched clothing.

Instead of seeking better shelter, they were required to enter the jungle and find food. Ange Pitou excepted, no one of the deportees had ever needed to bother about the provision of the essential comforts. If hungry, they went home or to a restaurant; if thirsty, they told a servant to bring wine or water; if caught in a rainstorm, they hailed a carriage and returned home for a change of clothes and a quiet hour before their own fire. It seemed impossible that men like themselves were really expected to battle for mere survival.

Dr. Florian was interested in seeing if the notables came out of the wooden building. They did not. Then he forgot about them and missed seeing the valet, Letellier, leave the building and walk in a southerly direction with the firm step of a man who knows where he is going. The newcomers followed the survivors into the strangeness of jungle. That was like a great cathedral devoted to devil worship. The rain stopped as abruptly as it had come, but the trees continued to shed large tears for a long time afterwards.

A hot sun came out. Though its rays could not reach them through the interlacing foliage, the oppressive heat deepened. They caught flashes of color among the trees, but the birds and small monkeys moved too swiftly to be captured. The survivors showed them banana trees and mango trees. They crammed the strange food into their mouths.

For Dr. Florian, this first day of hunting proved to be the last. A man screamed horribly. They milled around, trying to locate the source of the sound. He continued to cry out in pain and terror. Finally they found him in a pit the survivors had dug long ago, and camouflaged clumsily in the hope of trapping some edible animal, but then had forgotten about.

Dr. Florian had himself lowered into the pit on a rope of strong vine. Both ankles had been fractured. In the very first hours, the need for a hospital had been created. More vine ropes were sent down, and he tied one under the man's arms and another around his knees. When the hurt man had been hauled out, screaming in agony each time his broken bones collided with the walls of the pit, four men carried him back to the village, and Dr. Florian went too. Before he could finish setting the fractures, a snakebite case was brought in. One misadventure followed another and he was the only doctor, too often and too badly needed to be let waste his time in the endless search for food.

* * *

The days wore into weeks, the weeks into months, and time had no measure beyond the daily needs of stomachs and the burials of the dead. From the beginning, disease raged through the grass huts. Florian identified and treated cases of dysentery, ankylostoma, tropical anemia, Guiana fever, gangrene, and trachoma. There were the commonplace injuries incurred in the day's hunting: maulings from wild beasts, frond slashes that cut to the bone, fractures, heat exhaustion. The priests were kept busy burying his cases and, without him and the medical box, it seemed that all but a few would have died in those first weeks. His little hoard of drugs and herbs diminished with appalling rapidity. What in the world would they do when those supplies ran out?

Minor ailments plagued them. Vampire bats sucked blood from sleeping men, or tiny flealike insects buried themselves in the flesh under fingers and toenails and deposited eggs that swelled until the skin burst, leading to infections. Sand flies and mosquitoes tortured their flesh incessantly. Their diet was strange enough to make them sick if nothing else did. They roasted parrots, they ate iguana lizards, they boiled armadillos that they dug from their holes. Tapir was rare, bananas a staple. The survivors of Thermidor had volunteered their ideas of which of the glistening fruits were edible, and which dangerous; even so mistakes were made and men died of them, unless Florian's emetics could be made to work in time.

The notables in their wooden building baffled him. They lived apart from the rest of the colony; they did not hunt in the jungle, and they never seemed to become sick. Letellier came and went quietly on mysterious errands for them. Occasionally Florian caught a glimpse of him lugging a tapir into the building. A tapir was the most prized meal of all, a shy and gentle animal that is hard to find and kill. How did the valet manage to do it so often? A whole tapir boiled into a stew with bananas and palm cores would have fed the village, but the notables never shared outside of their own small group.

Someone in that wooden building—and Florian was convinced that it was General Charles Pichegru—owned such a gift for organization and management that they were able to create security for themselves in the center of deprivation and suffering. But the journalists and Deputies and priests grubbed in the jungle like pale, blunt-toothed animals, and daily, they became more like the piteous survivors of the first purge. In the medical box, very little of value remained.

❖ ❖ ❖

He noticed a growth just outside the village that looked like guaiac, the "Holy Wood." It was guaiac. He cut parts and dried them carefully in the grass hut he shared with Father Roger and Michel Fleures.

If there was guaiac, there might be other things as well. He asked Michel to come with him to look. At first they found nothing. They were handicapped by the fact that Florian himself was not accustomed to seeing the medicines he sought in their native state, and because it was hard for him to find time to get away to make the search. But eventually, persistence yielded good results.

They found *Jateorhica palmata*, whose root excels anything else as a tonic and stomachic, and digitalis leaves in the immense grasslands along the coast. Common seaweed was plentiful; when dried and burned, it yielded in its ashes a medicine he knew of empirically as beneficial in small doses taken internally, or when moistened and spread on external wounds, would stop suppuration and speed healing.

The great discovery came in a dream. He was accustomed to passing a stand of small trees on his way to the river bank to bathe. They were insignificant-looking, dwarfed by the jungle giants, and had a smooth bark of reddish cast. In his dream, he met his old mentor Antonio Scarpa on the path to the river. Scarpa, carrying his cane, looked as he always had, humane and studious and dignified. "Imagine having your own supply of cinchona!" Scarpa said, tapping one of the smooth-barked trees with his cane.

When Florian wakened he remembered the dream. Such good fortune could not be possible of course, cinchona bark was rare, expensive, and sought-after throughout the civilized world. Of all known medicaments, it was the most effective in all fever cases. If there really was cinchona on Guiana, its discovery would more than make up for what other drugs and spices could not be replaced. He went to the scene of his dream, knowing he was being foolish and yet not able to control his excitement. He peeled away a little of the bark, which he boiled. When it had cooled and he tasted it, his palate was assaulted with the characteristic bitterness of true cinchona.

The villagers were gathered around their night fires. Dr. Florian burst onto them shouting his news. He, always so reserved, was almost dancing with joy. At first they could not comprehend the importance of his discovery. When they did, their enthusiasm mounted with his own. This was the first happy moment the village had known.

There was cinchona enough at that one stand to have made all their fortunes, had the men of Sinnamarie been allowed to trade with the outside world. It could not be made to serve them in that way of course, but he enjoyed the irony. Cinchona, or Jesuit Bark, was so scarce and expensive that only rulers and rich men could afford its benefits. But France's castoffs, decreed to forfeit everything, had all of it they could ever use.

Without realizing it Florian had drifted into mere acquiescence to their sufferings, but now his attitude changed. Plans filled his mind, and the need to act. Fate had tossed a gift of great value at his feet as though to prove that human affairs are never without remedy as long as human hearts and minds stand firm. His old plan of a cooperative village life came back and obsessed him. He mentioned it again to Michel Fleures, who volunteered to help in sounding out the men of the village.

So heartened was Dr. Florian that he made a bid to repair his broken friendship with Ange Pitou, using the plan as an excuse for drawing him into conversation. He was sorry for Ange whose popularity had steadily dwindled. The singer was morose and hard-tongued, and even when he was moved to sing his growing misanthropy stood like a barrier between himself and his listeners. Ange had misplaced his ability for entering into the minds of others and then putting what they felt into his words and music.

Ange heard Florian out, then said coldly, "And who were you thinking of as suitable to become our master? Yourself?"

"Certainly not. I have more than I can do now, and I have no talent in that direction. I am thinking of General Pichegru."

Ange shrugged and said, "Why bother me about it? I don't care what you do."

"Doesn't it seem that we ought to forget our past misunderstandings, Ange? You wanted me to keep out of your way, and I've been very faithful about respecting your wishes. But in the situation in which we find ourselves, it seems to me that generosity toward each other is almost our only hope of survival. I would like to become your friend again, if you'll permit it."

"Friends?" Ange's mouth pulled down. "You and I, friends?"

"Why not?"

"A low clown like myself is not a fit companion for the first citizen of Sinnamarie."

This attack was so unexpected, Florian did not know any answer to make. Finally he said, "I have done the best I know how for them."

"I know you have, my dear doctor. I know that. Pay no attention to me. I hate useful men, Dr. Florian. Perhaps that is because I am so useless myself."

"Aren't you being foolish?"

"Don't pay any attention to me then, no one else does." He started off.

"Damn it, Ange, wait a minute."

"I am a rebel by profession," the singer said. "So far there is no authority here to rebel against except yours. If General Pichegru tries to make a little king of himself, I shall start hating him instead. Then, perhaps, you and I can be friends."

I think he must be as mad as Angélique was! Dr. Florian thought, watching Ange stride fiercely away.

Father Roger gave him something real to think about. "I support your idea enthusiastically, Doctor, but not your choice of a leader," the priest said. "There's an essential flaw in the man who would do what Charles Pichegru did."

"At Altkirch, you mean." Father Roger nodded. "But my feeling about that is it was the only way he knew of protesting the crimes of the Directory. I can't believe you're exactly loyal to Paul Barras and those others, and I certainly know that I am not."

"I agree that what he did would have been no great crime coming from you, or myself, but Pichegru was a soldier. In my opinion, Doctor, our work is a form of prayer. Our most complete contact with God is our willing performance of the work He permits us to do, to fulfill His glory on earth. I know you are not a religious man. But haven't you felt, after a particularly brilliant operation say, or a diagnosis of unusual accuracy under these difficult circumstances, a kind of kinship with something greater and wiser than yourself?" Florian admitted it. "Pichegru was a soldier," the priest said. "He should have found some other way to strike at Barras. He very nearly compelled the surrender of his whole Army without a shot being fired. No, in my opinion a general who would betray his Army and the people of his country is no better than a journalist who would take pay for writing lies, or a doctor who would consent to murdering the patient he pretended to save. Or for that matter, a priest who stopped Mass and began shouting that man was abandoned by God."

"Your point is a good one. But I don't know who else would be qualified, and the very fact that Pichegru has kept away from the rest of us would make it easier to accept dictation from him rather than from one of our own number."

"Why don't you administer the program yourself?"

"I have no talents in that direction, and no time."

"But you have so much more influence than he does."

"That's hard to believe," Florian said, embarrassed.

"But it's true. Your medical box has done more than anything else to keep us alive and whole in spirit."

"Father Roger, I couldn't possibly superintend the work crews and all the other details and keep my hospital work going."

"But you could superintend the men you appointed to take care of the details."

"No," Florian said, "I couldn't do it. I'm a doctor. Not a commander of men. I still think Pichegru is the right choice."

"You must do as you think best," the priest said.

*   *   *

When Florian and Michel Fleures had talked to enough of the men to be able to say honestly that the plan was acceptable, he presented himself at the wooden building where the notables lived closed away from the life of the colony. It was like entering another civilization.

The first thing he noticed was the only artificial light in Sinnamarie. It was of simple construction and looked like Indian work: a huge seashell, melted fat of some kind, and a wick of a dried braided substance. There were clean rush mats on the floor, and pallets that looked comfortable, and a real table with chairs. The empty windows had been masked by a kind of fibrous netting, evidently to discourage vampire bats, perhaps mosquitoes as well.

They were sitting down to their evening meal when he arrived. It amused Pichegru to invite Florian to join them, and the doctor ate the first real food he had enjoyed since the day a hatchway had been thrown down over him, imprisoning him with the men he had been told to examine. The valet Letellier had prepared the food and served it also. His deft quiet ways gave a touch of elegance and luxury. Altogether, the wooden building seemed at least a thousand miles nearer to France than the rest of Sinnamarie.

There was to eat a rice dish rich with tapir meat, baked bananas, fish, and for dessert, mangoes that had been preserved in a thick sweetish sauce. In place of wine was tafia, a potent native drink resembling rum that the doctor had not tasted before. Aubrey and Dossonville at least had drunk well of the tafia, and now ate enormously to overcome its effects.

Dr. Florian ate two platefuls of food in wondering silence, and drank tafia out of a cupped shell. He burst out, "How in God's name do you do it?"

The others at the table laughed at him. Barthélemy said contemptuously, "In any civilization, the superior man is privileged, Doctor." From him, the whiner, the remark was only ridiculous. Pichegru seemed to think so too.

"My snuffbox had as much to do with it as your superiority, Barthélemy. And General Willot's anus was of greater benefit yet."

He said to Florian, "It's a wonder a doctor would not have thought of that himself. General Willot came aboard with a small fortune in gold set in a wax cylinder. He replaced it just before we landed and recovered it after the search was over. It is our custom every night at mealtime to say grace, and invoke the blessings of heaven on the anus of General Willot."

Willot, at Pichegru's right, flushed and grinned. "That part is a story, Doctor."

"But what good is gold to you on Guiana?"

"It's true that we can't go to the marketplaces in Cayenne. But Indians in the village south of here can go. As long as the anal treasure holds out, the Indians will continue to treat us tenderly and supply all our needs. They have learned that a single gold coin can buy many beads, many bolts of bright material, much tafia."

So the mystery had an explanation as simple as that! Not genius, but gold, accounted for their comforts. He had been naive to think otherwise, he now saw. Even so, he sensed behind those oddly light eyes a firmer assurance than the diminishing hoard of gold could give. Florian had taken hope from the finding of the cinchona stand, but Pichegru had never lost hope. There was some inner certainty in him of things eventuating to his satisfaction. If only he could be persuaded to lend this quality of his to the community.

"But you are looking at me reproachfully, Dr. Florian. Perhaps you think my snuffbox, and General Willot's anal resources, should have benefited a larger number."

"I don't want to criticize my hosts," Florian said quietly.

"I am a mathematician, Doctor. At one time, I taught mathematics."

"Yes?"

"The morality of the matter aside, the mathematics of it is roughly this: The village could have lived in comfort for a week, or we few can live comfortably for six months. The spirit being unwilling and the flesh anything but weak, we voted to do as we have done. I trust you don't intend to mention this outside? As you say, you are our guest." He smiled.

Sated, the others began leaving the table. De la Rue put a captive parrot on his forearm and tried to teach it to say, "To hell with the Directory." Imbert-Colomes played with a young monkey. Four others started some kind of betting game involving squares marked out on the floor, and castor beans. Florian compared their gaiety to the grey misery of the others just outside, who were always hungry, always soaked in the interminable rains. In them, no spark of play existed. He very nearly hated Pichegru. But he told himself that kind of hardness, that stern knowledge of mathematics, was necessary to a governor of men.

Eventually Pichegru and Florian were alone at the table. The General poured himself another measure of tafia, then, as an afterthought, one for Florian. He said, "Why did you come here tonight, Doctor?"

"That day in Cayenne when I tried to suggest a plan for the colony —do you remember?" He nodded. "You didn't care to discuss it then. I am hoping you will have reconsidered."

"I'm willing to hear what you have to say."

His voice breaking with emotion, Florian described the life of the men outside. Pichegru listened with wandering attention. He was at least as interested in the outcome of the game with castor beans as in anything that Florian had to tell. The doctor broached his plan: divide the men into work crews which would take their turn at performing the various tasks for everyone. Crews to hunt, to haul water, to bring wood for the fires, to keep the village clean.

"Very sensible," Pichegru commented. "But why do you want me?"

"You are experienced in administration, General, and you know how to give orders and how to back them up. I'm afraid of a failure. Their morale is too low to risk that. Please consent, General, their need is so great."

"Why don't you administer your own reforms, Dr. Florian?"

"I wish people would stop suggesting that."

"Ah. So it's been suggested before. But why not? Judging simply from the concern you have exhibited tonight over their welfare, they must love and trust you."

"I'm not capable of doing it. I'm a doctor, not a leader of men."

"But you have a very valuable qualification that I lack."

"I do? What?"

"You care," Pichegru said simply. Florian looked at him with wonder. "You care what happens to them," Pichegru said. "And I don't."

"You can't mean that, General."

"I do mean it. You are an idealist, Dr. Florian. I was myself once but I have outgrown it."

"Is it idealism to say that if we don't work together, we'll perish together?"

"That is true for the rest of you, perhaps. It is not true of me."

"General Willot's funds won't last you forever, General. Then what?" He shook his head, refusing to answer. His eyes were as clear as water, as unreadable. Florian pressed him. "Do you really believe like Barthélemy that the men in this building are in some way superior?"

"I am not a fool, Doctor."

"I think you are if you can't see that this community is behaving exactly as the other one did, and will end exactly the same way."

"Let's not be insulting to each other. I am not a fool. I agree with you about the probable fate of the community. As I don't intend to participate in that, I'm not much interested."

"But I thought it was impossible to escape Guiana."

He lifted his grizzled eyebrows. "Did I say anything about escaping?"

"How else are you going to avoid the common fate?"

"I believe I have heard that one man escaped successfully. Fifty others lost their lives trying. Again, my mathematics informs me that the odds are poor."

"You must have some plan of your own, or you wouldn't be so indifferent to mine."

His attitude of tolerant good humor changed suddenly. He looked at Florian with hard dislike. "I don't know why you think you have the right to come here and question me. I believe you wanted me to assume certain responsibilities. I have refused you. That terminates the discussion." He stood up.

Florian was furious. He stood too. He said, "I'm sorry I bothered you about it. Thank you for giving me your time." He stalked out, seething. For days, he carried the mental picture of their easy way of life, while his friends and patients went without everything. But Florian was not a hater. He tried to put the General and his associates out of his mind, and in time, he found himself ignoring them and their doings as completely as they ignored everyone else.

When there was renewed need for a hospital, he forced himself to go back there and demand the wooden building for his miasma cases.

FIVE

Miasma

MICHEL FLEURES, the journalist whose indignation over the banishment of others had brought on his own, was the first miasma case. Florian took his sickness for simple Guiana fever. He dosed the journalist with cinchona and put him to bed, covering him with some pieces of tattered canvas and four coat-jackets sewn together with vines that had been donated as bedding.

"Tomorrow is Christmas Day," Michel said suddenly.

"It is? What makes you think so?"

"I made myself a calendar. I could be wrong a day or two either way, but I don't think so."

Christmas Day. Both men were silent, thinking of other Christmas times. All over the civilized world there was warmth and good fellowship between men, and between God and man, except here where no one so much as remembered. Michel with his made-up calendar was not really sure.

"I thought we had been in Guiana a much longer time than that," was Florian's only comment.

He visited his other cases. Nearly fifty men were confined to their huts from one ailment or another. Their hut mates fed them and gave them rough nursing, and he visited them many times a day.

He did not tell the sick men that this was Christmas Eve. He found no comfort in that himself, and doubted that they would. It was better to forget about things like that. Better, as the Governor had warned them, to forget that they had been men. The frog-face of Bénigne Keroual drifted across Florian's thoughts. Keroual had known what Guiana was like, yet had not been able to keep his vow of sobriety long enough even for the *Bonnet Rouge* to let off her condemned cargo.

Father Roger came hurrying after Florian. The priest's cassock had turned an evil shade of green. Even his beads were disintegrating. "Michel is sick!" he called.

"I know, Father. I've seen to him, didn't he tell you?"

"He's out of his head with fever."

"That's strange. He had a strong dose of cinchona. I'll come and see."

By midnight, Florian knew that Michel's fever was something foreign to his experience. This fever thrived on cinchona bark. Though delirium had passed, Michel's temperature remained alarmingly high. His breathing was labored, yet Florian could not detect any pulmonary disturbance either by the old classical method of using his ear or the newer, little-known method of percussion. The sound of a muffled drum that was elicited in that way was perfectly normal, yet Fleures was fighting for breath.

"Is he very sick, Doctor?" In his anxiety over Michel, the priest spoke to Florian as to an authoritative stranger in whom was locked the secrets of life and death.

"It is something new. I don't know what turn it will take next."

He stayed up all the night, watching the progress of the strange illness. Toward morning Michel became conscious and complained that he had lost the use of his limbs. Certainly there was a partial paralysis.

Whatever the sickness was, it seemed determined to run the gamut of symptoms. The fever rose and fell but never broke, in spite of quantities of bitter medicine he swallowed. Every day he was a little weaker. Then signs of dropsy became evident. Florian realized that he was not going to be able to save Michel. This was the first time that it had ever happened to him, that his dying patient was also his close friend, and he felt as useless and frantic as any layman.

Michel's death occurred ten days after the first onslaught of the fever. Florian was not given time to grieve for his friend. By then he had five new cases. He lost them all. Each time the killer, at onset, appeared to be simple Guiana fever. He would know differently only when it proved nonresponsive to cinchona.

He charted all the data faithfully, making his notes on the tattered canvas bedclothes that he had washed and bleached so that some records might be kept. Though his charts showed that the disease had a definite pattern, and was not as he had first supposed simply an individual example of nature on a rampage of rule-breaking, they told little else. Nothing in his medical box proved of much worth. He named the new disease the "Sinnamarie miasma."

Before the five cases could be buried, there were eight more. The epidemic continued to spread. He saved a few cases, he did not know how or why, and those remained disabled and dropsical.

It became impossible for Florian to care for so many dying men in their huts. He had to sleep sometimes. It would make his work easier and they would have better care, if all the victims could be brought together under one roof. The one building large enough to house them all was the wooden building where the notables lived.

He went there. In his exhaustion, he even hoped that he would be invited to their table a second time or given some of the relaxing tafia to drink. To his bitter disappointment, he was refused admittance. General Pichegru consented to come out. He stood a good distance away.

Florian was tireder than he had ever been in his life. He stood patiently, his shoulders sloping, and explained what he wanted. Unshaven, his hair grown out raggedly, he looked humble and beaten and years older than he was.

Pichegru said, "I have a theory that our isolation is the reason that none of us has become sick."

"The building would make it possible to isolate the miasma cases."

"But whatever it is you're all dying of, we don't want it introduced into our little sanctuary."

"That's all right," Florian muttered. He thought it was an apology to him for not inviting him inside.

"I'm glad to find you so reasonable." Pichegru did not bother to conceal his contempt. "And don't bother me about them again, because another time I'm not going to come out."

"Wait."

He paused, looking back over his shoulder. Florian took an angry step toward him and Pichegru skipped aside, saying, "Stay away from me, damn it! You look as if you're coming down with the thing yourself."

"You're very anxious to live, General."

"Why not?"

Florian spoke curtly, his square-shaped lips drawn hard against his teeth. "Until now, I have let myself be dominated by an immense respect for you. I don't know why, because there is nothing about you that deserves respect. I am going to ask for the support of the community in the very enjoyable project of throwing you out by force."

Pichegru laughed. It was a hearty, friendly sound. "I wondered when you would think of that," he said. "Very well, Dr. Florian. Is tomorrow soon enough for you to take possession?"

The victory had come too easily. Florian wondered if it were not a trick of some kind. "Yes," he said, "that's soon enough. I'm sorry I had to do it this way."

"Believe me, it was the only way you could have done it. To-morrow morning, then." He nodded, still friendly, and went inside again. Florian more than half expected they would barricade the place in the night and attempt to defend it.

By sunup the next morning, the wooden building was empty and the notables nowhere in Sinnamarie. There was no time to wonder where they had gone.

✽   ✽   ✽

As soon as he knew he had his hospital, Florian called for volunteers to clean it. The healthy population answered his summons to a man. Even Ange Pitou came. Some he put to cleaning the building, others to preparing beds of rushes, and others to constructing litters on which the sick would be moved. The remainder were sent into the jungle to hunt and to prepare food for the patients and the hospital workers.

The lamp he had admired had been left for his use. Of course it was invaluable. There was no way of telling if Pichegru had intended to be generous, or merely had reasoned that Florian in this new mood would remember having seen it and would send a party after them to demand it. And I would have, he thought.

The table and chairs were still in the building, but everything except the lamp that was easily portable had been taken, including the fibrous netting that had kept out bats and possibly mosquitoes. But the sick men were accustomed to those pests. By nightfall, all were moved in. Ninety-four miasma cases occupied the rush beds. Some of the volunteers stayed as nurses and Florian got his first unbroken stretch of rest since the miasma had struck.

Next day, he felt strong of heart and full of new ideas. Since others were so willing to help him, there was no reason not to launch an offensive war against the killer and all sorts of measures occurred to him. Ashes of seaweed in their food and water might help. It was worth trying. He could give the healthy men chinchona in light doses; if the drug could not cure, perhaps it could prevent. He considered bleeding one or two of the desperate cases but dismissed that idea. Generally speaking, he was against this most popular treatment of his times, because personal observation had convinced him that a patient is generally weakened after phlebotomy; anyway, the vampire bats bled them all, all too often.

In the days that followed, and almost without his noticing, he came to occupy the position he had planned for General Pichegru. Each morning, those who could still walk reported to the hospital for orders. He divided them, assigned captains, laid out the day's work. Ange Pitou was as faithful as a right hand. The doctor found time to be pleased at the restoration of their friendship.

The epidemic subsided. Either the preventive measures of cinchona and ashes of seaweed had been correct procedure, or the miasma had simply run its course. There was no way of knowing which it was. Nearly a fourth of their number had been wiped out; another, smaller group was left permanently dropsical and disabled. These he kept alive through tending them devotedly. They lay on the rush beds and stared stonily, and waited through constant pain for sleep's release. The partial paralysis that was characteristic of the disease neither improved nor worsened. They could with effort feed themselves, but little more. It did not occur to him to wonder if he served them badly by thus extending their days. It was his business to keep men from dying. It was not his business to wonder whether or not they could be happy with the kind of life they had.

One morning, giving the orders, he noticed that Ange was missing and realized he had not seen the singer for days. He inquired about him. "He hunts alone," one of the crew captains said.

Florian said, "I want to talk to him. Will you send him here, please?" After the captains were gone, he thought for quite a while about Ange. The singer's deliberate absence emphasized a nagging worry of the doctor's.

During the emergency, it had seemed natural and right for him to command the efforts of the others. The emergency was over, but they showed no desire to return to old ways. The hospital had become the seat of government in Sinnamarie, and he their governor. It made him uneasy. Not that he did not enjoy being looked up to and obeyed, because he did, he was human. But it seemed to him that his civil authority interfered with the pure concept of the healer's art. As their leader, he was accomplishing more toward allaying sickness and providing comforts than all of the secrets of his medical box had done. The food was better and there was more of it. The village was becoming clean and neat, the grass huts more livable. It was all working out as he had imagined it would, in improved conditions for

everyone. What distressed him was this mingling of two great enter-
prises in the person of himself.

But then hopelessness flowed over him in waves. How pointless it
was to fear the corruptions of authority in this place! Or, for that
matter, it was pointless to strive toward any kind of perfection. All
he could do, either as doctor or commander, was stave off for a
slightly longer time the obscure and meaningless deaths that were
inevitable for all of them. The survivors of Thermidor, four of whom
had been lost since, had made their little improvements too, until
all hope died and they reverted to animalism. You couldn't fight
Guiana for any long time. You could only endure her. When you had
endured to your limit, you succumbed to her. The *guillotine sèche—*
Guiana was aptly characterized in that phrase.

His black thoughts were interrupted by three of the men, dragging
Ange. The street singer's resistance was entirely passive. He simply
hung from their hands, dead weight. The doctor was astonished.
"What's this?"

"I see that your government is like all the others I've known," Ange
remarked. "Right away, the first thing, it's 'Arrest Ange Pitou.'"

"Let him go, you fools! You're not under arrest, Ange." But at once,
he was stricken with embarrassment. Why had he spoken to them
like that? He had never called anyone a fool in his life—until now.
They had tried to please him and obey him. They snatched their
hands away from Ange and remained looking at Florian stolidly,
their faces consenting to anything he might do. "You misunderstood
me," he said unhappily. "I didn't want him brought here by force."
The little incident had served to clarify the whole issue, and Florian
recognized in a flash of insight the quite remarkable danger he was
in. He wanted to plead with them not to make him responsible for
everything, but he saw that already they had shoved him ahead of
them, to a place where the only real communication possible was
commands from him and prompt obedience from them. "Go back to
your work," he said tonelessly.

When Dr. Florian and Ange Pitou were alone, the doctor left his
place behind the big table that had belonged to the notables and
since had bewilderingly become not his consultation desk only, but
the seat of justice in Sinnamarie. He placed a chair for the singer and
motioned for him to use it. Ange hesitated, looking at Florian out of
his suspicious, wild-animal eyes. Finally he sat down. Florian resumed his own place and sat there sunk in thought. "Why?" he said
finally. "I thought you'd got over hating me."

"I told you. I'm a professional rebel."

"But you were splendid. You worked harder than any of them."

"I saw how hard you were trying. I was glad to help. But that's over now."

"It will come back, or something else as bad."

Ange's mouth pulled down mockingly. "Are you excusing yourself to me? Why bother?"

Florian said, "They tell me you're still hunting alone. That's a waste of your strength, Ange. What about the rest of it, do you cook for yourself too?"

"And eat it alone, yes."

"I should think you'd be lonely."

"I'm a man. Not a herd-animal."

"The Governor said that none of us were men," Florian remembered.

"I chose not to believe him. I'm as good a man as he is."

But wild beasts hunt alone, Florian thought. Men form into social units, name leaders, submit to laws. He said, "I didn't want this. I don't like it any better than you do. I wanted Pichegru to do it." Ange did not comment. The doctor said, "I wonder what happened to them."

"They cleared a site a few miles south of here and put up a new building. It's smaller than this one by quite a lot. Big enough for them, though."

"Of wood, is it?"

"Yes."

"Pichegru is a talented leader indeed. To get that much work out of them!"

"The Indians did most of the work."

"You've kept close watch on them. Where did you find time?"

"I'm fascinated by them. Anyway there's nothing on Guiana but time. He's got some kind of plan, General Pichegru has. The others know enough about it not to have a worry in the world. They're just marking time here."

"I got the same impression. I wonder what his plan could be."

"And they have some kind of hold over the Indians."

"It's money," Florian said, "they have money."

"What good is that to them here?"

"None to them, but the Indians are allowed to cross over and go to Cayenne."

Ange thought that over and said, "If I were Pichegru, I'd spend my money to buy a little boat from the Indians. Maybe he could get away in it."

"Obviously his plan is a safer and better one even than that."

An oddly companionable silence followed. Almost dreamily, Florian found himself thinking over the whole history of their relationship. He imagined that Ange might be doing the same thing. "Ours has been a singular friendship," he remarked finally.

"We should never have become friends, that's all."

"Perhaps you are right. The fact remains, we did."

Ange said, "For some reason, I've got over being angry about what you did that time. Maybe I even understand it a little bit. I thought about coming to you and saying so."

"I wish you had. I have suffered very much over it."

"You have other friends, and everyone's liking and respect."

"What difference does that make?"

"Anyway, we're unlucky for each other. We're not through yet causing trouble for each other, I think."

"That sounds darkly prophetic." The dreamy quality of their exchange was heightened by the digression, and by the sound outside of heavily falling rain. "Will you work with the others now, Ange?"

"No."

"But you have got over resenting me. You just said so."

"I couldn't like anyone who had any authority over me. It's the way I'm made."

"The only authority I have is by consent, though."

"That's the worst kind," Ange said.

"Yes. It is. You are right." He brooded. "What else can I do, though?"

"I suppose there is nothing else you can do. Just don't ask me to be a part of it, that's all."

"You're evading. If you know, tell me. What else is there to do?"

Ange said sharply, "Do you understand that if you wished you could order my execution because I refuse to conform?"

"No such idea ever crossed my mind!"

"I didn't accuse you. I merely said it could be done."

"I'm tired," Florian complained, rubbing his forehead.

"I'll go then."

"Will you come back and talk with me again?"

"I'll come any time you send for me. But they will always have to drag me here."

"Ah, but why?"

"So you won't forget what you're doing," Ange said, and went out into the rain. Florian sat a long time, his head sunk in his hands, and listened to warning voices that spoke to him through the falling rain. Finally he roused himself to tend to the needs of his miasma cases. Humbly kneeling by them to bathe their swollen parts, he was sharply aware of the dual role he was playing. As physician, he guarded life and tended its least, flickering flame. But the weapons of a harsher authority lay to his hand and he was filled with a kind of dread toward himself, as though he might change overnight.

II

ROBERT LASNÉ's medical education meant more to him than anything in the world, excepting one. The exception was the person of Dr. Charlot Florian, who had taught Lasné and the others, who was responsible for every good thing in their lives. He learned from Dr. Scarpa that Dr. Florian had disappeared mysteriously. A desperately sad, short letter from Diane was the source of Dr. Scarpa's knowledge. She was trying everywhere to get news of her husband; seeing everyone, or writing those who lived at great distances, who had known him and might have learned in some way of his whereabouts.

Robert Lasné put in some thoughtful days. He remembered the time Diane and he and the other students had waited for Florian during the storm. They had been sure then that he had been taken and had faced it, each in his own way, what Florian meant to them. Lasné had been sorry for Diane, but soon forgot about her and went looking in the storm for Florian. His impulse now was the same, but stronger even.

He had this year to finish out, and his year-of-practice. Instead he applied for leave from the University, and for a passport back into France.

Dr. Scarpa summoned Lasné to his own quarters. "My poor boy, what is this you are doing? What good do you think you can be to him? If he were alive, isn't it obvious that he would have found a way by now to get in touch with his wife?"

"It seems I have to go, Dr. Scarpa."

"Finish out your year at least. You can make up the year-of-practice any time, or perhaps I can arrange something about that."

"Somehow I feel there isn't much time," Lasné said.

"You've worked so hard," Dr. Scarpa said. "It's such a waste."

"None of us would be here if it weren't for Dr. Florian."

"I know that, Robert, and I think a great deal of your Dr. Florian myself. But I don't see how you're going to do him any good. I see that you're determined, however."

"Thank you for everything, Dr. Scarpa. You've been wonderfully kind. Just as he said you would be."

Dr. Scarpa said, "I wonder if there is anywhere in the world a person who cares as much about me as you care about Charlot."

When Robert Lasné left Pavia, he was just two months away from finishing his studies that had been so hard for him, that he had attacked so doggedly, with so much patience and faith.

✿   ✿   ✿

On Guiana, the north wind had been blowing steadily for a month now. Its lashing attack on the village was an almost unbearable irritant. Even to walk against it, a man was required to bend himself nearly double. Its high, thin screaming beat against their ears. It scooped breathable air away from the nostrils. Everything in the jungle was in hiding from it, so that hunting was more difficult than ever. The repair crews worked hard to keep the grass huts from being blown apart. The wind did not relieve the heat, but intensified it. The aggravation to their nerves was perhaps its greatest curse. Their nerve-ends seemed to lie exposed on their skins while the wind blew.

The hospital was filled. Accident and fatality were frequent during the wind. Three suicides were followed by two murderous attacks within a day of each other. Dr. Florian found himself faced with the problem of punishing the murderers. The steady, hard-working members of the community expected it. Yet, looking into the dazed, sorry eyes of the pair, he saw his own soul looking out. How dared he add to their sufferings in any way? "Drive them out of the village. That's all I know to do," he said.

What little pleasure he had ever taken in being what Ange had called "the first citizen of Sinnamarie" left him then. He bitterly hated his new duties. But how to evade them, he did not know. Even Father Roger, when Florian tried to ask advice from him, answered in respectful phrases, and he praised the doctor for his great services. The words of praise stung Florian as insults could not have done; he sent the priest away brusquely.

❀ ❀ ❀

The north wind blew, and he became appalled at the idea that the wind might stir up the miasma poisons again. He got out his old notes, jotted half legibly on the pieces of tattered canvas, and went over them. But nothing emerged that seemed hopeful except a note he had made of what Pichegru had said, that the notables might have escaped the disease through isolation. Isolation was the classic method when the plague struck; the miasma took a similar toll of life. It might be a good idea to take temperatures every day and isolate those who showed feverish symptoms until cinchona could prove the presence or absence of the miasma. But what a task, to take several hundred temperatures daily with his clumsy, slow-working water thermometer. Could he construct more thermometers? There was so little material on Guiana to work with!

He was still working over the notes when General Pichegru strode in. It was the first time Florian had seen him since the seizure of the wooden building. "To the commander of Sinnamarie, hail!" He bowed mockingly.

"I'll pack my box," Florian said, without any surprise.

Pichegru, however, was surprised. "Are you really willing to attend to my friends and myself?"

Florian thought how spruce and clean-shaven he looked. His uniform was badly worn and had turned color on the seams; just the same, he was an almost unbelievable figure of full-dress elegance to be seen in Sinnamarie. Poor Letellier, the valet, must be very busy, Florian thought; all of them to shave and comb and wait on. He knew that he himself had grown a ragged beard, and that his hair was lank and unclipped. But they had to come to me in the end, he thought.

He asked Pichegru, "How many of you are sick, and what does it seem to be? Does it look like the miasma?" He was packing his box. He glanced back along his shoulder, saying, "That's my own term for it, but you know what I mean. The epidemic here that drove you out."

"The only epidemic that drove us out was yourself," Pichegru said pleasantly. "What are all these men sick of?" He gestured along the rush pallets.

"Everything along the right wall survived the epidemic. The others

are the usual thing, dysentery and snakebite and broken bones——"
He stopped talking to count over what was in the box.

"So you did save some. And this is what they are like." Pichegru
stood looking at the wretched men, naked in the heat, their bellies
and parts horribly protrusive and their wasted limbs slack. "Was it
worthwhile, Dr. Florian?" he asked softly.

"As worthwhile as anything else, I should think." He was only half
following.

"I can't agree with you. A zooful of living dead would be the least
worthwhile thing, in my opinion."

"Don't talk like that in here!" Florian swung around. His bearded
face was dark with fury.

"You are quite right. I apologize."

"You had better wait outside."

"But I enjoy noticing all the changes. I won't say anything more
to offend you."

"No. Wait outside."

"I wouldn't know you, Dr. Florian. You give orders very compe-
tently now." Amused, detached, quizzical, he bowed again and went
out.

Florian finished with the box. He seemed to have thought of everything that mischance could require. He gave brief instructions to
three hospital orderlies he was training, then joined Pichegru. Outside, the sunlight was hot and bright, the north wind stronger than
ever.

The General had been walking around and looking things over.
"Is this Sinnamarie?" he said, in joking amazement. "Are you trying
to rebuild Paris on the banks of the Kourour, Dr. Florian?"

"We're trying to make the place habitable, since we have to live in
it."

They began walking through the village toward the jungle. "But
didn't I tell you that they would take orders from you?"

"I don't give orders. I make suggestions."

"Well, perhaps. Though it is my experience that suggestions ac-
complish little, orders very much more. What are all those new buildings going up?"

"In time, we hope the whole village will be solidly of wood. After
all, wood is one thing we have aplenty."

"But how do you cut it down?"

"The north wind performs that service for us. We simply gather up
what is blown down."

"Are those drainage ditches I see being scraped out?"

Florian nodded. "We're flooded here all the time, as you must remember."

"When will the citizens start piling refuse in them, as we saw at Cayenne?"

"They are most conscientious about everything. There is an exception, but then he doesn't attempt to share in the benefits of the work either."

"Who is your exception? They are always a danger."

"His name is Ange Pitou, perhaps you have heard of him."

"The street singer, eh? You don't have to blame yourself over him. If he were mine, I'd make him knuckle under, however."

"No," Florian said, and did not elucidate.

They went quite a way into the jungle before Pichegru suggested they rest and finish their talk. Florian said, "But let me see my patients first."

"No one is sick, Doctor."

He was startled and angry. He held out the heavy box. "Why did you let me waste all that time packing this, and now I have to carry it around."

"But you seemed occupied, and if I had told you then you might not have come with me at all. I want to talk to you and it's important that what I say is not overheard. Please sit down." His manner had changed subtly; he had stopped treating Florian as his equal.

Curious, the doctor accepted the seat Pichegru was pointing out, an accident of flaring roots as noble as a throne. Pichegru sat down too and leaned back, gazing upward thoughtfully. "Beautiful tree. Think of the thousands of years it has taken them to grow to that height. And puny human beings attempt to reach heights of the spirit in less than a century of living." Florian was compelled to lean toward him in order to hear the musing voice over the screaming voice of the wind. "Has it occurred to you, Dr. Florian, that there is some of God and some of Satan in every man? Circumstances will bring one or the other of them into dominancy. Is that a new thought, Dr. Florian?"

"I don't believe so, General. As you said, I am busy."

"Now you, Dr. Florian. You serve others. You guide them and help them. The hours of your day are dedicated to the general good. That is why you are so busy. Doing Christ's work, let us say. I am sorry to have to tell you that the mere thought of you can cause in me a considerable resentment. That is because the devil in me has grown larger than the Christ. Circumstances, Dr. Florian. A soldier who has been caught in the act of betrayal has little choice but to incline toward dark places. You must live with yourself, after all."

Florian did not say anything. He was no longer impatient with the conversation. He felt sorry for Pichegru, and curious about him.

"I was a virtuous man, once," Pichegru said. "In those days, I never could see anyone wallowing in misery or shame that I wasn't compelled to try to get him on his feet. But since my own fall from grace, I find this characteristic in myself has turned perverse. Since that day, I have not dealt with a man of impeccable virtue that I haven't plotted to bring him down where I am. It is the devil's business to tempt just as it is the Christian's to uplift and save. You offend me very much, Dr. Florian. You are too virtuous by far."

I'm not, Florian started to say, I'm far from being pleased with myself, either.

But Pichegru was saying, "Do you want to escape Guiana with me, Dr. Florian?"

        ❖   ❖   ❖

His voice louder now, and as mocking as the wind's, Pichegru said to Florian, "When you betray your country, you make new friends outside her borders. You make friends among her enemies, for example. In my prison room at Rochefort, I received a message that an attempt would be made by the British Navy to rescue me. But if we missed each other, or if the escort was large enough to make a fight costly, then I was to rendezvous with these new friends in the third week of March, at a place designated by them. I was to bring whom I liked with me, but not to exceed eighteen. There are seventeen men in my party including the valet, so there is room for one more. I am offering the place to you."

So this was the explanation of what Dr. Florian and Ange both had noticed, that Pichegru had never accepted his fate, that he was only marking time on Guiana. Florian said slowly, "But I don't understand. You don't even like me. You have just said so."

"I could like you very much, if you were willing to creep away in the night, abandoning your sick men and your little project of cooperation. In short, going to certain safety yourself, while you left them to certain death."

Shocked past clear thinking, he merely stared into that clean-shaven pleasant face dominated by curiously light-blue eyes that were mocking and sure.

Pichegru went on, "Perhaps you begin to understand why I was not interested in administering any improvement program in Sinnamarie. And why I have avoided mingling with those outside my own party. I am not, like yourself, a man of high moral rectitude, Doctor. But even I shuddered away from a betrayal as heartless as that."

"I see."

"For my own peace of mind, I was careful to make no friends that I could not take with me."

"Yes. I see."

"Do you want to come with us, Dr. Florian?"

"You said yourself you couldn't do a thing like that."

"I know. But I wondered if you could be made to."

"No! How could a British warship rescue you off Guiana?"

"Yes, I will explain that. I don't want you to have any doubts about what is being offered you. Some seventy miles from here, the mouths of two large rivers meet and form a bay sufficiently large and deep for a warship to enter, and quiet enough to permit the use of smallboats. Of course there is no one around there to observe anything."

"I think you're making all this up."

"Perhaps you can't believe the word of a man who has broken his service oath. If you can believe mine, I give you my word. I'm not making anything up, I mean it."

Florian stared at him helplessly. Escape Guiana! A man would be a fool to refuse. Any other man in Sinnamarie would seize the chance, he knew. But then, no other's leaving would deprive the community in the same way. He alone was indispensable, both doctor and leader. Pichegru knew that. If he had been planning the monstrous proposal as far back as the days of the epidemic, how he must have smiled to himself the night Florian took the wooden building by force from him; smiling and watching Florian build the pit for himself that Pichegru in time would bait. A kind of pity mingled with growing hatred. The man must live in hell to need to do a thing like this.

"You don't have to answer right away," the General said.

"I've already answered. I'm not going."

"If you change your mind, join us in our new quarters any time tomorrow. We'll start early the following day. Do you know how to find us?" Florian nodded. "You can tell them in Sinnamarie that we are all sick and you're going to remain with us a day or two. That way, they won't start worrying about you and sending out search parties that might embarrass us."

"You have it well planned!" Florian said bitterly.

"Well, I'm anxious that everything goes right. Don't try to bring your medical box, that's too heavy for a hard march. Choose a few things that could be useful but are easy to carry."

"I told you, I'm not going!"

"That's up to you, certainly. You'll be very welcome in case you change your mind."

Florian said quickly, "Would you take Father Roger in my place?" Pichegru weighed it. Florian was sure he was going to refuse.

Pichegru said, "I'll take anyone you send. Though I'd prefer the singer, because I would enjoy finding out if I could compel the obedience from him that you could not. But I'll leave that up to you." He stood up. "Think it over carefully, Dr. Florian. Ask yourself who will be most missed if he dies here, the celibate priest or the man who has a wife or mistress, as it may be, in France. Ask which of you would be of greater service to the outside world. Ask why the priest has more right to life than you do. And then decide." He started away.

Florian would have gone too but Pichegru turned and said, "Don't go back yet. The jungle is a fine place for thinking. If you go back there now, you may rush into a decision you will regret. This is your last chance to get out alive. You know that as well as I do." Mocking and spruce, he bowed to the man he had called the commander of Sinnamarie, and walked away briskly in the direction of their new building.

*   *   *

Florian watched after the compact, soldierly figure, until Pichegru disappeared in the deep shadowed aisles of trees. The north wind blew and the jungle screamed from it. Parasitic growths whipped like the tattered flags of beaten regiments. Strange fruits fell and smashed. Monkeys jabbered their fright and irritation. A snake, brilliant as a rope of jewels, slid over his foot. Where am I, what is this place? He asked it of himself in new, deep alarm. What could Dr. Charlot Florian, the consultant physician of the Hôtel Dieu and the Bicêrte, the former Medical Inspector of France, be doing here? The lover of Diane, here! The horror of what had been done to him was

now as strange and shocking as it had been when first he realized it.
Escape Guiana!

To whatever far corner of earth the British warship would take
him, there would be opportunities for finding his way back to France.
Diane's lovely, haunting face rose before his inward eye. Her mouth,
soft, trembling; her eyes, silver-colored from deep emotion, begged
him. He heard himself crying out to her, "I can't leave them, Diane!
Not even for you." She glanced at him reproachfully before his vision
of her faded.

But then the moment aboard the *Bonnet Rouge,* of acknowledging that he had been a self-deluded fool, returned vividly. Was he
going to be a fool again, a worse fool than ever? What madness had
made him think for a while there, as he talked with Pichegru, that he
would willingly choose to live with howling monkeys and the never-
ceasing north wind? Of course I will go with them, Florian told himself.

He felt that he was justified in putting himself first this one time.
Already through life, he had made more than his share of sacrifices.
Florian, the twelfth physician to be sought out by the medical students, had been the first to practice both the letter and the spirit of
the physicians' Oath; eleven other doctors had refused the risks. He
had stayed for their sake when a way out of France was offered to
him, and had remained in the danger a second time in the hope of
serving French medicine. All that time, his idealism had been leading him here. It's enough, he thought. Certainly I'm going.

Driven by the wind, a giant jungle butterfly flew past rapidly. It
must be nearly night, since they appeared early-morning and late-
evening only. That one, or another, flew past again, wavered, lit
gently on the arch of his foot. It clung there. The wind tore at its
wings. It clung to him as though to safety. It was unusual to see one
of them at rest. Target-butterflies, the men called them, because of
circular white spots, even and true, centering their wings. If he
pushed it away from him, it would be blown down the aisles of trees
until it was smashed against one of the trunks. He recognized the
symbolism. All of the miserable exiles clung to him in the same way,
and he had permitted it, never guessing that a chance for himself
would come.

They forced me into becoming something I never wanted to be,
he thought. I'm a doctor, not a leader of men. Here is a way to get
out of these duties that are against my whole nature. But the plan
of a strong leadership had been his to begin with, and he had played

his dual role for many weeks now. . . . Escape Guiana! I am *not* going to be a fool again, he told himself. He raised his hand angrily against the butterfly clinging to him for life. But he could not do it; his hand dropped.

Ange or Father Roger, then, he thought wearily. "Ask yourself why the priest has more right to life than you do." But that was not the point. Father Roger would not be much missed in the community, there were other priests. But the men are condemned anyway, he told himself. If I go or stay, they are condemned. He could buy them a few extra months of life if he stayed, no more. Their end would be the same. Mock heroics again, he told himself angrily. First it was the medical students. Then French medicine. And now these few hundred doomed men. Always, always, you have to find something to put before your own safety and the desires of your heart. Fool! By God, I will go. No, I can't, he thought.

Why had Pichegru approved the idea of a substitution? It seemed uncharacteristic and generous. Father Roger or Ange—why not Ange? He had known Ange the longer time and had done Ange a grave wrong that had never been righted. But the seeming generosity actually would be exquisitely cruel, since he knew the characters of both men. Pichegru had to be obeyed, and Ange had to withhold obedience. Ange would never be allowed to mount that free sweet British ship. Pichegru would kill him when he couldn't make him submit. It would have to be Father Roger after all.

Florian realized why Pichegru had consented to the substitution. With cold horror, he understood just how deep the General's antagonism went. Pichegru had not thought of it by himself, but when Florian suggested it, had seen at once how that could be used to make the decision harder; his surrender, if he did surrender, more abject. It would be so easy to argue yourself into thinking that it was madness to waste the extra life, even though that life was only your own. But if a substitute were acceptable, that would not come into it. No rationalization would excuse him. Either he was going to sacrifice the others to save himself, or sacrifice himself to save another and help others.

The longer I think it over, the harder it is going to be, Dr. Florian thought. I had better find Father Roger at once and ask him to take the place. He started through the darkening jungle, feeling a sense of well-being, of peace. But the north wind ripped at his resolve, and rain came suddenly, melting every intention but the great one of getting away from Guiana. "Ask yourself why the priest has more right to life than you do"—why indeed?

III

DIANE FLORIAN was a familiar figure to French officialdom. Every week or two, she called back at the police bureau to ask if anything had been learned yet. But her husband appeared to have dropped off the face of the earth somewhere between Paris and Rochefort. Such happenings were far from being uncommon. The roads of the provinces were infested with highwaymen. They did not murder travelers often, but it had happened. The police could tell her no more than that.

After weeks of trying, she finally was received at one of the public audiences presided over in turn by the various Directors. She had tried to see Paul Barras, who seemed more knowing than the others and had lasted a longer time, but was fobbed off on François de Neufchâteau, a latecomer. He patted her shoulder kindly and said that the situation about the highwaymen was terrible. She could not decide if he knew more than he was telling. Certainly his eyes were clever about avoiding her own.

She attended a number of social gatherings, stalking important people, trying to enlist their aid. But the new, gay, self-conscious society wearied quickly of such commonplace emotions as loyalty and grief. Invitations to Diane slowed to a trickle, to nothing.

Among the few friends she had left, Dr. Pinel was always glad to receive her, but he did not know any wise advice to give her beyond counseling that she try to believe that Charlot must be dead.

"But sometimes I have such a strong feeling that he is thinking about me, and trying to reach me."

"Then you do believe he's alive."

"I believe he's alive somewhere, and suffering dreadfully."

"I wish I could help you, Diane," he would say. And then, after she left, Dr. Pinel would worry that someday he would see her in the Bicêrte not as a visitor who could come and go, but for the rest of her life. Oddly, grief had not tampered with her fragile beauty. Her face was a little too thin, her eyes a little too large, but the effect was not at all unpleasing.

Sometimes Diane envied Fidèle because the red-haired girl at least knew where Ange *was*. But then they would hear terrible stories about the *guillotine sèche,* as Guiana was beginning to be called, and Fidèle would cry and Diane would comfort her, and feel grateful that at least Charlot was not there. In spite of having little in common except their grievings over the men they loved, Fidèle and Diane had drawn close.

Robert Lasné arrived in Paris, a little older, a little more mature, but stumpy, short-sighted, plodding and anxious as always. When Diane comprehended the sacrifice he had made for Charlot—and its uselessness—she took him in her arms and cried.

The next day, Robert began the dreary round she was so familiar with, of the official bureaus, and he too applied to be admitted to one of the public audiences.

*   *   *

Dr. Florian, on his way to the notables' encampment, felt deep astonishment that his body continued to move purposefully in that direction, while the whole resolution of his good mind and strong will was to move in an opposite one. He told himself that all he wanted was to see for himself if they really were going. But in that case, he would be back in Sinnamarie by nightfall, so why had he made all those careful explanations about illness among the notables, his promise to stay with them until the crisis had passed? Why the little packet of drugs carefully chosen, mostly cinchona, and a few instruments? And especially, why the short intensive course he had given his hospital orderlies in the rudiments of medical practice, and the turning over of his administrative duties to Father Roger? He shook his head, honestly puzzled by innumerable deceptions of his own.

It was after noon when he started out. The wind was at his back and seemed to push him along like a hand, to this place where he had no intention of going. Except for the wind it was a fine day with no rain. Finally he saw the outlines of their new building. He halted abruptly. It was time to turn back.

It occurred to him that Pichegru might have lied about the delay. It would tickle the General's sense of humor to think of Florian hanging back, fighting his decision over and over, only to yield in the end but then find he was too late and they had gone. He came closer, to see. There were movements about the building, so they had not stolen away. He was noticed before he could make up his mind to start back. He was hailed in a friendly way, and told that the General was indoors and expecting him. So he went inside.

Pichegru glanced up long enough to say, "We are glad to have you with us, Doctor." Then he went back to what he was doing. Florian stood in the middle of the floor, his hands hanging starkly, his face racked with unhappiness. He had about made up his mind to start away when Pichegru pressed him into service as his secretary in the work of checking the contents and approximate weights of eighteen small light packages.

While he was kept busy, Florian was less unhappy. He noticed that the valet was not expected to carry a burden any heavier than the others. From this small fact he deduced that Pichegru expected the journey to be a hard one, since the valet had been worked mercilessly while life was easy for the others.

"Where did you get the machetes?" he asked.

"We made a check trip. You can't keep any kind of direction without cutting your way through stands of cane and the vine mats."

"I suppose so, but where did you get them?"

"Indians."

"General Willot's gold again?"

Pichegru straightened, satisfied, and nodded agreement. "We couldn't have lived this way much longer. We spent the last of the gold getting the expedition ready. But I considered it a good investment. The men are in excellent condition."

"Not if they have been drinking tafia as steadily as on the one occasion I saw them."

"I put a stop to that more than a month ago. How about you, Doctor? Are you in good physical shape?"

"I've been overworked, of course. I don't think I've had sleep enough since I arrived on Guiana. And our food ration has not been as varied or sufficient as yours. There's nothing organically wrong with me, I don't think."

"You must do your best to keep up," Pichegru said. "I can't allow for anyone holding us back. Each day will weaken us a little more, and as we can't go overloaded with food we will have to eat lightly or hunt on the way. Do you think you can keep up?"

"I'll keep up," Florian promised grimly, and heard his own words with startlement amounting to terror. It sounded as though he really were going!

"You will get a good dinner tonight," Pichegru said.

As they worked, Florian realized how well everything had been planned. His own experiences at command had equipped him to appreciate the ability in others, and Pichegru was one of the best.

Finally all that could be done was done, and they sat down to eat. If the others in the party knew anything about the temptation of himself by their leader, they dissembled the knowledge perfectly. They were extremely friendly and kept pressing food on him. But nothing tasted good to Florian, who so loved good food. A bitterness lurked back of his palate, poisoning every other taste. He thought he read understanding of his feelings in Pichegru's light-blue eyes, and something that was very near to sympathy. Yes, Pichegru would understand; he had eaten of savorless food, had drained the bitter cup, himself.

I can always go back to Sinnamarie in the morning, when they leave, Florian told himself. But next morning, he took his place in line with the rest of them, putting the light pack over his shoulders. Pichegru and Willot had taught them to march with maximum speed and minimum effort. Florian soon fell in with the rhythm. For a time, they made good progress. But the jungle was thicker west of Sinnamarie than it was to the east or the south. Soon the machetes were in use almost constantly.

Since their line of march paralleled the coast, occasionally there were easy stretches of grassland. But again and again, they were driven back into the thick of the jungle by mangrove marshes or flooded savannahs that only the birds dared cross.

The steady north wind had blown the butterflies out of sight. Every living thing in the jungle was in hiding from it, except mosquitoes. At their backs the wind would have helped them, and walking against it would have halted them entirely, but it blew from right to left and was like an invisible ball and chain that they dragged wearily mile after mile.

Pichegru had allowed nearly a month for the trip, with the idea they could make a leisurely walk of it and still be early at the rendezvous. But he had not reckoned sufficiently with the wind and the deeper jungle, and he began to push them mercilessly. Dr. Florian welcomed the physical exhaustion; it prevented him from worrying about what was happening in Sinnamarie and stopped his endless questionings of himself as to what he was doing here at all. The exertions and challenges of the journey swallowed up all else but the necessity of keeping pace with them, though they were so much stronger. Pichegru, he learned, had compelled the party to take strenuous exercise morning and night in preparation for these hardships, but Florian had gone without sleep and proper food and his work had been within-doors and sedentary.

Their worn boots and shoes dropped away; their feet turned into shapeless masses of tortured flesh. Each night, Florian made poultices of mud and ashes of seaweed to draw out soreness, and this was all that permitted them to resume the journey next day. "It was a good thing for us that you decided to come, Doctor," Pichegru commented.

Rain came torrentially every other hour, driven against them like shot from the force of the wind. After each rainfall, mosquitoes buzzed out in infuriated, wind-propelled clouds. Finally, at Florian's suggestion, they began covering their exposed parts with black jungle mud. It was a discomfort as it dried on them, but helped considerably to ward off both mosquitoes and frond-cuts.

Barthélemy, not Florian, was the laggard and he complained incessantly. Pichegru put up with this for a surprisingly long time, then, using a machete, he hacked savagely through a vine that was rope-thick and rope-strong, and threw it down at Barthélemy's feet, saying, "The next complaint out of you, you'll be tied to a tree and abandoned." The ex-Director fell into a total silence that lasted the better part of the day.

Rivers intervened. In themselves they were not large rivers, but were flooded from the rains. The men walked along their banks for tiring miles, looking for a place to cross. At the crossing of the second of the rivers, alligators were sleeping, their fierce armored heads propped on the bank.

Barthélemy quavered and pointed. "What in God's name are they!"

"I don't think they'll bother us. They look too lazy," Pichegru said.

"No power on earth could compel me to advance a foot nearer to them."

"Suit yourself about that. I'm going on. I'd rather be eaten quickly by monsters than die by inches back there." He walked fearlessly into the yellow water. Florian was first to follow him, and won a swift glance of approbation from Pichegru. The alligators turned their heads and watched from glazed eyes the color of the water. Otherwise they did not move, and General Pichegru and Dr. Florian clambered out on the farther bank, safe. Then the others followed.

The jungle became thicker yet. The men crawled down tapir trails on their hands and knees, hacking with the machetes when the trails swerved. They had covered two thirds of the distance by Pichegru's calculations, and he believed they were still on schedule. Pichegru let no one rest except during official halts called by himself.

❀   ❀   ❀

In all their minds was the dream of the trim British ship, her decks clean, her officers span, her route away from Guiana. She was an obsession, so much thought about that she had an actual physical existence as though already under their eyes.

Constant exercise had created abnormal appetites that their lightening supply packs could not begin to fill. Pichegru, as hungry as anyone, doled out supplies with rigid parsimony. Nightfall the end of the third week, Willot threw his machete at something moving in the foliage, and had the fantastic luck to have hamstrung a tapir. They were hours cooking it because nothing in the jungle was dry enough to burn, and then they ate it half raw.

Pichegru said they were very near to the rendezvous. How he could be so sure no one knew, and no one asked him, but his words gave them courage. Snarled tough stubborn vines held them back. Apparently no human foot ever had traveled this way. Every tree was an enemy, closing out the sky, pelting them with ripe fruits that splattered nastily, or green fruit capable of knocking a man senseless. Or they stumbled into hummocks of soft ground and sank thigh-deep, and had to be pulled out by their tiring companions. Mangrove swamps became frequent and drove them heart-aching distances out of their way. The wind never dropped. They fancied it was screaming words of threat and mockery. Even the vision of the trim British ship began to fail, and stubbornness rather than hope kept them going now; and dread of the army ants. The men crawled as obsessively as if their Creator had fashioned them to no better purpose than this endless marching on hands and knees, along beast trails, and under the lashing wind.

They reached the bank of the Mana and did not even know it as their goal. It seemed only another, more impassable obstruction in their predestined hell of endless crawling. They stared at its smooth waters with blank uncaring eyes, their jaws slack from weariness. Then Pichegru whispered hoarsely, "It's the river. It's the Mana."

Even then they could not bring themselves to caring. They fell down on her banks and slept, Pichegru too. The tireless driver of men had had his will broken at last, by success.

Florian was the first to waken. He lay quietly and watched the river surge past. They must be downstream from the rendezvous, and he wondered how far. When he saw that Pichegru was awake, he asked him.

The ex-commander of the Army of the Rhine yawned and stretched. "Not far. I kept bringing us back on course."

"It will be hard going."

"We'll make it."

A kind of admiration, affection even, for Pichegru, started in Florian. What a leader he was! The qualities Florian had imagined in him when he asked him to govern Sinnamarie, had been abundantly displayed through these days that would have devoured them all had Pichegru been less. Florian was able to believe that they were not far because Pichegru had said so. His heart eased, he slept again.

But the General felt strong and life-filled. He got up and began to climb one of the taller trees, using ropes of vine to help his ascent. He climbed tirelessly. Sweat poured into his light eyes. He blinked and climbed on. For nearly an hour he climbed and rested. Near the top of the tree, he could see out for miles. Behind him was a swaying mass of greenery that represented the impossible journey they had made; before him, and not three miles away, was the body of quiet water that was formed by the combined mouths of the Mana and the Maroni. He wiped the sweat from his eyes to look again, but from him there were no tears of joy. He descended and went from man to man, waking them, telling the news. "It's an easy distance, and we're in plenty of time because the ship isn't there yet." They wept unashamed.

They finished the journey in a few hours, hunting food as they went. On a grassy savannah dotted with occasional trees, they made their camp. It commanded a full view of the natural harbor.

They waited.

They caught fish in the Indian manner, spearing them with pointed stakes. Lizards and bananas and palm cores were easy to find where no other hunters had been. They rested, and tirelessly they scanned the harbor for the ship that was so real to them.

A week passed. The ship was now overdue. They blamed the wind. Another week passed. They stared at the blankness of water as if they could cause a ship to form there through the force of their staring. They did not talk about it, because once the thing was said aloud, it became true, that no ship was coming for them. They waited, and rested, and fished, and stared.

Pichegru himself broke the long silence. They were all sitting around an oven dug into the earth, from which came succulent odors of fish wrapped in palm leaves, baking. He spoke in a level voice, with no trace of regret.

"It would not do for a traitor to complain that he had been dealt with treacherously." His hard glance swept their faces. "What do you want to do now?"

The sudden yielding of responsibility frightened them. No one answered. Then Dossonville said, "The wind is keeping the ship back."

"Do you really believe that?"

"Yes," he muttered, looking away.

"I have no objection to further waiting if that's what the rest of you want. After all, food is far more plentiful here than it is around Sinnamarie. But you are telling yourselves bedtime stories if you really think things are going to come out right for us. There's been no ship yet simply because no ship was sent here."

"But why would they do that to you, General?"

He shrugged. "Who knows? We've had no news of the world. Anything could have happened. Perhaps France and England have made peace. Perhaps there's some big naval operation afoot and they can't spare a ship. Or else they simply decided that I was not of that much value to them."

"We're giving up too soon," de la Rue said.

"Then we'll wait another week. Or however long it takes you to accept the obvious."

"And then what?" It was Barthélemy's bitter whine.

"What indeed?" He stared solemnly over the blank waters of the river mouths. "If I had a little boat—!" he said.

To all this, Dr. Florian paid little heed. His heart was beating out a slow sad message, that his betrayal of the men in Sinnamarie had gone for naught. There is more than one way of making a fool of yourself, he now saw. And surely the man who had hurt so many others in order to buy escape for himself, but instead found himself miles from everywhere, with nothing accomplished and nothing ahead but the necessity of making the fierce journey back, was a bigger fool than any he had ever known before.

In the hopeless days that followed, while others watched for the British ship that wasn't coming, the notion of a little boat grew in Pichegru. None of the rest of them felt anxious to risk their lives in any such escapade; neither did anyone want to be left behind, in case he found a boat. His was the only sound knowledge of geography among them, and he explained how the south equatorial current flowed directly past the Guiana coast into the Caribbean. Even a pirogue would travel briskly once it reached the current. Of course there was danger that they might be cast up on one of the French islands, Martinique, for instance, or they might be run down by a French ship. But chances were equally good of landing on British or Spanish territory, or being sighted by a ship of theirs or of the United States.

General Willot said, "I don't like to be the one to confess an inability, General. But I'm damned if I can make the trip back there and then back here again, and we can't launch a boat off the Sinnamarie coast because of the breakers."

"Maybe we could find an Indian village around here," Imbert-Colomes suggested.

But Pichegru vetoed the idea. Since they had nothing left to trade with, their dealings would have to be with the Indians who knew them, and in this unfamiliar section of jungle, they would become hopelessly lost if they started wandering around looking for a settlement. "I'll find a way to launch it from the Sinnamarie coast, if I just find a way to acquire it in the first place," he promised them. "We made a serious mistake when we spent General Willot's anal resources so freely. Or if I had my snuffbox, the Indians might give us a boat for that. But it's gone."

When they had rested on the riverbank three weeks and four days, they turned their faces back. All the way, when the butterflies made their rare appearances, Pichegru spent ebbing strength to catch them. He saved them carefully. It seemed an uncommon thing for a man like him to do.

IV

DR. BÉNIGNE KEROUAL, ship's doctor of the *Bonnet Rouge*, twisted his little fat hands in his lap and looked anxiously from one face to another. He wanted them to understand everything, and yet he did not want to tell them everything. For instance, he did not want to tell them what Sinnamarie was really like. Diane Florian, so worn and tired-looking: her beauty reminded him of a tall candle that has burned a long time, through nights of particular darkness. If Fidèle had a last name no one had thought to tell him what it was, but her little pointed face was sharp with yearning. And Dr. Lasné. The women insisted on calling him "Doctor," but he had said he was not one. What his relationship was, to them and to Florian, Keroual had not figured out.

"Then he's been on Guiana for over a year," Diane said.

"Over a year, Citizeness. I expected to be here six months ago. But the ship had unexpected orders, which delayed my leave." Her eyes were frantic. He spoke into them urgently. "I'm here to help him, Citizeness."

"Help him. But how?"

Robert Lasné said, "If he was tricked like that, the Directory knows he's there and they mean for him to stay there. Short of overthrowing the government, I don't see much that can be done." His blunt, honest face was puzzled. "I'd do anything," he added.

"I have three months," Keroual said. "That's a long time. I'll find a way."

He spoke grimly. He was haunted by an idea that Dr. Florian might have seen him drunk on the day of disembarkation. That had been an innocent mistake. He had simply reasoned that there was no real need of swearing off until his ship reached France, and it had seemed a good idea to finish his supplies during the voyage, then liquor would not be around to tempt him. But if Florian had seen him like that, he would have little reason to put much stock in Dr. Keroual's promises. Dr. Keroual knew it was important for Dr. Florian to have believed him, because he knew what happened to men who had been on Guiana for a long time. The lucky ones died quickly. The others ceased to exist as men. Florian's faith in him was to have been Florian's talisman against the evil spirit of the land, and as soon as Dr. Keroual recovered sufficiently from his bout to realize that he might have been seen in that condition, he astonished the crew of the *Bonnet Rouge* by bringing out the remaining bottles in armloads, and throwing them into the sea. A handsome gesture, but one made too late, perhaps. These were the things he did not want to tell the anxious wife, and the friends. Instead he repeated, "Don't worry. I'll find a way."

Fidèle said harshly, "But what about Ange?" Diane Florian's face changed. She looked shocked, as though something of major importance had been overlooked.

"Fidèle, forgive me!" she said, "I forgot about him." She said to Dr. Keroual, "Fidèle lives with me. Her husband is on Guiana too."

Dr. Keroual was impatient at the blunting of his bright purpose. "Is he a doctor too?"

"No, Doctor, but Ange is quite remarkable, and it's important that he be rescued——"

Keroual broke in disapprovingly. "I wonder if you know how much of an impossibility it is to rescue one man. I have sworn myself to perform the impossible, very well. I'm not going to do it twice over."

Diane Florian started to say something, and so did Fidèle. Robert Lasné stopped them. "There is a way," he said. "Now don't upset Dr. Keroual any more. It isn't fair." He seized Keroual's hand and dragged him out of the room unceremoniously. "She's gentle and grateful, but she'll scratch your eyes out over Ange," he said in an undertone.

"I can't help that." He sounded, and felt, querulous. "I wish you had some idea of what I have given up to try to help Dr. Florian." Brandy was what he had given up, but he had the confirmed inebriate's fierce secrecy on that subject.

"Will you sit down here just for a minute, and let me tell you about Dr. Florian and myself?"

"On the stairs?" Keroual said, affronted. (He had slept on wharves, in brothels, and once, he had found himself after sleeping in a hog sty.)

"Just for a minute, please. I would do anything for Dr. Florian, Dr. Keroual." That was touching on Keroual's own obsession, so he sat down on the stairs in a practiced gesture and waited to hear what it was that Lasné had to say.

❋   ❋   ❋

Dr. Keroual said slowly, "But you don't know what it's like there."

"I know what he's like. He would never leave them. They will all be his patients by now. He stayed here for the sake of myself and the other students when he could have left during the Terror. He sent her away, but he stayed. I only found out about that a few weeks ago, from her. We didn't know Dr. Contarini's true purpose in coming. But you see how it is, he wouldn't leave them, unless there was someone to take his place with them."

"Will you please tell me what your status is? I'm confused about you. Are you a doctor, or aren't you?"

"I had two months to finish, and my year-of-practice."

"Why didn't you finish, then?"

"I had to find out if he needed me."

"I—see. So I am not alone in being impressed by Dr. Florian."

"No, Doctor, you're not alone."

Keroual said fiercely, "Do you want me to tell you about Guiana?"

"I may as well find out for myself. I've always been slow, and seemed stupid," Robert Lasné said. "I know just as much as the others do. I think I know it better. But Dr. Scarpa himself warned me that patients won't like me. Maybe the men on Guiana won't care."

If either of us is going to do this mad thing, it ought to be me, Dr. Keroual thought. Because once Florian has been rescued, I'm going to start drinking again. This young man might be really useful. Then he remembered that in Sinnamarie there was nothing to drink, and no way to get anything. He flinched back from the sacrifice and was grateful that Lasné was willing. Keroual might have been tempted to the same folly if Dr. Florian refused to leave whatever rude hospital he might have set up. "All right," he consented, "you can come along and take his place if that's necessary."

"It will be," Lasné said with soft, devoted assurance.

"But the green-eyed wench, how does that solve anything for her?"

"Ange can come out on my papers."

"What?"

"He can come out on my papers," Robert Lasné said patiently. "I'll still have papers, won't I? He can come out on those."

For a moment, a rocket of excitement flared in the brain of Dr. Keroual. Certainly! Granted a willing sacrifice, a rescue can always be made. Florian could come out on Lasné's papers. But the rocket burned itself out and fell without fire. A ship would have to be sent to Cayenne harbor; what sacrifice was going to motivate that? The Governor would have to dispatch men from the garrison, and a smallboat. What sacrifice would influence him? No. Sacrifice works in the quiet ways that Lasné had chosen. It replaces, but it does not create. To create, there must be power, force. . . . If the ship were sent and then the smallboat, for Florian, Ange whoever he might be could come out on Lasné's papers. But no one would come out unless a ship was sent.

"All right, Dr. Lasné," he said, "I'll keep it in mind." He was perfectly aware of using toward the other a title that had not yet been earned. Dr. Keroual was fiercely indignant toward the false doctors who had no degrees, but it seemed to him that Robert Lasné's degree was earned on that staircase.

❋ ❋ ❋

No lives had been lost on the trip toward the Mana because the men were strong and fit and buoyed with hope, but the hardships repeated had been too much for eight exhausted bodies and despair-blackened minds. Pichegru himself, the valet, and Dr. Florian were among the survivors. Five of the escape party had to be hospitalized as soon as they arrived back at the notables' building south of Sinnamarie. Florian drove himself to care for the others, although he was as thin and weak, as badly in need of rest, as anyone.

"You ought to have your medical box," Pichegru remarked, watching him move among the sick men.

"They need it in Sinnamarie."

"But they don't know how to use it."

"I taught the orderlies something. They'll get some use out of it." He spoke curtly. He did not want to discuss Sinnamarie with General Pichegru.

Life was not easy for the notables now that they had nothing left for sale or exchange. The months when they had not hunted in the jungle told against them. Pichegru gave orders that nothing was to be eaten that had not been inspected first by the doctor. They were obedient about that, but when Florian would advise them to throw away most of what they had brought, in their hunger they would cry weakly like children. He had joined his fortunes with theirs just at the time when their exertions and sufferings became worse than what was endured in Sinnamarie itself. He did not feel chagrin, but acceptance, as of justice having been done him.

When the sick members had improved sufficiently, he took a food party into the jungle to show the notables what he knew could be eaten safely. He very much hoped to find another stand of cinchona bark because he was out of that, and he could not bring himself to risk meeting a party from Sinnamarie at the old place by the Kour-our River. Florian and the food party did not return until evening. They had had good luck finding food, but no cinchona.

General Pichegru was sitting at the table, and staring into Florian's Leeuwenhoek with avid interest. The medical box, opened, was on the floor beside him. "Where did you get that?" the doctor demanded angrily.

"I walked over there and got it. Come and look. It's better than I thought it would be."

"I told you I wanted them to have it!"

"I know you did," General Pichegru said mildly. "But I wanted to have it myself. I have good use for the things in your box. Come and see."

"Did they really give it up without a word of protest?" He knew how much it meant to them.

"I said you had sent for it. It's your box, after all."

"I know, and I think it's damned temerity on your part that I can't dispose of it as I wish."

Pichegru leaned back and looked at Florian coolly. "Do you want to go back to Sinnamarie yourself, Doctor? If you do, take your box and go on. I won't stop you."

"No," he said in a low voice. "I don't want to do that."

"If you intend to stay with us, then you owe us what loyalties and possessions you have. And I do think it's wise for you to stay, because you're not exactly popular in Sinnamarie any more."

"I didn't suppose I would be," he said.

"Then it can't hurt your feelings to hear it from me. Now stop sulking, and come here and look." He made room, holding his hand so that Florian could not see what kind of specimen he had mounted; with the other hand, he guided Florian to a bent posture over the lens.

"I'll be damned! What is it?"

"Can't you guess?"

"What a beautiful thing!"—like a great blue canyon of immense depths and distances, in which every shade of blue had been brought together.

"It is. Isn't it?"

"I never saw anything like it. What is it, General?"

"It's a butterfly wing," Pichegru said. He took his hand away from Florian's back and the doctor, straightening, could see the wing of the Morpho, the most common butterfly on Guiana.

Pichegru replaced the blue wing with the wing of a target-butterfly, kin to the one that had clung to Florian's foot for protection on the day he had been invited to escape Guiana. But he pushed that memory aside, and bent and looked. It was like staring into a most brilliant moon surrounded by the softest night the world had ever seen. And then the black wing of the Heliconius, which, to the naked eye, showed mere flecks of red, green, yellow, violet. Through the lens, the Heliconius wing resembled a firmament ablaze.

"I wonder why I never thought of doing that," Florian said.

"You were accustomed to using the microscope as a tool, rather than a toy. But I'm delighted that you're so impressed. Surely an ignorant Indian will see magic in it if you do. Even I see magic when I look at these beautiful wings. Do you know what I see, Dr. Florian? I look into your microscope and I see a little pirogue with a good stout canvas sail, outfitted with oars and stocked with supplies." He patted the instrument lovingly. "Tomorrow, Dr. Florian, we will go to the Indian village, you and I. We will traffic in magical things, with the Indians."

Florian's flash of resentment over this calm disposal of his property did not last. The only important thing was to leave Guiana. Though he owned the box, he never would have thought of trading it for something really needed, like a boat.

Pichegru had been watching him. "I see that you're no longer angry with me," he said. Both men smiled. We have come to understand each other very well, myself and General Pichegru, Florian thought. But then he remembered Pichegru saying, 'I could like you very much if you were willing to creep away at night, abandoning your patients—' His friendship is an insult, Florian thought. And my own is no better now.

He said in a low voice, "What is it like there?"

"In Sinnamarie, you mean?"

"Yes."

"The work parties have broken up. Building has stopped. Your drainage ditches are filled with refuse. The orderlies you say you trained are in the hospital only at odd times, or not at all. The hospital is full, but the sick have no care beyond the clumsy attentions of one man who seems to have no idea of procedure. He gave me your box. The village is incredibly filthy, and they never even finished the palisade." He related the details with a kind of enjoyment, watching Florian's face.

"I ought to go back."

"Would it do any good?"

"I could tend the sick, at least."

"You could do that," Pichegru agreed.

But they both knew he was not going back.

*　　　*　　　*

After all, Florian did not accompany Pichegru the next day to the Indian village. Months of hardship, the terrible journey across

Guiana and back, and the fact that he had driven himself to care for the others instead of taking rest himself, all had collected against his health. He felt light-headed, and suspected that he might be feverish. Aubrey and Dossonville and General Willot went with General Pichegru to the Indian village, with Florian's medical box.

As the day lengthened, the doctor realized that he really was sick. He dosed himself with tafia and a little mercury and went to bed, thinking that it was ironic that he should develop a high fever himself on the very day he let his fever gauge be traded away. Ironic, too, that the discoverer of cinchona bark on Guiana should be the one to go without cinchona, but he never had found another stand.

His memories of Pichegru coming back and telling of success were not detailed. He was too sick to share the excitement.

The Leeuwenhoek, with the collection of butterfly wings, had been traded for a thirty-foot pirogue large enough to hold them easily, and cleanly and stoutly built. The Indians had been glad to trade their best canoe and four paddles to have such a wonderful thing in their village as the Leeuwenhoek. During the trading, Pichegru had seen a sailor's canvas hammock improperly hung, that they had come by somehow and did not know how to use, but respected because of its uniqueness in their experience. They did not want to let the hammock go. But it would make a fine sail. After long bargaining, the Indians consented to take the fever gauge in place of the hammock. After all, the hammock was old magic.

The medical box itself, with its jumble of odd instruments, had gone cheaply for a water container and some dried food. Six Indians had carried the canoe from the village to the notables' building, but after they were gone Pichegru insisted that the boat be carried to another place, and well hidden.

*   *   *

When consciousness came back, Dr. Florian was not aware of any lapse of time. He realized that he was lying in the most familiar place on earth, the wooden building that he had taken away from the notables and made into a hospital. He was not at all surprised at being there, and drifted back into healing sleep, a little smile of homecoming on his bearded mouth.

When he wakened the second time, Ange Pitou was sitting tailor-fashion on the floor by his bed of rushes and watching him. "Do you know me, Charlot?" Dr. Florian himself did not notice it, but this was the first time the singer had ever used his name like that. "How do you feel? Could you drink a little water, or eat a banana?"

"Just water, please, Ange." He brought some in a gourd, and Florian drank it all.

"More?"

"Not yet." It had been a real exertion to swallow the water, and he was trembling with weakness. "How long have I been sick?"

"About six weeks, here."

"Is it the miasma?"

"Like in the epidemic, you mean? No, I don't think so. You didn't act the way they did."

"How did I get here?"

"Why don't you sleep again," Ange said. "We can talk later. We have plenty of time. We have all the time there is." The bare suggestion was enough, and he fell asleep.

But eventually he was told all that had happened. Ange had been walking along the beach looking for shellfish when he saw the notables march down carrying the pirogue, and the sail and the paddles. They had been too far away for him to count them or recognize them as individuals, but he knew their number had much decreased. He had watched, fascinated, while they readied their little boat for the sea, and run out with it into the breakers. He had lost sight of them before they crossed the last line of whitecaps, so he could not say for sure whether or not they had won through. But he had patrolled the beach several times since and seen nothing of theirs cast up by the tide. Probably they had made good their escape that far anyway.

Their sick member they had ruthlessly abandoned. Ange had gone around to the new building to see what they might have left that would be useful in Sinnamarie. Florian, unconscious, high in fever, was what he had found. Traveling in easy stages, he had brought the doctor back and given him cinchona in what he thought was right amounts. But the fever had gone untended so long, it was stubborn and Ange had given up hope. Overnight it seemed, signs of mending began.

"He traded my medical box away to get the boat," Florian told Ange.

"So that's why I couldn't find it. I looked all over. I didn't see why they would take that and leave you, and I knew they had it because I was here when he came for it."

174

"But I didn't send after it," Florian said, "I didn't know anything about him having it until I saw him using the microscope to see butterfly wings."

"I imagine those were pretty," Ange said.

The orderlies Florian had trained had deserted the hospital when they realized he was not coming back. The miasma cases had died one by one, from lack of care. Ange had done what he could, but he could not do much and hunt for himself too, so they had died.

"Has the whole thing really fallen apart, then? Couldn't Father Roger keep them in line at all?"

"He's dead," Ange said. "He couldn't believe that you'd go off deliberately. He was sure you had become lost, or fallen into a pit. After the others stopped looking for you, he went on by himself. One night he didn't come back, so we went looking for him. We found him all right. He had tripped over a vine and broken his ankle. He had crawled a part of the way back, before the army ants scented him."

"Oh, my God!"

"There's no point trying to keep it from you."

"But that's terrible!"

"Yes," Ange said remotely. "I imagine he found it so."

For a long time, Florian lay rigidly without saying anything. His dark eyes were filled with a kind of suffering he had never known before. "Forgive me," he said finally, in a broken voice. A curious happiness filled Ange Pitou's heart. He rose and went out. He was smiling.

❊   ❊   ❊

Lying in bed, gaining strength daily from rest and from the food the singer brought faithfully, Dr. Florian had plenty of time to go over his own actions, and the actions of General Pichegru. His first bitterness toward the General was lost in the realization that Pichegru had acted on his own pattern. It would have been out-of-character for him to wait around for a sick man to recover since that would have cost them what little chance they had of escaping, as they consumed the supplies they had got from Indians and weakened daily under the rigors of Guiana life. To have sent word to Sinnamarie that Florian was there, ill, would have attracted notice to more important activities around the boat. It would be so easy to take the boat away from them if the men of Sinnamarie guessed that there was one. Pichegru had done the best he knew for himself and the others in his party. And what had Pichegru said about himself, after days of staring over the blank waters of the harbor where no British ship had been or would be? "It would not do for a traitor to complain that he had been dealt with treacherously," Pichegru had said. The remark was as just when applied to Florian, so resentment passed into bitter understanding of what kind of man he had accepted as his leader.

More than escape from Guiana, Florian came to want escape from himself. He wanted to become virtuous again. But the instrument of his virtue had been the medical box. And the box was irrevocably gone.

He had not realized that the box was more important as a symbol than it was in intrinsic value, even though its value had been great. The medical box had been like the Ark of the Covenant that had held the ancient Jews together through every kind of misfortune. It had been the source of authority, the emblem of a civilization to which they still belonged as long as they possessed it. The things in the box were so obviously constructed to help suffering mankind, to lift pain, ward off disease, correct nature in her rare faults. The medical box had been a rallying point, but had been sacrificed to provide transportation for Pichegru and the notables. Its loss was the final blow to endeavor, and the village looked now as it had when the victims of Fructidor first came there and found the surviving victims of Thermidor crouched like animals amid the ruins.

After he could be up and useful, Florian, with Ange's help, maintained a dispensary, and those who were sick still came to the wooden building to sleep. But these services, which might have stood as a symbol had there never been a medical box, were insufficient in the face of its loss.

Pichegru had lied or been mistaken about the resentment the men felt toward Florian. Or else resentment itself had died away in a climate of total indifference. No one said anything against his defection; no one reminded him that he had bartered away their last chance to remain men. Perhaps they had forgotten that such a chance ever had existed. Perhaps the days when Sinnamarie built, and planned, and held hopes, were as far back in their memories now as the golden days when they had lived in France and made laws, and argued cases, and written brilliantly for publication by newspapers. There would have been less pain to him in their hatred than there was in this, but nothing he could do now would revive them. They had slipped past the call of his commanding voice, and the mercy of his serving hands. He felt himself drowning in the same dark tide, and after a while he yielded to it, and found a measure of peace in the darkness of not-caring.

SIX

Bonaparte Again

Dr. Pinel knew a Dr. Desgenettes slightly and, since his appointment as physician-in-chief to the new Expeditionary Army, Desgenettes had become important and influential. Dr. Pinel gave Dr. Keroual a letter of introduction to Dr. Desgenettes, in which he asked him to listen to the story and to intervene if he could.

The chief physician was closeted with Dr. Larrey when Dr. Keroual arrived. Dr. Larrey was the new Army's chief surgeon. They were splitting a bottle of wine while they outlined their responsibilities to each other and to the several thousand men being entrusted to their care. They were anxious that no taint of the old hatred between medical doctors and surgeons be allowed to intrude on their real work. It was not the best time for Keroual to have come, but Dr. Pinel's letter excited curiosity and the servant was directed to show Keroual in.

The important doctors were touched by him. There was something appealing about this little fat figure, flaming with purpose. The ugly trickery by which Florian had been sent to his doom roused indignation.

"I believe I met the Medical Inspector once," Dr. Desgenettes commented. "I was impressed. He seemed young for so important a post, and I remember being somewhat envious. If Carnot had lasted, Dr. Florian would have had a great destiny. So he's on Guiana! That's a clear lesson against envying anyone, isn't it? I'll find out what I can, Dr. Keroual. Do you want to come back, say, next week at this hour?"

Dr. Keroual said in strained voice, "A week on Guiana is a long time."

Dr. Desgenettes was disagreeably surprised. He started to answer sharply, but something on Keroual's face held him back. The little man looked ready to cry. "Tomorrow, then," he consented.

Keroual spent the remainder of the day restlessly. The desire to drink had never left him, though it had been more than a year since he had given in to it. It would have helped him to spend the time with Florian's wife and friends, but he was resolved not to see them again until something real had been accomplished. He got through the day somehow and went to bed in his room on the fringe of the Palais Royal, convinced that Dr. Desgenettes would have good news for him on the morrow.

Instead, Desgenettes said, "There is nothing to be done. I didn't learn the details but while the present government lasts, Dr. Florian will do well to stay out of France. I'm sorry, Dr. Keroual. I wish I could have helped you."

"You were my last hope!" Keroual said.

"I'm sorry," Desgenettes repeated.

"Even if he can't come back to France. Isn't there some way of getting him off Guiana? There's such a shortage of doctors. It seems there ought to be a place for him somewhere."

"Oh, a place, yes, I'm shorthanded myself, I'd be delighted to have him. But you don't seem to appreciate the difficulties, Dr. Keroual. I thought seriously of trying to interest General Bonaparte in his case, but then I realized a ship would have to be sent for him. It's simply too much trouble to go to for one doctor, however qualified."

Dr. Keroual said, "If General Bonaparte has the authority to send a ship to Guiana, I am going to see him about it. Whether or not you help me, I'm going to see him."

Dr. Desgenettes looked into his resolute face, and shrugged. "I'll do what I can for you. I admire you very much, Dr. Keroual."

*   ✳   ✳

"I dislike refusing people," Bonaparte said to Desgenettes, "and especially in a case like this, where my sympathies are with the victim. I ought to say yes, but I can't afford to say it, so I prefer not to be asked. Paul Barras tells me that life at Sinnamarie is far from unpleasant, that the men are given every freedom and consideration, and they're far better off than they would be in prison here."

"That certainly doesn't match with what Dr. Keroual seems to believe. He calls it the *guillotine sèche*."

"That's a singularly chilling phrase!" Bonaparte said.

"I gather his ship has been used several times to transport prisoners. He seems to be well informed."

"If Barras has lied to me again, I may as well know it. Dr. Keroual may come here to breakfast, Thursday at eight. But make him understand there is nothing I can do for his friend. I'll appreciate it if he doesn't ask me about that."

Dr. Desgenettes started to tell him that Dr. Keroual would almost certainly be out of his depth at one of the General's breakfasts, and moreover, could not be depended on to respect the General's prohibition. But Bonaparte, his decision given, had turned his attention elsewhere.

*   *   *

When Dr. Keroual was presented, he said eagerly, "I plead the cause of Dr. Charlot Florian, the former Medical Inspector of the Republic, who——"

General Bonaparte was not accustomed to having his wishes set aside. He interrupted. "This is not the place to make such a plea, nor am I the man to hear it." He turned away, under the impression that he had been remarkably forbearing. But he left Keroual in a state bordering on consternation.

The other guests were famous; the only obscure name here was Keroual's own. Monge the mathematician, Volney the philosopher, Talma the tragedian, and others tried to draw him into conversation. He rebuffed them with the frantic rudeness of an embarrassed man. Now they were leaving him alone. He sat, head down, staring into his plate, only occasionally darting swift shy glances toward the man at the head of the table. He did not attempt to eat; he was barely capable of lifting his coffee cup. He did not hear a word that was being said.

The General had finished his breakfast quickly and now was leaning back in his chair, listening to the others and smiling slightly. Only occasionally did he speak himself, usually in the form of a question. But he guided the conversation expertly, with a firm hand. In Bonaparte, listening was very nearly a creative art.

It seemed to Keroual that the breakfast had lasted a long time. The hour must be drawing to its close. Maybe he was not going to be given another chance to speak. Dismayed, he put down the coffee cup so quickly that its frail china smashed. A brown stain started across the white cloth. Keroual, in horror, watched it spreading. So did everyone else.

Bonaparte made a deft attempt to rescue his guest. "Dr. Keroual's bid for our attention is justified. So far he's had no chance to contribute, though he's the only man of my acquaintance who claims to have actual knowledge of conditions at Sinnamarie, the settlement on Guiana where our political offenders are confined. You have the floor, Doctor."

He said in a high, trembling voice, "I plead the cause of Dr. Charlot Florian, the former Medical Inspector——" But memory of the earlier rebuff pinched off the words in his throat. He began plucking helplessly at the tablecloth with his little fat hands, as if he could remove the stain with his fingers.

"Well?"

The harsh syllable spurred him into saying the first thing that came into his head. "I'm a drunkard, General Bonaparte."

Their startled laughter he endured head down, his eyes filling with ashamed tears. Why had he imagined that he was capable of appearing in company like this, and acquitting himself? All he wanted was to get away.

"That's a more adequate excuse for smashing my china than it is for sending a ship to Guiana," Bonaparte said mockingly. Keroual bolted up from his chair and started blindly across the room. The harsh voice flashed out, pinning him. "Sit down, Dr. Keroual. I haven't finished with you."

He stood, alone, cynosure of eyes, his head swinging slightly like a baited bull. He was too hurt to know or care what he said. "Haven't I given you enough to laugh over?" was what he said.

"You have indeed. But what point were you trying to make? Perhaps you think it's wrong for a man with your failing to be at liberty, while a better doctor is being wasted on Guiana."

"Yes!" His relief at being understood was immense.

"Perhaps you even had some idea of saving him to make up for your own shortcomings."

"That's it exactly!" His round, tear-marked face beamed with delight.

"Then why don't you say so? I'm not going to do your pleading for you. Are you drunk now, Dr. Keroual?"

"I haven't had a drink for a year," he protested.

"That's interesting. Why not?"

"I promised him I wouldn't. I wanted him to trust me. No one trusts a drunkard, you see, because we're forgetful. Anyway, no drunkard believes anything is very important except getting another drink. When he's drinking, that is."

Someone—not Bonaparte—laughed, and Keroual's spate of words stopped. The General frowned slightly at the offender, who was

Talma, and who grinned apologetically. "Go on, Dr. Keroual," Bonaparte said. Keroual stood mute, his mind emptied. "How long have you and Dr. Florian been friends?" the General prompted.

"I met him just that one time."

"So. He was a total stranger to you. Yet you stopped drinking for his sake. Wasn't that a handsome sacrifice to make for a stranger?"

"I wanted him to trust me," Keroual repeated.

"Why was that so important?"

"I know what Sinnamarie is like."

"So. We approach the subject you were asked here to discuss. What is Sinnamarie like, Dr. Keroual?"

"It would be better to kill them outright." He took a forward step, thrusting his hands out toward the other. "Please help him. There is no one else to turn to."

"That's true, isn't it," Bonaparte said in a musing tone. He appeared sunk in thought. His guests watched him tensely, and none of them felt like more laughter. Keroual's sincerity, and his obvious horror of that far place of exile, had impressed them. Finally Bonaparte said, "Do you appreciate the difficulties of getting your Dr. Florian off Guiana?"

"Dr. Desgenettes warned me, yes."

"Did he encourage you to think I'd consent?"

"No, General. He seemed to think you wouldn't."

"And Desgenettes knows me. But you don't know me, and so you believed that I might. That doesn't speak very highly for the way I meet my responsibilities as a court of last appeal. Does it, Dr. Keroual?"

He did not know what to say. He shook his head dumbly.

"What ship is yours, Doctor?"

"The *Bonnet Rouge*, General."

"Under my orders, is she?"

"Yes, General. She's to proceed to Toulon harbor as soon as she's been overhauled."

"How large a ship is she? How many guns?"

"Just one gun, General. She's a merchantman third class." He hardly dared to feel hope, yet the turn the conversation had taken certainly seemed to imply room for hope. He watched Bonaparte anxiously. His sight had cleared, and he could see how young and sad the bronzed face was. He felt another's gaze, and shifted his eyes slightly. From the important seat at Bonaparte's right, an old man wearing rusty black was watching him. His eyes and his lined, wattled face were remarkably sweet-tempered. This would be Monge, the great mathematician, who nodded slightly to Keroual and smiled. *You're doing fine, I'm on your side,* was the message silently conveyed.

Bonaparte said, "Does anyone here know anything about this Dr. Florian?"

"I remember when he was appointed, General," one of them said.

"Medical Inspector. That would be a political appointment. It doesn't say anything about his abilities as a doctor."

Keroual said eagerly, "He was licensed at both Pavia and Leyden."

"Pavia. Was he?" The intonation was peculiar, as though that word caused him pain, and Keroual regretted having mentioned it.

He added quickly, "Dr. Florian taught at Montpellier for a year. Then during the Revolution, he instructed students privately with such success that they were admitted to third year classes at the University of Pavia." That name again, it had slipped out. He paused, alarmed at the look of pain crossing Bonaparte's face a second time.

Monge intervened gently. "It was admirable of Dr. Florian to teach medical students. No doubt he foresaw what I've been warning you about, the end of medical knowledge in the next generation. He sounds like a valuable man."

"Are you taking sides against me? I need that ship."

The old man spoke to the young one as though to a beloved son in danger of committing a fault. "I'm on the side of wanting you to do the right thing. Always."

"But a really good doctor would hesitate about abandoning the others, I should think. Most of them will be his patients by now."

Keroual said eagerly, "One of his medical students is in Paris, and he's willing to take his place there."

"Dr. Florian has loyal friends," Bonaparte commented. "I need that ship, Dr. Keroual. But I'll commission the *Bonnet Rouge* to Guiana for the purpose of rescuing one medical doctor. I don't like it, but I'll do it. Tell your Dr. Florian that I will expect much from him."

Keroual tried to stammer out thanks. Bonaparte stopped him with grim good humor. "God help you if Florian is dead when you get there. I'll take you instead, and I'll make a good doctor out of you, since you want it so much." He made a little gesture of dismissal, and Keroual fled as though before grave danger. He had an idea that it would be a painful process indeed, to be made a good doctor out of by Bonaparte.

❖   ❖   ❖

On his way to see Diane Florian, Dr. Keroual realized that he had
no idea where the Expeditionary Army was being sent. Neither Dr.
Desgenettes nor General Bonaparte had mentioned it; in fact, they
had skirted the topic in what seemed to him now a very questionable
manner. He decided to see Desgenettes first.

He was kept waiting for minutes only. Dr. Desgenettes received
his tidings without much surprise. "I am delighted for you, Dr.
Keroual. And for Dr. Florian of course, who will be my colleague,
and I look forward to meeting him."

Keroual said, "I'm on my way to see his wife. I would like to be
able to tell her where he's being sent."

"That's a closely guarded secret, Dr. Keroual. I can tell you this
much. I don't believe Dr. Florian will be unhappy when he finds out.
But I rather imagine he won't be told about that until your ship
returns to Toulon harbor for new orders. Please convey to Madame
Florian my most sincere wishes for a happier future for them both."

Diane, when she opened the door to his knock, said, "I thought
you had forgotten us, Doctor."

He came inside, saying, "Far from it. I've been busy every minute.
And I didn't want to inflict my presence on you until I could bring
you good news." Enormous self-satisfaction radiating from him seriously impugned the modesty of this remark but Diane, who so
loved the ridiculous, did not even notice. "Where is Dr. Lasné?"
Keroual asked. "This concerns him too."

"He usually comes about this time. But please don't make me
wait!"

"Very well. I won't." His imitation of Bonaparte's clipped way of
speaking was entirely unconscious. "The *Bonnet Rouge* has been
commissioned to Guiana for the express purpose of picking up Dr.
Florian."

Diane looked at him wonderingly. "It isn't a joke. You wouldn't
joke with me about that. Would you?"

"Indeed I wouldn't. I told you, I have been very busy!" He swelled
importantly. The memory of those awful moments of being out of
his depth, the butt of laughter from famous and important persons,
was now only a nervous tic in the back of his memory.

"When is she sailing?"

"Right away. I'm to report aboard her within two weeks. It's costing me the rest of my leave, but I'm glad to sacrifice that."

Fidèle said in her harsh husky voice, "I'm glad for you, Madame Florian. Very glad. But what about Ange?"

"I think Robert should tell you himself. But Ange will be rescued if the doctor is," Diane said.

Dr. Keroual said, "It was a lucky thing that Dr. Lasné confided his plan to me, because that was brought up, how Dr. Florian would naturally hesitate about leaving his patients. If I hadn't had an answer ready, the whole thing might easily have gone the other way. General Bonaparte was looking as hard as he could for a loophole. He needs the ship, you see. He was definitely unwilling to part with her. But I simply refused to take no for an answer."

"General Bonaparte is sending a ship after Charlot?" Dr. Keroual nodded and beamed. "But why?" Diane asked. "He's not like that. He's hard and cruel."

"Perhaps you misjudge him, Madame."

"I know what he's capable of. I saw Pavia after he had finished with her."

So he had not been mistaken in thinking that word had particular significance to the General. Keroual started to ask about Pavia. Diane was saying, "I shall certainly look for some way of thanking him, but other than that I hope Charlot and I need never have anything to do with him again."

"I don't want to cause you distress, Madame. Especially now, when you should be enjoying your happiness. But I'm afraid your hope is a wasted one, since your husband has been appointed to the medical corps of the General's new Army. It's a long step down on the professional ladder for Dr. Florian. I realize that. But a man like him will make his way up quickly."

"Is there any way of getting Charlot out of this appointment?"

"I'm afraid not. He gave up a ship, you see. That was a lot for him to do. I'm disappointed, Madame. I thought you would be pleased with me."

Diane realized that she had robbed him of his triumph. She was ashamed. "That part of it came as a surprise, but after all, a medical doctor won't be having much to do with the Commander-in-Chief, will he? It was silly of me to be alarmed about it." And suddenly, realization that Charlot was really going to be rescued, that she was going to see him again, swept her. It had simply taken her this much time to comprehend the good news. She said in a soft voice, "Good fortune can stun you too. I didn't know that. Dr. Keroual, in the last four years, Charlot and I have been together exactly four months. I can't believe this is really happening. Can we go on your ship? Can Fidèle and I go? Please say we can!"

"We can certainly ask the captain, and I myself think it's a good idea. He'll be under Army orders from the moment he boards her, and he might not be able to get leave to come here. It will cost money. Do you have enough? As well as your passage, you may have to pay a rather large bribe."

"I have four thousand livres."

"That ought to be more than enough."

Robert Lasné knocked and came in. He's only a boy, Dr. Keroual thought, and among us, we have contrived to send him to the *guillotine sèche*. Some of his self-satisfaction drained away.

When Fidèle understood what it was that Robert planned to do, she ran to him and threw her arms around him. "Ah, Robert, I love you better than anyone else in the world."

"You know that's not true, Fidèle." The tenderness on his ugly, shy face as he looked down on her copper-colored head pressed against him, made Keroual realize that the boy was going to death-in-life without ever having known love. It seemed unbearably sad, even sinful. "It's Ange you love, and we all know it," Lasné said.

"But next to Ange I love you, Robert. I was hating all of you because all you can think of is the doctor. I don't like it when you forget about Ange. Why didn't you tell me, Robert? I was so unhappy, so full of hating."

"It seemed like silly boasting when we didn't know if Dr. Keroual could do anything. It's magnificent, Doctor," he said, holding Fidèle and looking over her head at Keroual. "You have done a great thing. I don't know why I didn't think of going to Bonaparte myself. He does things like this rather often."

"It wouldn't have occurred to me if Dr. Desgenettes had not mentioned it. And you deserve more credit than I do. You're the one who is giving up everything." It was a generous speech, though lacking in conviction. Dr. Keroual's heart was singing with joy.

I have given a good doctor to the world after all. A really good doctor, he thought.

II

Dr. Bénigne Keroual stood on the sloping muddy bank of the Kourour River and stared into its yellow waters. "The river Styx," he said softly. He did not feel there was anything exaggerated in this image. To bring back to life one of the condemned men of Sinnamarie was not unlike bringing a man back from death. But then his eye fell on Robert Lasné, standing a few steps away from him. The boy looked frightened. He was beginning to realize, perhaps for the first time, the true nature of the fate he had accepted for himself. It was the river Styx to Dr. Lasné too, and he was crossing it not to come back.

Feeling guilty about Lasné, Dr. Keroual watched an officer and four soldiers who were their escort preparing to slide a smallboat into the water. If I'm not too late! he thought. It had been more than a year; a long time for a man to live on Guiana.

Now don't expect him to share your joy right at first, Keroual told himself. It will take a little time before he can understand. Keep it to yourself about his wife, let that be a surprise later. You don't want to overwhelm him. But I never could keep a guard on my tongue, Keroual thought. I'll probably run at him shouting, telling him everything, I'm so pleased with myself. I don't believe I have overlooked a detail that will make his happiness complete.

The officer beckoned that the boat was ready. Lasné entered it first, then Keroual, clumsily because of the package he was holding, which he refused to release into anyone else's care. It contained clothes and shaving things for Florian. They began rowing across. The river Styx, the river Styx, the oars seemed to chant it rhythmically, and Keroual continued to avoid Lasné's eyes.

The boat nudged the opposite bank. A soldier climbed out, waded, and beached the boat so that the lieutenant and the doctors could leave it without wetting their feet. While the soldier secured the craft Keroual, too anxious to wait, started toward Sinnamarie. He did not realize that the officer was following him.

He became aware of an inappropriate sound, of someone singing in a voice astonishingly joyful and pure. He was a nearly naked man, who was carefully stripping pieces of bark from a stand of small trees. His head and chest were forests of hair, his skin was strange as a reptile's, and his bare feet were not quite human in shape and

187

color. He carolled joyfully, laying the pieces of bark aside in a neat row.

Ange's song was without words, a series of musical shouts of well-being. His outlaw heart had found peace at last. Ange would have been ashamed to realize that the break-up of authority and respectability in Charlot Florian was the source of his joy, but he was not introspective enough to know that. Vaguely he understood that his ways had been justified, that he was now the strongest man in Sinnamarie since he was the most successful hunter and because his body and spirit alike seemed indestructible. His kindnesses to Florian were unremitting and each one that he performed seemed to increase his strength, while Florian was driven lower. The doctor seldom left his hospital. He brooded there cloudily, occasionally rousing himself to tend one of the sick, who accepted his ministrations with an indifference matching his own. The only person who was real to Florian now was the one who was not there, his tempter, Pichegru. He held long silent conversations with Pichegru, but talked very little to anyone else. His descent had been rapid and complete, and Ange sang his wordless songs joyfully, justified in all that he had ever done.

The officer spoke to Keroual, startling him. "My orders are to shoot every one of them I see outside of Sinnamarie."

Horrified, Keroual began shouting warnings. His squealing voice echoed shockingly through the jungle. The singer wheeled and ran. They could hear him crashing through the underbrush somewhere to the left of them. The officer said, "You're in command of this party, sir. Why don't you just countermand the order?"

"Can I do that?"

"You're in command," he said patiently. His hard young face wore a faint smile.

"Don't shoot anyone," Keroual said. "For any reason. Unless they attack us." That was a possibility, he knew.

"Very well, sir," he said, saluting.

Robert Lasné came up, puffing. His eyes had a fixed look. The soldiers were behind him. Dr. Keroual began walking up the path toward Sinnamarie. He did not speak to Lasné; he did not know what to say to him.

Keroual had prepared himself for any kind of a reception from Dr. Florian. Though he had made up a scene of reunion which he enjoyed very much, in which the two doctors fell into each other's arms, he knew any such exchange would be most unlikely. Florian was more apt to faint, or simply stare at him disbelievingly.

But what actually happened was odder than anything Keroual had imagined. They found him in the only completed wooden building in Sinnamarie, an old building, falling into ruin. It was used for a hospital evidently, because men who looked ill were lying on rush beds that were foul with dirt and crawling with vermin.

Dr. Florian was sitting at a table, slumped forward, holding his head between his hands in a gesture as old as human despair. When he heard their footsteps, he looked up and Keroual felt a shock of pity and fear. The drawn face was a map of inward torment, the eyes clouded over. He showed no surprise at seeing them, though it must have been a year since fully dressed human figures had been seen on the Sinnamarie side of the river.

He looked past Dr. Keroual, obviously not recognizing him. He did not recognize Lasné either, but he knew the officer in charge of the escort party. He looked at the officer for what seemed a long time, his face working, and finally he said in a broken voice, "You should not have let me keep the medical box, Lieutenant. I traded it away to Indians after all."

Whatever he was talking about, the officer understood and answered, "A man isn't responsible for what he does here, Doctor."

The little piece of understanding seemed to hurt Florian in some new way, because he rose abruptly and staggered off as far away from them as he could get, where he leaned against the wall of the building and stared at his splayed, naked feet. Robert Lasné sobbed harshly. He was remembering his beloved Dr. Florian, whose mannerisms he used to copy in order to feel closer to him. He could not believe that this terrible figure was the same man. Florian wore nothing but a piece of tattered canvas roped to his waist by a drying vine. Keroual, approaching him gently, saw there was faded writing on the soiled canvas. Medical notes, it looked like, so he had tried at one time to be a good doctor.

Keroual put his hand on Florian's shoulder, and was shocked by a sensation transferred to his palm from the thick, roughened skin of the other man's body. "Don't you remember me, Doctor? I am Dr. Keroual. I have come to save you."

He did not even look around. "Save me." He repeated it wonderingly. "How can anyone do that?" The gaunt, roughened shoulder shook from the force of inward grief. "I belong here now."

Dr. Keroual said to the officer, "Please have your men build a fire and heat water. I won't believe it. It is not too late." But he very much feared that it was.

❖ ❖ ❖

The good fortune of finding Florian almost alone in the village except for sick men too defenseless even to fight off the vermin that were devouring them alive, made Keroual hopeful that they could get in and out of Sinnamarie without being seen by the others who, no doubt, would be hunting in the jungle. The idea that they might, in their desperation, turn on the rescue party and massacre them had grown stronger now that he had seen Sinnamarie with his own eyes. For truly, it was an incredible place, and though he had been so fond of saying, "I know what Guiana is like!" he saw now that he had not known, he had not even guessed the extent of its horrors.

He went after Robert Lasné, who was wandering in and out of the ruins of grass huts, walking with difficulty in the slick, offal-soiled mud. "I think it would be a piece of wisdom for us to leave without being seen," Keroual said to him. "After a year of living like this, it's impossible to predict what they might do when they find us here."

"I guess it's goodbye, then." He held out his hand.

Dr. Keroual said, "You may as well come back with us, Robert. There's no point in your throwing yourself away here. He understands now that he's being taken out, but he hasn't even mentioned them. That was the whole idea behind the sacrifice of yourself, after all, but he doesn't care one way or the other."

Lasné's voice was wretched. "I can't believe it of him."

"Don't blame him too much. He has endured what we can't even guess at."

"I'm not blaming him," Lasné said. "It's only that I can't bear seeing him like this. There is nothing about him that reminds me of what he was."

"But I thought there was considerable improvement after we shaved and dressed him."

"He acts more like a man, yes, but he doesn't in the least act like Dr. Florian."

"That will pass," Keroual said, "and I'm glad that the necessity for leaving you here does not exist, because I can't tell you how guilty I've been feeling about that since we decided it."

"But what about Ange?"

"You don't really want to throw your life away for the street singer, do you?"

"But I promised Fidèle."

"My dear boy. You see now what Sinnamarie is like. No promise made in ignorance deserves to bind you now. I wouldn't dream of permitting it." Lasné's ugly face blazed with relief. "You're a brave young man," Keroual said, patting his arm.

The lieutenant, too, had been wandering around the village. They met him looking over the wreck of some partly completed wooden buildings. "Odd," he said. "They started a number of projects to make life more bearable. At one time, they began a system of drainage ditches. Of course they had nothing to dig with but pieces of wood, but if they were bold enough to start, what kept them from finishing? And they started a palisade, but they didn't finish that either. And now these. It certainly makes you wonder."

Keroual said, "I think it would be a good idea if we got out of here before they return and find us."

"You're in command, sir. But I strongly advise that we stay here for tonight. It's nearly nightfall, not a very good time to start out. There wouldn't be any light at all when we reached the river. Also, if you start now, we'll have to rig up some kind of litter for the doctor. He's exhausted, he couldn't walk farther than a kilometer or two."

"I'm rather afraid of the others," Keroual confessed.

"You needn't be, sir. We're armed, and judging from the ones I've seen so far, their spirits are broken."

"I want very much not to have to see them. But we'll stay if you think that's wise."

"I do indeed, sir."

The hunters began straggling in shortly after that. Keroual was appalled by them. Their awful bodies were capable of movement and speech, yet were oddly unoccupied. All of them were nude or nearly so. They seemed totally indifferent to the idea that their doctor was leaving them. Though they crowded around Florian, it was the miracle of his clean-shaven, fully clothed appearance that drew them. They were equally interested in Keroual and Lasné and the soldiers, who stood quietly and submitted to being touched by their shy, wondering hands. The men of Sinnamarie were like a herd of gentle beasts into whose grazing pasture something curious had wandered.

"The ones who came here first were Terrorists," the lieutenant said, "but these were all professional men." He was speaking before them as though they were not there, or incapable of understanding him. "Not criminals at all. So they went this way when the breaking point happened, instead of brawling amongst themselves, as you might expect. Sad, isn't it? Those who sent them here have a lot to answer for."

Their little flurry of interest subsided quickly. The day's hunting had exhausted them; they wanted to eat what they had brought back, and then sleep. Many were emptyhanded. What fruits and berries they had found they had eaten on the spot. Others more fortunate had brought meat: a dead monkey already stinking in the awful heat, a lizard, a parrot, and fuel enough for small fires. The lieutenant was much interested in their method for keeping fires alive throughout the day. They packed seashells tightly with some kind of fungus that would smoulder for hours. The seashells, when placed under a little fuel, would ignite after much blowing.

The rescue party withdrew into the wooden building, and apparently Sinnamarie forgot about them as soon as they were out of sight. Inside it, few words were exchanged. Keroual, Lasné, the lieutenant and his soldiers, bore an immense burden of guilt. To see such misery, but then to walk away, saving one man only out of some three hundred who were left, was like spitting in the face of the Christ. But their authority stopped with the salvage of Florian.

Dr. Florian had nothing to say. He roused himself occasionally and went among the sick men, whom he tended with dreamy motions. The other doctors, Keroual and Lasné, did not try to assist him because the medicaments he was using were unknown to them, nor did they have much idea what the various sicknesses might be.

"How do you get food for yourself and the men in the hospital?" the lieutenant asked Florian.

"Ange brings it. He'll come soon."

Keroual and Lasné exchanged glances. Lasné had said earlier, "I hope I don't have to see Ange Pitou face to face. Not to recognize him, anyway."

He came shortly afterwards, his arms filled with provisions. Keroual recognized the naked singer he had startled away in the jungle. "We are friends," he said quickly. "We mean you no harm." Ange dropped the provisions on the soiled floor and stood lightly on the balls of his feet, a look of almost crazy suspicion stamping his swarthy face. Then he saw Florian in his fine clothes. Astonishment wiped out every other expression.

Florian knelt by the provisions and began sorting them. "Nothing to cook today. That's good. I'm so tired."

"But you've eaten already, Doctor, you and your patients," Keroual reminded him.

His face cleared. "That's so, isn't it. I had forgotten. There was bread, Ange."

Ange said in an ugly voice, "What the devil is going on here?"

"Gently, there," the lieutenant said, touching his sword. He had spoken sharply, but on his face there was nothing but pity.

"Who are you? What are you here for?"

He was not like the others. He was still a man. Keroual said placatingly, "We'll be gone by morning."

"What's he dressed up like that for?"

"We're taking him away with us," Keroual said.

"Ah." It was hard to say exactly what he was thinking, but Keroual had an idea he was not pleased.

He chose from among the provisions, then went out through the doorless opening. Keroual rather imagined he would not be back. Florian went to sleep quickly, pillowing his head in his arms at the table. The lieutenant, scratching himself briskly, said, "I'm damned if I'm going to lie down in here. I'm beginning to wish we'd gone when you wanted to, Doctor."

"We'll get an early start," Keroual said.

After a while, Ange came back. He moved silently past the sleeping patients, to where Keroual was trying to imitate Florian by sleeping in a chair. But none of the rescue party had found sleep yet. Ange hunkered down beside Keroual's chair. "Are you his brother or something?" he said in a hard voice.

"I am Dr. Keroual."

"Oh. A doctor."

"He must have told you about me." Ange shook his head. "That surprises me," Keroual said. "You see, I promised him on the crossing that I would do this. Really, didn't he tell you?" Keroual was disappointed. The singer's not-knowing made it seem that Florian had not put much stock in Keroual's promises to him. Again, the tubby ship's doctor wondered if Florian had seen him drunk that day the condemned were disembarked, if that was a partial explanation for what had happened.

"Were you the doctor on the *Bonnet Rouge?*" Keroual nodded. "I've seen you before, then. At Rochefort."

That old shame came back. "I was drunk," he said, looking down. "I didn't know what I was doing."

The naked man was thinking hard. He said, "Did Rochefort have anything to do with your deciding to save Charlot?"

"Yes indeed. It had everything to do with it."

"You doctors are a race apart. Aren't you?"

"I don't know. It would be wrong if we were."

What kept this man whole? he asked himself. I would have expected Dr. Florian to outlast the street singer, he thought. I wonder why it worked out like this? He acknowledged to a bitter feeling of having been robbed. I kept my part of the bargain, he thought. But there had been that day he had not, like a shadow athwart his sacrifice.

Ange said, "Charlot is going to be rescued because of the old men I held up in the cart and let sleep. You were too drunk to see how old and sick they were, so it is Charlot who is going to be rescued. Well, I'm glad, I suppose. It's strange, though."

And it is stranger yet, Keroual thought, how you were to have been rescued too, had not Florian become so changed that he cannot care about what happens to the men here. He was aware of glancing briefly into some dark twisted pattern of human affairs beyond his understanding. "I'm afraid the doctor will be much missed in your little community."

"Don't worry about it. There are no indispensable men in Sinnamarie. We are all dying, but it takes time."

Keroual said recklessly, "Someday, someone will come here with the same good news for all of you."

"No."

"Try to believe it, I'm sure it's true. Barras can't last."

"None of them last, but they keep getting worse."

"That has to stop somewhere," he said helplessly.

"Where is Charlot going? Or should I ask?"

"I don't know either. He has been attached to the medical corps of the Expeditionary Army, which probably has sailed by now from Toulon, and we won't know where it went until we get there. Officially it's being said this is an attack on the British, but on the streets they're saying——" He broke off, at first aware of being indiscreet, and then embarrassed to realize that the receiver of his opinions was as though dead.

"Yes. Tell me what they're saying on the streets. That's the kind of politics I understand."

"They say Barras has grown jealous of Bonaparte, and afraid of him, that he's sending him to some far place to be rid of him."

"Bonaparte. I thought he was in Italy."

"He won all his battles and made peace. We're at peace with everyone but England."

"And Charlot is going to serve under Bonaparte."

"Yes."

Ange Pitou laughed. It was an ugly, mocking sound, and full of hatred. Keroual shivered. "I guess I don't envy him so much after all," the singer said. He stood up.

"Why did you laugh like that?" Keroual was angry.

"Men of affairs, and generals in particular, are Charlot's Nemesis, that's all."

"Why do you say so?"

"I have an idea that Sinnamarie without Pichegru might be an improvement over the unknown with Bonaparte." He went out, stepping lightly, an agile, naked figure still chuckling with hateful mockery.

*   *   *

"Tell your Dr. Florian that I will expect much from him," Bonaparte had said. But how could the poor broken creature endure the demands and disciplines that flinty young man would exact? I think it would have been better for everyone if I had stayed drunk that whole year, Keroual thought.

But the next morning, his worries about Dr. Florian's future were resolved as easily as if Heaven itself had intervened. On their way to the Kourour, Keroual noticed the stand of small trees where he had first seen the naked singer. He mentioned it idly. "Why tree bark? You haven't been reduced to eating tree bark, surely?"

"It's cinchona bark," Florian said.

"No!"

"It's why so many of us stayed alive."

Since more than a half of their number had died that first year, the calm statement should have been horrible. But Keroual was too excited over the presence of cinchona to react to it. "But we must take it with us! Why, there's a fortune there. Several fortunes."

"No," Florian said sharply. "It's ours. It's all we have."

Robert Lasné, who had been listening to them, brightened. That had sounded like the old Florian. Keroual said humbly, "You are quite right. I'm glad you reminded me. There's such a hunt on for cinchona, I would have forgotten myself and taken it all." He turned to the lieutenant, saying, "Tell your men to help me strip one or two of these trees. The bark is a medicine of remarkable properties."

When two of the trees had been stripped, Keroual hesitated

briefly, then nodded for them to continue the work. Lasné looked to Florian for words of protest, but after that one outburst the doctor from Sinnamarie seemed to be indifferent as to how much was taken. So Lasné appealed to Keroual himself. "It's cruel to rob them of the one thing they do have."

"But there's sure to be more than one stand. They can find another, and probably they already have."

"It isn't right, just the same," Lasné said unhappily.

"Robert, I know what I'm doing, and it's for his sake. I believe I have earned a share of it for myself, but it's really for him that I'm doing this. If he can go to his new duties with a large supply of cinchona, don't you see, he will have performed an important service from the beginning. In time, his ability to command respect on his own merits will return to him. I'm sure of that. But in the meantime, he will have presented his Army superiors with a gift of great value. They will be grateful, it will make them more patient with him. And what a mercy that is, because while I am greatly encouraged about him, I must confess that he is strange."

A stunted tree on the fringe of the stand was left for the men in Sinnamarie.

III

HE *is* improving. He improves every minute, Dr. Keroual told himself. The four days of their journey from the Kourour to Cayenne had worked a remarkable change. Florian noticed things, and commented on them. He listened to the words of others, only occasionally his attention seeming to wander. He walked straighter, and he seemed to fit better in his clothes.

But there were puzzling lapses. For instance, he had not once mentioned his wife. Keroual, afraid now that Diane's presence aboard the ship was a mistake, had not mentioned her either. The meeting would make an emotional demand on him for which he did not seem ready. Certainly Diane ought to have some warning that there were changes. Keroual began plotting how to keep Florian in Cayenne long enough for Robert to go aboard the ship and talk to her.

He told Robert, "Make her understand how important the cinchona is, how it will pave the way for them. She's frightened about the future. Tell her that's going to be all right. And then, as gently as you can, get her to understand that she mustn't expect too much just at first. Though he *is* improving, Robert, every minute."

To Florian, Keroual said, "It is simple courtesy to present ourselves to the Governor before we leave for our ship. Do you have any objection, Doctor?"

An odd expression crossed Florian's face. "No," he said. He asked himself, Will the Governor remember how he advised us to forget that we were men? Will he see that I have followed his advice? Perhaps he will tell Dr. Keroual, "This is a shell you have brought back. There is nothing inside. You had better leave him in the only place on earth where he can belong." If the Governor did say it, Florian would admit that it was true. There was no stir in his blood at all, no joy, no hope for the future. Keroual seemed as important as one of the chattering monkeys. The soldiers of the escort were from another race. He was already homesick for Sinnamarie, where men like himself were, the walking zombies alert to nothing but food and weather. Since seeing Keroual and Lasné, he had tried the doors of his mind. They were all locked. All the complex knowledge carefully stored away was out of his reach. I can't practice as a doctor, not even an Army doctor, Florian thought. I can give only cinchona and *Jateorhica palmata* and ashes of seaweed, the things we found on Guiana. My other knowledge is gone. I don't remember what surgical instruments look like, I have no idea how to go about doing an operation.

The Governor, when Florian saw him, did not look like a living being; he looked like a suit of clothes, elegant and inhuman. Humans sweat, go hungry, fall ill; they slap continuously at the torment of mosquitoes and vermin. The Governor did none of these things. Florian stood stiffly, his arms hanging, and looked at the Governor while Keroual pattered on.

The Governor was feeling nearly as strange as Florian. I helped do that to a fine man, he was thinking. This man is so excellent that General Bonaparte wanted him enough to send thousands of miles for him, but I ordered him away in gyves to die in the jungle. He did not die. He is here to reproach me. He looks so stern. What sufferings—! The Governor felt sudden kinship with another governor whose rôle in history he had not understood before today, Pilate of Judea.

"I am glad to see you safe and whole, Dr. Florian," the Governor said.

Safe—there is no safety in a world where Sinnamarie is permitted to exist. Whole—there is no wholeness when one has lived through it. "Thank you," Dr. Florian said, "that is gracious." Who was speaking? A familiar voice was speaking out of his mouth, in courteous words whose shapes and sounds he had forgotten. It was Pichegru who spoke, he decided.

The Governor relaxed slightly. "It is generous of you not to hold a grudge against me for my part in what was done to you. Truly, I could not help what I did, but no one deplores Sinnamarie more than I do."

The voice of Pichegru speaking for Florian answered smoothly. "I bear no grudge against anyone. I am glad to be recalled to the world and I intend to serve faithfully and well in it."

"That is excellent, that is what I would expect from a man of your stamp. If it should ever happen that you were in private conversation with General Bonaparte, I would appreciate it if you would mention my name to him. And tell him——" But Florian lost the rest. Though he gave every appearance of listening, he was not hearing anything beyond the rise and fall of the mellifluous voice.

How well it is going! Dr. Keroual thought. Really, he handles himself very well. And yet there were those puzzling lapses. His absence of curiosity about his wife was the most significant, but there were others. He had never asked about the mechanics of his rescue, though Keroual had looked forward to telling it. He had not asked about national affairs. So much had happened since Fructidor: the peace of Campo Formio, and the congress at Rastadt that had given France peace at last with all of her enemies except England. He had not even asked the simple, though unanswerable, question as to where he was being sent.

When the audience with the Governor was over, Keroual led Florian through the hallway of mirrors. At first the doctor from Sinnamarie did not notice his reflection, but when he did he began to walk with slow steps, looking into the mirrors and frowning. Keroual was careful not to speak.

"Is that what I look like now?" Florian said finally.

"Impressive, don't you think?"

"I—don't know."

"Your appearance inspires confidence. The white patches on your temples seem to add years and authority."

Florian remained looking at himself, the little frown still between his eyes. "Yes," he said finally, "I look very impressive. Nature is odd." He was thinking of mutations of foliage and fur that protect those jungle beings who cannot protect themselves in other ways. Nature had moved swiftly to camouflage the most helpless of her children, this doctor who had forgotten everything he knew, and moreover, did not care. He looked handsome and self-assured, even wise, and it was no wonder the Governor had not seen through him, to the phantom of Pichegru who spoke for Florian out of a handsome mask.

*   *   *

"He's in Cayenne with Dr. Keroual," Robert Lasné said to Diane. "He hasn't been told that you're here. I suppose that sounds odd to you, but so much coming so quickly, Dr. Keroual thought that it was best. But he's all right. He's gaining every moment. Don't look like that, Madame! I wouldn't lie to you."

"But isn't he anxious to see me?"

"He doesn't know you're here," Lasné repeated.

"What did you say when he asked about me?"

"It will sound odd to you, I'm afraid. He hasn't asked."

"That hurts me," Diane said, after a moment.

"You don't understand," he said helplessly.

"Is Ange with Dr. Keroual too?"

"I couldn't do it, Madame. That place is horrible."

"You mean Ange is still there."

"Will you tell her? I can't. Where is she?"

"Asleep in the cabin. The poor child has been too excited to sleep at night. Yes, I'll tell her. Don't reproach yourself, Robert. It was too much to sacrifice, I always did think so. But what did Charlot say about leaving them without medical attention?"

"He didn't say anything, so we didn't bring it up either."

"I think you are telling me that he's much changed."

"I have good news," he said, "we found a stand of cinchona. We brought most of it out."

The doctor's wife did not have to be told how important the find was. "Yes, that is good news," she said slowly.

"Dr. Keroual said to tell you not to worry any more about his future. He owns a fortune in cinchona. His superiors in the Army will be grateful at having such a supply available."

But you're talking of places and things, Diane thought. Her eyes begged him for news of a different kind. Lasné, driven to it by affection for her and devotion to the man Florian had been, said an unbelievable thing.

"He's beaten down, and terribly tired, and he looks much older. I think he must have been sick at one time, and never completely recovered. Please don't turn against him, Madame Florian."

"Turn against him! What are you saying? What kind of woman do you think I am?"

"I didn't mean anything," Lasné said, horribly embarrassed. He turned away, his face working. "I was trying to help. I don't want to talk any more."

"All right, Robert," she consented. She was deeply hurt.

She entered Dr. Keroual's cabin which had been turned over for hers and Fidèle's use. The red-haired girl lay in warm sleep, a little happy smile curling her pale mouth. Diane did not waken her. Fidèle needed the sleep and Diane was glad to put off the hard task of telling her.

From where she sat, she could see herself dimly, a pale waiting figure. So much waiting in our lives, she thought. The dress she was wearing had been chosen with an eye to pleasing Charlot. It was simple, of white muslin banded with silver that clarified the light tones of her hair. But when she leaned nearer to her reflection, she could see how careworn she looked. Robert had mentioned Charlot looking older, and I do myself, Diane thought. She rubbed the little lines around her eyes and mouth. But no soft fingertip would smooth those away, they were the marks of endless nights. He can't have changed, she thought, not Charlot. The men are letting themselves be deceived by fancies. But Lasné's return was no fancy, and Diane knew that the real Charlot Florian would never have consented to leaving men who were dependent on him. Robert had said that had not been mentioned even. . . . Fidèle stirred. Her eyes came open gently. She saw Diane, and sat up. "Is there news?"

The kind thing was to say it quickly. "They are back, but Ange is not with them."

"You mean Ange is dead!"

"It's not that bad, Fidèle. He's alive, but he didn't come out with the others." Diane took a deep breath, and said, "Fidèle, you know that was a lot to ask of Robert. He's young, he has his whole life ahead. When it came to staying, he didn't want to, that's all. I'm sorry we deceived you with false hopes. Robert was sincere when he offered, you know he was, but he couldn't do it after all."

"The doctor got out, though," Fidèle said.

"Yes," Diane admitted.

The red-haired girl swung off the bunk. "Well, this is where we part company, Madame Florian," she remarked. She went to the mirror and began dressing her hair loosely. "That's always the way, isn't it? Everything can be made to work out for the important people of the world. It's the little people who get hurt. And somehow I knew it was going to turn out this way. Even while I was going around feeling happy and telling myself I'd see Ange soon, all the time I really knew that the doctor would get out but Ange wouldn't."

Diane said in a moved voice, "I know how hurt and disappointed you must feel. But I don't think you should blame Robert."

"I'm not blaming him. I can't help but wonder why Dr. Keroual couldn't have asked General Bonaparte about both of them. He was willing to send a whole big ship to get one man, but no one even asked him if there wasn't room on it for two." She swung away from the mirror and began throwing a number of small personal objects onto a scarf. "You've been good to me," she said. "But I had to learn sometime that no one was going to watch out for Ange and me except ourselves. So that's what I'm going to be doing from now on." She knotted the scarf skillfully and stood in front of Diane, swinging it, and said, "Well, goodbye, Madame Florian. Maybe we'll meet again someday, but I guess we won't."

Diane said blankly, "Are you going somewhere?"

"You didn't think I'd sail into Cayenne harbor and out again, did you? I'm as close to Ange now as you can help me get, so I'm dropping off here."

"Fidèle, my dear, you can't take care of yourself in this terrible place."

"I don't know what I can do. You never know until you try, do you? It was different for you, you didn't have to save your man by yourself. You had Dr. Keroual, but Ange has no one but me. Goodbye, Madame Florian." She walked out.

Diane paused only long enough to divide evenly what money she had left, then she followed Fidèle. Her emotions were mixed. Her responsibility seemed to be to stop the street girl, and yet this was what Fidèle wanted to do, and when Diane put herself in Fidèle's place, she realized it would be unendurable to have come so close to Charlot in physical distance but then let others drag her away again, thousands of miles away. Had it happened like that, she would want to do the same thing. Diane found herself remembering that long-ago incident when Florian, to protect Pinel and the inmates of the Bicêrte, had tricked Ange into losing his hold on the Paris crowds. From that moment the singer had been a doomed man. And Ange had not been rescued although a ship had been sent. Something had gone very wrong.

Fidèle and the captain were talking on his bridge. Diane climbed there, the assignats fluttering in her hand. The captain saw her, and Diane heard him say, "I'll put it up to Madame Florian as to whether you get a boat or not. You came along as her companion, after all. She paid your passage." So even in this desperate venture, Fidèle was being forced into dependence on the good will of the Florians. The girl's green eyes darkened with anger.

"Please give her the boat, Captain," Diane said. "I would have had to do the same thing, in her place." She thrust the money into Fidèle's hand. "Good luck. I wish with all my heart that things had worked out differently."

Diane remained on the bridge to watch the departure. There was something hopelessly gallant about the little vivid figure in the prow of the rowboat, on her way to adventures so bizarre that they could not even be guessed at. Tears stung Diane's eyes. Theirs had been a strange companionship, and now it was ended strangely. Goodbye, Fidèle, good luck, God keep you, she said silently.

❧　　　❧　　　❧

She heard hails from the ship and fainter, echoing hails off the dark water. He was coming! He was nearly here! She sped through the star-studded twilight, to the door of the cabin which she wrenched open to enter. She managed the lamp with shaking fingers. No one must witness this meeting. She stood in the center of the floor, watching the closed door of the cabin. It seemed to her she waited a long time. She was trembling.

The cabin door opened at last, slowly, as though the man who was trying it had forgotten how to perform the commonplace action. It swung back, and she saw a man standing there who looked remote and sad, rather as she had always imagined the King might have looked on the day they told him he must die on the guillotine. The face was terribly self-contained.

Then he saw her, and his face began to alter, his emotions following each other too quickly to be read by her. She held out her arms. He made a hoarse noise in his throat, and plunged toward her, onto his knees. She felt the weight and heat of his head against her thighs. She dropped her hands, fondling him, willingly exploring the scaly thickness of skin that did not feel quite human. "It's all right, Charlot. We're together, and we'll never be separated again."

He repeated it wonderingly. "I'll fight the whole world. We'll never be separated again."

So keen of edge was his happiness, it hurt him. The wrench was as extreme as dying, it was dying reversed. It was being hauled back to life in seconds, although the state of death-in-life had become accepted and familiar over months. His happiness was a kind of anguish, as the empty inner places filled suddenly with strength and desire and need.

IV

DIANE FLORIAN wakened early that morning, with a sense of excitement. The ship would enter Toulon harbor sometime today. Then they would learn at last where it was they were being sent. Charlot was deeply asleep at her side. She watched his sleeping face. It was relaxed and untroubled. Perhaps you know best, my dear, she thought again. Certainly it seemed to be working out; yet their pretense that the months at Sinnamarie had never happened meant that they were living a lie.

The two months' voyage had been perfect, the weather bright and calm, the sea as glassily quiet as an inland pond. The reunited couple had been together almost every moment; in fact, he became restless if she was out of his sight, as though he believed that should he look away ever so briefly she might disappear like a creature of wind. But this dependence on her seemed to be the only lasting change Guiana had made in him. That and his fierce secrecy about everything that had happened there.

Once she had begged him for his confidence. Holding her wrists, looking deeply into her face, his own thin and intense, he had answered, "I'm fighting this the only way I know how, simply by saying that it never happened. Don't make me admit that it happened. Please don't." Deeply moved, she had promised, yet it worried her. He was a reserved man but he had never been secretive before, not toward her at least.

Keroual and Lasné had learned not to mention anything about that to him. How they felt about it, she did not know, because out of loyalty to him, she could not bring herself to discussing him with the others. I'll miss Robert, she thought, what a comfort he has been. But it was time for him to take up his interrupted studies. He had sacrificed half a year, and he had been very useful. Was there ever a sight so odd as that of watching Robert Lasné teach medicine to Charlot Florian?

Four hours a day, those two sat over battered and obsolete books of Keroual's, and Robert lectured to Charlot in his dull, stumbling way. Charlot would listen carefully, faintly puzzled, until something was said that jarred his memory. Then his thin face would come alive. He would break in on Robert and finish the lecture himself in his old way, brilliant, concise, definite: the exact word, the well-turned phrase. Robert Lasné was simply giving back what Charlot had given him so many years, so many events, ago. And Diane, watching and listening as she had in those far-off days, would applaud them both silently in her heart.

She was propped on an elbow, and looking into his sleeping face. He did not look much different than he always had, except for the white patches on his temples. Luster had returned to his hair that had been dry and brittle; his skin was almost smooth again; the skeletal emaciation was nearly gone. God bless you, Dr. Keroual, she thought, you have earned your drinking bout you keep saying you're going to have when we get to Toulon. For your own sake I hope you don't, but you deserve to stay drunk the rest of your life if you want to. So much cruelty in our world, she thought, but so much kindness too. Dr. Keroual, Robert, even the captain, so kind. I wish this weren't ending, I wish it would never end, she thought.

Suddenly Charlot's sleeping presence was not enough. She needed the reassurance of his glance, of words exchanged. She touched him, murmuring his name. His eyes came open promptly. He smiled, and laid his hand against her cheek. "Lovely, lovely," he whispered. Then, in firmer tones, "But why are you awake so early?"

"It isn't early now, and it's docking day. Aren't you excited? Will we be allowed to go ashore, do you think?"

"I doubt that I will, but we'll see. Do you want to go anyway?"

"You know I don't."

"Good. I don't want to let you out of my sight. How did I ever bring myself to sending you away from me?"

By now she was accustomed to his habit of speaking in a way that wiped out everything between that time and now, and she fell in with it easily. "That boy in the garrison asked me the same thing."

"He made a deep impression on you. Shall I become jealous?"

"But he's dead, Charlot."

"I used to wonder if Conte wouldn't fall in love with you while you were there."

"He's dead too," Diane said, "let's talk about today."

"So now we find out what's going to happen to us, eh? This is the first time I've wondered much about where we are going. Do you have a particular choice?"

"Greece," she said promptly, knowing it would please him.

"That would be wonderful. Wouldn't it? But more probably it will be some savage place like Tripoli or Morocco, and I shall be frightened every minute that some giant native is carrying you off. I ought to insist that you stay in France, I suppose."

"Now don't start that again," Diane said sharply.

"Don't worry. I won't. I need you more than you need me." Before she could speak, denying it, he rose and began dressing. "I'm hungry again. I can't seem to get enough to eat," he said. Actually, he ate less than she did, but he needed to eat frequently. A dozen small signs like that reminded her daily of the fact of his exile, which he so determinedly maintained had never been. She began to dress too.

The docking was shortly before noon. As Florian had expected, shore leave was not offered to him. Some sailors whose turn it was for leave were rowed over, and Dr. Keroual had a place in the captain's gig. A look of high purpose decorated Keroual's round, froggish face; he was thinking on the subject of his first drink in nearly two years. When he mentioned it, "I'm keeping a different kind of ship these days, Dr. Keroual," the captain said darkly. "Don't forget that."

"But surely you wouldn't begrudge me my little glass?"

"You can get as drunk as you please in port, but if you try to bring anything aboard my ship I'll throw it over the side, and likely I'll put you in after it."

He was indeed keeping a different kind of ship. The élan of serving under Bonaparte, if it had not gone to his head certainly had gone to his heart. The *Bonnet Rouge* was as tidy a ship as could be seen in the teeming harbor.

Robert Lasné stayed behind with the Florians. More than likely, the orders waiting would be for immediate departure. He was not going to surrender his last hours with his friends for the lonely joys of sightseeing in Toulon. The trio remained on deck in the brilliant spring sunshine, watching the harbor activities and straining their eyes toward shore. When they talked, it was of Robert's future; their own was too shrouded in mystery to make speculation about that profitable.

❋   ❋   ❋

The captain of the *Bonnet Rouge* was not by nature a sympathetic man, but the married pair aboard his ship had touched him. It seemed a sad thing to part them. He felt very sorry about it when he heard. Meanwhile there were practical things to be done. Casks of drinking water, and new flour and fresh cured meats to be ordered and sent out; a cook to replace the one he had fired this morning for being the kind who creates succulent meals for the captain's table but turns out inedible messes for the men. The sailors of the *Bonnet Rouge* were going to get the best from now on.

The faces of the pair continued to intrude on his thoughts. He remembered the stark fleshless man who had come aboard his ship that night at Cayenne. It was hard to believe that Florian now was the same person. A good woman's love, the captain thought sentimentally. The good food of the dismissed cook had had something to do with it but food, which can pad bones harshly protruding and fill out cheeks gaunt and dark under their high-planed cheekbones, cannot bring light back into hooded eyes, or smiles to a mouth as grim as a healing scar. The simplicity and strength of Florian's happiness now was as clear as the sun rising, and no cook had done that for the man who had come aboard looking like a symbol of what the dreaded *guillotine sèche* can do to one bold enough to survive it. Well, she can come along as a passenger again if she wants to, the captain thought, that will give them another few weeks. I won't charge her any fare either, he decided; probably she couldn't pay, after that fistful she gave to the little red-haired spitfire who deserted her in Cayenne. His generosity having lessened his concern, he went briskly about the business of supplying his ship.

For dinner, he went to one of the waterfront places frequented by men of his trade. Keroual was there, drinking but not drunk yet. The captain joined him and signaled for drinks for them both. Keroual began a remarkably graphic description of what he was feeling. The captain listened tolerantly. As he had said, it was all right with him, as long as Keroual's drinking stopped when they lifted anchor.

The captain interrupted. "What made you stop, anyway? I never told you to. I didn't care, then." Keroual began to explain. The captain interrupted again. "But you told me you'd never seen Florian until that time you were sick and you sent for him." Keroual finished his explanation, the captain's wonder growing.

"You doctors are a race apart," he said finally.

Keroual's startled movement knocked over his glass. He looked at its contents vanishing into the rough surface of the table, and finally asked, "Why do you say that?"

"I wouldn't do it for another captain, that's all. Providing I liked drink as much as you do, which I don't."

Keroual began drawing with a forefinger into the moisture of the spilled drink. "One of them at Sinnamarie said the same thing. The same words, I think."

"Pretty obvious words," the captain said, yawning. "Considering." Keroual continued to draw in the moisture. "Don't you want another drink?" the captain said. He ordered drinks and said, "You'd better be the one to tell him. I don't want to."

Keroual was saying, "But it isn't right if we are. I think those were my words too, but it *isn't* right. Doctors are supposed to be important to their patients. Not to each other."

The captain said, "Yes? Is that so? What is there around here to eat?"

"Have you ever been sick?" Keroual said. "Not while I've known you, anyway."

"And let you around me?" he said with heavy jocularity. "Certainly not. Better to stay healthy. Not that you haven't been fine lately."

"There's a bond between the sick man and his physician," Keroual said. "For the time the sickness lasts, the pair ought to be as close as brothers. But if you've never been sick, you don't know what I mean."

"No. I've never been that sick," he said.

"A really good doctor can make a sick man believe in his right to live. He can be made unafraid of his disease, because he knows it is understood by the other and can be mastered by him. He feels the doctor will fight for him to the limit of his knowledge and will, and they are almost limitless. But should it happen that he's maimed or killed instead, his doctor's grief will be earnest and lasting. A really good doctor makes his patients feel like that."

In spite of himself, the captain was impressed. "If you are like that, I haven't known you before," he commented.

"I am not like that. I am not a very good doctor. But Dr. Florian is a good doctor. From now on, every grateful patient of Dr. Florian's will owe something to Bénigne Keroual too. He will not know that, but it is true." His new drink came and he lifted it, saluting the captain.

"They're going to be separated after all. It doesn't seem right somehow, the way they feel about each other, but that's the way it is."

"Charlot and Diane—separated?"

"General orders, no women. I'll give her free passage to Alexandria, where he's to report himself. That's three weeks, a month at the most."

Keroual started to drink from his glass but then set it down, and began making circles with its base on the spilled drink. "General orders, you say. No way out, then. Do you know, I had stopped worrying about him. But now I wonder. Alexandria, did you say?"

"He'll be all right," the captain said.

"Right from the beginning, she was frightened. She asked me if there wasn't some way of getting him out of the appointment. I was disappointed in her. I had done something rather remarkable, after all, but instead of being pleased she was frightened. Women show an odd, other sense at times. There's a word, prescience."

"I never heard it," the captain said, "what does it mean?"

"It means knowing what others don't, or knowing what will happen before it does happen."

"Aren't you going to drink that? I want you back on board at midnight."

Keroual looked at the full glass sharply. For a moment his eyes were shiny with desire. But then he pushed it away from him. "I'll go back with you," he said. "Do you know that until now they had been together exactly four months out of the past four years? Why is fate so determined to keep them apart, I wonder? Did you say you were eating here? I'll eat something too and go back with you. I'm worried about them."

✳   ✤   ✤

It was after sundown when the gig returned. Florian and Diane were leaning over the rail, and when the little boat was in hailing distance Florian shouted, "Where?"

Keroual, cupping his hands, called back, "Egypt!" But his squealing voice did not carry. The captain condescended to trumpet it after him.

Egypt! He was startled, then gratified. The most ancient civilization of them all, the land that had seen more great history than any other. "Ah, Diane, we are fortunate!" he said. Her imagination was stirred too. Egypt was better than Greece even.

He was thinking that he would see the medical schools of Alexandria and Cairo, where Hippocratic medicine had been preserved then given back when, at last, the western world tired of superstition and incantation and demanded real physicians again. If there was any place on earth where Charlot Florian could recover his lost areas of knowledge and his passionate love of his art, that place was Egypt. He felt the compulsion to kneel and thank God, but he did not believe in God. He clung to the rail, his dark sensitive face dreaming.

✻   ✻   ✻

Keroual asked Florian and Diane to come into the cabin with him. His flustered manner warned them something was wrong. He knew no way to tell it except to blurt it out brutally. "She isn't going to be allowed to land. She'll have to return with the ship."

Dr. Florian was as shocked as if he had returned to consciousness a second time to find himself in the wooden building at Sinnamarie. Dr. Keroual read his naked, stricken face and said quickly, "You have at least three weeks yet. The captain is willing for her to continue on as a passenger, and you must remember to thank him."

"I can't give Diane up," he said.

"No," she said in a clear frightened voice. "We promised each other."

"There's no help for it, I'm afraid. No women at all were allowed to come with the Army. No doubt he had good reason."

Florian stood starkly, his arms hanging. "You don't understand," he said. "*I can't.*" He knew the mocking, light-eyed phantom was only waiting a chance like this to come back, to walk always at his elbow and speak out of his mouth: Pichegru the tempter would come back if Diane were not there to exorcise its awful presence. He felt that his only chance to become a good doctor again was to drive the phantom away from him, but he could not do that alone. Diane's loving faith kept the tempter at bay, but he was not strong any more by himself. That day he had followed Pichegru away from Sinnamarie in a lonely effort to survive at the cost of the others who depended on him, he had become another man, a man whom he could not like, whom he could not trust. But Diane trusted him, and while she was near him and gave him her trust, he had strength enough left not to fail her. He told Keroual the truth; he could not give her up, he could not.

The tubby doctor spoke kindly of the future. "In time, when the conquest is assured, no doubt General Bonaparte will relax his order. Then you can send for Diane."

But that might be too late. He dared not expose himself again. He said sharply, "If I can't take her with me, I'm not going to stay there either."

"Great heavens, Doctor! What gave you the idea you had a choice about that? He sent halfway across the world for you, he gave up a ship. It was a lot for him to do. Be a little reasonable!" Florian, who had not given a thought one way or the other about Bonaparte, now saw him as a figure of menace and power intent on snapping the main thread of his life.

Keroual tried to think of new words of reason and appeal. But Florian's face was as adamant as the remembered face of the commander. He appealed to Diane. "You reason with him."

"Charlot is right," she said. "We have consented to too many separations as it is. Perhaps we are being unreasonable, I don't know. But it seems to me that human hearts have some rights too. If General Bonaparte doesn't want me in Egypt, then let him release Charlot. There's been nothing in our lives almost since our marriage but renunciations and sufferings. It's too much, Dr. Keroual. We're asking very little after all, only the right to be together, as God intended."

Keroual said uneasily, "I suppose there's no harm in requesting an exception. Perhaps he can be made to appreciate your feelings. But don't hope for too much, either of you. He's not a lenient being, exactly."

"I know that," Diane said, "but I can't afford to be afraid of him, and I'm not going to be."

He shrugged. There was nothing more that he could say. It lay between them, the couple's reckless passion for each other against the harsh authority of that man who had said, "Tell your Dr. Florian that I will expect much from him." He went out, shaking his head. He was remembering the remark the naked singer of the jungle had made. "Generals are his Nemesis," Ange Pitou had said, mocking and hateful. "Perhaps Sinnamarie without Pichegru would be an improvement over the unknown with Bonaparte," he had said. I wonder if there's time for me to get drunk after all, Keroual thought.

SEVEN

The Oath Broken

DAWN, the *Bonnet Rouge* approached the anchorage at Aboukir Bay, where she had been ordered to rendezvous with the French fleet. Because of the earliness of the hour, no one was on deck but the watch, the helmsman, the captain on his bridge, and Dr. Keroual, whose nervousness over the immediate future had increased as distance between it and them shortened. The little stout doctor clung to a deckrail and stared disbelievingly. If he had been drinking, he would have suspected a trick of liquor, but he was quite sober.

The floor of Aboukir Bay was filled with the corpses of ships. Burned masts and spars broke out of the clear waters. *L'Orient* the flagship listed idly, her four decks scarred with flame. Aboukir Bay was the graveyard of the French Navy.

For a long time Keroual clung and looked, trembling, for it was too much to take in all at once. Finally he noticed the captain beckoning him from the bridge. He climbed up, sweating. The captain's face was empty of any expression except mere surprise.

"It looks like the whole of the fleet," he whispered.

"Who did it?" Keroual whispered.

"The English probably, how should I know? What am I supposed to do now?"

Keroual understood that the question was rhetorical, that the captain of the *Bonnet Rouge* was not actually asking his ship's doctor to log out their next move. He did not make any answer. Astonished and uncomprehending, the two men watched the dawn flower in shades of rose and pearl and gold, as they tried to accept the disaster.

The captain began thinking aloud. "If the Army got off, we hold Alexandria. Then I ought to go on in and drop anchor. But if there is no Army of Egypt any more—I have heard that the Beys put their prisoners to death by torture."

It was a new shock to Keroual, whose thoughts had not gone that far. No Army of Egypt any more!—it was possible, and that frightening young man might be dead. He glared into the enigma of green waters, and thought that Alexander had looked on this same scene, and Caesar had, and Bonaparte might have been greater than either. Over the coffee cups Bonaparte had alarmed him only, but now he was aware of an odd wild grief at the idea of that loss.

"I think there's some movement ashore." The captain began using his glass. "Yes. They're sending out smallboats. But I can't tell——" He leaned over the bridge and began yelling orders. The sailors turned out of their hammocks and milled around until the sharpness of his voice penetrated their sleep-haze. Her sails slanting, the *Bonnet Rouge* tacked around. There was one gun aboard, its muzzle now aimed squarely at the little boats dipping and floating toward them over the jeweled waters. The captain went on using his glass. He made a sound of satisfaction and handed the instrument to Keroual. "French. I'm sure of it. Look for yourself."

But his hands were trembling too much. He gave the glass back, and now he could see with naked eye. The men in the boats were unquestionably European. Although it crossed his mind that Turks could have dressed themselves in the clothes of drowned soldiers and sailors, or that Alexandria might be occupied by the English, he did not really credit these thoughts. The captain called new orders and the ship swung around again, her sails dipping in salute.

Dr. Keroual saw Dr. Florian and Diane, their arms around each other's waists, just below the bridge. The realization that this brilliant man had been freed from one circle of hell only to enter another, humbled Keroual. He started down to them, forgetting, and the captain did not notice the little breach of etiquette either.

"Your destiny lies in strange places, Doctor. The Army is cut off," Keroual said.

Realization came slowly to Florian. It would be years before France could build another Navy. In all that time there would be no troop replacements, no shipments of food or ammunition. The Army would need to survive by its own efforts in a hostile country. These few thousand men were adrift among alien millions, and his lot was cast with theirs.

❖   ❖   ❖

The Commander-in-Chief and an escort had ridden from Cairo as soon as news of the disaster reached there. Bonaparte and his staff were at the summer palace of the Murad Bey, where Florian was told to report himself. Keroual supervised his dressing and the arrangement of his papers fussily. Florian said to him, "He can't refuse Diane and me now. There wouldn't be any chance of bringing her back."

Dr. Keroual said gently, "Are you sure you want to try to keep her? The Army's situation is much worsened, and it seems to me that she might be in real danger."

He turned his tormented face. His voice was low and harsh. "Don't you understand yet? I'm trying to save myself. If he takes Diane from me, he'll have to shoot me in the end."

He was rowed over on one of the ship's boats. The youngster in command promised to wait for him. "Until nightfall, Doctor. You'll have to be back here by nightfall." Since it was barely noon, that did not seem to be any problem.

Florian, a trained observer, remained noticing in spite of his preoccupation. He saw that energy, rather than despair, was the dissevered Army's answer to calamity. Already diving parties were being sent out to recover what they could from the holds of sunken ships. Sailors were building a flotilla of barges in which to transport the salvage to headquarters at Cairo. Even spent shot was being collected against a day when ammunition would run out. These men were not being given time to realize that their homes and families had just been lost to them.

General Bonaparte's chief secretary was a good-looking young man named Bourrienne, narrow of face and eye, but pleasant in his manners. He checked Florian's papers and confirmed his appointment, and assigned a billet not far from the Bey's palace. "But don't become too fond of your new quarters, because we won't be staying in Alexandria," Bourrienne said. "Aren't you the doctor from Sinnamarie?" Florian said in a low voice that he was. "Yes. Well. General Bonaparte is willing that you don't assume any duties right away. That's up to you, of course." Florian looked at him uneasily. "We've heard such tales about Guiana," the secretary went on. "Those may be exaggerations, of course." He waited but the doctor could not bring himself to make any comment. Their silence stretched out. Bourrienne began to look irritated. "Why don't you say something?"

"I have a favor to ask."

"All right, I'll hear about that in a moment." He was consulting his notes. "General Bonaparte directs that you be made to feel welcome, and be assured of his deep interest in you. You are not to misunderstand his suggestion that you occupy yourself at first in leisurely ways. Battles were won on the second, the thirteenth, the twenty-first and the twenty-third of last month, and that ends the fighting for the present as we hold all of the Nile valley and Murad and Ibrahim have withdrawn their troops further than we care to follow. Later we can expect more trouble, especially when news of the naval disaster becomes known, and then your services will be needed badly. In the meantime, you should be allowed to do pretty much as you please. You've had a bad time. Or he imagines that you have," Bourrienne added, looking up.

This remarkable piece of empathic understanding from Bonaparte came as a surprise. Dr. Keroual had not led him to think that his commander was sympathetic and sensitive. He no longer dreaded being refused about Diane, and started eagerly to phrase the request. But one thing more was in the notebook. Bourrienne snapped it shut, saying, "He does not have the time now, but when things have settled down he wants you to make a report to him about conditions at Sinnamarie. As I said, we hear many different stories, but you are the first we have seen who has been through it."

"I can't!" It was torn from him. Bourrienne looked at him curiously. An aura of stark suffering came from the gaunt man whose clenched hands hung stiffly at his sides.

"Am I to understand that you are refusing to make this report?"

"No. No! I'll make it if I have to." He was trembling. His mind was planning evasions wildly. If it became necessary, and he held on with all his force to the notion that he had observed the life there without participating in it, perhaps he could acquit himself without betraying himself. "I'll do anything he tells me to," he said raggedly.

"That's better. I assure you, it would not have been wise to refuse. Was there something else, Dr. Florian? There was a request you wanted to make, what was that?"

"My wife is aboard the *Bonnet Rouge*, I'm asking that she be allowed to land."

"Sightseeing trip, Doctor?"

"I want to keep her with me."

"I'm sorry, that's not possible." He pulled some papers toward him and began to write rapidly.

Florian said, "We have been separated for a long time. This means a great deal to me. Please listen."

"I am listening, Doctor. But I can't do anything for you. No wives. No camp followers. He's very definite about it."

"Will you arrange for me to ask him about it myself?"

"It wouldn't do any good, and he's too busy to give interviews now."

"But when he gave that order, he must have planned to let the wives come as soon as our position was secured."

"I believe so," Bourrienne agreed, writing again.

"With no fleet, that won't be possible."

"Yes. It's too bad."

"In view of that fact, don't you think he might make an exception?"

"He doesn't care much about making exceptions, Dr. Florian."

Florian was acquainted with the need of subordinate natures to indemnify themselves in mean ways. He suspected Bourrienne of a petty seizure of authority under the cloak of zealous obedience, and said coldly, "I think it would be better if you let General Bonaparte make his own decisions, Citizen."

The secretary looked up. For a moment, his face was exposed and antagonistic and Florian saw that he had read him correctly. Then Bourrienne controlled himself. His neat eyebrows lifting, he said, "I am employed to handle his business of routine nature. I should think that would be obvious."

"But I am not business of a routine nature. I am a human being, asking a very great favor of another human being. I think the General should know."

"I'll make a note," Bourrienne said, and made one.

"But I want to see him myself."

"If he wants it, he'll send for you."

"I don't trust you to tell it right!" Florian said desperately.

It was the secretary's turn. He looked the doctor up and down in a way calculated to drive the most level disposition into frenzies of indiscretion. He said, "Dr. Florian. If you will take my good advice. Stop antagonizing the very people you will need to depend on for what favors you may get."

The advice was good. Florian knew it. "I'm sorry," he muttered.

"That's better. Come around tomorrow if you wish, I'll try to have an answer for you then. Meanwhile, as long as the ship remains in harbor, I see no real objection to you staying aboard her yourself. Now if you'll excuse me—"

Florian went out. He was shivering. The secretary's contemptuous treatment of him had made him understand what Keroual had tried without success to explain. It was not true that he could prevent Bonaparte from taking Diane away from him. He could not even prevent the secret of Sinnamarie being wrung from him, if the other commanded. To repair, with Diane's help, the break in his own spirit was a demand as grave as he felt he could meet. He had not reckoned sufficiently with the fact that as an Army doctor, he was not his own man, but Bonaparte's. Only in a man's absolute integrity was there any defense against that overweening power. Integrity was what he had sacrificed on the lost and secret day when he had followed Pichegru instead of himself.

Diane, waiting with Dr. Keroual, saw that he looked troubled and ill. The news was bad, then. She thought recklessly, I will hide myself in some way until the ship is gone. Then they can't send me away. I don't think even Bonaparte would drive me out on the desert to die. A picture formed in the back of her mind: Fidèle, bright-haired and hopelessly gallant, being rowed toward that mysterious place of exile that was called the *guillotine sèche*.

But when Charlot told his story, there seemed every reason to think that the commander would grant what they asked. Dr. Keroual thought so and said, "The fact that he specifically mentioned to his secretary that you were to be assured of his interest in you is a convincing reason to hope. Frankly, I had expected him to take another attitude altogether, and be impatient toward the idea of any special consideration. After all, you're deeply in his debt already. But apparently he doesn't feel that way. I can't imagine why you're so depressed."

"It seems to me too that he's practically said 'yes' to any reasonable request you want to make," Diane agreed. Their combined optimism lifted his spirits, and he began to see that it had been ridiculous for him to give way to despair because a secretary was rude.

"I sadly regretted cutting short my little hour of revelry in Toulon," Dr. Keroual remarked. "But this news is so good, it seems I might allow myself a few hours ashore here."

Diane kissed his cheek lightly. "Dr. Keroual, I think you deserve to become as drunk as Bacchus. Only please take good care of yourself, we love you very much." The little man turned scarlet and hurried away.

Diane said, "What puzzles me is that the man who commanded the Pavia massacre has shown such delicacy and generosity of spirit. He must be a very complex person. I still find myself hoping that we won't have much to do with him."

"I hope so too," Florian said in an ashamed voice. "I learned today that I'm afraid of him." Diane was startled. She could not remember that Charlot ever before had confessed to being afraid of anything.

❊   ❊   ❊

He presented himself to the secretary a second time. "Oh, yes, Doctor." Bourrienne's eyes were twinkling. "I have your answer for you." His good humor was so obvious, Dr. Florian decided that he had misunderstood him that other time. It was kind of Bourrienne to feel gratification at relaying good news. "I took care to take his exact words down," the secretary went on, opening his notebook. Florian waited, his gratitude including them both.

Bourrienne read out, "'Louis, get this Dr. Florian to understand that I appreciate his feelings, and I would like very much to do as he asks. I don't feel that I should. Exemptions seldom serve any purpose save to increase the disappointment of others, and morale is particularly important now since the loss of the fleet. I will do everything I can to bring the wives here when it is feasible. Tell him that.'" Bourrienne closed the notebook and laid it aside. His eyes were still twinkling.

Florian was stark and speechless. He had become so sure of a hearing, at least. When he continued not to speak, the secretary prodded him. "It might interest you to know that the *Bonnet Rouge* has her sailing orders for day after tomorrow." He's enjoying this, the doctor realized. "I am sorry for you," Bourrienne said, "but I warned you what his answer would be. Another time, perhaps you can trust me to act for him in these—ah—matters of routine nature." He gloated openly.

Without having spoken at all, Florian turned and went out.

II

Dr. Bénigne Keroual was enjoying his first friendly hangover in years. It isn't the sickness that makes you so sick, he thought, lying in his bunk and playing with his fingers as though he were an infant. It's the remorse. I am never going to feel that again. I drink; very well, is that so bad?—many men do. Yes, it makes me a bad doctor, but then I do as little doctoring as possible and the crew knows better than to present themselves when I'm drinking. Really I do very little harm. And in Egypt, among the homesick men of that unfortunate cast-off Army, Dr. Florian will work zealously. He will never be drunk when he is needed, and he will save many lives.

217

A half interest in all his good works belongs to me. I purchased half of the good works of Dr. Florian when I went without drink for more than a year, for his sake.

That intoxication had prevented him from saying farewell to the Florians did not disturb his peace of mind. Their affairs had come out all right, since the *Bonnet Rouge* was in motion and Keroual had wakened in his own cabin. Diane would be using the cabin had they been refused. And what happier farewell could there be to remember after her gentle kiss, her saying, "We love you very much." He lay in his bunk, playing with his fingers and smiling.

The cabin door opened and the captain strode in. His face was wrathful. Keroual started to remind him how he had said he didn't care how drunk his doctor got in port. But in his cups, Keroual might have bribed a sailor to smuggle liquor aboard. He waited apprehensively to hear that he had done so.

"How much did you have to do with getting Madame Florian off this ship?"

Keroual felt a deep pang of alarm. "I don't even know what you're talking about."

"She's nowhere on the ship."

"He was trying to get permission for her to land, sir."

"I know that, but he was refused."

"Oh, my God," Keroual said.

"What was I supposed to do when I found she wasn't aboard?" the captain asked, rhetorically again. "Lose two days' sailing time going back for her, when my orders are to go straight to France as fast as I can sail there? General Bonaparte wouldn't have liked that any better than he's going to like finding out for himself that she's there, and thinking I connived at it, probably."

Keroual groaned and turned his head away. His hangover had taken a sick turn.

"Damn you, Keroual, I told you when you asked me about taking her on as a passenger, that a woman is unlucky on a ship. Superstition, you said, crazy nonsense, you said. Get out of that bunk and get dressed. I'm damned if I'm going to let you lie there nursing yourself. Report to me in fifteen minutes unless you want to recover in the brig." He stalked out.

Unsteady on his feet and queasy in his stomach, Keroual began to dress. But the painful situation in which he found himself was the smaller cause for unhappiness. Diane was in Egypt, in disobedience of orders from that severe young man. It would be impossible to hide her successfully for any long time and that Bonaparte would react swiftly, terribly, Keroual knew. Bonaparte would not take into account that the good works of Dr. Florian were to be the passport for two souls; he would take nothing into account, except that he had been disobeyed the very first thing, by the man whose rescue he had effected halfway across the world. If only I had stayed sober, I might have talked them out of this madness, Keroual thought. The remorse he had been resolved never to feel again swept him like a black tide.

           *   *   *

Dr. Charlot Florian started to take his wife's arm to help her, but then he remembered. He brushed past Diane haughtily, leaving her to follow with both their bundles. His own was light and flat, merely a change of linen, his shaving things, and the cinchona bark he had brought from Guiana. But Diane's package was bulky.

The sailors manning the barge helped the doctor, respectful and courteous. She was left to clamber aboard by herself. She lost her footing; before she could recover, she was soaked to the waist. Diane hauled valiantly at their two bundles while a sailor cursed her, and Florian suffered it. Though the beloved looked alien, so attuned were their bodies, the rough treatment she was receiving was physical punishment to him. The loose garment Diane wore gave perfect concealment, and her face had been coated with a bronze dye. Under the bournous hood, little drops of sweat gathered on her upper lip and stood out on her forehead.

Florian was given a comfortable place to sit, but then had to watch while Diane was thrust down roughly on soaked bales of material that had been salvaged from the sunken ships. Their eyes met; no trace of resentment showed in hers, and he sank back. The journey along the Nile to Cairo was not a long one. She was so much safer as a young, native male servant, among these boatmen lonely for their women in France. But his heart stormed protest at every fresh insult of hands and harsh words.

The barge moved slowly along the majestic Nile. The sailors poling it were survivors of the wrecked ships; water travel like this must seem odd and primitive to them, though they poled along skillfully. The sun sank behind the great rock cliffs, and the river changed from clear green to a deep purple as the stars came out. Cleopatra had traveled this way on a barge laden with flowers and the riches of the east. These same stars were in the sky when Antony made love. Florian and Diane sat apart, and to them even words were forbidden.

✿   ✿   ✿

The latecomer, Dr. Florian was given as living quarters what no one else had wanted. Headquarters was the palace of the Elfy Bey in the square of Esbekye'h, and all of the houses in that district had been taken up. Five incredibly dirty, though nobly proportioned, rooms on the outskirts of Cairo were assigned to him. No one but the incurious natives was around to observe them.

He found two servants who seemed trustworthy and were quicker than most at understanding the signs of their hands. "Servants again!" Diane said, lifting her eyebrows. "The Army certainly lives better than people at home do." He shopped in the bazaars for things they had to have; the beautiful things he saw would have to wait until his salary began. But Diane's gift of creating loveliness from little had not left her. The place became a true home almost as soon as it had been cleaned.

The necessity for concealing herself prevented Diane from ever leaving the house. All companionship except her husband's was denied her, and there would be many lonely hours in store for her once he went on active duty. Charlot fretted about this more than Diane did. It was happiness enough for her that they were together, she said loyally. But as invitations to him continued to come and interesting activities claimed him more and more often, he felt that in time her loneliness and isolation would become a real problem.

He was invited to a meeting of the Institute. The prospect excited him; he had just learned what the Institute was. A number of scientists and savants had joined the adventure, feeling that their work could be pursued better in a far place under Bonaparte than at home under Paul Barras. They had modeled themselves on the French Academy of the King's time, but had divided into sections for chemistry, physics, astronomy, botany, medicine, and mathematics.

When he approached the palace set aside for their meetings, he was overcome by shyness. He wondered if he would be welcomed. The feeling was new to him and hateful; in his professional life, he had never been in need of reassurance until now. He had to force himself to enter the palace, and then he avoided speaking to anyone. The starkness of modern scientific instruments amidst all the Oriental luxury caught his eye, and also gave him an excuse for remaining by himself, defensively occupied in looking at the instruments.

An aged man started across the room toward Florian. He was sober as a crow in rusty black, but remarkably sweet-faced. He introduced himself as the president of the Institute, and welcomed Dr. Florian in warm terms. It was some time before Florian comprehended that he was talking to Gaspard Monge, whose work he had admired for years. No greater name existed in the world of mathematical speculation. Florian was deeply moved. He said so.

"I am not less pleased to meet you," Monge said. "I became interested in your affairs months ago, before this expedition started out. It was at a breakfast at General Bonaparte's house in Paris. You had a strong advocate in the person of a small round physician whose name has escaped me."

"Do you mean Dr. Keroual?"

"Precisely, it was he. He spoke of you with the largest warmth, yet he had met you but one time. On his ship, I believe. It is unusual for a man to make so lasting an impression on so brief a meeting, and I thought the good doctor's emotion was a not inconsiderable factor in evaluating your case. Not that I had any voice in that, but I did become curious about you."

"Dr. Keroual never told me about this." Florian was ashamed to realize that he had never asked. "He has done a great deal for me. I don't know why."

"I know why," Monge said. "He admired you for being the doctor he would have liked to become himself, and would have perhaps, had it not been for that fatal fondness for drink."

"Did he really tell you about that?"

"He did indeed, in his anxiety to convince us you were worth rescuing. After he left us, we did not know whether to be amused by him, or saddened at the waste he had made of his life. I remember General Bonaparte saying he was tempted to take him and make a good doctor out of him, since he desired it so passionately. The General is gifted that way. Now, Dr. Florian, I want you to start considering which of our projects would interest you most. Not all of our work here is speculative. A good many practical projects have been turned over to us. We have to earn our way, you know! But the Paymaster-General informs me that you have not been collecting your salary."

"I'm not on active duty yet," Florian said.

"But you have to live. You are on half pay from the medical corps and on half pay from the Institute, which makes up a full salary."

"I didn't know," he said, embarrassed. "That's very generous."

"Do you know Dr. Desgenettes? He's your superior in the medical corps."

"I know his name. I may have met him years ago."

"He and Dr. Larrey are too busy to come around here as often as they would like, but I believe I noticed that Desgenettes is here tonight. You will want to thank him for his part in your rescue off Guiana." Monge began moving away, his wrinkled hand lightly on Florian's forearm. Florian had stiffened at the mention, but he controlled himself. He could hardly impose his law of silence about that on these important strangers, but he could continue to tell himself that they were mistaken in believing he had been there, because he had not.

"I'm astonished that Dr. Keroual knew so many important people," Florian commented.

"I believe he made a point of meeting them, because of you."

I don't remember that I even so much as thanked him, Florian thought remorsefully.

They entered several of the rooms without finding Desgenettes. Each room contained its interesting jumble of Oriental objects as well as the newest and finest scientific instruments. Florian mentioned his delight in this startling incongruity, and Monge halted, his seamed face glowing.

"Yes. It's exciting, isn't it? A real meeting of two civilizations. My hopes are high that our work here will not be forgotten while human memory persists. Our commander summed it up best when he said, 'We will perish in this land, or we will depart her as great as the ancients.' That's a fair statement of what the destruction of the fleet means to us."

Florian was enchanted. The aged man could not have fired a round of shot if the entire French venture in Egypt depended on him, yet he had repeated those harsh words of challenge with joy. "You don't seem disturbed by so exacting a prospect, Citizen-President."

"Disturbed, no indeed. I never enjoyed myself more." Behind the wrinkles, the eyes clouded over with age and cataracts, lived a high-spirited youth who was in love with the world. Florian began to understand why Monge was a great man.

Monge said, "The story of mankind has been the story of intelligence kept back, or indeed destroyed utterly, by brute force. I had come to accept the pattern as inevitable. But now I see my boyish dreams being splendidly fulfilled. Intelligence governs force here. The mailed fist is lifted to drive home the enlightened thought. But you will come to see what I mean. Ah, there's Laplace. Have you met him, Dr. Florian?"

"Is he in Egypt?" Laplace, geometrician and astronomer, was as well known as Monge himself. It occurred to Florian that he would not have aspired to meet these international figures were they and he still in Paris. The Egyptian adventure began to assume an Aladdin-like air. Florian said jestingly, "If Berthollet were here too, we could truthfully say the center of the world had been shifted."

To that, Monge said, "He's not here tonight. He's doing some work at Headquarters. You know we are faced with the need of manufacturing everything ourselves, now that we can't depend on shipments from France. I believe I have heard that Berthollet has nearly concluded his experiments in the large-scale manufacture of gunpowder. But I do wonder if the botanists will ever find a way to make beer. There isn't a hop grown in Egypt, yet you can't keep soldiers happy without beer."

"That seems rather trivial to me."

"Oh, that's our motto here, no problem too little and none too large. Human happiness is purchased through a number of little things, and especially when the great joys are irrevocably lost, homes and wives and children. But I forget myself, Doctor. The man who once lived in Sinnamarie would understand that best." Florian looked at him resentfully, but Monge did not notice. An officer had come into the room and Monge was watching him.

Florian would not have remarked him: youthful, inconspicuous in his field uniform, but Monge's old seamed face glowed with the love and pride a man feels toward a favorite son. Yet he did not try to go over there. The officer finished his conversation and started away but felt Monge watching him; he turned his head, smiling, and sketched a friendly salute. Then he went out.

"I would have liked to present you to our vice president, Dr. Florian. But tonight was not a good time, as he was obviously in a hurry."

"I'm surprised that a military man would show that much interest in a scientific society."

"Oh, General Bonaparte is probably the best all-around scientist of us all."

Now Florian wished that he had looked at the officer more closely.

The impressions he retained of Bonaparte were of extreme youth and a slightness of figure, and the depth and strength of the affection Monge felt for him: no more.

*   *   *

High on the list of practical projects which the Institute had been directed to solve was the development of a substitute for cinchona bark. Florian, smiling broadly, said, "If you will assign me to this tonight, Citizen-President, tomorrow you can move me on to something else."

"You mean, you know of a substitute?"

"Not a substitute, no. But I brought a rather large supply of cinchona with me. I think I can safely say there's enough for the entire Army for a year anyway."

"Dr. Florian, you are a gift from heaven! Where did you acquire such a supply of cinchona bark?"

Florian said quickly, "I'll turn it over to the medical corps tomorrow. I should have done so before this. Frankly, I forgot I had it."

"I don't know that there's enough money available to pay you fairly for it. If you're satisfied to do it this way, perhaps you can be paid now for half of what it's worth and the rest can be owing to you."

"I don't want any money," Florian said, "let it be a gift." The decision, though made quickly, was a wise one, he was sure. His generosity now would be held in his favor later, if he and Diane were discovered.

Monge beamed. "I hardly dared to hope that you would feel that way. But it would be a serious embarrassment to try to pay you, I know, and also, your spirit of generous cooperation is what is demanded of us all by this sudden turn in our fortunes."

Florian's was the largest single collection of cinchona ever seen in those days when a gram of the powdered bark was worth more than that in gold. His superior, Dr. Desgenettes, then Dr. Larrey, and the head apothecary, a man named Royer, called on him in turn and thanked him in behalf of the Army. Diane, wearing the bournous, concealed herself among the servants during these visits. The love and pride on her face ought to have given her away, but it seemed that she went unnoticed.

An ovation at the Institute was accorded Florian. He had no further reason to feel shy at the meetings, because he was known to all and highly regarded. Climaxing the results of his generosity was a warm note of appreciation from the Commander-in-Chief. Florian smiled when he realized that the antagonistic secretary, Bourrienne, had been compelled to pen that.

The other projects of the Institute ranged from small to staggering. Good minds were as busily engaged in engineering the construction of portable baking ovens for the Army, as they were in studying the Rosetta stone which had been unearthed and brought to Cairo, or planning a canal to cut through the isthmus of Suez. A solution of Cairo's sinking and drainage problem was being sought; an analysis of fish and flora was underway; the exploration of the lakes and the Nile mud was being conducted. On a printing press whose construction had just been finished, a weekly newspaper was being printed and a complete French-Arabic dictionary would be run off when it was finished.

Not since his student days had Dr. Florian been given the opportunity to live in a completely intellectual climate like this. Daily, new excitements of the mind brought him further along in the rehabilitation of the man he had been. The cinchona project having been moved from the top of the list to its bottom, Florian enlisted with a group of doctors studying the causes and treatments of Oriental plague and trachoma, the twin scourges of the East, and of ophthalmia and blood fluke infection, the common diseases. His life was now full of everything that was good. If only he were allowed to take Diane around the city with him, and introduce her to the new friends he was making—that too will come in time, perhaps, he thought. He had made such a good start in his new life, it did not seem impossible to him that he might eventually strengthen his position to a point where discovery of his infraction would be powerless to harm him.

❂   ❂   ❂

Louis Antoine Fauvelet de Bourrienne had not forgotten about the existence of Dr. Florian, but there had been no reason to trouble himself over the obscure physician until a warm note to the doctor was dictated by Bourrienne's former classmate in military school, Bonaparte. The secretary chewed his lip reflectively. He did not like the idea of Florian having been brought to Bonaparte's attention in so favorable a light. He knew that his chief's habit of mind was to reward generously when pleased, and it occurred to him that the doctor might be as fond of exacting petty revenge as Bourrienne himself was. The thing to do was to circumvent Dr. Florian before he could win more favor. The secretary put his quick shallow mind to the enjoyable task of plotting the ruin of a man who had attracted his dislike.

Bourrienne remembered an oddness in Florian's manner when Guiana was mentioned, as though it would be painful, if not impossible, for him to talk about that to anyone. That might do, the secretary thought.

He sent a note requesting Florian to present himself "at his convenience" to General Headquarters. Nothing about the wording indicated who had inaugurated it, so Florian hurried there as soon as he received it, late that afternoon.

Bourrienne was a master at contriving a deliberate piece of rudeness that would resemble exquisite courtesy. He received Florian with supercilious affability—and forgot to ask him to sit down. He said, "I believe I mentioned that General Bonaparte was interested in whatever you might have to say about Sinnamarie. If you will be so kind, Doctor. Suppose you relate your experiences to me, and I will take down as much as I think might be of interest to him."

Florian was shivering. He said in a low voice, "But I understood that he intended to see me about that himself."

"That was the original plan, yes. But then he's been busy, and I am so well acquainted with the turn of his mind. There is no real reason for him to waste his time with you. I can just as well draw out the facts and arrange them neatly in a report. Please go on, Doctor," he said, poising his quill over one of the inevitable notebooks.

Florian's voice, though still low, was tense and hard. "Listen, Bourrienne. I'm perfectly aware that an Army doctor is about the lowest thing on earth. I know that any field officer can compel me to leave dying men, to act as a barber and shave him. But a man's past belongs to himself, and I choose to keep mine." He strode out.

He was too angry to think clearly, but it dawned on him he had reacted magnificently to an exquisite needling. There had been a gleam of triumph in the secretary's eyes. Obviously Bourrienne planned to use the incident to hurt him. What countermove could he make? Monge was so friendly, could he explain the affair to Monge, and ask him to mention it to the other? But the Commander-in-Chief of the Army and the president of the Institute had too much on their minds to be bothered by the apologies of an unemployed doctor who had lost his temper with a secretary.

He asked Diane's advice. She thought that going to Monge would merely focus attention on what otherwise might go unnoticed. "Even if the General does hear about it, which I doubt, he will probably think that Bourrienne deserved exactly what you gave him."

"But what prevents Bourrienne from claiming that what I said was a message to Bonaparte himself?"

"That would be dishonest."

"But he had some reason for provoking me like that. I know it!"

It grieved her to see Charlot so upset over what was, after all, a trifling matter. The old Charlot would have handled it so easily. He would not have lost his temper in the first place, but if he had done so he would have ignored the incident until there were actual consequences. "If the General is angry, he will let you know. Then will be time to explain yourself," Diane said.

"But I can't afford to make him angry. Someday he's going to find out about you. Nothing must happen before then to prejudice him against me. That's why I gave them the cinchona bark. They would have paid me for it."

"I'm glad you didn't let them. None of us will get out of here alive unless we all contribute what we have."

Her simple words jogged old, painful memories. He said roughly, "You don't know what you're talking about. We're well off here." He had never used that tone to her before. She looked at him wonderingly, and he was as puzzled as she was.

Diane realized for herself that what she had said must have approached the forbidden topic of Sinnamarie. She said quietly, "Charlot, what's going to happen if you're compelled to talk to him about that?"

"I don't know." He turned away and slumped into a chair. She crossed over to him and quietly laid her hand on his cheek. She knew there had to be some good reason behind these seemingly purposeless bursts of anger. The logical reason was that he was ashamed to talk about it. Then he had done something shameful there. It was hard to believe that of Charlot, but no other explanation seemed to serve.

But a man who has been shamed once is in danger from the whole world. Some automatic defense against evil has been taken away, and he is vulnerable. She felt that he was in grave danger, but she did not know how to help him so she merely stood quietly, stroking him, and wondering about Sinnamarie.

*   *   *

After Florian's outburst the secretary wrote busily in his notebook, then sat quietly, lacing and unlacing his fingers, and smiling. Finally he gathered up some other papers, and the notebook, and tiptoed to the door of the next room, on which he scratched gently. He opened it a little way and looked inside.

"Come," a voice said, roughly good-humored. Bourrienne went in. The lamp had not been lighted yet. All the windows in the room were thrown open, so its occupant could hear the calls and bells of the mosque. Bonaparte always had loved the sound of bells.

Bourrienne laid his papers unobtrusively on a corner of the desk. "These are ready for your signature, General." He stepped back a short distance and stood holding the notebook.

"Well?"

"You're busy. I'm sorry." He made as if to go.

"Come back. What is it?" Bonaparte glanced up and smiled. "More gossip, I suppose. Where you find time to rake up all that stuff, I never will know. But I'm afraid I share your weakness for enjoying the secrets of others. To me it's a form of relaxation, but what do you get out of it?"

"I think it gives me a feeling of power," Bourrienne said, with rare candor.

"Power. I don't see it."

"My little stories cause you to notice people that otherwise you would not. And the notice of a man like yourself is a form of Destiny, General."

Bonaparte said drily, "You turn phrases like a courtier."

"Well, I live in a palace like one," Bourrienne said neatly.

He laughed. "Get on with your yarn spinning."

"It has come to my attention that your order barring wives has not been carried out in every case. One wife was smuggled in and the happy couple have coolly set up housekeeping. Naturally, some others are beginning to wish they hadn't been so scrupulous, and there's quite a lot of talk about it."

"Name and rank?"

"Sub-lieutenant Fourès of the artillery, sir."

"He shouldn't have done that." Bonaparte stabbed at the desk

idly with the point of the quill he had been using. When it had
been rendered totally useless, he tossed it away. "How did they manage it?"

"She was dressed as an equerry, sir. But now she has resumed her
own wardrobe, so I imagine he feels there is no further danger to
their arrangement."

"He might be mistaken about that. Though it's romantic and
charming, don't you think so?"

"She is, anyway."

"Ah. You've seen her."

"At the bazaars, General, and she is remarkably pretty. Violet
eyes, black brows and lashes, hair very blonde. No more than twenty,
I would say, and most symmetrical in her figure."

"Aren't you adopting a new profession, Louis?"

The secretary lowered his eyes. "I don't believe I understand you,
sir. I merely wanted you to get the picture."

"I get it clearly. Well, that was interesting, what else?"

"Captain Lanusse and General Junot were involved in an affair
of honor last night. At the Tivoli Gardens of course, and both had
been drinking. Perhaps it's been reported to you already."

"Not yet, no. Were they hurt?"

"Lanusse no, Junot slightly."

"What was that about?"

"The ostensible cause was when Junot refused to lend Lanusse
money, but there had been high words before that, about you. I think
I have mentioned before how Captain Lanusse is a leading spirit in a
little clique of grumblers and complainers who——"

"You're repeating yourself. I remember."

"I imagine you'll feel you want to discipline Captain Lanusse.
Junot was being his usual loyal self."

"But you are quite wrong. It is Junot who will be disciplined."

Once in a while it turned out that way, that he made mischief
for his own friends. As many years as he had known Bonaparte, he
was never quite safe at second-guessing that logical mind. Quickly
he tried to mend the damage. "But Lanusse was really insulting toward you, General. He certainly knows how Junot feels, so he must
have been egging him on."

"Junot should have kept his temper. He's my friend, he knows
what I'm trying to do here. Captain Lanusse is a troublemaker but
he is also a good officer. I wouldn't have thanked Junot for killing
him for me, and if he had killed Junot I'd have had him shot. So I

stood to lose two good men because that simple head won't contain any higher idea of loyalty than brawling about with his sword in a nest of crocodiles. Was it swords?"

"Yes, General," Bourrienne said, giving up. "And the others held lanterns for them. The story I heard was that Junot tripped in the dark and fell on the captain's blade, but I really can't be sure about that part."

"What others?" Bourrienne read their names from his notebook. Bonaparte nodded and said, "The next time there's a quarrel down there, I'll close their Gardens for them. Well, enough of that. You're more than usually interesting today. Anything else?"

"It doesn't amount to much. This Dr. Florian. He sent you a rather odd message."

"Ah, our donor of cinchona bark. If I can do him a favor, I'll be glad. What was the message?"

"Do you remember that you wanted a report from him about conditions on Guiana?"

"Yes. I haven't found time. Next week, perhaps."

"He was in here today and I mentioned it. His reaction was—unexpected. I took his exact words down, so you can judge for yourself." Straining to see in the growing dusk, Bourrienne read out, "I am well aware that an Army doctor is about the lowest thing on earth. I know that any field officer can compel me to leave dying men, to act as a barber and shave him. But a man's past belongs to himself. I choose to keep mine." Bourrienne closed the notebook. "Then he walked out, General." He waited confidently.

Bonaparte was frankly puzzled but not yet angry. "Why did he feel that way?"

The secretary answered with soft viciousness, "He's arrogant and opinionated. He derides authority of any kind. He fiercely resents having been refused about letting his wife stay. I saw at once what kind of man he is. You're sure to have trouble with him."

Bonaparte was silent. The last of the day's light failed. "You had better light the lamp," he said finally. "Make an appointment for Dr. Florian to come here. You know better than I do what free time I have. Don't put it off too long." The wick caught, and a soft yellow light washed up. Bonaparte said musingly, "The officers can be excused, perhaps. I wouldn't be too happy myself about a commander who let himself get cut off like this. But Dr. Florian has no reason to complain of me. We'll hear what he has to say." He looked up. His eyes were depthless and serene.

Bourrienne knew that look. If Florian did not step carefully, he was going to fall into an abyss. A thrill of pleasure shot through the secretary's body. He lowered his eyes, the tip of his tongue darted around the rim of his mouth. He much enjoyed standing by while his schoolfellow Bonaparte broke the hearts and wills of men. It paid something back to him out of lost years, the deep hurts of childhood, of misery without understanding. Then Florian's tormented face intruded itself on the pleasure he was feeling. That man had suffered unreasonably already. If you confessed that his resentment really had been aimed toward yourself— He paused at a crossroads.

"That's all, Louis," Bonaparte said. The opportunity was gone, and he went out.

III

AT ONE TIME, Dr. Florian had admired General Pichegru's competency; he came to know that he was now looking upon the miracle of perfect leadership. Scrupulous himself toward the laws and customs of the conquered country, Bonaparte compelled his soldiers to respect them too. His measures for the general good were both idealistic and intensely practical, benefiting all classes except the deposed Beys. The miserable Copts and the large Arab population were better off now than they had been in living memory. Oppressive taxes had been slashed, the country's economy stabilized. Bonaparte behaved as though determined that his conquest should be remembered forever, and with gratitude, by the conquered.

The doctor ·was particularly impressed when instructions were given himself and the other members of the Institute to halt all other work until the survivors of the disaster at Aboukir Bay had been dealt with. The sailors had started out as a tight little community of lost souls: shipless, rudderless, held in contempt by the more successful Army. Stealing here, begging there, eventually they were sure to cause trouble enough that they would all have to be imprisoned or shot. But then they were ordered to report in lots of twenty at the Institute, where the trained minds of the savants easily uncovered the bents of the various men. Funds from the Army chest were made available to set them up in the businesses of their choice. They became locksmiths, joiners, cartwrights, carpenters, ropemakers. Those without knowledge of the crafts were employed in the construction of saltpeter works, power mills, a foundry. When they were not building things more significant, they made billiard tables, decks of playing cards and confections, for which there was a brisk sale. The sailors had become happy and useful because the man on whom all depended had remembered all.

The doctor thought, If only Sinnamarie had never been! Then he could have looked forward to meeting that giant intellect, perhaps even befriending it. Instead, he found himself standing in the center of a magnificent apartment, rubbing his sweating palms along his flanks and telling himself that if he were forced to speak, he must control himself, be evasive, hide. . . . Bonaparte must never know that there had been a ripping straight through the admirable tapestry of Florian's professional life, a monstrous tearing that Diane's love and trust had patched, but which would tear again if there were real strain.

The hangings parted and a beautiful young woman wearing European clothes stepped in. Florian was too astonished to speak or move. "I'm sorry," she said. "I didn't know anyone was waiting." She withdrew quickly.

Where in the world had she come from? She was French certainly. Her unusual coloring would have made her attractive anywhere; here, among the dusky-skinned native population, she was beautiful as a vision. He recalled the briefly glimpsed face; violet eyes rimmed with long black lashes, and masses of hair so blonde as to be nearly silver. His nervousness was almost gone as he continued to speculate about her. There could be but one explanation: Bonaparte had not included himself in the order depriving the men of female companionship. It lessened him. Florian wondered if knowledge of the little secret could be made to work in his behalf if he were found out about Diane.

The hangings parted a second time. Bonaparte's appearance was anything but military. He had thrown off his coat, his tunic, and his sword, and was wearing nothing but a white cambric shirt, regulation trousers, and a pair of lightweight shoes. He looked Florian over coolly. The doctor was uncertain what to do and merely stood quietly, his hands at his sides, and looked back. So much hardness in so young a face repelled him, yet the head and the features were beautifully modeled. Bonaparte looked like one of the warrior angels, Gabriel, or Michael perhaps. Or Lucifer, Florian thought.

He said brusquely, "I received your message, Dr. Florian."

"I'm glad of the opportunity to explain about that!"

"I'm glad you have an explanation. Let's hear it."

"I lost my temper, General. I heartily apologize. I know how deeply I am in your debt."

"Are you always so quick-tempered?"

"I don't believe so, General. I'm convinced that your secretary deliberately provoked me, and I'm ashamed he found it so easy to do."

"That would not excuse insolence toward me."

Florian said desperately, "I swear nothing like that was intended. He asked me for the information himself. What I said was meant for him."

Bonaparte looked thoughtful, watching Florian from penetrating eyes whose glance was hard to meet. "Then Louis misunderstood you completely," he said, "or else he was trying to hurt you with me. Do you have an opinion as to which it was?"

"It could have been a misunderstanding, General," the doctor said quietly, though he knew better.

Bonaparte was pleased. He smiled slightly. "That's very generous. Or merely tactful, but in any case I prefer it to talebearing. Sit down, Doctor." When Florian obeyed, he was startled by a sensation of falling. The plump cushions were as though filled with nothing. Bonaparte, on the other end of the long divan, lounged easily. He asked in a conversational tone, "Where did you acquire the dramatic notion that you were going to be summoned from the bedsides of dying men, to barber my officers?"

"Everything I said was hasty and foolish, but I was under an impression that I had heard somewhere it was common practice."

"There were incidents in the old Army. Nothing like that has been tolerated since. Is this your first experience as a military doctor?" Florian said it was. "You won't like it much. It's rough hard work, and the suffering you will witness is frightful. On the other hand, if you feel a sincere regard for your profession, there is no limit to the amount of good you can do. But you're not on active duty yet, are you?"

"No, General. I much appreciate being given time to adjust myself."

"Let Desgenettes know when you think you're ready. Meanwhile I might have a more enjoyable project in mind for you. Who was responsible for your appointment as Medical Inspector? Paul Barras?"

Florian very much wanted to say yes. He had it in mind that to have known Carnot was to condemn yourself. Bonaparte was not easy to lie to and Florian answered correctly, but then began to describe the innocent nature of their relations.

"I admired him very much," Bonaparte interrupted. Florian, abashed, halted the explanation. "Tell me about yourself, Doctor. I know very little about you, except that you gave time to some medical students, which impressed Monge."

For some reason, Florian's mind promptly emptied itself of all but Guiana. Finding nothing to say, he tried to smile. "It's hard to talk about yourself when you've been told to," he said, his thin face wistful and disarming. When Bonaparte answered the smile, it became easier to talk to him. Florian heard himself describing the results of his survey of the closed medical schools and the emptied hospitals; of his work at the Hôtel Dieu and the Bicêrte, of Pinel's revolutionary treatment of the insane, and his own part in it. He began to enjoy himself as the other's searching questions kept him digging back for buried mental treasures.

"I taught for a year at Montpellier, then moved to Paris shortly before the Revolution. My real reason was that I had stirred up a hornet's nest with some experiments I was making, that I thought were valuable."

"What kind of experiments?"

"Folli and Colle had done some work involving the transfusion of blood from healthy persons to dying ones. Emeret of Paris took it up, but then the practice was put under interdict both by the Parliament of Paris and the Holy See. I had seen the literature, and I resumed the experiments, using only animals at first. There were some astonishing results."

"Before the Revolution, this was?"

"Yes, General."

"It was courageous of you. And what did you decide? Were Parliament and the Holy See mistaken?"

Florian weighed it carefully. "In extreme cases, where death is certain anyway, the transfusion of blood ought to be attempted. Otherwise, no, because there is an unknown factor that occasionally intervenes and causes painful sudden death. I had hoped to learn why, and how to avoid that."

"You had hoped—have you lost interest, then?"

He felt himself flushing. "There's been no opportunity to do any more about it." His unfortunate break in tenses, so quickly seized on by the other, had ended his new confidence in himself. I must be more careful, Florian thought. He's dangerous, he very nearly reads your mind. He began casting around for something, anything, that would lead that searching intellect away from himself. "Another method that might interest you is the opening of the windpipe in patients dying of malignant croup. Surgeons never do it any more, but I can't say why, since it is almost always successful."

"You seem to know what you're talking about. Go ahead with the use of your unique methods, but don't take unnecessary chances with any man's life in the interests of research. I don't want to threaten you, but every soldier in this Army is to have devoted care of the kind you would give your best friend or your brother. I know that honest mistakes will occur in a science as inexact as yours, but I won't permit careless or lazy mistakes, or malign ones. But you have your own honor and pride. I don't wish to rob you by pretending that orders from me should take the place of your conscience. Are your quarters comfortable?"

"Very comfortable, General, thank you."

"About your wife. I am sorry I could not have obliged you. After a year on Guiana, it must have meant a great deal to you. But it would have caused bad feeling among the others, and it was not strictly just, either."

Florian wished with his whole heart that the subject had not come up. In the face of such steady kindness, his guilty secret disconcerted him; also, he realized that his silence now was tantamount to a lie. Much more than the original disobedience would be held against him if he were found out, after this. The memory of the lovely blonde Frenchwoman at Headquarters was all that kept him silent.

"Are you finding your life of continence difficult?"

"No," he said, looking down, "not really."

"I could help you about that. The sheiks continue to send me beautiful veiled women as gifts. Do you want one of those?"

"My God, no! I mean, thank you, but I don't think so."

He laughed. "I share your feelings. To force myself on a slave girl would make me ashamed of being a man. My officers are less scrupulous or more realistic, I don't know which. If you change your mind, let me know."

I can afford to be scrupulous too, General, Florian thought, steeling himself to the lie.

"Are you willing to tell me about Sinnamarie, Dr. Florian?"

He felt his mouth drying. He answered with difficulty. "I will obey you in everything, General."

235

"But I don't want to command you to speak. A confidence that has to be forced is not worth having." He read the trapped, helpless eyes trying to avoid his own and said kindly, "All right, Doctor. I see that you don't want to. That's all, then." He stood up.

That he had failed with Bonaparte, Florian knew, because there had been no further mention of the half-promised assignment. He rose, feeling that he had been brushed by the fleeting wings of opportunity. His face revealed his disappointment. A little smile of understanding softened the commander's mouth.

"Dr. Desgenettes will explain the work I had in mind. See him tomorrow about it." He sketched a friendly mockery of salute, as he had to Monge at the Institute, then stepped out. An aide-de-camp appeared at once, and led Florian back through a maze of hallways and arches.

*　　　*　　　*

General Bonaparte's loyalty to persons he had known in his early, difficult days, was well known. This trait in him had protected Louis de Bourrienne before, who was banking on it now, for his chief was angry with him. The letter to Dr. Desgenettes concerning Dr. Florian, the General dictated while standing immediately in front of Bourrienne's desk. His eyes never left his secretary's face. Bourrienne struggled to keep all emotion hidden.

Bonaparte finished and Bourrienne sanded the paper, very conscious of the fact that his commander was still standing there, still watching him.

"No comment, Louis?"

"Sir?" Bourrienne said, blandly innocent.

"I thought you might have something to say about Dr. Florian's advancement. It was you who went to the trouble of arranging his evening after all, though with an opposite end in view, of course." The expression of the wide-spaced, deep-set eyes, warned Bourrienne that the danger was real.

"I don't believe I understand you, General," he said, knowing his pretense was hopeless.

"I've watched you trying to play on my emotions, to get me to punish or protect according to your interests. It seemed harmless enough, you're so easy to see through. Outright lying is something else. I hate a liar, Louis. What pleasure were you going to get out of seeing that man ruined? Tell me."

"Did he accuse me of lying to you? Then he was lying himself, General."

"If you want to get out of this with a whole skin, be careful of what you say."

"I didn't lie to you! I didn't! I took down his exact words."

"But words addressed to you, not to me."

"I didn't understand it that way."

"Why did you want to ruin him? Answer me!"

In a voice no louder than a whimper, the secretary said, "He was rude to me, General. He was loud and insistent and he treated me as of no account."

"Louis, I saw tonight a man of great charm and talent, whose only flaw would appear to be an excessive reserve. I find it hard to believe that he was rude to you. I think it far more likely that you were rude to him. You'd be wise to admit it, because I'm running out of patience."

Bourrienne capitulated. "Please forgive me. It won't happen again."

"See that it doesn't." Then Bonaparte dropped the matter, and he seemed to have forgotten about it. But Bourrienne had been too deeply startled to regain command of himself easily. How much damage had he done to himself? There was no way of telling. He was always claiming how well he understood Bonaparte, but he didn't understand him; no one did. His hands were shaking and it was impossible for him to keep up with the General's rapid dictation.

"What the devil is the matter with you?" Bonaparte said irritably, the fifth time he was asked to repeat himself.

"I am chagrined to have annoyed you, General," Bourrienne said, fawning.

"For God's sake, Louis. You're around here so much, of course you're going to annoy me. Forget about it, I have. But when are you going to forgive the world for those few unhappy years at Brienne?"

The secretary hung his head. He knew himself how that was the heart of his sickness. But he was ashamed at being found out.

Bonaparte said, "It is pardonable in schoolboys to plot revenge for hurt feelings. But that was a long time ago. You don't need to defend yourself in that way. The other day, you mentioned enjoying a feeling of having power over others. Power's twin is responsibility, Louis. Don't you know that yet?" His voice turned hard. "If I can't trust you, I'll have to replace you."

"You can trust me. You know you can!"

"For myself I believe it, but that is not enough. I expect you to be the generous advocate of others. You know I am severe by nature. Then bring to my attention those details that will help me become more lenient. I am too quick to punish. Remind me of that when you see I'm becoming angry. I ask it as a friend."

The shallow man was moved. He said impulsively, "I'll do it, Napoleon. You can trust me. Truly you can." Then he became afraid that he had overstepped. He blushed violently.

"Do you think we might get a little work done now?"

Bourrienne, his nerves under control again, kept pace easily. He felt warmth and satisfaction at the idea of playing the generous role Bonaparte had outlined for him. But in the back of his mind was the determination to see to it that Dr. Florian paid, paid high, for the fright he had had.

❖   ❖   ❖

Dr. Desgenettes explained to the translator what was wanted, and asked him to wait in the next room until Dr. Florian had arrived and the three could discuss it together. Slim and haughty in his white robe of the Imaum class, the translator bowed deeply to Desgenettes and glided out. The doctor sat on at his desk, tapping it thoughtfully. He was a badly disappointed man.

He liked Dr. Florian, and he had the good superior's loyalty to subordinates, the desire that they should acquit themselves well in everything. But he had never wanted anything in life as much as he wanted what was being taken from him and given to Florian. Desgenettes supposed it would be impractical for him to take that much time from his other duties; just the same, it had been his idea in the first place and was not easy to give up, so strong was its appeal to him.

Florian was announced and came in. Desgenettes stood up and shook hands with him, saying, "I envy you, Doctor. I had very much hoped to make this study myself. It may well be one of the most important and far-reaching projects being carried on in Egypt. But General Bonaparte feels that I ought not to give that much time, and also, because of the preliminary work you did at home as Medical Inspector, you are better qualified. Let me bring the translator back in here." He went to the door and summoned him. The priest came in and acknowledged his introduction to Florian in the pure French of Racine and Corneille, liquid, polished, a delight to the ear.

Dr. Desgenettes said, "Briefly, Dr. Florian, it is this. General Bonaparte is as deeply interested as we are in your old project of seeing the medical schools of France reopened one day, and the hospitals functioning again. But then certain superficial observations that I had made and reported to him started him to thinking along more ambitious lines yet. Of course, all this is dependent on our getting back to France someday, but he seems confident. He wants to see the schools and hospitals reopened, and also renovated."

"Renovated in what way, Doctor?"

"Yes, that's the crux of it. When I took over this hospital, it became clear to me that the Egyptians had at one time been far in advance, in their medical facilities, of anything that exists in Europe today. I believe there is much of value to be learned from them. I requested permission to take time to make a study of their methods. But I have been instructed to hand the assignment over to you."

Florian's dark eyes glowed. His thin, hard-planed face came alive with delight. "I can't imagine anything that would have more appeal to me."

"I can believe that, since I feel the same way." But actually, he had surrendered the last remnant of his vexation at being robbed. Though he would have derived much enjoyment from it, it was not a lifeline to him and obviously was to Florian. There's no use talking, Desgenettes thought; our General understands the human heart as no other man ever has.

He said to Florian, "Goma-el-Azbar is the school; you'll find it built around the mosque. A number of original manuscripts there should prove of great interest. Also, you will want to interview native physicians and officials. There are several hospitals. Most of them have been closed for years, but judging from my experience with this one, it will not be difficult to reconstruct many practices that existed when this civilization was at its height. You may begin as soon as you wish. Today, if you like."

"Yes. I'm eager to start!" Florian said.

The older doctor rose and shook hands with the young one, and wished him success in generous terms. The little sigh of a disappointed heart went unnoticed by them both.

*　　　*　　　*

The first of the manuscripts that he chose to have translated was the *Al Tadhkira*, the work of a long-dead physician, Dâwûd-al-

Antâkî. There did not seem much of value in it for modern times, and he was about to move on to something else, when a description of treatments for both ophthalmia and blood fluke infection came to light. His colleagues at the Institute were still looking for effective methods of treatment, so far without success. There could be no harm in trying these old recipes on a few control cases. The cases were easy to find: almost the entire native population was afflicted with one or the other of the diseases, and their incidence was high among the French as well.

In a matter of days, there was improvement in his control cases; in a little longer time, there were actual cures. Gratified and excited, Florian prepared a full account of this rediscovery of lost medical knowledge, with detailed descriptions of the pathology observed in his control cases. He read the paper at a meeting of the medical division of the Institute, and later, he was asked to read an abbreviated version at a general meeting attended by all the sections, at which General Bonaparte was present. The dead physician Dâwûd-al-Antâkî was thus responsible for his living colleague's second ovation by the Institute, an honor sought by all the savants in Egypt. Bonaparte said nothing to Florian personally, but his order extending the benefits of the treatments to the native population was proof that he realized the importance of what Florian had accomplished.

Other valuable manuscripts translated in part or whole were the works of Alî-ibn-Redwân, whose description of the poor hygienic conditions in Cairo was as apt as if one of the French savants had completed it but yesterday and whose medical topography of Egypt was a mine of wealth for the report Florian was to make: the fourteen thousand drugs indigenous to the country as listed by Ibn-al-Baitâr, and the pharmaceutical book of Al-Kûhîn-al-Attâr-al-Isrâ'îlî.

Not all of his work was with dusty manuscripts, however. He was embarrassed by riches; there was too much to see and understand. Every hour brought a new adventure of the mind.

At the beginning, he was somewhat in awe of his confrère, the priest-translator, but the priest was also a physician and they were not long making friends. From him Florian learned how the great physician Rhazes had determined the sites of hospitals by hanging fresh meat at various points in the city; where the meat took longest to putrify, there a hospital should be. The best preserved of these buildings had been founded in 1283. It had been divided into wards: for the wounded, for those suffering from diseases of the eye, for fever cases, and a special ward for those whose ailments escaped diagnosis. The wards had been cooled and freshened by running fountains whose ruins still existed. Airiness and space and light were important features. Florian remembered the dark, airless wards of the Hôtel Dieu, which, before the Revolution, had laid claim to being the finest hospital in Europe. It was customary at the Hôtel Dieu to thrust patients four and five in a bed together, the contagious cases lying side by side with those who were not. Nursing in France had been done by rough brutal persons hired from wineshops and street-corners, but in the old hospitals of Egypt where the nurses had been regarded by the doctors as more important than their own left hands, training had been extensive.

The squirming life of Cairo was unrolled before Florian's dazzled eyes with all the beauty and suddenness of one of their jewellike rugs. He walked in the poverty-stricken places, and saw general misery like nothing his Occidental eyes had ever rested on. He entered the palaces and saw the luxuries of an opium dream. He talked with priest-physicians, and with men of law called ulemas, and cadis and sheiks, and visited them in their homes. He became accustomed to sitting crosslegged on fat cushions thrown down on the floor, and to choosing from trays those delicacies that appealed to his palate. Even, he became accustomed to the barely stirring curtains behind which the women waited for their lords. Several more times, he was given the opportunity of refusing a beautiful slave to share his bed.

Everywhere Dr. Florian went he heard praise of Bonaparte. Actually the excellence of the General's rule endeared him less than his own personality did. This vanquished people required to be dazzled, and he dazzled them. He ruled with imagination; there was dash and fire to everything he did. Sultan el Kebir, they called him. The Lord of Flame.

Except for Diane's enforced isolation, the Florians were very happy. He had little time to spend with her now. Sometimes whole days went by during which she never spoke or was spoken to and her meals, though well-cooked and deftly served, were eaten alone. He felt that it was wrong to ask her to go on any long time like this, and yet, when he remembered how he had lied to Bonaparte, he was terrified at the idea of being found out.

One thing he could do for her was to make her his secretary. She took notes on his conversations, thus relieving him of the work of assembling notes; and during the day, while he moved on to fresh wonders, Diane reworked her notes and put them in order. She would not have been able to do this had she not listened with so much attention while he lectured the five young men who had been his medical students during the Revolution. While she loved the feeling of having a part in the great work he had been given, the problem of her loneliness was not entirely solved by it, he knew.

IV

THE LOVELY blonde Frenchwoman at Headquarters was not being kept a secret after all. Dr. Florian saw her several times riding horseback with Bonaparte or with a small escort of armed men or shopping at the bazaars. Actually, the doctor was about the last Frenchman in Cairo to know all about the affair, because his time was being spent with the native personages who never had acquired the European habit of gossip.

One day when he was walking with the translator on a street near Headquarters, he was stopped by a youthful officer. "Excuse me, sir, but are you a physician?" Florian said that he was. "Would you come with me, sir? It's an emergency."

As the day was far advanced, Dr. Florian said goodbye to the priest after making an appointment for the next day. He followed the soldier, questioning him.

"My friend keeps trying to kill himself, sir, and no one can stay with him any longer because we have to go on parade."

"Then I had better stop for something to help him sleep," Florian said.

Six young men, low-grade officers all, were staying with the suicidally minded patient. He was a good-looking young man with a fresh, open face, but the face was oddly collapsed when Florian saw him. He was Sub-lieutenant Fourès of the artillery, the other officers told the doctor, and yes, he had been drinking most of the afternoon. But he had talked about killing himself before he became so drunk, and they believed that he would because he had been prevented in two attempts already.

"I'll have to make a report of this," Florian said, stirring a powder into a glass of wine. "Do you know what reason he has to want to kill himself?" And then he heard the story that brought down his joy of life with the suddenness of Jericho's walls falling. Stripped and shocked, he stood there, the glass in his hand, and comprehended the awful danger he was in, the punishment he had escaped this far through sheer luck, but that might yet be exacted.

The blonde woman he had seen at Headquarters had not been brought along for Bonaparte's pleasure, but for Lieutenant Fourès', whose wife she was. Like Florian, Fourès had smuggled his wife into Egypt in a disguise, an equerry's uniform in her case. They had lived happily at his billet, an idyll of conjugal relations triumphing over stern military authority—but then the wife's presence had become known. The commander had sent the husband to France on a mailship, with dispatches. He had blandly taken possession of the wife.

The mailship on which Fourès was traveling in blissful ignorance of developments at Cairo, was stopped by the British patrol. The ship and her cargo were taken as prize, but the sailors and passengers were released at a point near Alexandria. The British were ignorant of the efficient measures taken by Bonaparte and his Institute, and supposed that the Army would be starving and that the extra mouths would provide extra embarrassment. So yesterday, Fourès had returned to Cairo, but found his wife gone. His brother officers had had to tell him what had happened. Early this same afternoon, he had gone there and while his chief had consented to see him, he had refused to discuss Madame Fourès at all. It was against his orders that she was in Egypt and so he would make such disposition of her as pleased him. Fourès had been drinking, and trying to kill himself, since.

Florian could see it all. Only the characters were different. It was Diane who was imprisoned behind the swaying curtains at Headquarters; it was himself hearing Bonaparte say that, powerless under the cool stare of those challenging eyes. A crueler punishment for a husband whose crime was that he loved his wife too well could scarcely have been devised.

Diane was badly frightened when he told her. But she tried to be sensible about it. "If he's found a woman who pleases him, he won't be looking for another one, Charlot. He isn't a Turk, after all."

"You can't tell what he'll do. He's capable of anything, evidently. He might decide to give you away to one of his officers, as a punishment to me. It has certainly been made plain that he won't let us off if he finds out, so we'll just have to see to it that he never finds out."

He dismissed the servants. He and Diane would have to do the work of the house themselves, but no one must know anything about their affairs. He became possessed by an idea that he might come home one day and find her gone, and he began taking advantage of every possible excuse to stay with her. Though he dared not stop work on the report entirely, his interest in it was ended and he did as little as possible. He did not enjoy Institute meetings any more; he attended few of them.

Diane tried hard to persuade him to different behavior. "Charlot, you will break my heart if it turns out that my being here ruins you. I was as anxious to stay as you were to have me, but not as your burden, my dear, not as a cause of your destruction. Please, please go back to your duties. You'll attract more attention to us this way, can't you see that?"

But he was captive to his obsession. He followed the Fourès story with the passionate interest of self-identification, to the point where the young officer came to accept the monstrous retribution and now served as faithfully as before. But the hatred that Bonaparte had earned from Fourès, he received full measure from Florian. Alert, suspicious, misanthropic, Florian drew back from the brilliant life that had been opened to him, in fierce lonesome guardianship of the woman who was his touchstone with life. The man who had escaped Sinnamarie now drew its vacuum around him. Diane, desperate in his behalf, began to toy with the idea of surrendering herself in order to set him free.

❋　　　❋　　　❋

The Ottoman Porte declared war on France in Egypt. The troops of Djezzar occupied El Arish, and even Gaza. Bonaparte announced plans to divide his Army, leaving half to garrison the Nile valley, organizing the other half into five squares which, Monge said, were mathematically conceived to insure a maximum result with a minimum loss of life. Desgenettes, Larrey, Royer, and the greater part of the medical corps were going with the fighting Army.

Desgenettes sent for Florian. He asked if Florian were ready yet for service on the field. One of the other doctors would be grateful for the easy post in Cairo, he said.

Florian was in a terrible position. To refuse would be a flagrant case of shirking his duty. But no one else knew about Diane's presence in the city; she could be abducted by natives while he was gone, and sold on the slave market. His thin face racked with unhappiness, Florian pleaded dizzy spells, then the importance of the study which engaged him.

"I thought you would have finished that by now."

"No, but I'll finish quickly."

"All right, but you'll have to go on active duty here, and if there is great need for more doctors at the front, you'll be one that I send for." Florian withdrew, relieved to have gotten his way, but that he had not convinced Desgenettes, he knew. The disappointment the other doctor felt in him had been made plain.

"It's your duty to go," Diane said, when he told her.

"I want to, I'm a doctor after all. But my first responsibility is to you."

"No," she said, "it's to yourself. Please go back and ask Dr. Desgenettes to take you."

"I won't leave you here without protection of any kind. That's final."

Diane thought recklessly, I don't care what happens to me. But I won't be the cause of Charlot's destruction, I won't!

*   *   *

Wearing the concealing bournous over the prettiest of her European dresses, Diane Florian slipped through the hot dirty streets. This was the first time since her arrival months ago that Diane had been outside of the house. There was much to see, much that would normally have interested her. Nervousness prevented her from taking any notice of things outside herself.

Her first plan, of surrendering herself at Headquarters, she had given up. She was too frightened of Bonaparte to do it. From what Charlot had told her about his immediate superior, Dr. Desgenettes sounded like someone who might help them. He was in charge at the hospital and she was hoping to find him there. If she could enlist his aid, it might be possible to go on concealing herself until Bonaparte had gone with the Army; in that way, Charlot would be free to go to the front.

Desgenettes was pointed out to her on the steps of the hospital, where he was engaged in conversation with a good-looking young man whom she took to be another of his staff doctors. Diane approached them shyly. Desgenettes, a man in his mid-fifties, excused himself to the other, saying, "Let me hear what the fellow wants. Perhaps it's an emergency."

She glanced around apprehensively. She seemed to be alone with them. "I need your help, Doctor," she said, letting the bournous hood back long enough to show her shining hair, the tender pure lines of brow and cheek. "I am Dr. Florian's wife," she explained, drawing the hood forward again. "Because of me, Charlot refused to go with the Army, but he must! It's his duty."

"How in the world did you get into Egypt, Madame?"

In her nervousness, she began explaining too fast, asking him to understand too much, too soon. "I left the ship in this disguise when Charlot did. We had asked for permission for me to stay, but General Bonaparte refused us. We had been separated such a long time— I know we shouldn't have done it, Doctor. I wish you would try to understand."

"What I don't understand is why you are giving yourself up now."

"He knows it's his duty to go, but he won't consent to leaving me here without protection. I'm not going to let Charlot ruin himself for my sake."

"You're a very brave young woman," Desgenettes said. She felt that he wanted to help her, yet there was something reserved and strange in his manner.

"And a beautiful one," the younger man said. He was watching Diane closely, from amused eyes. She paid him little attention, looking at Desgenettes trustfully.

"Why are you confiding in me?"

"I need your help," she said again.

"Just what is it you want me to do?"

"If you would help me conceal myself until the Army leaves— Once General Bonaparte was gone, I wouldn't be afraid to ask for protection at Headquarters."

"You should have waited to do this, Madame."

"But I'm trying to surrender myself so that Charlot will feel free to go with you."

"Your husband was given permission to stay."

"But you were disappointed in him. He told me you were."

"Yes, I was disappointed, I couldn't imagine why he was behaving so. I understand now." He said to the other man, "Well, Louis?" That look of amused delight deepened. "I see no real reason to report her," Desgenettes said, his tone pleading. "The Army will be gone in a week. Don't you think we might overlook it for that short time?"

"Be careful, Doctor."

"I am trying to be careful. But what she has done is brave and conscientious. I would like to help her. Don't you feel some little stirring of pity for them, Louis?"

"I'm afraid I don't."

Too late, Diane realized that the young smiling man with the narrow head was a threat to her. Her eyes on Desgenettes were filled with appeal. But he was helpless. He said, "Permit me to present him, Madame Florian. This is Louis de Bourrienne, General Bonaparte's secretary."

She took a backward step. Her face was stricken. "Come with me," Bourrienne said, taking her elbow.

"I won't!" She tried to get free.

"You have no choice, Madame."

She looked at Desgenettes wildly. He said, "I'm afraid you must."

"Come," Bourrienne said again, urging her with his hand. Shaking with terror, she permitted Charlot's enemy to pilot her through the hot streets, toward Headquarters. There, by Bourrienne, she was placed under formal arrest. Expecting a cell and her wrists shackled, instead she was led through palace hallways to a luxurious apartment. For hours, she was left alone except when food that she could not eat was brought to her. The door, on trying it, was not locked, but when she opened it and looked out, the corridor was guarded. The windows of her apartment were too high and too narrow to permit escape that way. Scenes she had witnessed at Pavia returned vividly, and haunted her. It was nearly midnight when General Bonaparte came.

❖   ❖   ❖

Exactly as his obsession had warned him, it happened. Dr. Florian came home, and Diane was not there. The frenzied man raced from room to room, looking for her in impossibly small places, calling her name. He would drop into a chair, exhausted, hiding his face with his hands, until a new seizure of wanting to search the rooms he knew to be empty would drive him through them again.

It had been a mistake to dismiss the servants. At least they could have signed to him something of what had happened. But having no idea what had caused her disappearance, he was afraid to act lest he only provoke what he was trying desperately to avoid.

Much later, Dr. Desgenettes came around to the billet, having guessed how worried Florian would be. One look at that drawn, sick face told Desgenettes that "worried" was a pitifully inadequate description of what the younger doctor was feeling. He felt sorrier for Dr. Florian than he had ever needed to feel for any other human being. How they love each other, he thought. He told Florian what had happened.

"Any other man of my acquaintance would have kept her secret. But it had to be Louis de Bourrienne," Desgenettes finished. Florian started away. "Where are you going?" Desgenettes said.

"To Headquarters, of course."

"I've already seen the General. There's nothing you can do."

"I won't stand back and let her be harmed."

"She's here against orders, Doctor. He has a perfect right to dispose of her in any way he likes." Florian started past him. "Florian, listen to me! If you provoke him any further, he may have both of you executed."

"Damn it, let me go! I'm going to Headquarters and get her."

"Doctor, please let me advise you. I've been in Army work for years. It's not a bad life as long as you obey orders, but once you're afoul of authority, you simply have to make up your mind to accepting whatever is handed you. You'll get nowhere going there and making a scene and you may do yourself, and her, irreparable harm."

"Are you seriously suggesting that I behave as if nothing had happened?"

"Not exactly. Your one chance now rests in distinguished service on the field. At least you can be grateful that the campaign is starting so soon."

"For God's sake, Desgenettes! I'm not going to wait around here, wondering what is happening to her. I can't! I'll throw myself at his feet, I'll do anything."

"But it wouldn't do any good. He dislikes that sort of thing."

"That night I saw him, he seemed more than ordinarily kind. There must be some way I can rouse his pity."

"In other circumstances, perhaps, but he doesn't have time for you now, with a campaign starting. If you had any real explanation to make, I would advise you differently, but he has a right to be angry. No one enjoys the feeling of having been deceived."

"Is there really nothing I can do?"

"Believe me, nothing. Not now. As I told you, your best chance, your only chance in fact, is distinguished service. If you keep your head, things may come out all right for you yet."

"Why doesn't he arrest me instead? Why does she have to suffer for my mistakes?"

The practical Desgenettes said, "You're too valuable, Doctor, now that a campaign is starting."

After his superior left, the empty house seemed about to crush Florian. He left it, walking the streets, not aware of taking any direction. But his steps led him unerringly toward Headquarters. He stood a long time, his eyes stabbing at the lighted palace, as though he could force its secrets from the sheer need to know. He fought with himself. The advice Desgenettes had given him was good, but to follow it was very nearly beyond his strength.

While he was standing there, he became aware that he was not entirely alone. The shade of Pichegru had been biding its time. The mocking light-eyed phantom had never given him up, and was waiting, and had drawn close.

V

DISTINGUISHED SERVICE—if it would help Diane, he was ready to perform impossible feats. Dr. Florian drove himself past the efforts of the other doctors, and all were working nearly to the limit of strength. "You'll kill yourself, Dr. Florian," Dr. Desgenettes warned him, but did not press the point. He knew that what Florian was doing was necessary.

The battles followed each other quickly. El Arish and Mount Tabor; Gaza was taken, Jaffa. They pushed on to the bloodiest work of all, the siege of St. Jean d'Acre. In his exhaustion, Florian hardly noticed what was going on around him. He lived through a welter of shattered limbs, of hoarse screams of agony; he scarcely slept.

Opportunity came finally, during that siege. General Caffarelli, Bonaparte's personal friend, was brought into the hospital with a shattered arm. Dr. Larrey decided on amputation. Though Caffarelli had survived a leg amputation years ago, his condition steadily worsened after the removal of the arm. After many days, Larrey told the commander that his friend's case was hopeless, that Caffarelli was dying. Bonaparte said, "Ask Dr. Florian to attempt transfusion."

None of the other doctors had ever witnessed a transfusion. Several of them asked to attend, including Desgenettes and Larrey. He read their fascination as they pressed near, watching his every move. He came to a quick decision. Although he really preferred the syringe and basin method, feeling it safer, in this case he would use Folli's direct transfusion, and his own blood. He justified the less accurate method to himself on medical grounds, but his real reason for wanting to use it was because it was effective drama. If he could save the life of Bonaparte's friend in this dramatic way, perhaps Diane would be restored to him.

While he assembled the equipment, he gave quick instructions to his superiors, Desgenettes and Larrey. Florian had not attempted a transfusion since Montpellier, although he had carried the equipment since Bonaparte had given his sanction to the lawless maneuver. The literature of Folli and Colle and Denis, the experiments he himself had made in Montpellier, passed rapidly through his mind, as he unwrapped the oily coverings that kept the blood vessel soft and moist. Next the trocar, around which the bone cannula fitted tightly, and the silver tube for insertion in the donor's artery.

He jerked off coat and shirt, exposing the tender flesh of his shoulders and upper arms. He jabbed the silver tube into the artery of his wrist. The pain was as though he had severed his hand. He pressed the sharp point of the trocar against Caffarelli's wrist, until the cannula entered the vein; then he released the trocar and withdrew it. The dying man watched him with patient, wondering eyes. But Florian hardly thought about Caffarelli and what he was feeling, his real attention was on the impression he himself was making. Distinguished service—this was his big chance.

Florian stood up, the tube from his spurting wrist leading to the vein he had opened in the dying General. "Quickly," he said to the other doctors, who began raining blows down on him with sharp little whips. The whipping of Florian's flesh would make his blood run faster, lessening the danger of clotting, which was always a possibility in direct transfusion. His skin began to rip and bleed. The pain was exquisite. He paid no attention to the blows or the pain, watching Caffarelli for the signs he dreaded.

When he saw the rash starting, and Caffarelli's breathing becoming labored, he knew transfusion had failed. The mysterious factor he never had solved had intervened in this case that was so important to him. Light-headed from loss of blood, and so bitterly disappointed that it was an effort not to break down, he explained to the other doctors what was happening. In the back of his mind was a bitter wonder as to whether, if he had chosen the safer method, Caffarelli might not have lived after all.

General Caffarelli died in convulsive agonies a short time after the transfusion. Florian, gaunt and tight-lipped, continued to drive himself.

*   *   *

The Army, victorious in so many battles, met an enemy they did not know how to fight. The scourge of the Middle Ages struck at the French in Syria: plague. Bonaparte raised the siege and withdrew his stricken Army back to Jaffa.

Not since the Sinnamarie miasma had raged through the little desperate colony on Guiana had Dr. Florian worked so hard and selflessly, and so hopelessly. Jaffa bore an unholy resemblance in his mind to Sinnamarie. Mud huts instead of grass, desert surrounding instead of jungle, the known killer plague instead of the unknown, the miasma—these were the differences, but the likenesses outweighed them.

Bonaparte was resolved not to bring the Army back until plague had been stamped out. He did not want the dying heroes of El Arish and Mount Tabor to infect their healthy companions in the Nile valley. So the Army camped, and sickened, and died, and only the doctors, a handful of worn-out men, fought for them.

The doctors inoculated themselves according to the dangerous, uncertain methods of their time. They powdered the scabs of plague sores and introduced the horror into their own veins. One doctor died of plague after inoculation; the others, Florian among them, developed mild symptoms and then recovered. It was a day's work to inoculate one man, so there was no thought of making the practice general. And in spite of their hoped-for immunity, they continued the use of the old, superstitious measures advanced in the Middle Ages. Plague was not a thing to experiment with, and all their human instincts bade them preserve themselves in every available way.

The greater part of their work was not in the overcrowded hospital filled with its dying, but in the camp itself. Segregation of the stricken from the healthy had been named in the Florentine laws as one measure that yielded real results. The doctors were kept busy moving among the bivouacs, looking for new cases. They tried to be careful, yet each of them knew he had sent men ill of dysentery or simple fever into the sure death of the plague wards.

The sick soldiers pleaded not to go to the wards, and the doctors had to bundle them off forcibly. Medical care provided there was minimum; rough nursing by natives or Army criminals forced to it at swordpoint, under the supervision of one doctor and an apothecary. They took the ugly duty by rote, Desgenettes serving his turn without trying to evade it.

Even in this outpost, the hospital building was better designed, larger, lighter, airier, than anything in Europe. In his half fainting state of utter exhaustion, Dr. Florian felt regret that he had not concluded the report that might someday have made such a difference to the civilization of the west.

✻ ✻ ✻

When General Bonaparte learned that his hospital was more dreaded by the soldiers than the plague itself was, he began to wonder just what went on there. He decided to find out for himself. He was not at all unaware of the risk he was taking, but a mutual emotion existed between Bonaparte and his soldiers that was compelling and powerful, and he was not willing that they should die apart from him. Also, some move toward restoring confidence was going to have to be made, because his fear-filled Army was on the verge of stampeding.

Accompanied by four aides, he went to the hospital, but to their immense relief he excused them before its doors and entered alone. A remarkable apparition met him, a doctor, swathed head-to-toe, wearing long gloves, who moved slowly and with a gliding motion, not to stir up plague poisons. His nose and mouth were bandaged by a thin layer of lint soaked in vinegar and ground cloves, and an atomizer containing vinegar and rose water occupied his hands. It was Florian.

This was the first time during the campaign that Dr. Florian had seen his General face-to-face. He was nearly overcome by mixed emotions—dread, hatred, and a horrible dependence, because no one else could be trusted to defend the French in Egypt. His dark eyes blazed behind the cowls and masks, and his hands were shaking. Behind that bronzed, impassive face, existed what intimate memories of the captive beloved? He wanted to throw himself on the Army chief and demand with his fists an accounting of what she had suffered. "Please go back, General," his muffled voice said. "You shouldn't be here."

"Who are you? What the devil are you doing in that rig?"

"Dr. Florian, General. Please leave at once."

"Florian. So." He inspected the spectral figure before him with those hard eyes Florian remembered too well. "You're enough to frighten a man to death yourself," he observed. "Is there any point to all that?" He listened to the explanation with his usual close attention, but then said, "Is your duty to yourselves, or to the sick men?" Florian flushed behind his masks, and did not try to answer. A mocking little smile hardened the commander's mouth. "All right," he said, "come, show me what you're doing here."

"I can't permit you to go into the wards, General."

"You can't permit me, Doctor Florian?"

Florian spoke in the low voice he used when moved or deeply disturbed. "You are my commander, sir, but this is a medical matter. Your personal safety is far too important to us all. You haven't been inoculated, you're not protected in any way. Please withdraw."

"I'm going through every room of this hospital and see for myself what's going on. You will please conduct me."

"General, I must forbid it."

"You've registered your objection, Doctor. That's enough, come along."

"Let us inoculate you. Then when we know it's been effective, you can make your inspection."

"How many of my men have you inoculated?"

"We don't have the facilities nor the time for that."

"Then you don't have the facilities or the time for me. Come along."

Florian snatched off his robes, saying, "Wear these, anyway, it's madness to expose yourself as you're doing!" His emotion was genuine. Behind his hatred of Bonaparte was respect, and even attraction. Also, if the General died of the plague in Jaffa, what horrors might happen to those left in Cairo—to Diane? The robes outthrust on his hands, he followed the other toward the nearest archway.

Bonaparte threw over his shoulder, "By all means, take your witch's garments off. But don't expect me to assume them."

The impression of hard authority that seemed so much a part of him disappeared as soon as he entered the ward. Florian was amazed at the change in him. He was tender and compassionate as he went from pallet to pallet. He sat down on the edges of pallets, or bent and touched the men with his hands, never showing fear or horror. Though he joked with them more frequently than he sympathized, his concern was as plain as their plague sores. As for them, pride and a sort of fierce joy replaced their listlessness, at seeing him. They did not appear to share Florian's concern that he was exposing himself. It was as though they believed him immune because immortal. Florian followed from ward to ward, still shaking with fierce, mixed emotions.

They approached a pallet on which a weeping boy was lying. Bonaparte knelt by him. In a warm, expressive voice, he said, "Don't do that. Whatever happens, you did the best you could. That's all that counts." The simple words struck at Florian, who felt tears prick his eyes.

"But I'm so ashamed, General."

"Ashamed. Why?"

"No one will touch me, they can't even bear to look at me. The doctor comes around here holding his nose, and the others hurry past, and they can't wait for me to die. I'm trying, General. I'm trying to die!"

"But I don't want you to die."

"But the maggots have got to me, General. Look." He showed the face he had been hiding. There was a peculiar silence.

Bonaparte said over his shoulder, "Bring warm water and vinegar and a linen cloth. Quickly." Florian went over to an orderly who had been leaning against the wall indifferently when they came in, and now was standing at attention. He repeated the command, adding rosewater and cloves. He went back and stood behind Bonaparte, who was still kneeling. He steeled himself to the ugly idea of having to bathe the maggoty sores.

The basin of water and the cloth were brought almost as soon as requested. Orders that Florian and the other doctors gave went unfulfilled for hours, if they ever were carried out. The orderly brushed by Florian and went down on one knee beside Bonaparte. "What do you want me to do, General?"

"Just hold the basin. Like that, good." He side-glanced. "Weren't you in Italy with me?"

"Yes, General Bonaparte."

"What are you doing here?"

"I was caught trying to desert, sir."

"Why?"

"I was afraid."

He was dipping and wringing the cloth. "I didn't think my veterans of Arcole and Rivoli were afraid of anything," he said.

"I didn't think so either, until the plague."

"You don't seem much afraid now."

"I am not afraid now," the deserter said, watching him.

"Return to your regiment when we have finished here. Don't be so foolish again." He began stroking the cloth over the raw, crawling sore. His movements were gentle, yet firm. He neither flinched from the pain he was inflicting, nor caused any unnecessary pain. Florian was transfixed. What a doctor he would have made! Florian was thinking. When maggots dropped onto his hand, Bonaparte shook them off as if they were as innocuous as dust specks. There was no trace of disgust, not even when a putrid bleeding began.

Florian noticed the boy's hand groping toward his commander's wrist in a gesture of shy trust. He began to realize the unconscious brutality with which he and the other doctors had treated these men. Fear, and an overriding weariness, had made them forget the first teaching of Hippocrates—that the patient feels. He feels more than pain. He feels fright, insecurity, and even shame of his sickness. But no one of the men of healing had remembered, and toward them the plague-stricken had made no gestures of any kind. They had lain down torpidly and prayed to die and relieve the world of them. He stood starkly, his hands hanging at his sides, his remorse clawing him.

Bonaparte finished and stood up. His voice was savage. "What the devil was the idea of letting a condition like that go untended?"

The accusation on top of his own remorse was too much. A man who has been trying to the end of his strength can be put in the wrong only so many times before something in him snaps. Florian said, "He's dying. We have too much to do to waste our time with him."

His feeling then was of standing alone in a storm and a bolt of lightning falling almost where he stood. A thrill of fear so inordinate that it resembled ecstasy shot through him. His ears roared; his stomach rose against his throat. Then the outside world rushed in on him. He heard the dying boy sob harshly, he heard the would-be deserter's snort of contempt. And he heard Bonaparte, level and icy, say, "Leave the wards, Dr. Florian. Don't try to come back."

*　　　*　　　*

The spectre of Pichegru had triumphed after all. Pichegru had robbed Florian of his identity, substituting Pichegru's own. Once Florian had ordered Pichegru out of the wooden hospital in Sinna-marie, for making very nearly the same remark that Florian had just made. The light-eyed General was smiling coldly; he was much pleased with himself.

255

Dr. Desgenettes came late that night to Florian's tent. His face was blank and drawn with weariness. His eyes, though curious, were still kind.

"Florian, I'm afraid you're finished. Did you really say to him, there in the wards, that a dying man was not worth our bothering about?"

He thrust out his hands. "Have you never been driven to saying something that you certainly did not mean, that you will regret to the end of your life? Yes, I said it. He persisted in going through the wards, and I was frantic at the risk he was running. There was no one but myself to take the responsibility. He disagreed with virtually everything we were doing, and he made it seem as if I personally was at fault."

"Your irritation was natural, I suppose. I confess to congratulating myself that I wasn't on duty there today."

Florian said furiously, "It never would have happened if the General had stayed outside of the hospital where he belonged, and left me inside it where I belonged."

To that, Desgenettes shook his head. "No, Dr. Florian. Not only did his visit restore confidence to the men outside the hospital, but remarkable as this will sound to you, every case within it shows definite improvement. Some we had given up are on the mend."

"Is it possible?"

"I've just come from there. If you live to finish that report on hospital procedure, you might include a paragraph advising doctors to stamp out medical fetishism, and replace it with that genuine concern and love for the sick that Hippocrates advocated. It still works miracles, Dr. Florian."

"If I—*live*," he said wonderingly. "Do you think he means to have me shot?"

"It wouldn't surprise me. He's Corsican, and he loves those men in a way we can't understand."

"But—I don't deserve that—anyone could have said it. You could have said it yourself." He was stammering from the physical chill of true fright.

"I know. Well, I'll do what I can for you, but don't expect too much. After all, he's under an even greater strain than we are ourselves. Meanwhile I have no instructions regarding you, except that you're not to go to the hospital again. I'm too shorthanded to let you sulk in your tent brooding about your future. Report on the field tomorrow, six o'clock as usual. Leave your robes and mask off, none of

us are being allowed to wear those." He nodded and shambled out,
weariness riding his shoulders.

* * *

Now Florian worked harder than ever, harder than a man should
work. No summons came for him; no blow fell. Finally, the doctors
knew the plague had been stamped out. There were ninety-seven
cases still hospitalized, but a new case had not been reported for
days.

The camp was electrified by news of a hard-riding courier from
Cairo. Rumors flew. The plague was in Cairo. The Turks were in
Cairo. Paul Barras had sent a big fleet to bring them all home. Bonaparte's custom was to share his information and general plans with
his soldiers, and he did so now, stopping the rumors with facts.

The Ottoman Porte had landed a large army near Alexandria, and
a second army under the Murad Bey was threatening Cairo itself. It
was necessary to go at once to the defense. The camp bustled with
preparations.

Dr. Florian, who had had nothing to do with the hospital since the
day of inspection, was spared the anguished harassment of the other
doctors as to what ought to be done about the plague cases. It would
be criminal folly to bring them to Cairo. The six thousand survivors
encamped at Jaffa had become immune, but plague would start up
quickly among twelve thousand troops garrisoning Cairo, as well as
the native population, if it were introduced there. Desgenettes and
Larrey and the others felt sick at the idea of abandoning the dying
men to furious Turks, who were sure to spend their pent-up wrath
against everything French upon these helpless bodies. But really,
there seemed no way out of that.

Florian waited eagerly for the march to begin. Diane's life was safe
as long as the French held Cairo, but certainly would not be if Turks
took the city. Now he became aware of the extent of his admiration
and respect for Bonaparte, because the one thought in his mind was
that the General must get there in time, that only he could save the
city—and Diane. They would begin the march at twilight, when the
burning sands had cooled somewhat, and would march all that night
and many nights. The officers' horses, Bonaparte's included, had
been commandeered for the transportation of men wounded in battle
and those ill of noncommunicable diseases.

The commander's summons surprised Florian but did not alarm

him unduly. If retaliation were intended, it would have happened sooner than this. He knew he had been working heroically and self-lessly; he even hoped for a word of commendation. When he arrived Royer, the head apothecary, had been summoned along for the same meeting.

Florian and Royer waited outside the tent, their feet slowly baking on an oven of sun-scorched sand, and watched the aides and officers going in and out. Finally it was their turn.

Bonaparte nodded to both impartially, but it was Royer to whom he spoke. "How does a man die easiest?"

"In his sleep, I suppose, General. Or have I misunderstood you?"

"I think not. How do you produce this effect?"

"I *don't* understand you, General." Royer seemed to be begging him. Florian had no idea what this was about but he felt sorry for Royer.

"Opium?"

"That's one way, General," he said unwillingly.

"Do we have enough?"

"Please, sir——!"

"Just answer my questions. Is there enough in your stores?"

"Yes, General Bonaparte," Royer said in a hurt tired voice.

"Give me your keys." Silently he produced them. Bonaparte nodded toward the desk and Royer laid the keys there, five of them on a thin gold chain. "That's all. Forget about it. Your keys will be returned to you." Royer, his face blazing with relief, went out. Bonaparte and Florian were alone.

Florian was thinking that he had never seen a face so adamant. Young as he was, the man seemed ancient, as timeless as the Pyramids themselves. Apparently without feeling of any kind, as though in a dream or a trance, he sat staring at the keys. He seemed to have forgotten Florian. But at last he lifted his eyes, depthless, serene.

"All right, Dr. Florian. Pick them up and use them, and when you're done, give them back to him."

"What do you mean, sir?"

"There are ninety-seven plague-stricken who are too sick to re-cover. I can't try to bring them into Cairo, I won't abandon them. This is what I would want for myself."

Florian leaped from not understanding anything, to understand-ing everything. "No," he said. He was not even agitated. He was merely definite.

"That's an order, Dr. Florian."

"I won't do it."

Bonaparte searched his face, then resumed looking at Royer's five keys spilled on the desk, linked by the thin golden chain. "You seem to mean that."

"I do mean it."

"But I'll have you shot, you know. I have put up with enough from you."

"I'd rather be shot than do what you ask. There must be some other way."

"Then tell me what that is. I'll be eternally grateful."

"But I'm a doctor," Florian said. "If it must be done, get one of your soldiers to do it. I took a most holy Oath, General Bonaparte. I can't break it."

The other quoted in a grave and beautiful voice, " 'I will follow that system of regimen which, according to my ability and my judgment, I consider for the benefit of my patients, and abstain from whatever is deleterious and mischievous. I will give no deadly medicine to anyone if asked, nor suggest any such counsel.' " His voice fell away. There was silence in the tent. The sage of Cos seemed almost to be there and Florian felt lifted and strengthened by the wise, loving words, so familiar to him, so newly heard now.

"Desgenettes was just in here reciting that with his tears running. I let him off. I couldn't bring myself to forcing him. But the sick men are the responsibility of the doctors. I am not going to require of one of my soldiers that he poison his comrades."

"But you require it of me."

"Yes."

"Why am I singled out?"

"One of the doctors must. Surely the one who could throw it into the face of a dying man that he was not worth bothering about, is the one who would be troubled the least."

Florian looked at him from stricken eyes. Bonaparte looked back serenely. Slowly, as though dreaming, Florian picked up the keys.

✻   ✻   ✻

He stole through the nearly empty wards, death in his hands, the oldest and highest of oaths a broken column in his heart. At his elbow, a phantom walked, the barrel-chested man with prematurely grey hair and curiously light-blue eyes, who had been offended once at the height of Florian's principles. General Pichegru was smiling broadly.

The purplish desert twilight crawled through the wards of the old hospital like a darkness that was always going to follow the footsteps of Charlot Florian. Palestine's purple dusk spreading behind him was the stain of great sin.

Some of the men took the poison unknowingly, but others understood. Again and again, he heard such words as, "I knew he wouldn't forget about us." They meant Bonaparte, who cared about everyone, who remembered everyone, who had singled out Florian to destroy.

Dr. Florian had loved Diane more than life, and medicine more than either. Life remained; all else had been taken away. Ninety-seven times he slew himself as a doctor, and the twilight was complete, the stain of sin was all around him, before he was through.

EIGHT

The Oath Fulfilled

I'M TIRED, Dr. Desgenettes thought, and old. I can't go on campaign again so soon. One full night's sleep here in Cairo scarcely makes up for a hundred sleepless nights in Syria and Palestine. He thought resentfully, The soldiers are being excused from further duty. Why not the doctors?—we shared the same hardships. He leaned against the wall, rubbing his eyes which were glazed from exhaustion.

The remnant of the Army had spent its last strength getting here, yesterday the fourteenth of June. To fight the gathering enemy, there was only the Cairo garrison, six thousand men. Many of the staff officers were on the verge of mutiny. They wanted to negotiate. "We may get terms of some kind," their spokesman, Klèber, had told Bonaparte. "If you insist on fighting and we're beaten, it will end in massacre, if not death by torture." Bonaparte had answered, "Negotiate with what? The enemy knows our position. But I believe I can beat them at that." Bonaparte shared the hardships too, Desgenettes thought, yet he can look rested and fresh, and sure. In his presence, you believed he could win; apart from him, you remembered that six thousand men were surrounded by more than twenty thousand. It was hopeless.

Desgenettes saw Diane Florian crossing the crowded room, apparently intending to speak to him. For a moment, he allowed himself to take pleasure in her beauty, her graceful walk, the simplicity of her sheathlike dress. She and Pauline Fourès were the only Frenchwomen in Cairo and the men watched for them, somehow feeling less strangely adrift in this alien land when they glimpsed these lovely reminders of home. But then Desgenettes realized what the future held for the women. At best, it would be harem life until their attractions faded—the worst was outside the realm of his somewhat limited imagination. Had there been time, he would have escaped before she could reach him.

"Where is Charlot, Doctor? I can't find him anywhere!"

Madame Florian, he thought, when you leave Cairo with six thousand men, and you return with something under two thousand, some faces are sure to be missing. Aloud he said, "I'm sorry, but I don't know where he is. I lost track of him after Jaffa."

"Where shall I enquire? Whom should I see?"

"Madame, we're going to fight it out. We leave Cairo before night-fall. No one can help you now. Excuse me, but I have a great deal to do." He turned away. She followed him.

"Doctor, you must tell me what to do. You're his superior, you know how to go about looking for him."

Suddenly he felt toward her an emotion resembling anger. It was not anger, but even he could not give it another name. He was seeing those nights and days of forced marching; himself and his staff stumbling past dying men, not pausing to help them lest contact be lost with what remained of the Army. Desgenettes said brutally, "Your husband is dead. You may as well accept it." He knew what Florian's terrible orders had been, and he guessed that death would be easier than living with yourself, after that.

All color had drained from her face. She looked ready to faint. "Are you ill?" he said, supporting her. "There's no point in grieving over him!" Was it possible that the woman did not understand yet what their position was? "He's lucky to be out of it. I confidently expect every French person in Egypt to be dead before the week is out, and likely by torture. The Murad Bey is at Natron Lakes with an army more than twice the size of our own. I don't know how many armed Turks have been landed at Aboukir Bay under the protection of British ships, but their number greatly exceeds the effectives we have here. We're simply between the jaws of a pincer, but he's going to force us to fight. I know you loved your husband. Then why not be grateful that his sufferings are over? Go to your quarters, Madame Florian. No one has time for you now." Dimly, Desgenettes felt shame at treating her so badly, but he was tired, and frightened for her and for himself. He left her like that, a stricken, still-graceful figure watching after him with stunned eyes.

*   *   *

He is dead. Charlot is dead. The words kept forming themselves in her mind and yet carried no real conviction. God, whom she had loved and prayed to all her life, could not have permitted it to happen like that. Death itself, yes, perhaps, but not his lonely dying in some far unmarked spot, in the bitter belief that his need of her and his impetuous love had brought her to disaster. Knowing him so well,

Diane also knew that whatever physical agony might have been in-flicted on him before he died would have been less than his mental torment over her.

Her thoughts went back to the day of her arrest and that midnight of pure fear. At last the Army chief was standing before her, his hand lightly on the hilt of his sword, looking into her face. She thought of kneeling and begging for his mercy, but since he had none why abase herself pointlessly? She wished she could faint; since she never had fainted, such a reprieve was unlikely. He said with marked impatience, "It would have been simple good sense to re-mind me that I was in your debt when you petitioned to stay here. It was you who saved my wounded soldiers at Pavia?" "Yes," she whispered. "Then you have my friendship. But don't go behind my back again. Ask me for what you want." He started away; he was nearly out of the room before she could collect herself and call after him, "Am I under arrest?" "No," he said.

In her eagerness to see Charlot and reassure him, Diane had left the apartment running. Her ardor had been a mistake, because she overtook Bonaparte in the corridor. "Where are you going now?" he asked. "To the billet, General, Charlot will be worried." "Ah, the husband." His large eyes narrowed with amusement. "We'll leave him in doubt, I think. It might have a salutary effect." Diane had started to plead with him, but he cut her short. "I'm being very lenient, Madame Florian."

From a military point of view, he *had* been lenient. Diane thought now that nothing he could have done in anger could possibly have hurt them more. Bonaparte understood the human heart very well. But married love like theirs was outside of his experience.

The commander, the medical corps, and the Cairo gar-rison marched away shortly before nightfall, and the awful waiting began. Two thousand emaciated survivors left in the city were in-capable of any kind of a defense. The waiting was unbearably hard, but there was no help for that. Diane and Pauline Fourès and what soldiers could stay on their feet kept an endless watch from the walls, waiting for the horrors they knew to be in store for them. Diane was the least troubled, for she had no real desire to live. Death by torture had scant power to move her.

* * *

Bonaparte shattered the Bey's Army in a second Battle of the

Pyramids. He arrived on a midnight at Alexandria, and by morning, had routed the strongly placed Turkish Army in a second Battle of Aboukir Bay.

In a single month of summer, he dissipated the clouds of his enemies and restored full security to the French in Egypt.

II

THE VICTORS RETURNED. A kind of hysterical gaiety gripped the French. There was a continual round of parties and celebrations. At Headquarters, two persons only held themselves aloof from the rejoicings: Bonaparte, because he never had been in real doubt, and Diane Florian.

To escape the tense, febrile excitement of the others, she thought of going to the old billet that she had shared with Charlot. If she could sit quietly for a few hours in the silent rooms that had known them both, some relief to the unbearable pressure of mourning might be granted her. When she saw that the place was occupied, she very nearly turned back. But perhaps the new tenants would not object to her using one of the rooms for an hour or two. She knocked timidly. "Come," a voice said, speaking French. What tricks grief plays on us, she thought, that sounded like Charlot's voice. She pushed the door open slightly, and looked in.

Charlot, looking tired but otherwise fit, was sitting in the chair that always had been his favorite.

❀   ❀   ❀

His clothes were neat, and the house was scrupulously clean. Diane had no way of knowing that it had not always been like that. He had lived here alone, stark and seedy, while others of the medical corps performed miracles of heroism under the fire of enemy guns. Left to himself, he would have starved to death, indifferent to his own needs. The priest-translator who had worked with Florian on the medical report had learned where Florian was and in what condition. From that time on, cooked food was brought to him; his garments were washed and mended while he slept; his house was cleaned while he sat in it, brooding.

Diane hurried toward him, her arms held out. He half rose, to

264

meet her, she supposed. Instead he thrust out his hands awkwardly, as though fending her off.

"Why didn't you come to me, Charlot! Don't you realize that I have been thinking you were dead?" Her frantic hands were trying to unlock his arms so that she might enter their familiar haven. "How long have you been here, my dear? You didn't come with the Army. I know, I saw every man." But then she stepped back, her hands falling away from his. His face was the same self-contained mask that she had seen the night he came aboard the *Bonnet Rouge* after the months on Guiana. That other time, his face had changed on seeing her, but not today. The frightening notion came that he had not even recognized her. "Don't you know me, Charlot?"

"Of course," he said dispassionately. He sat down in the chair again. "How have you been, Diane?" he said politely.

The automatic response rose to her lips, *Very well, thank you.* She forced it back, wondering if she had gone suddenly mad, or he had. This was grotesque. "You can answer that yourself, I imagine. Dr. Desgenettes told me you had been killed."

"I am sorry you ever found out differently."

"Charlot!" The man she knew and loved would not have punished her like this because he believed she had been forcibly possessed by another. She started to be angry with him but she fought back the feeling. She said gently, "I wasn't harmed, Charlot."

He accepted that silently, as though puzzled, then he nodded and said, "I'm glad about that. I brought you here, after all." He dismissed it and her; she saw in his inward-looking eyes that he had forgotten she was there.

Could this really be happening? She stood uncertainly, biting her lip. But the inward struggle lasted for moments only. She was an emotionally mature woman to whom only one choice was possible between hurt pride and love. She knelt with unstudied grace and began stroking his hands, attempting by the physical contact to recall herself to him. Slowly he became aware of her. He sighed, an infinitely weary and heartbroken sound. "Please go. Don't come here again," he said.

"Let me help you."

"No one can help me, Diane."

"You were like this after Guiana. You let me close to you then."

"But now I've simply taken everything I can. I never want to feel anything again."

She said steadily, "I won't ask you to feel anything toward me. Perhaps that will come back, in time."

"I think you should get a divorce."

She concealed her shock, answering in a quiet voice, "I don't want a divorce. I love you."

"People who love can be hurt."

"It's worth it."

"Not to me, I won't be hurt any more."

"I understand," she said, as though soothing a child.

"Promise you'll leave me alone!"

The desperate note in his voice forced her attention. He meant it; it was important to him. If she persisted, he might be driven to some sad final act. For now she had better humor him, and trust that time would work its miracle of healing. She rose and remained looking down on his bent head.

"I love you, and I always will. I'll be waiting for you, darling. Don't keep me waiting any longer than you must. I'll be expecting you every hour of every day, so please hurry and come, Charlot." She went out, her feet dragging.

They had been through so much together. The one thing in their stormy, tragic lives that had been unassailable and unchanging, had been their love for each other. She felt a stranger to the whole world without his love. Her own body did not seem to belong to her, and her face in the mirror reflected a person she did not know.

* * *

At a supper party given by the Chief of Staff, General Bonaparte crossed the room to speak to Diane. He said without preamble, "Is there anything I can do to make you happier?"

She had always disliked the idea of discussing Charlot with others, and she very nearly turned his question away with a tactful rejoinder. But the need to confide in someone was strong, and she had come to like and trust Bonaparte. She told the full story.

He listened attentively. When she finished, all he said was, "The advice is good. Will you let me give you a divorce?"

"All our married lives, Charlot and I have endured sorrow and separation and terrible fear for each other's safety. Even so we were happy, because we loved each other. Nothing, *nothing*, ever could change my feelings toward him. I don't want to divorce him, I want to know what happened to make such a tragic change in him. If I knew, perhaps I could help him."

"I think not."

"You must mean that you know what happened to him."

"It was a hard campaign," he said remotely. She saw that he did not want to talk any more. She even imagined that he might be feeling uncomfortable.

"I have to know, General," she said.

"He was told to obey orders or be shot."

The brusque words, and this outspoken man's determined reticence, warned Diane that the thing being concealed was too dreadful to say. But she had to go on with it; she had not given up the idea that, knowing, she could help Charlot. "What were the orders, General?" He looked her over coolly. "I don't want to be impudent," Diane said. "But you told me I have your friendship."

"You do. Don't abuse it."

Her voice was low and frightened. "You have complete authority over us all. We must trust you to use it wisely. I can understand why you might be ashamed." She waited quietly, rather welcoming the idea of being hurt by this man who had annihilated Charlot.

Bonaparte rested his hand lightly on her neck. "It's done," he said, "I can't change it." And she saw in his practical eyes that he was truly sorry.

III

DR. FLORIAN received his wife's request to come to the palace with the indifference he now showed toward everything. He supposed that his signature on the divorce papers was required, though this was late evening, an unusual time for the signing of papers.

He was brought into the palace through a back entrance. There was something odd and stealthy about all this. Florian was aware of it without feeling real curiosity. He was taken to a room where Diane was standing by a window and Pauline Fourès was lying on a low bed, weeping.

Diane's lovely face came alive with joy when she saw him, for she believed that her waiting was over. "I knew you'd come, Charlot!" She started toward him, but saw quickly that he did not want her to touch him. She halted, delight draining out of her face.

"I sent for the doctor, but I used your name," Pauline Fourès said in a blurred voice. "I wanted you to be here because I want you to tell him that I've always been kind to you, as kind as I know how."

Even in her own suffering, another's could touch Diane. "Of course, Pauline. You've been very kind to me. What do you want from us?"

"I want him to go to General Bonaparte and tell him I'm to have his child."

Diane, puzzled, said, "Why don't you tell the General yourself?"

"He would know I was lying. He might believe the doctor."

"Why do you want it believed if it isn't true?" Florian asked.

Pauline Fourès rolled on the bed and turned her face up. Diane saw her misery. "He means to leave me behind, Doctor. But he would take me with him if he believed it about the child. Please say you will, please!"

"The doctor couldn't do that, Pauline."

"Is he going away, Madame?" Florian said.

"He's going back. To France."

"But the British have been patrolling the Mediterranean since they cut us off. Even if we had ships, we wouldn't stand a chance of getting through."

"He *told* me he was going. There are two frigates in the harbor. It's all very secret, of course."

A look of exaltation came over Florian's face. "He told you he was deserting the Army!"

Diane moved to the bedside and began stroking the crying girl's hair. "I wish you had told me about your plan before you bothered the doctor. No reputable doctor would do such a thing, Pauline."

"I'm willing to say what she wants. Why not?"

Diane's hand dropped. She filled with new pain. Charlot's eyes noticed her, then went past her indifferently. "I suppose you wouldn't have brought me here unless you knew you could arrange it," he said to Pauline.

"Bourrienne will help us about that."

"Bourrienne." He repeated it with a questioning intonation as though believing the name should have some meaning for him, but then he shrugged, giving that up. "Tell Bourrienne I'm waiting in the garden. I don't mind saying what you want."

Diane stared after his strange-familiar person until he was out of sight. What he planned was like a giant fist smashing her hopes. She had never given up the belief that someday he would come back to her. But this indifferent, careless man, casually promising to violate medical responsibility to please a woman, was tissue-blood-and-bone, another being, a stranger to her. She had thought that she plumbed the depths of loss when he rejected her love. Now she saw that the loss of his love was only a facet of the incredible and irremediable loss—of Charlot himself.

*   *   *

He remembered having made some kind of promise, but what the promise had been and to whom given, he no longer knew. He had made it in the first place because it was a way of getting to Bonaparte. He wanted to see once more that unforgettable face as smooth and strong as an obelisk, while hugging to himself his secret knowledge that the worms of the immoral decision already would be working, silent and unseen. He who had wanted never to feel anything again was shaken with emotion. Every sense of his, the very cells of his body, quivered to the pitch of his hatred.

Bonaparte was the perfect leader of men, he was the flawless governor, the wise administrator, the soldier without fear and without reproach. He was deserting his Army. Men had trusted him enough to follow him to the rim of the world. He was abandoning them, sneaking away from them secretly. Clusters of low stars winked back at Florian. Gigantic joke!—the commander of Egypt was made of the same clay as the commander of Sinnamarie.

How neatly my soul fitted the palm of his hand, as he slew the sick soldiers with his love and my despair! I knew then that I never could fight him, never fight back; because the action he forced on me was eminently virtuous in a commander. I had no way then of knowing that this moment was waiting for time to uncover it.

Dr. Florian's eyes had never seen colors with such clarity, and his senses were bathed in perfumes of self-satisfaction. The cruel joy mounted in him, crazing him, while the hot fierce moonlight of Egypt beat down on the darkness. Florian shook his fist at the moon. "You too, Bonaparte," he muttered. He rocked with inward laughter.

Hatred passed into an ecstasy that drove his body to action. He began running. His gaunt stark figure fled down pathways bordered by exotic, never-sleeping flowers. Pichegru's phantom was close at his side, and the same dark laughter bound them as close as twins. "Bonaparte too!" Florian cried out in mad glee. "Bonaparte too," Pichegru echoed, chuckling.

*   *   *

He felt himself pass over the barriers of sanity into the strange world that lies just beyond the limits of the intellect. He was not alarmed because, being damned already, happenings to himself were without significance. This lovely phantom gliding toward them was, like Pichegru's dark existence at his elbow, a trick of the African moonlight and his own deranged ideas. Yet he was grateful, because in phantom form Diane could be looked at by him. He had not trusted himself since Jaffa to look at the actual woman, lest her beauty rouse him to new torments of loss. "You look so real," he said, marveling.

"I am real. I'm here, loving you, knowing there's a way yet for us if you'll only help me find it."

You're too late, Madame, Pichegru said. *You are late by many weeks. If you wanted to fight me for his soul, you should have been at Jaffa too.*

"I don't know what you mean, Charlot. Try to explain."

Come away, Pichegru said to Florian.

"But I like to look at her. She is so beautiful. She looks at me with so much love and trust."

She does not know yet that you are no longer a doctor, Pichegru said.

"Of course you're still a doctor!" Diane said. "As long as you live, you'll be a doctor. Nothing could change that. It's in your bones, your blood."

Pichegru asked her, *Does a doctor steal away from his patients? Does he poison sick men?*

"My dear, you are ill. You imagine all that. You could not have done those things." Pichegru laughed at her words of simple faith while Florian's eyes ran tears of blood. "Stop it, Charlot!" she said sharply.

Suddenly he wanted to speak the whole truth about himself. The words came readily and poured out of him. Dr. Florian said, "I was a virtuous man once. I never could see anyone wallowing in despair that I wasn't compelled to try to get him on his feet. But since my own fall from grace, I find this characteristic in myself has turned perverse. Since that day, I have not dealt with a man of impeccable virtue that I haven't plotted to bring him down where I am. It is the devil's business to tempt, after all, and I am on the side of the devil, now."

Word for word, the speech was the one Pichegru had made to him on Guiana. Those words coming back to him out of his own mouth had a profound effect. Illusion ended; the cloak of madness was jerked away, and his soul stood alone, naked and shivering. Diane— no phantom—held her hands out in a pleading gesture. Her face was desperately white. The trees and walls of the garden seemed to grind slowly into new, sane positions, and the moon and stars wheeled in a rational sky.

Great fear laid hand on him. He cried out in a voice of agony, "Now I have truly become Pichegru."

IV

"—a touching sight!" Louis de Bourrienne said in a light malicious voice. "They were kneeling together, their tears mingling, and she was teaching the good doctor to pray. They were perfectly in earnest."

"I would not have expected them to pray in any other mood," Bonaparte said mildly.

"I watched and listened a long while before they realized I was there. He prayed for you. He forgave you."

Bonaparte digested that and said, "You are amused?"

"Very."

"I am not." The warning emphasis was slight but definite. "Did he ask to see me?"

"Yes, but you won't like what he has to say."

"So?"

"I don't presume to advise you. In your place, I wouldn't waste any time locking up Dr. Florian and his beautiful wife in the most inaccessible dungeon in Egypt. He knows what you're planning and he's not in the least inclined to be discreet."

Bonaparte cursed softly. "How did he find out?"

"I don't know. Pauline, perhaps. Naturally the women confide in each other."

"Who has he told?"

"God—and in a voice designed to carry the whole distance."

Bonaparte said sharply, "Watch your tongue if you don't want to be left behind. I'm not going to try to sail through the blockade with a God-mocker aboard."

"I didn't mean anything!" Bourrienne said in deep alarm.

"Can you be sure there were no other eavesdroppers?"

"I made a careful check. Shall I write out an order of detention?"

The commander paused, weighing it. If word got around, the venture would be blocked by his own soldiers. On the other hand, the Cairo jails were worse even than those of France. Since he would not be here to see to the couple's release, there was a good chance of their dying in captivity. But he was a practical man. The arrest of the Florians was almost mandatory.

Briefly he considered buying their silence by offering to take them along. But the two small ships at his disposal were overloaded now with men who for one reason or another he wanted with him. Room had been made for the savants as well as for those who might be helpful in case he really decided to overthrow the corrupt government of Paul Barras and govern France himself. In a less important matter, he would have been content to accept their promise of silence. But there must not be any slip-up about this.

"It must be done, I suppose," he said slowly.

"I'll write out the order now for your signature. The sooner the better, I should think."

"Where are they?"

"In the anteroom. I thought it best they not be left to wander around."

Bonaparte was remembering that Diane Florian had saved the wounded soldiers at Pavia. "Send them here," he said. Facing them, telling them himself what must happen, was an unpleasant duty he was willing to accept only because he had told the woman that he was her friend.

The change in Dr. Florian, Bonaparte noticed immediately. This was not the shivering wretch he had forced at Jaffa. This man possessed deep spiritual reserves. At that, he might live through what was ahead of him without breaking. Certainly Florian had overcome a great deal both inside and outside of himself to be able to stand like this, squarely on his feet, neither humble nor bold. Bonaparte found himself admiring and liking Dr. Florian.

His eyes went on to Diane. She had never looked lovelier. A new sweetness was on her gentle face. The love and trust she felt toward the gaunt man at her side would have been obvious to a far less sensitive person than was General Bonaparte. He checked the little sigh that rose to his lips, acknowledging that Florian, for all of his misfortunes past and future, was the luckier man. Self-pity was not a feature of Bonaparte's disposition; he banished the small regret efficiently.

Bourrienne came back almost on the Florians' heels, waving a drying paper. He did not lose much time, Bonaparte thought coldly. He wondered again at the fury of his secretary's persecution of the luck-less physician. He had known for a long time that there was some-thing cruel and twisted in Louis. He nodded, and Bourrienne put the paper on his desk and went out.

"Do I have permission to speak?"

"In a moment, Dr. Florian."

He dipped a quill, and began reading the paper. I'll be damned, Bonaparte thought. He scored out the lazar-house named as the place of detention. He promised himself that Louis would pay for that. He started his signature, but then threw down the pen. He had no reason to imitate his secretary's savage haste.

He leaned back, watching them. Diane's face was stamped with the deep exhaustion of long emotional strain. In Bonaparte, the pro-tective instinct of the male was peculiarly strong, and he felt its tug on him now. He conquered it. His rule over himself was complete, and was his secret of ruling others with such ease.

"All right, Dr. Florian. I'm listening," Bonaparte said.

*　　　　*　　　　*

For Bonaparte's sake, he tore his heart out for the other to read, understand—and be warned. He gave up every secret to the man who had harmed him so. For Bonaparte, one more time he walked through the screaming jungle and was bent nearly double from the force of the north wind. He ate strange offensive things; he wakened on hot damp nights and found the vampire bats sucking his blood. His clothes rotted and fell away. He watched himself and his fellows disintegrating, becoming less human daily. The walking dead of Sin-namarie were aware of nothing but food and weather.

Bonaparte, watching Diane, saw that she followed the story as new. He wondered about that. They seemed so close. And if Florian had kept it locked in himself all this time, why was he telling it now?

For Bonaparte, Florian watched his little friend, Fleures the jour-nalist, dying of the strange malady the doctor did not know how to treat. The notables played their gambling game with castor beans in the pale light of the only lamp in Sinnamarie. Pichegru surren-dered the wooden building. The faces of the other exiles gave con-sent to anything Florian might do, while rebel Ange hung from their hands, dead weight.

"If you abandon the men you brought here, you'll regret it to the end of your life. I know that, General."

But why are you so concerned about me? Bonaparte wondered, fingering the paper reflectively. He did not break his silence.

For Bonaparte, one more time Florian sat down with General Pichegru under a tree as tall as a church spire, and he listened to that fatal question, "Do you want to escape Guiana with me?" He followed Pichegru across Guiana, and back. Father Roger perished again in the pinching jaws of army ants. Pichegru looked at butterfly wings through the Leeuwenhoek, and refuse filled the half-dug drainage ditches while work on the palisade was stopped.

Not heroic, exactly, the General thought, but very human, and I wonder how many men could say honestly that they would have done otherwise. I wonder about myself. Florian was pleading, "Don't fall into the same trap, General Bonaparte. Don't destroy yourself, I humbly beg you." Bonaparte looked back unblinkingly. He made no reply of any kind.

Florian, his voice rough with emotion, told the end of the story, how the betrayal of the men of Sinnamarie became the seed that flowered so horribly at Jaffa. An hour of madness, in which he had put too high a regard on his own life, inevitably had led to another hour when he was compelled to keep his life although the easier choice would have been to lose it.

At last Bonaparte spoke.

He said crisply, "That's nonsense. You could have refused me. You were told as much."

"But you were determined that a doctor must do it."

The commander made no sudden gesture, nor did any particular expression cross his face. He merely sat there, glaring into Florian's face, and waves of raw power seemed to emanate from him, charging the atmosphere with so intense an excitement that it approached pain. But he himself was first to look away, bending his head slightly over the desk. He said expressionlessly, "You were trying to spare the other doctors, you mean."

"I had broken the Oath already, voluntarily. It couldn't possibly have hurt me to break it a second time as much as it would have hurt one of them."

The silence lasted too long, and Florian became afraid that the point he was making had been lost. He looked at Diane for reassurance. Her sparkling eyes told him that she, at least, understood. But it was Bonaparte who must become convinced. Though he hesitated to interrupt the commander's meditations, somehow he must drive it home to this powerful man on whose will so many obscure destinies depended, that the first steps toward evil are the significant ones.

He spoke shyly. "Do you have nothing to say, General?"

"What do you want me to say?"

"That I richly deserved what happened to me at Jaffa because of the thing I did at Sinnamarie."

Bonaparte said in a level voice, "Dr. Florian, what you did at Jaffa was the highest moral action I have ever known."

❋   ❋   ❋

He sent them away finally, their faces glowing, their bodies filled with new strength and their hearts with pure joy. All their wounds had been healed by him; all they had ever hoped for, he had granted. But his own body was a cold dark temple in which he lived in distrust of himself.

Amazing, he thought, incredible. There were differences between what I did at Pavia and what he did on Guiana, but for each of us, those were first crimes. Yet he took the materials of moral failure and fashioned them into a magnificent action. And I proceeded from Pavia to—this. He picked up the paper, not reading it—his memory was excellent—but considering the weight of its indictment against him. At one time he would not have considered mistreating human beings as a convenience to himself.

He had not looked at his memories of Pavia for a long time. He did so now, sparing himself no detail. Dr. Scarpa repeated his entirely intellectual appeal while, just outside, the slaughter and rape that Bonaparte had unleashed maimed and destroyed human beings. Dr. Spallanzani held out his bone in a childlike trusting gesture, and insisted that the world of men lived to the right or the left of that most ancient object. Bonaparte himself was a sick exhausted youth telling the professors and learned men of the University that he had never committed a crime before now. Out of his great knowledge of men and things, he had guessed then how easily the crimes would follow each other once his pride in his clean hands was gone. Most vivid of all was Dr. Contarini with whose fate Bonaparte had identified himself as with a brother's, as Contarini passed through the guard voluntarily to increase his brother's shame.

He discarded Pavia in order to look at Jaffa. He had supposed that Dr. Florian had obeyed the order to save himself. In that case, Florian would have been guilty of an action somewhat more corrupt than what he had done at Sinnamarie, though not murder. But Dr. Florian had not obeyed for that reason. He had distributed the poison himself because his commander's frantic concern over the soldiers had led to a wrong and impossible demand being laid on the doctors. Bonaparte should have realized that the duty, while inescapable, was his own. They were his men, after all. But he had not been able to see that, and his abuse of authority had produced in his victim the highest possible action of sacrifice. His logical mind continued the analogy to now. Tonight, Florian's love of his fellow-man had triumphed over the very real hatred he must have felt personally toward his commander. Bonaparte, hating no one, not angry even, had consented to the drafting of the paper that lay now on his desk, his signature half drawn.

It was an ironic footnote that Florian's coming here had been to try to prevent an action of bold generosity. Bonaparte knew now that nothing was being done at home toward rescuing his cast-off Army. If the Army were to be saved, he must save it. He had brought the men here, and he accepted his responsibility for getting them home again.

He well knew how small were his chances of success. No ship of his had been allowed to pass the British patrol for weeks. Yet he felt scant concern over the venture. His two poor ships *would* slip through the patrol. They *would* stay afloat though they were patched and seamed and only half rebuilt from the disaster at Aboukir Bay. He *would* gain France, and if he wished, he would govern her—the just wise rule he had given the Egyptians. If only Pavia had never been.

He started to crumple and throw away the document condemning the Florians, but stopped himself, and smoothed it out carefully. I will never finish the signature, he thought, but I will never destroy this either. It is an excellent reminder.

❋   ❋   ❋

Gehenna was an enchanted garden now, in which Charlot and Diane wandered hand in hand, their love at the same pitch and their whole future before them. Every dream of his, every hope he owned, had been fulfilled tonight. Another man grandly making such promises while poised on the brink of a most uncertain venture, would not have convinced anyone, but when you looked into Bonaparte's calm face, his sure eyes, you knew all would come to pass exactly as he said.

That the Guiana system ever would be ended, had never crossed Dr. Florian's mind. To him, Sinnamarie was immutable, as fixed as natural law; to him, the sufferings of the men who were there could only be stopped by their deaths. Bonaparte had sworn tonight that he would put an end to it. No fresh victims would be sent to the *guillotine sèche,* and those who still endured its living death would be brought home by him.

There was Charlot's appointment for the pair to rejoice over, Medical Intendant of the French Republic. "I will send for you and Madame Florian on the first ship. You and I are going to open the hospitals and medical schools of France, Doctor." Since the Florians had no more doubt of Bonaparte than he himself did, these wonderful promises could be savored as accomplished facts.

Charlot chuckled ruefully. "I should be feeling miserably embarrassed. What he's planning is splendid. He must have thought me a complete fool."

"I don't think so," she said tenderly.

"But I tried so hard to get him to see a comparison that did not exist."

Diane said, "General Bonaparte is a very complex human being. I don't pretend to know what he was thinking. But I felt that he was deeply moved, and I don't for a minute believe that he thought you were foolish. In his way, he seemed to be—well—honoring you."

He laughed joyously before he kissed her. It was such a loyal, loving, absurd thing to have said.